THE CURSE OF FIRE

THE STEEL CITADEL SERIES
BOOK TWO

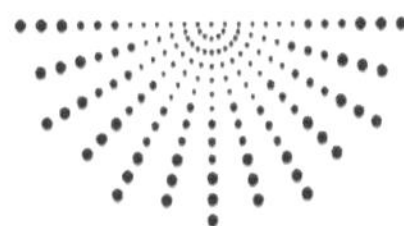

WHITNEY WELSH GIBBS

This is a work of fiction, and the views expressed herein are the sole responsibility of the author. Likewise, certain characters, places, and incidents are the product of the author's imagination, and any resemblance to actual persons, living or dead, or actual events or locales, is entirely coincidental.

Copyright © 2025 by Whitney Welsh Gibbs

Cover by Whitney Welsh Gibbs

Edits by Hannah Hayek, Sarah Detrich, and Kirsty Murdoch

All rights reserved.

Human Authored™, Reg #: 7965877, https://authorsguild.org/human

To Megan. I have been lucky enough to call you 'friend' from the high school bleachers on cool fall nights to the barrens of Tinemallacht and the halls of the Steel Citadel. Thank you for journeying through life as my partner in crime. May we never stop exploring this crazy world together.

TRIGGER WARNINGS

Abuse (off page), Attempted murder, Death, Drugs, Hallucinations, Infertility, Murder, Profanity, Sexually explicit scenes, Violence, Sexual Assault

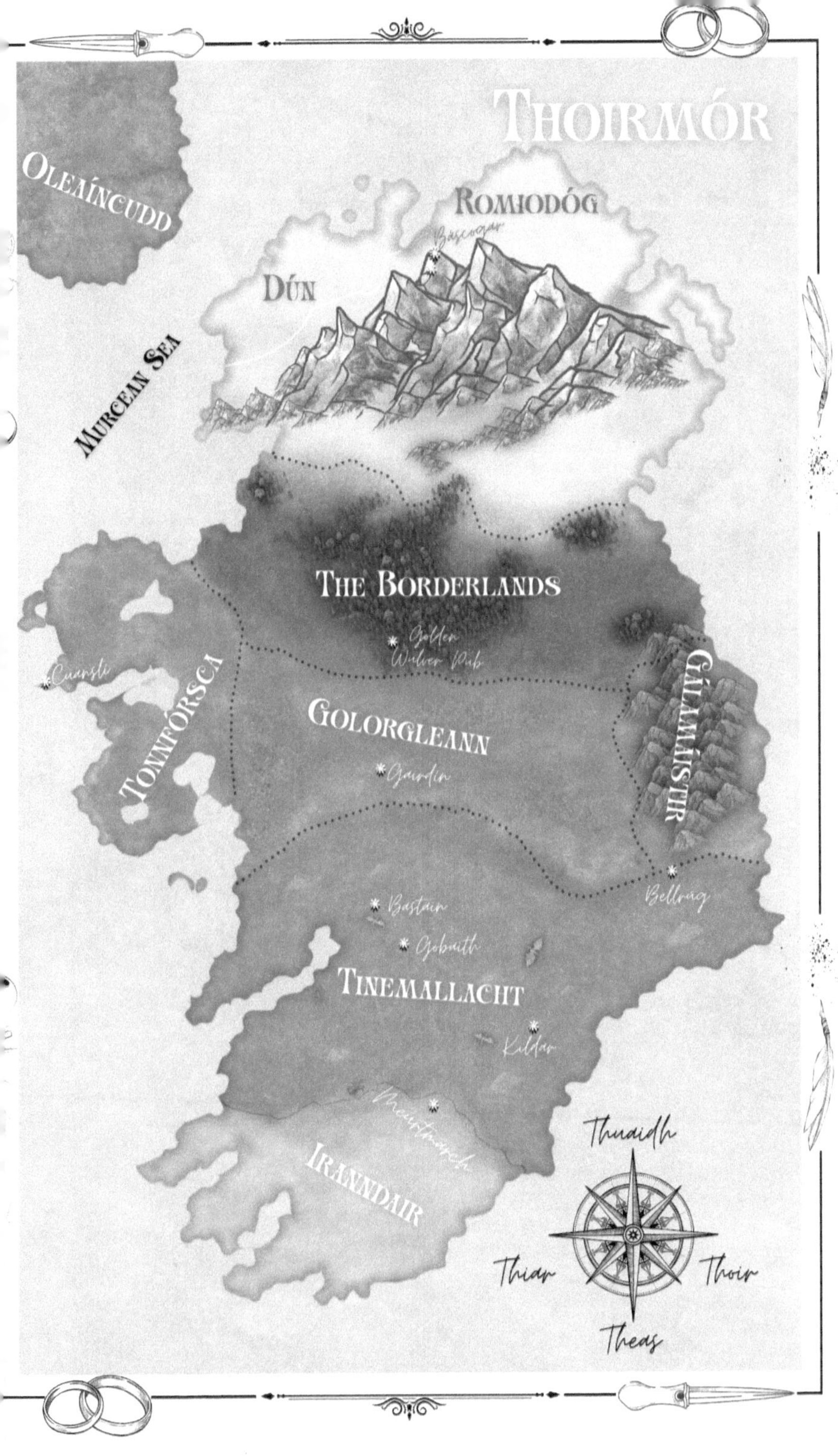

THOIRMÓR
OLEAÍNCUDD
ROMIODÓG
DÚN
Bascogar
MURCEAN SEA
THE BORDERLANDS
Golden Wulver Pub
Cuansli
TONNFÓRSCA
GOLORGLEANN
GÁLÁMÁISTIR
Gurdin
Bellrúg
Bastain
Gobnith
TINEMALLACHT
Kildar
Meartmurih
Thuaidh
IRALNDAIR
Thiar
Thoir
Theas

PRONUNCIATION GUIDE

Áine Moran
On-yah More-ann

Alia Darwish
Uh-lee-uh Dar-wish

Arran Sullivan
Air-un Sole-i-ven

Bode Buell
Bow-dee Byoo-uhl

Bréanainn Doherty
Brenn-ann Doh-er-tee

Bryn Kael
Brin Kay-ehl

Dedra Blos
Dee-drah Bloss

Eoghan Kael
Oh-wen Kay-ehl

Finn Rhodes
F-in Row-dz

General Osian Kael
General Oh-shan Kay-ehl

Gálgalesh Devenallt
Gahl-ga-lesh Dev-en-alt

King Cashel
King Cash-ehl

Lowri Kael
Low-ree Kay-ehl

Maeve Moran
Mayve More-ann

Mari Kael
Mar-ee Kay-ehl

Ovidia Dalca
Oh-vid-ee-uh Dall-kuh

Prince Cai
Prince K-eye

Rian Doherty

Ry-ann Doh-er-tee

River Hayes
Ri-vr Hay-z

Sawney Ore
Sonn-ey Orr

Seren Lago
Seh-ren Lah-go

Sir Oli Raven
Ser Ah-lee Ray-ven

Theo Moran
Thee-oh More-ann

Tiernan Damaris
Tear-nan Duh-mare-is

Trystan Price
Triss-tan Pryce

PLACES

Báscogar Prison
Boss-ko-gar Prison

Bastain
Bass-tain

Cuanslí
Coon-shlee

Caisleán Rialú
Cash-lan Ria-loo

Fáintìrean
Fane-ter-ain

Gairdín
Gar-deen

Gobaith
Go-bithe

Murcean Sea
Mer-sea-uhn Sea

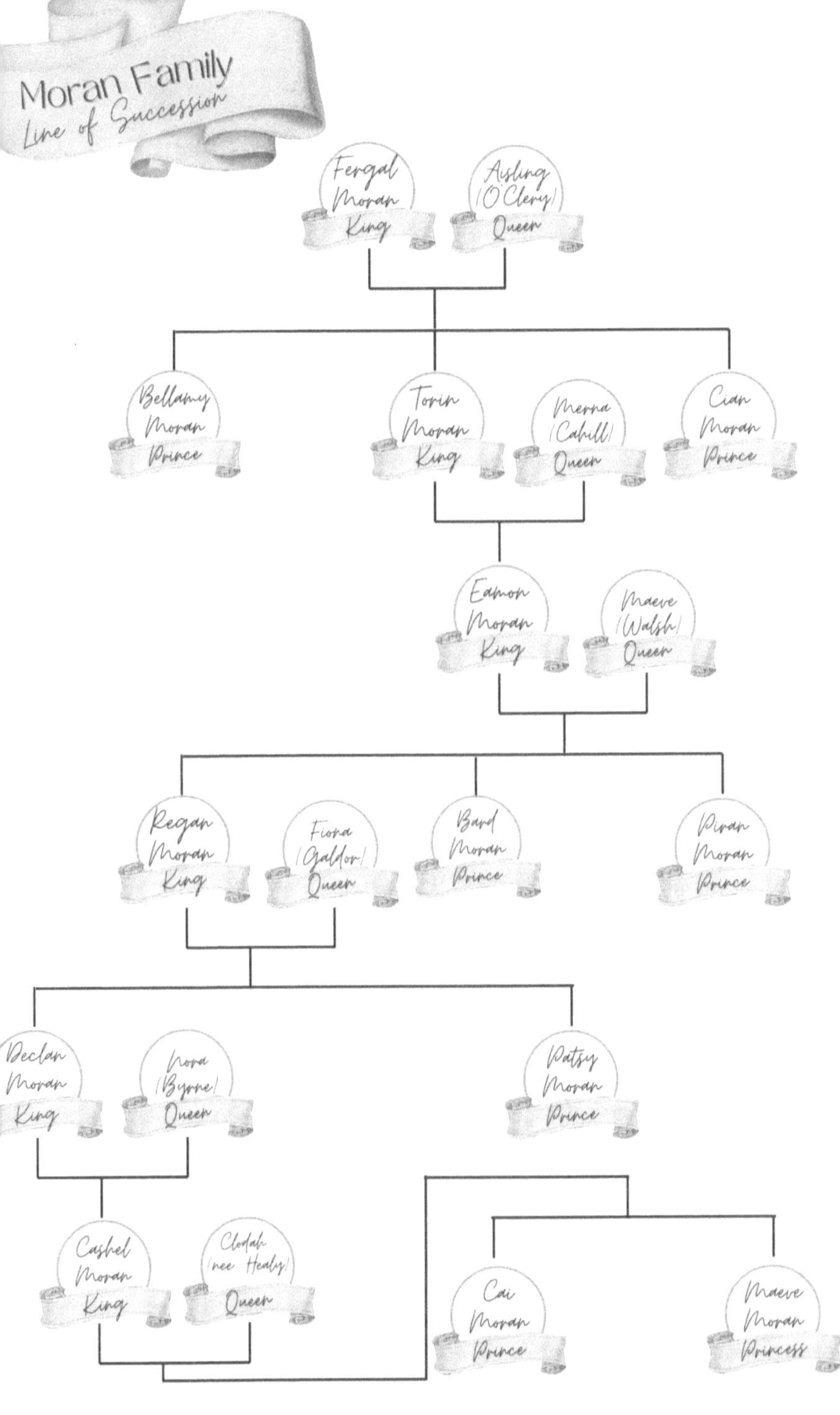

Moran Family
Line of Succession

Fergal Moran King
Aisling (O'Clery) Queen

Bellamy Moran Prince
Torin Moran King
Merna (Cahill) Queen
Cian Moran Prince

Eamon Moran King
Maeve (Walsh) Queen

Regan Moran King
Fiona (Galdor) Queen
Bard Moran Prince
Piran Moran Prince

Declan Moran King
Nora (Byrne) Queen
Patsy Moran Prince

Cashel Moran King
Clodah (nee Healy) Queen
Cai Moran Prince
Maeve Moran Princess

CHAPTER ONE

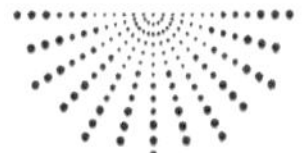

*H*e killed your family. He left you for dead. He took the *crown for himself.* Rian Doherty, the first man I ever loved, stands, breathing, in the courtyard, a wicked smile pulled across his face, as though nothing in the world can touch him. He should be dead, buried under the cobblestone streets of Gairdín; yet, here he stands, more alive than I have ever seen him. He's the vision of health, with his fattened stomach and rounded, pink cheeks, parading around in fabrics that cannot possibly shelter him from the Romiodóg winter chill.

I fight the arm laced firmly around my waist and hand glued to my mouth. Eoghan pulls me back from the arched opening that looks down onto the courtyard and into the shadows of the upper corridor.

"Maeve, you have to stop screaming before I let you go."

I had not even registered that I was. I stop my thrashing and fall silent, and he eases his grip. He steps into my line of sight and crouches so his gorgeous, green-gold eyes are level with my own. I cannot breathe for the wild hammering of my heart in my chest. I feel the familiar warmth of tears as they track down my freezing cheeks, and Eoghan brushes his thumb lightly across my skin to wipe them away.

"That's..." Panic makes my voice shrill as it echoes much too loudly through the dark passageway. Eoghan holds his index finger up to his lips to quiet me. "That's," I begin again in frantic, hushed tones, "Rian! That's my Rian!"

"I know," Eoghan breathes, the fire in his eyes at the sound of my former lover's name betraying him.

"You know?" My hands shake at my sides. He reaches for them, but I pull them from his grasp. "How do you *know*?"

"Maeve, calm down." He reaches for me again, but I step back into the dimly lit corridor. He sighs. "Gálgalesh received word a couple of months ago that Bréanainn Doherty had been crowned king, his son Rian named heir. He didn't think it would be wise to tell you until—"

"Until you took me to Fáintìrean and fucked me like a common whore? Did you think I wouldn't miss him then?" My words pour out like venom, and I watch as Eoghan's mouth falls open in surprise. "You knew, and you pretended you didn't! You pretended to be so interested in hearing about how much I missed him and loved him, knowing full-well he was alive! Gods be, I'm an idiot to think you actually loved me!"

"Damnit, Maeve! I do love you! I didn't hide it from you to fuck you. I hid it from you because he wants you dead!" His voice rises, and the corridor fills with heat as the crowd in the courtyard settles for the first time. He stands to his full height and takes a step toward me, but I hold up my hand to stop him.

"You're lying. He wouldn't."

"He already tried, Maeve. Don't you remember, or have you conveniently forgotten why you're here?"

From below, the long silenced voice of Rian rises through the frigid air. "Prisoners of Báscogar! I thank you for your warm welcome to this icy mountaintop." My mind spins, my head light as the memory of him comes flooding back, and with it, every desire in my heart to be near to him—to have my arms around him. It's as if the crowd senses it too as the anger of their murmuring voices softens. I push past Eoghan, back toward the arched opening overlooking the courtyard. Eoghan lets out an almost possessive growl from deep in his chest as Rian continues. "I have come to extend my hand as a gesture of good faith, to show you that my father, the king, and I mean you no ill-will. We understand just how gravely you have suffered under the hand of a tyrant for much too long."

I reach the stone pillar, leaning against it for a better view. How had I not seen his handsome face for what it was as soon as he walked into view? Time. Time had clouded my thoughts of him, had taken me away from his love. I step a foot up onto the ledge. *If I jump, perhaps I will fall into the snowbank beside him, like an angel from above. He would come to me then and sweep me into his arms.*

"Maeve..." Eoghan's voice is softer now, nervous, as though he's debating the merits of trying to convince me to step down.

"Leave me alone, Eoghan." I do not take my eyes off Rian as I take another step onto the ledge.

"I'm not going to do that," he purrs in that low voice that would have had me melting just an hour ago, and I feel his warmth near my back.

Rian clears his throat elegantly as he lifts his hand to his lips and then addresses the men once again.

"I have also come here on another, much more important mission, and I wonder if perhaps the fine prisoners of Báscogar could help me." Help him? I'd open a vein if he so desired. "I am told a woman has come to live among your ranks. She goes by the name of Alana and has hair of crimson. The first woman these walls have ever held, if the history of this prison is to be believed. She is said to have been brought here just before the roads closed and the winter snow began to fall, but I have been informed that perhaps this is not true." The prisoners begin to chatter in interest—no doubt exchanging surprise at the lies Gálgalesh spread about my arrival—and a smile curves Sir Oli Raven's lips as he eyes Rian. Rian's mouth ticks up as well, and then he nods, his guards calling for silence as he continues. "That is so very interesting. You, like my trusted confidant, have confirmed the worst. I have come to believe the woman who goes by the name of Alana and hides within these walls is masquerading as another. That the woman is someone much more important, to me and to Draíocoinnigh, than one might ever imagine. She is, in fact the—"

Shouting stops Rian mid-sentence as the guard who left to find Drustan Anwyl runs through the men lining the courtyard and pushes his way into the stoney center, where Rian and Sir Oli Raven stand. His face is mutilated, black with bruises, and he nearly falls to his knees. He staggers, and Rian's guards in the courtyard rush forward to hold him upright. His hands clutch his abdomen, deep red blood pelting the snow-flecked stone.

"What has happened?" Sir Oli Raven shouts as he steps back from the pool of blood accumulating near his feet. The injured guard's voice is so low, I can't hear what he's saying. He slumps into the guard to his left, and red sullies their pristine uniforms. "DEAD?"

The courtyard erupts, the sound of voices so deafening, I can no longer hear Eoghan's low breathing behind me. Sir Oli Raven whispers wildly to Rian and the guards, whose faces have all gone the same shade of ghostly white. They drop the bleeding man, and I realize he is no longer clutching at his middle. He won't be moving at all anymore. Sir Oli

Raven says something, waving his hands dramatically before they break apart and he clears his throat over the din.

"SILENCE!" he shouts. All heads turn in his direction. "It seems Drustan Anwyl has been found dead in the belly of the prison, along with two of his guards, all drained by a shadow lurker. However, I have it under good authority that Drustan Anwyl had taken two prisoners who had threatened the safety of this prison: a Tinemallacht warrior named Eoghan Kael and the woman known as Alana. I have no doubt they are to blame for this…atrocity!" He splays his hand out to the dead man on the ground. "All of you are ordered by His Royal Highness, Prince Rian, to find them both and bring them here. Immediately!"

Chaos erupts, and I feel hands on me again as Eoghan throws me over his shoulder and barrels down the corridor at lightning speed. The men have scattered as quickly as we have, in every direction through the vast labyrinth of the prison, hunting us. I am all too aware of the stories of these men's crimes and the horrors I will face if they find me here. Even with an armory of weapons, I don't think I stand a chance.

"Take out the torchlight!" Eoghan orders as he runs.

"What?"

"You heard me. Take out the torches—all of them, in the entire prison!" He rounds the corner, and I hear feet racing toward us from somewhere in the distance.

"You're insane, Kael! I can't do that! My magic isn't powerful enough to take out every torch!"

"Yes, you can, and you will, unless you want us both to die!" I feel his hands tighten on the backs of my thighs as he turns down an unfamiliar corridor. "Do it, Maeve!"

The panic in his voice tells me there's no more time for arguing. Even if I can't do it, I have to try. I reach for the thread of faerie magic that hums awake in response. I have used the spell so many times, the symbols and sequences are second nature. Still, I've never tried to command the magic on such a scale. *I need this to cover the whole prison. I don't know how, but please, please help me*, I whisper down the line, and it hums a little louder this time. A response? I can only hope. Eoghan's boots slide against ice that has formed on top of the stone floors, indicating the we are somewhere in the depths of the prison's basements. He swears under his breath, and I feel him grow hot under me. He apologizes weakly as I turn my attention back to the magic thread, trying to ignore the burning of my skin against his. *I need this to work. Please, let it work*, I beg, and then I hurl the sequence of symbols and words down the line.

The effect is immediate. The entire prison plunges into darkness. Eoghan keeps running, removing one of his hands from my thighs and throwing it out in front of him to keep us from crashing straight into the walls. Shouts rise like thunder, confirming the magic has answered my request. Eoghan slows his pace in the darkness.

"Eogh..." I whisper, and the spinning in my head that had started when Rian had first spoken begins to cease.

"I knew you could do it." He stops walking and sets me down on my feet beside him. The passageway is silent. No one has followed us this far into the prison's underbelly. "Light just this one."

He taps on something metal as he indicates to the torch beside him. I reach for the magic again, and this time, a low light illuminates the small space. I take in his face, those beautiful, green-gold eyes. There is fear written across every inch, the kind I only ever saw on death's doorstep. He takes me in, his fingers flexing as though they want nothing more than to reach for me, but he hesitates. My own hands shake as I hold them at my sides.

"Tell me." My voice is a quiet demand. "Tell me everything, Eoghan Kael, or I swear to Danu, I will light all the torches in this place and let them kill us."

He stares into my eyes, and I fold my arms across my chest, waiting for him to speak. How dare he promise me there would be no more secrets between us and then keep the biggest one of them all? We had spent so much time together, just the two of us. He could have shared *something*, yet he said nothing. He drops his head and places his hands on his knees.

"Just before the roads closed, Gálgalesh received word that the Doherty family had orchestrated the coup and were acting as the new sovereign. It wasn't until he had gone to the Borderlands for supplies that he had confirmed the Four Seats officially recognized Bréanainn's rule. He told us when he arrived in Fáintìrean after his run—right before I found you bleeding to death in the snow."

The Four Seats. The four families of the four territories of Draíocoinnigh. The lords and ladies of the land turned their backs on my family and fell into line with the usurpers to legitimize their hold on the throne. Every territory. *Except Tinemallacht*, I remind myself. *Tinemallacht is the lost Fifth Seat —Eoghan's family.* They have no say anymore, but would they have followed suit?

"You've known that long?" My mind races back to the day of the secret meeting all those months ago. Someone had spoken of a 'wretched man and his son'. They were speaking of Rian and his father.

Eoghan nods, though he does not speak.

"The entire time we have been paired together, you could have told me, and you chose not to. You asked me about him! You let me cry to you about how much I missed him, and you let me think he was *dead*!"

"What else could I do? Tell you that bastard was alive and was the one who tried to kill you...the one who killed

Cai…and let you run back to him so he could finish the job?"

Fury boils through every inch of me at his words. I pull back my hand and swing it hard across his face. He stands frozen, and I do it again. He doesn't even flinch as I release my anger onto him. I can't be sure my blows hurt him, but his cheek blazes red in the low light, the imprint of my hand stamped across it.

"How dare you assume I would be stupid enough to go running back to the person who killed my family? How dare you not trust me to make an informed decision as if I'm a child? I. Am. Not. A. Fool." We are silent for an excruciating moment as we take each other in. "Did Gálgalesh ask you to keep it from me? All of it?" He stays quiet and still, as though worried about implicating another person in our quarrel. "Did he ask you to kiss me? To keep me distracted?"

His eyes grow wide, as if I've said something so terrible, he can't comprehend it.

"Of course not. Don't be ridiculous! He was furious!" I shrug, and this time, he does touch me, his hands on my arms with the same softness I felt during our fight in the village, before Kruz Lanzo tried to kill me. "Maeve, I'm sorry. I'm so sorry I didn't tell you about Rian and that you had to believe he was dead all these months. You have to know that you and I…we aren't just a distraction designed to keep you here. When I told you I loved you, those weren't just words."

"You promised me you would share your secrets, and you didn't, Eoghan. Men are so stupid. They say stupid things and think women are too naïve to hold them to it. You lied to me, and you thought it didn't matter. You did not trust me, even though I have never given you any reason not to. I don't care what Gálgalesh told you to do. I had a right to know."

"I know. You're right." His thumb brushes my elbow, and everything in me says to pull away, but I remain. He drops his hand to his side. "Let me at least get you out of here. You can hate me all you want after that."

"Don't worry, I will," I huff nearly under my breath, and Eoghan's lips ticks up on one side despite himself. *If he thinks for one minute that his adorable smile changes anything at all, he is dumber than I thought.* I reach for the magic and extinguish the torch so I don't have to look at him anymore. He lets out a purr of a laugh this time, and my cheeks heat.

"You better be able to find your way in the dark, Kael." I feel him grab my hand. He does not entwine our fingers, though, as he starts off along the black corridor.

"Where are we going?" I ask as he picks up his pace, and I wonder if I will be able to keep up if we have to run.

"Bode said to meet him at the Eastern Tunnel if anything went wrong. I'm sure he's waiting for us there."

"The Eastern Tunnel lets out along the jagged ridgeline and is nearly impossible to traverse. Lovely. So we die today either way then?" My heart sinks into my stomach at the faint sound of footsteps somewhere in the distance.

"I told you, I'm with you, Moran." Eoghan wheels me around a corner, and I pray the darkness has not beckoned the shadow lurker to venture from his corridor.

We make our way down the sloping passages, dipping into darkened meeting rooms and through trap doors as the sounds of prisoners grow louder and more frantic. We sneak through the food storage building, and I lead the way this time, through familiar shelves I spent countless days organizing with Boyle Martin, listening to his stories of how he slaughtered wealthy countrymen like me. I never thought I would long for those days again.

We reach the corridor leading to the Eastern Tunnel—the only other exit in the entire prison, save for the main gate— and Eoghan stops as his foot makes contact with something lying on the stone floor. We look down at our feet, our eyes adjusted enough to the darkness to see a handful of dark masses strewn across the corridor.

"Fuck." Eoghan releases my hand and bends down to the one nearest us to examine it closer. I hold my breath; nothing good can come of lifeless bodies laid out in front of our only hope for escape.

"If you are going to say a prayer over them, I suggest you're quick about it, Kael," a voice from a few yards ahead through the tunnel entrance teases, and I recognize it as belonging to the guard who kept me alive in the dungeons.

"I was just making sure it wasn't you before I stepped on it, Price." I can hear the relief in Eoghan's voice as he stands and urges me toward the tunnel. "Alana, this is Trystan Price."

"We've met," the voice says, stoic and even. "Bode and the others are waiting at the gate. I was sent to finish off anyone who came this way. You're lucky I can recognize this one in the dark by now—though I might have taken one or two shots at her already."

"Appropriate." Eoghan tucks me closer to him instinctively as we continue toward the faint illumination of the snow at the end of the tunnel. I can feel the phantom sting of Trystan Price's fist colliding with my jaw relentlessly in the dungeons below our feet, and I ghost my hand softly across my cheek. As we approach the end of the tunnel, dark figures come into view. We stop in front of them. "Just this one… please." Eoghan taps the torch on the wall, and I light it for him. The faces of half a dozen men are illuminated by the soft yellow glow of the fire, Bode standing at the center.

"How did she…?" one of them begins to ask as they size me up.

"Not important," Eoghan replies. "Do you have every-thing?" Bode nods, and I notice two enormous packs at his feet. He crouches to pull forth daggers from one of the pockets and hands them to Eoghan, who sheathes them one-by-one at his sides. Then, he hands over a large sword Eoghan straps to his back. When he finishes, he turns to me and hands me four daggers I recognize as my own, and I fasten them to my thighs. "Ready?" Eoghan waits for Bode to rise. "Good. Let's get the hell out of here."

CHAPTER TWO

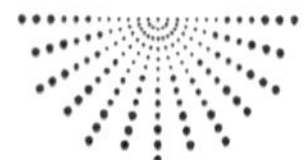

E oghan reaches for my hand once more. He hesitates, heat radiating from him before he turns to the group to count us off. He pairs us off, keeping him and I together. We will be escaping through the gate of the Eastern Tunnel that lets out against the jagged rocks. That's the first challenge. The second is the warning siren that tolls when the gate is opened, alerting the guard towers and the rest of the camp to an escape. The only one who knows how to disarm the siren is Gálgalesh, who could be anywhere now. The third, Eoghan reminds us, is what we will face when we reach the front of the prison. The main entrance sits on the western side of the fortress, which would not be a problem if we were to escape across the ridgeline and down the mountain, but we aren't. We would be caught in the mining village sitting at the foot of the range—if we made it that far at all. Besides, we have others waiting for us in Fáintìrean…which happens to be five kilometers west of the prison.

"So, we fight." Trystan is sure of himself to the point of arrogance, but I suppose now is not the time to be timid.

"We can wield as soon as we set foot outside the walls,

and most of us wield stronger magic than any of the guards the prince brought with him," another man, someone I recognize though I cannot name, adds. Eoghan nods.

"Fight. Stay in your pairs and head to Fáintìrean. We'll wait until dark for you there if we get split up. Do not forget what Gálgalesh—" Eoghan begins, but an explosion rocks the prison walls, and we all stop and listen.

"THE BARRIER IS DOWN! WE CAN WIELD! SOMEONE REMOVED THE ENCHANTMENT ON THE PRISON!"

Voices rise up like a nightmare through the corridors. Someone had been fighting and tried to wield, with success. That should never happen.

"Eogh!" I turn to Eoghan and instinctively lace my fingers through his. *How long has the barrier been down?*

"Fuck! We have to go, *now*! This place is going to turn into a slaughter house if everyone in here can wield. Go! Run!"

We rush toward the gate, and I push it open before we reach it. A high-pitched shriek fills the prison as the warning siren blares. My ears ring, and I can't hear anything except the harsh banshee-like cries reverberating off the mountain peaks. We race through our exit, Eoghan half-dragging me to help me keep his stride. When we all stumble out onto the ice and snow, I reach with the thread of magic and push the gate closed, the siren falling silent. It's too late, though. Everyone is aware we've escaped, not least of which being Rian and his men.

I step forward, but Eoghan yanks my arm, dragging me back. I make to protest just as I look down…and I stumble, grabbing at him to stay upright. Mere inches from where my toes perch precariously atop a broken, shaky boulder is the edge of the ridgeline, dropping mercilessly one hundred feet to a bed of protruding granite stakes below. The impossible ridgeline. The one no one has been able to make it down in fifty years.

"We are going *that* way, Maeve," he whispers as he holds me steady and points with his free arm to the others traversing the slender cliffs. I swallow hard as a lump sticks in my throat, and I grip him tighter. "You can do this," he reassures me as he takes a step. I clutch his biceps. "It's okay. I've got you."

He guides me across the rocks one-by-one, our pace agonizing. The only relief is that no one has been crazy enough to exit the Eastern Tunnel after us. Eoghan wields his dragon fire, clearing the ice from the rocks where we—I —might run the risk of slipping. Eoghan has no such fear. In fact, I'm sure he would be halfway to the winter village by now if not for me. We reach the edge of the fortress, the others already long disappeared around the stone walls, and Eoghan stops as frenzied wails and angry shouts rise to meet us.

"You wield whatever you have to. Use your daggers if anyone gets too close. Do not hold back, no matter who is in front of you. Kill all of them, or else they *will* kill you. Got it?" He pulls my hand to his lips and kisses it softly.

"Where will you be?" Even if he is a lying bastard, I do not want to face a single person without him.

"Haven't I told you already? I am *never* leaving you. I'll be right by your side, keeping you safe." He drops my hand to reach for the sword on his back. He waits for me to grab my daggers from the sheaths at my thighs. "Let's leave this hellscape behind, shall we?"

We round the corner, only to be met with chaos I have never witnessed in my life. A war has broken out at Báscogar Prison. The gates, rid of their enchantments, have fallen open, and prisoners have rushed out into the snow. Killers, siphons, blood-thirsty maniacs, all engaged in the fight—for revenge or pleasure. The king's guards rush forward, pushing men out of the way as they search for us, their targets. I watch as two of our companions engage a pair of guards from the towers, and I wonder if the guards' lack of wielding practice has made them slow and less capable. It does not seem to be a problem for the Leader's men.

A prisoner races toward me across the barren clearing, throwing his hands in front of him as a green ball of light shoots from his palms, hurdling in my direction. I freeze, panic-stricken. Eoghan throws his hands out, and the green light slows its trajectory just before it hits me square in the chest. The impact does little more than force me back, and I cough weakly as a dull, bitter taste creeps into my mouth. The prisoner looks at me, disappointment written across his face, his eyes transfixed on the spot where his poison should have consumed my lungs in an instant. Eoghan pushes me behind him, and I watch as his hands move with expert, lethal grace and speed. He wields, and with the force of a cannon, the offense finds its mark in the man's center, tearing him apart so brutally, his limbs fall fifty yards away from one another.

"Did you just...?" I gape as half a dozen men fall around the prisoner.

"I don't have my damn wielding cuffs," he mutters, as though disappointed. "Next time, one of your blue shields might work, Maevie." He winks and cracks his knuckles, as if he didn't just brutally kill someone. "If we are getting out of here, we need to get rid of some of these idiots." With inappropriate grace for the moment, he trudges forward, slicing, maiming, and blowing prisoners and guards away.

The level of power he possesses is terrifying...and so wholly captivating, I pause and watch as he crosses the clearing. His sword rises and falls with a power that had been stripped from him behind the walls. His blows are like thunder, shaking the ground with a force no man could match. His opponents' attacks fall lamely, as if they hold no power at all, and I realize he has perfect control of that too, the god of war incarnate. This is the legend, the warrior who made men quake and run in fear at the Battle of Buaeth. I was never told how they won victory so swiftly, but now, I see it with my very own eyes.

Men fall around him as he engages the king's guards, and my concentration is broken by the sound of a man hurling himself toward me, his fist in the air. Instinctively, I analyze his weaknesses, finding he left his chest exposed completely. I grab the front of his shirt, as Eoghan has so often done to me in our sparring matches, and I roll back, pulling him over me and throwing him to the ground. I land on my feet, pinning him with my foot to his chest. He thrashes in rage, like a wild beast trying to break free. I pull my thread of magic binding his arms to the ground before running my dagger through his chest. He gurgles and coughs underneath me as his lungs fill with blood. I release him when he stops thrashing and race toward Eoghan.

I fall in line beside him and throw a punch at a guard who reaches for me, catching him square in the jaw. I push him back with an offensive spell, and he hits the stone exterior of the prison before crumpling. Then, I release my dagger toward him, and it barrels through his eye with a force I know I had not placed behind it. I look over at Eoghan, my brows pulled together in a scowl. He chuckles lightly as he runs his blade through another man in front of him, barely even breaking a sweat. It seems unfair as the raggedness of my own breath stings my lungs. I summon my now blood-coated dagger and wipe it across his cloak.

"I don't need your help," I bark at him while dodging a heavy stone hurtling through the air from somewhere in the madness.

"Clearly," he laughs. "But it's just way too much fun. Take that guy out for me, would you?" He points to an Iranndairian prisoner standing amongst a sea of bodies, and my hands fall slightly as I recognize the face. Tómas, Kruz's closest friend and one of the only truly kind prisoners I have met at Báscogar. I take a step forward as I drop my dagger to my side.

"Tómas, you need to run! Try to make it down the ridgeline while everyone is distracted and get to the bottom of the mountain range. If you do, you'll be free to go back home to Iranndair. Those are the rules." I am only an arm's length from him when his eyes darken, and I freeze. "Tómas…"

"What happened to Kruz, Alana? He went after you, and he never came back. What did you and Kael do to him?"

"I-I-I didn't do anything to him, Tómas. He tried to escape and died along the ridgeline—"

"Bullshit! Do you really think I would believe Kruz was dumb enough to try to escape down those cliffs? He was a prisoner here for twenty years. He knew better!" I try to open my mouth to speak, but he spits on the ground in front of me. "You really are the biggest bitch I have ever met." He lunges toward me.

Well, fuck. I jump away from his grip, and he falls forward, giving me time to reset. He hurls himself in my direction again, but I am ready for him. I crouch, slicing my blade into his knee, tearing through his ligaments. He cries out as he stumbles over his footing. I round on him, and he swipes at my own legs, but I catch his hand with the end of my dagger, blood spilling onto the snow. I close the gap between us and drive my knee up into his unprotected nose. The familiar crack of bone and cartilage breaking echoes through the space. This time, I am swifter than the torrent of blood pouring from him, and I kick my boot into his chest, splaying him onto his back. He gasps for air as I stand above him, and something about it makes me feel *good*. I am not a damsel who needs to be rescued. I am in control.

"A shame. I really liked you," I say down to him while he sputters out incoherent profanities. "Quiet; you're making a mess." I stomp my boot against his chest once more. He coughs and cries out as the pain grips him before I take his final breath.

I step away from Tómas, and Eoghan is at my side, sheathing the sword into his back holster. I didn't even notice everyone had either fallen or retreated into the prison for safety. I turn to see the Leader's men racing down the brown gravel road toward Fáintìrean. I try to count them, but their black masses are huddled too close together. Eoghan looks down at Tómas and nods in contemplation.

"Remind me of this the next time I piss you off." He places a gentle hand on my elbow as I return my daggers to my thighs. "We need to get going."

As we begin to leave we hear the clanging sound of the metal gate cracking as it sways. We stop and turn at the sound of a throat clearing behind us. Rian stands between the metal gates, his soft shoes sliding against the ice and gravel, looking down at the bodies covering the landscape. Then, his eyes rise to lock on mine.

Rage and pain well up inside me, and I reach for the faerie magic thread. *Let me blow this bastard straight to Donn.* I pull every symbol and sequence toward my inner concentration, willing anything powerful enough to kill him to unleash itself. My breathing becomes heavy, and my fingertips glow red. Then, I feel a hand on my chest, and I lose the thread when I come tumbling back into the present. Eoghan's palm lays against my sternum, his other thrown up, outstretched, driving out all sound around us.

"Do not let him see you wield," he warns. I can see out of the corner of my eye that Rian speaks just beyond the silencing charm. I push Eoghan's hand away, and he drops his other to his side.

"Mae—" Rian begins when the faux-silence falls away, but that primal sound rips from Eoghan again, and he throws out his hands in front of him. Rian flies through the air, barreling into the prison wall, where his body goes limp as it crumples to the ground.

"Eoghan! You didn't—" I shout.

"No. He'll be fine, unfortunately. He just needed to shut the hell up." He lightly grasps my elbow again and turns me away, toward the gravel road. "Come on. We have to go."

CHAPTER THREE

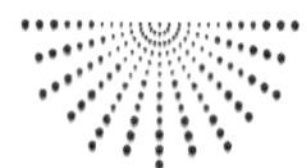

I pick at a piece of chocolate cake on a plate of white porcelain and gold trim as Rian speaks to my mother at the far end of the table. It has been like this since my father gave in to our engagement two months prior. Rian never speaks to me about wedding plans; he prefers to coordinate with my parents or the staff. I haven't had a single opportunity to choose anything at all—not even my wedding dress. I was informed yesterday that the seamstresses will be crafting something for the day, and it will be delivered to my rooms the night before the ceremony. Perfect. It'll be that hideous midnight blue we Morans are compelled to wear, no doubt, overly cumbersome to make me seem delicate beneath the endless layers. I hate feeling delicate and weak, as though I am one of the voiceless porcelain dolls that crowded every inch of my room as a child. They all seem to prefer me this way—my parents...and Rian.

I stab my fork into the cake and shovel a mouthful past my lips. It is actually quite good, though I would never choose a chocolate cake for a summer wedding. It is too rich and heavy on the stomach; something with strawberries would make much more sense. If I were in charge, there would be no cake at all. Flavored ice in pale *pinks and purples, smelling of wildflowers, would be what I would serve—and the entire kingdom would be invited, not just our families and the palace staff.*

My mother's laughter rises from across the room, and she clutches her necklace in that way she always does when someone has charmed her as Rian clearly has. She gently pats his forearm, and I roll my eyes. Perhaps they should be married if they adore each other so much. I shovel more cake into my mouth, working my jaw loudly; irritated, Rian and my mother turn in my direction.

"Darling, that is disgusting. Close your mouth while you chew," my mother admonishes as she rises from her chair. "You will scare Rian off with your poor manners."

Rian follows suit, and my mother plants a kiss on his cheek. She says something to him, too low for me to hear. He nods and gives her a handsome smile before she leaves. Rian watches as she goes and then walks casually toward me, dismissing the staff with his hand, emptying the room.

"You are displeased? I thought you adored cake." He brushes a strand of hair behind my ear before he drops into the chair beside me.

"It's not the cake." I push the plate away. "I don't have any say in any matters of importance when it comes to the wedding."

"Don't be silly, Maeve. You have all the say in the world. The topic of conversation was simply tiresome, and I did not want to bore you with it. Do you really want to look over the plans in case of trouble on our wedding day?"

I reach for his hand, and he tucks it into his lap, as though touching mine might be disgusting in some way. He leans forward instead to plant a kiss on my cheek, and I close my eyes at the softness of his lips.

"There will not be any trouble on our wedding day," I say simply. I cannot imagine what issues might arise behind the castle walls. It would take a mastermind to get past the guards and into this place. "Besides, if there were any issues," I continue, as his lips

move down my neck, "I would be perfectly fine. I know all the secret hiding spots. I would hide, and no one would find me."

"Oh really? And will you share your secrets with me, just in case?" he whispers against my skin.

"No." I laugh softly. "What if you are the trouble? I would want to hide from you then."

"Do you think I'm trouble, Maeve?" I can feel his lips pull into a devilish grin.

"Not at all," I say as I pull his mouth to mine.

———

WE WALK DOWN the dirt and gravel road, the walls of snow rising around us, as if pushing us toward our one destination. Eoghan walks on the opposite side of the road, far enough away from me so I cannot feel his warmth. I carry on straight ahead. My thick wool cloak, which has become overwhelmingly large after my weeks of being held in the dungeons of the prison with little food, is pulled around my shoulders, my feet aching in my boots.

My mind won't stop racing. How is it that everything I think I know is never as it seems? How is it that I do not know anything at all? Rian clearly knew I was alive, but how could he? It still doesn't seem as though my existence is common knowledge. Besides, I've been locked away in a prison for nearly six months with almost no contact at all with the outside world. Who would have told him?

I turn my gaze toward Eoghan, who's walking silently. The sound of gravel beneath his boots is the only audible signal of his existence. *He* has had plenty of contact with the outside world. Tinemallacht warriors at Báscogar are the only other people within the walls of the prison who can come and go as they choose. I drop my gaze to my boots and shake my head. *Stop it. He wouldn't do that to you*, I reason. *I've been wrong about placing my trust in men before, though, clearly.*

"Are we just not going to speak?" Eoghan grumbles quietly, and I straighten at the sound of his voice.

"What is there to say?" I have no desire to rehash my anger; he knows perfectly well how I feel. "You lied to me and told me Rian was dead, even though you knew he wasn't."

"I did not!" Eoghan stops walking. I have half a mind to keep going without him, but the sensible part of me slows my feet in response. "You believed he was dead long before we ever even spoke. I didn't tell you he was dead. I simply didn't correct you when you said he was—there's a difference."

"Oh, do not try to save yourself with semantics! You knew he was alive, Eoghan! You could have told me!"

"Would you have believed me if I did?"

I hesitate. "What?"

"You heard me, Maeve. If I told you Rian was alive, that he led the coup that killed your family and tried to kill you, would you have believed me? You didn't even want to believe me when I told you about Cai! How was I, after months of you thinking I wanted to kill you, going to get you to trust me enough to tell you that your former fiancé had turned on you? You don't trust anyone to begin with!"

I take a step toward him, anger rising within me again. I point my finger as I round on him, but he stands his ground. "That's bullshit! You could have tried!"

"Is it?" I can feel the heat of his dragon fire radiating from him now. "You can't even believe me when I say I love you—which is something I have never told anyone else, by the way —even when I know you can see that it's true. You don't trust me, or Gálgalesh, or anyone, and I don't blame you for it. Be honest with yourself, Maeve. There was no winning in this.

You had to find out this way, and we have to figure out how to move forward now."

I drop my hand to my side as his eyes penetrate me. I tear mine away toward the snow. He's right. There was no way I would have believed him without seeing Rian standing with Sir Oli Raven in the courtyard. My distrust would have pushed him away, and then I would not even be here now. I'd be dead in the prison dungeons or taken to the Capital for my execution. He steps toward me, and I still as his arms cautiously wrap around me.

"I'm sorry," he whispers as he kisses my hair.

"For what?" I sigh into his chest. Defeat and shame sink in as I intertwine my fingers behind him.

"For not finding you and loving you first," he replies, and gods be damned, my heart melts again.

————

WE WALK the rest of the way to the village, his fingers interlaced in mine and his body closer to me than a whisper. I don't want to talk about Rian anymore. Even if I refuse to believe he had played a part in the coup, there is no denying he had a hand in Peadair's execution. He is the reason why Gálgalesh is on the run. For that, I could not forgive him. For that, I'd make him pay one day.

We reach the familiar fourth cottage on the right, where Eoghan leads me up the short steps to the door. The tiny sitting room is packed with faces, the Leader's men all gathered around the hearth, warming themselves by the fire and drinking ale in the early morning light. I scan the room, counting the men. I find Bode lounging against the far wall with Trystan Price, in deep conversation. From the looks of it, at least one pair has not made it from Báscogar. We had not passed them on the road, and my heart sinks at the thought. Eoghan motions for my cloak. I draw it from my shoulders, its warmth replaced by the cozy cottage fire, and he hangs it by the door. He indicates for me to sit on the low dividing wall that separates the sitting room from the bed. I pause. *He is trying to take care of you. Let him.* When I relent, he crouches to unlace my boots.

"Rhodes? Hayes?" His voice rises as he massages my feet softly. From the kitchen comes the familiar frames of three Tinemallacht men: River Hayes, Finn Rhodes, and Arran Sullivan. Relief overwhelms me as Eoghan stands to greet them, their arms lacing around each other. "All right, then?"

"We didn't expect the company, but Bode says all hell broke loose at the prison," Finn begins. "Glad to see you brought Alana with you. Less glad to see your ugly mug." Eoghan smirks and rolls his eyes. "You're looking thin. Care to fill us in on the past month?"

"In a minute. Get Alana something to eat while I speak to the others." He runs his fingers through my hair and then raises my chin softly so my eyes meet his. "Go rest while I figure a few things out." When I raise an eyebrow in question, he lowers his lips to hover over mine. "I promise to tell you all about it when I'm through." He presses a quick kiss to my mouth and then walks off to join the others, River and Sullivan following behind him.

Finn helps me to my feet before we make our way to the small galley kitchen. It has been a month since Eoghan and I left the village, but it has felt like an eternity. I've missed this place, missed the warmth that is ever encapsulated within the walls, heated by the fire straight from Eoghan's large hands. I've missed the kitchen, where the food is not gray mush or stale bread. I've missed the sofa where I can sit and read while warming my feet. I've missed the bed where Eoghan and I had found each other for the first time. Finn walks to the stove, turns on a burner, and places a pan on top.

"Do you like eggs?" he asks. I nod in silent acknowledgement as he pours me a cup of hot tea and places it in my hands. "Anything but porridge, right? I think I'd rather starve than eat one more bowl of porridge."

I lean against the counter and inhale the earthy scent from my cup. The first sip warms me from my lips to my stomach. How normal this all seems when it is anything *but* normal at all.

"How has everything been…since you escaped, I mean?" Finn keeps his eyes on the pan as he cracks eggs into it.

"Quiet, boring. We received a raven from Gálgalesh as we arrived, informing us he and Peadair were being sent to the Capital and to wait here until either you or Eoghan or you both arrived…or we received word everyone was dead." He looks over at me and smiles weakly. "It seemed like Gálgalesh assumed you making it here alone was the most likely outcome and wanted others to be here if you did. Is he—?"

He hesitates, and I shake my head. "No. Still alive, as far as I know."

"Good. At least there's that, then."

He places a piece of bread on top of a plate before finishing with the eggs and sliding them on as well. He rummages in a drawer for a fork before he hands me my breakfast, and I remember, for the first time, that it must still be early in the day. I take it from him and begin to eat as silence falls between us.

"I'm glad he's alive," Finn finally says, inclining his head toward Eoghan. I look over my shoulder into the sitting room and watch as he checks on all the others with the same care he had when he checked on the sick in the village. "I'd hate to have to tell his mother he was dead…and I'd hate telling Lo even more. Gods, I'd probably leave that one to River and spare myself."

He lifts his own mug to his lips as I turn to face him, curiosity written all over my face.

"Lo?" I question. He opens his mouth to speak just as Eoghan enters the kitchen, and he shuts it again. Eoghan reaches my side, placing his arm protectively around my waist. He looks me up and down for any signs of injury, as he had the others.

"All right then? You're lucky Finn made you breakfast. River would have burned this place to the ground," he laughs as River joins us.

"That's a fair assessment, though it's not a kind one," he adds. "Are you ready to tell us what is going on, Eogh?"

Eoghan looks to me, and I nod my head. He indicates to my plate, assuring me he will wait until I'm finished. When I have eaten my fill, he places my dishes in the sink and takes my hand, leading me into the sitting room with the others. The room falls silent. Eoghan clears his throat.

"What happened this morning," he begins as everyone listens with interest, "was not expected, although it was also not entirely unforeseen."

"Well, for those of us hidden away for the past month, would you mind filling us in on what exactly happened?" River cuts in, and Eoghan raises a hand in acknowledgement.

"The usurper pigs showed up a month ago with a man named Drustan Anwyl. They sent Gálgalesh and Peadair to the Capital and turned the entire prison into a work camp. Of course, they tried to get any and all information about Gálgalesh from whoever they could," Trystan explains, his voice gruff. "I was placed on duty as one of his guards, as was Bode."

"We are grateful for that too," Eoghan adds. "Anwyl realized Alana and I were not actual prisoners of Báscogar and decided to separate us to try to get information from us about why we were there. Bode was assigned to me up in the South Tower, and Price was assigned to Alana in the dungeons. I will say, they played their parts well."

He indicates to them, a mischievous look in his eyes, and Trystan Price locks his gaze with mine.

"Sorry." He shrugs, and I lift my own shoulders in dismissal. What is done is done now—at least it's better than being dead.

"And Anwyl found out nothing?" Sullivan asks from somewhere on the sofa.

"No. I don't think he was an idiot, I'm sure he had at least a guess as to why we were there, even if misguided. He did alert the Capital about us, after all, though he got nothing from us."

"So he just let you go? He couldn't have. Eogh, you can be pretty persuasive, but not even you could talk your way out of something like that..." River leans against the divide between the sitting room and the bed.

"No, of course not. Alana killed him." My heart falls into my stomach at the words.

"Actually, I made a deal with the shadow lurker, and *he* killed Anwyl," I say, as though there is any sort of need to defend my actions. "I had no choice."

"Damn, Alana! Making deals with the shadow lurker? We knew you were brave, but I'm not sure any of us would even try that." River whistles.

"At any rate, the Capital sent the new King's Hand and the Heir, and they showed up this morning," Eoghan continues as he rubs his thumb along the backside of my hand.

"Why did they come?" Finn asks this time.

"To deliver Peadair's head on account of 'good faith'." Trystan Price scoffs.

"No!" the Tinemallacht men exclaim in unison.

"Gálgalesh is on the run. The good thing is, he's alive—at least for now."

"And they sent the new Heir all the way to Báscogar for what purpose exactly? As a warning? From what I've heard, he isn't all that terrifying," Sullivan speaks, and my stomach churns.

"For me," I say, and everyone in the room turns. "They were looking for me because…" Eoghan squeezes my hand and shakes his head in warning, though I wave him off. "It's fine, Eoghan. Trust, remember?" His eyes hold only worry as I continue. "Because I am Princess Maeve Moran. They thought they killed me once, but I survived, and now they found me here…somehow."

The room plunges into such silence, the crackling of the fire is like thunder. No one moves or speaks, and Eoghan's temperature rises as he watches the room with a steely glare, threatening anyone who might step even an inch closer to me. We remain frozen in time as long moments pass, and then Finn drops to his knee, bowing his head toward me. River and Sullivan follow suit. One-by-one, the occupants of the room reach toward the floor in a reverent yielding to me. My cheeks turn pink, and I turn away, embarrassed by the sight. Eoghan clears his throat, and for a moment, I remember him down on his knees for me in this cottage as well. My cheeks burn crimson at the thought.

"If any one of you even thinks about hurting her or giving her up, I will burn you until all that is left is ash. Do you understand?"

A resounded confirmation fills the room. Eoghan wraps his arm around my waist and pulls me into his side.

"How did you get out without getting caught?" Finn continues, as if I hadn't just let them all in on the kingdom's biggest secret.

"The Eastern Tunnel. Bode was sent with some of the

king's guards to find Anwyl, and when they found out he was dead, the King's Hand ordered all the prisoners to hunt us down. We were escaping through the tunnels when someone realized the prison enchantments were down, and that's when all hell broke loose."

"Someone took the enchantments down? Who would be dumb enough to do that?" River's jaw falls slack in surprise.

"It had to be Rian. The instructions to disarm Báscogar are hidden in a vault at the military base in Gairdín. I heard the castle guards speaking about it once..."

"But why? Whoever did it would have to be a damn fool. That's akin to suicide," Trystan Price says.

"To wield." Eoghan's low purr makes me jump slightly as he speaks. "The bastard wanted to wield inside the walls. He thought no one else would know what was happening."

Rian wanted to wield, so he endangered himself and everyone else to do so. What must he wield that might be so important? I survey Eoghan's expression, and I can see him weigh the same thoughts.

"What a stupid man," one of the men I cannot name says under his breath. "So, what's the plan now?" Everyone watches Eoghan closely for direction, making it obvious that with Gálgalesh gone, he is in charge.

"We wait until nightfall, as we promised we would—hopefully, Macy and Beck will join us, and then we will head out to the coast toward Tinemallacht, where we know it's safe." Everyone is silent, as though no one has a mind to disagree. *Tinemallacht. We are really going to Tinemallacht.* I swallow my fear as I trace my fingers along Eoghan's sides. "For now, get something to eat, ditch your prison uniforms, and find something to occupy your time."

———

THE MEN from the prison take their turns bathing and changing in the small cottage bathroom while Eoghan and I lay in the darkness on the bed, staring up at the ceiling. He traces his fingers along my spine and down my arms lightly. We don't speak, the only sound is the running water as the men wash this morning's battle from their skin. Once the last of the men have finished, the cottage empties, and Eoghan and I are left alone with the quiet snapping of the firewood, like the peaceful song crickets sing on summer evenings.

"We should change," Eoghan speaks to the ceiling, and his chest vibrates with his words.

"Into what? I only have these damn wool clothes."

"That's not true." Eoghan makes to move, and I sit up to allow him to slide off the side of the bed. He stands and walks into the sitting room, his feet bare against the wood floor. He picks up something from the corner of the room before walking back to the bed. With one hand, he dangles one of the packs Bode carried with him out of Báscogar over the bed. It is nearly empty now as Eoghan lets it drop to the mattress. "Every prisoner at Báscogar surrenders their personal belongings when they arrive. Their clothes are laundered and stored in a closet in the unlikely event of their release. Bode grabbed yours before we left."

I wrench the pack to me and yank it open, diving my hands deep into the canvas bag. Eoghan smirks and turns to the dresser, pulling open a drawer. From the pack, I pull forth my dark traveling pants, shirt, a green cloak, and a brown one as well. I feel the leather of my boots Tiernan laced to my feet before we left the shared room. I pull them out and drop them to the side of the bed. I stand to pull off the black prison uniform. I drag the pants up my legs. They feel snugger now, as though all my training has widened my thighs. I huff as I button them with minor difficulty, and Eoghan snickers in the corner. I turn to face him, taking him in as I do. His black pants have been replaced with tan, cargo-style military ones Cai had worn so frequently in his final years. He yanks a matching tan short-sleeved shirt over his head, leaving his biceps exposed. As he pulls a light-brown leather jacket adorned in dragon scales from the lower drawer, I find I have never been more attracted to him.

"Why were you laughing?" I exhale, feeling suddenly self-conscious.

"You really were frail when you arrived, weren't you? I think the fit of those pants is an improvement." I stick my tongue out at him, and he rounds the bed. I pull on my shirt and then my boots as he laces up a pair of his own. He meets me as I stand. He picks up the cloaks on the bed and buckles the green one around my shoulders. He pauses as he holds the other between his fingertips for me to see, fire dancing in his eyes. "Why do you have a man's cloak in your belongings?"

I reach for it, but he keeps it out of my grasp. "It's Tiernan's. He was worried I might freeze on the way to the prison."

He lets out a sound that makes it clear he wants me nowhere near another man's clothing before he pulls it around me and snaps the metal fastener.

"It'll be warmer once we leave Romiodóg, and then we can throw Damaris's cloak into the sea." He runs his fingers through my hair and plants a kiss on my lips. "Unless you would like to just stay in my arms the whole journey. I can keep you plenty warm."

I love how jealous he can get, even now, when he has me captivated. I throw my arms around his neck, his own snaking around my waist.

"First, to Tinemallacht." A smile dances across his lips, and we head for the door.

CHAPTER FOUR

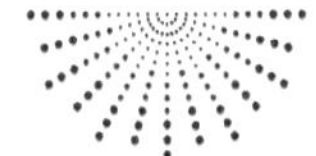

Macy and Beck do not arrive before nightfall, and Eoghan maintains it's best not to leave a note about our whereabouts, in case unfriendly parties come to call. I hate it. I cannot imagine leaving anyone behind, yet I know staying for even one night is dangerous. The group decides to travel to the coast, then to Tinemallacht by way of the sea to avoid run-ins with anyone who will undoubtedly be looking for us now. Eoghan reckons we might be able to reach the seaside by tomorrow evening—if we don't stop moving to set up camp and rest.

"What about the faeries?" Finn asks.

"Faeries? What faeries?"

I am aware the faerie kingdom of Dún lies northwest of Romiodóg, on the other side of the summit, with at least one faerie camp in the mountains near Fáintìrean. I have not seen any signs of them yet, though, and had begun to wonder if they were legend.

"There is a faerie camp nearby, but I think we will bypass them this time to the south. There is also a faerie camp at the mountain's descent. That one will be harder to avoid, as their camp blocks the path to the coast on nearly every side." Eoghan rubs his forehead. "We will need to just be careful and stay together. No stragglers. You'll be as good as dead if a faerie catches you alone. We will place Maeve at the center for safety. Nothing gets to her, understand?"

The others agree. I put my hand up to quiet them and turn to Eoghan.

"That hardly seems fair. I'm not allowing another person to be harmed on account of me. No, I'll travel at the front of the pack, in the open."

"Out of the question." Eoghan motions to the others, and they circle me, as though hiding me inside a human treasure chest.

"Eoghan, stop! I am not going to be treated like a fragile child. I am going to travel at the *front* of the pack with you, and I will not hear any more discussion about it. This is not your decision to make! We are leaving. Now!"

He is absolutely *not* going to treat me as though I am not capable of surviving a group of faeries when I already killed one in cold blood on my own. I push my way through the men and grab Eoghan's hand, dragging him through the snow.

"Maevie," he says, his words full of amusement that makes my eyes roll.

"What?" I snap as I continue walking.

"Oh, nothing. I just thought maybe you would like to know the coast is that way." He points behind us and smiles. "But by all means, lead me wherever you would like to go, and I'll follow you there."

I stop moving and loosen my grip around his fingers. He pulls me to his chest, planting a kiss on my forehead before walking me back to the group. I feel like an idiot.

"Okay. Mayhem and I will lead the way. Stay close, and maybe we will clear the mountains without being eaten."

———

THE FIRST NIGHT of travel is endless and freezing. I am starting to miss my heavy wool cloak that pulled at my shoulders and weighed me down so much, I was shorter by an inch or two every time I wore it. Even with Eoghan beside me, his heat does not penetrate the winter chill of the mountains.

"Would you like my jacket?" he asks as a violent shiver runs through my body.

"I'm fine," I lie. I cannot even feel my feet anymore, and my legs are heavy with cold.

"You are not fine. Your lips are blue, for gods' sake. Let's stop and make a fire. You need to warm up. We can rest for the night and start to move again in the morning."

"It'll take us days to reach the coast if we stop every time I am cold." I know at some point, I will let him win, but I was hoping to make it through the night at least before I did.

"We will never make it to the coast if you freeze." He slows his pace and turns to the others. "We are stopping for the night. River, Finn, Sullivan, light some fires. Everyone else, conjure up some tents."

Eoghan wraps his body around mine, and my skin stings as he heats my frozen core. I melt into his touch, a welcome break from the unbearable arctic Romiodóg temperatures. He is always there, my constant dragon fire to protect me and warm me, just as he had that first time he found me in the snow. I lean my head back against his shoulder and watch as the stars move in a circular motion around the sky. I've never seen so many stars before, and, despite the cold, I imagine I'll never see anything this beautiful for the rest of my life—including present company.

"At the top of the world, the stars never pass across the sky. They simply spin endlessly while the northernmost stars stand still," he explains as he points up at the deepest black. "I was seventeen when I saw my first star, on my first night at the military academy in Gálamáistir. They were not as bright as these—too much light from the buildings nearby—but I had never seen anything more amazing...or dark. A bit frightening when you're used to the sun never setting."

"Are you telling me you are afraid of the dark, Eoghan Kael?" He simply smirks. "We could not see stars with the naked eye from the castle, with its bright lights and towers that obscured the view. When Cai and I were children, he told me of a group of scholars who had built a tube of steel and enchanted it to bring the stars closer when looking through it. I had to have it. I begged Cai endlessly to get one for me, so we stole a bit of gold from one of the castle vaults, and he snuck into the city to the private academy to purchase one for us. We stayed up on the roof all night looking through it, studying the constellations and filling our minds with wonder of the gods we did not believe were more than bedtime stories."

Our chests rise and fall in perfect unison. Eoghan's thumb caresses my chin softly as he holds me transfixed in his gaze.

"I love you," he whispers. "If I could bring every star to you, I'd string them into a necklace to illuminate you with their light; though the truth is, they'd never compare to what I see when I look at you. When I saw that...idiot in the court-yard today, I wanted to tear his heart from his chest. It wasn't out of jealousy or fear that you might want him more than you want me—it was because I knew he had stolen the light from you. I couldn't stand to think about someone hurting you like that." I forget to breathe for a long moment and then inhale audibly with a soft gasp. "Before I found you outside the village, I used to hear you crying in your room in the evening. I wanted so badly to stop your crying, I just didn't know how. I tried so many times. I was sure I would frighten you, or you would send me away. I should have tried. I'll never let you feel so broken and alone again, Maeve, not if I can do anything about it."

I remember the night I sobbed into my pillow in my freezing room at Báscogar, the footsteps outside my door forcing me to sit in silence until they had retreated. Had Eoghan thought to come and comfort me then? What would have happened if he had?

He lifts my chin to bring my lips to his and kisses me with a tenderness that feels like coming home. His scent fills my nostrils, and I take his face between my hands as the world fades away around us. I love him, and despite how angry he makes me or how hard it is to trust him, I love him more than I have loved any other. And he loves me—I can feel it every moment he is near.

We pull away as the others shout for us to join them at camp, where they have begun to pull out food from their packs and warm themselves. Eoghan guides me toward a fire, but when we reach the first tents, I shake my head in protest as desire devours me in waves. I do not want him to stop holding me, stop kissing me. If I don't feel his touch for another moment, I might simply die.

"What's the matter?" he asks as he examines me, as if I might be ill or hurt.

My lips curl into a sensual smile. He pauses in his confusion, and I grab the front of his shirt, pulling him wordlessly toward one of the tents the others have just conjured up for us to stay in overnight. I hear River shout something playfully, and Eoghan gestures toward him, his eyes never leaving me. I duck and crawl through the entrance, and he follows, his hands falling on either side of me while I push myself backward on the makeshift bed. I plant small kisses against his lips one-by-one as I lead him further inside. Once we are completely encapsulated by the canvas shelter, I draw him near to me, and he scoops me up toward himself.

"Now is not the time," he whispers, though he does not pull away.

"I do not care who hears," I reply, my lips trailing across his jawline.

He grabs my hands and softly pries them away from his body. I stop moving, shocked by his dismissal. I pull away to find his face in the dark.

"You are not a conquest, Maeve. I don't need anyone else to hear me claim you and make you mine. You are everything, and one day, we will be bound to each other as one heart and one soul. Let me get you to safety first, though. Not here." I make to protest, but he seals his lips to mine. I feel his hands move up to the clasp at my neck, pulling the outer cloak from my shoulders. "Especially not in Damaris's cloak."

Ah, so his jealousy still remains, even now. I laugh as his lips reach my neck, and fire rises in my abdomen at his hungry yet measured affections. How I wish he would balk his self-control, even just once.

"Tiernan and I slept like this." His roaming stops as he listens, his breath against my skin. "The last night before I left with Gálgalesh to Báscogar. I woke up against his naked chest with his arms wrapped around me, keeping me warm… keeping me to him throughout the night."

It wasn't a lie, though I know it had meant nothing more than survival to either of us. My words hit their target, however, just as I had hoped they would. The guttural sound of frustration that escapes Eoghan echoes against the trees outside the tent, and an owl startles from its perch into the night sky. He doesn't care anymore where we are or who else is around.

———

THE NEXT MORNING, with little sleep and an abundance of heat, we pack up our camp and head toward the coast. Eoghan and the others stop periodically to check the map we took from the cottage, seeking alternative routes around the faerie camp, but to no avail. We will have to walk right through the center of it if we are going to make it to the only seaside village in Romiodóg.

"How bad can it be?" Sullivan muses from somewhere behind us as Eoghan melts our path through an especially high bank of snow.

"We could die," River scoffs. "Eaten by a camp of faeries with razor sharp teeth and terrible breath."

"Faeries do have terrible breath," I concede, remembering when Gálgalesh intruded underneath my cloak's hood all those months ago.

"If we had something to bargain with, they might spare us," one of the others suggests.

"Give them River so we won't have to listen to him the entire trip," Eoghan grumbles, and Finn laughs.

"No one is going to get eaten. We just have to have a plan," I admonish, even though I'm not sure how anyone could bargain with a faerie, especially if faeries are as mean as Peadair was.

"Faeries are fearful of banshees," Trystan says from against a tree, where he lounges as he waits for the path to clear. Eoghan stops wielding and looks at him, tilting his head to the side.

"What are you talking about, Price?" he says as I blow on

my hands to warm them. He walks over to me, taking them in his own, and they heat pleasantly at his touch.

"I heard Gálgalesh and Peadair speak about it once. I was in the warden's quarters one evening when Peadair burst through the door in hysterics that took me by surprise. I'm not sure I had ever even heard him speak before that day. I excused myself from the room, but I stood outside to listen while he spoke of hearing what he thought was a banshee. They were so worked up, they almost placed the prison on lockdown."

Trystan Price finishes, and the men burst into fits of uncontrollable laughter.

"You have got to be kidding me! You really think any of us would believe that?" River wipes tears from his eyes as Bode pats Trystan on the shoulder, shaking his head. "Peadair would have eaten a banshee for dinner. Do you even know what a banshee is? It's a wailing woman of the forest. Are you telling me Peadair was scared of a wailing woman?"

Peadair, scared of banshees? That hardly makes sense. Peadair did not seem to fear anything at all. Although, that night in the forest when he and his men had tried to kill me, I had cried out at the top of my lungs, and Peadair hesitated and backed away from me. And then there was that time, in Kruz's room before he had confessed his hatred for my family... What was it that I read about faeries and banshees?

"Wait," I shout over their voices, and Eoghan stops laughing. He turns his attention to me. "In the book of legends I found in the prison library a few months ago, there was a poem about banshees and faeries that was underlined twice. It said, 'in moonlit hills where faeries tread, banshee wails fill their hearts with dread.'"

Eoghan and the others fall silent in contemplation.

"Well, that's great, but even if faeries are afraid of banshees, what are we supposed to do? Catch one and drag it into their camp? There can't be many in these mountains." Sullivan takes over melting the snow along our path as Eoghan stands silently, gazing off somewhere ahead.

"Maybe we don't need an actual banshee. Maybe we just need someone to *play* a banshee long enough for us to pass the camp." His eyes fall on me, and I scoff. *He cannot be serious. Maybe I exhausted him to the point of lunacy last night.* "Come on, Mayhem. You up for causing a little trouble?"

I step back as I roll my eyes. As if I know the first thing about banshees! I have never even seen or heard one. My father used to take annual hunting trips to the Borderlands so he and his men could hunt them for sport, but none ever made it through the castle gates.

"I wouldn't know how to imitate a banshee even if I tried. I'll get us all killed." Eoghan's eyebrow ticks up, silently challenging me while someone else speaks up.

"I do." Bode's voice is delicate and does not match his menacingly large frame. "I'm from the southern village of Cathcru along the Romiodóg border near the Borderlands. Banshees terrorized our village growing up."

"Will it work? Could you help her?" Bode nods. Eoghan turns to the others. "Well then, let's make a plan."

———

BODE and I climb onto a low hanging tree branch just outside the faerie camp as the sky begins to darken. From our vantage point, we can see each of our companions and the twelve tents that make up the faeries' impassable domain. The sounds of singing and fighting in Anquonda—the language of the faeries—fill the air as Eoghan and the others approach.

Our one hope is that the faeries will postpone killing us until we can scare them off. An almost unreasonable request, when faeries are the most dangerous threat to human existence. They are faster, stronger, and smarter in every way, and this bunch seems particularly driven by their stomachs and their taste for human flesh. My eyes scan the outskirts of the faerie camp, and I note a dozen human skulls on stakes surrounding the perimeter, a warning to anyone foolish enough to think they might pass through. It's a warning we should not ignore; nevertheless, we have no choice if we have any hopes of escaping this mountain.

Eoghan reaches the boundary of the camp, the others tucked in closely to him on all sides, their weapons sheathed —though easily accessible. He looks over his shoulder in our direction and spies us hidden among the branches. He nods, almost imperceptibly, before he turns his eyes back toward the camp. He wants to know I'm safe before the madness begins. Even Eoghan, in all his bravery, cannot deny this is a stupid plan that will probably get us all killed. We should just have mercy on ourselves and roll around in butter while praying for a quick death.

"Gentlemen," his voice rises up in the forbidden language, and the singing and fighting cease.

I watch as a blur of a figure sweeps through the camp and stops in front of Eoghan. Faeries are dangerously quick. I had almost forgotten how fast Gálgalesh could move during our training sessions. What the hell are we doing? This is a ridiculous, stupid plan concocted by truly ridiculous, stupid people. There is no way this plan is getting us anywhere but the grave.

Eoghan—to his credit—does not flinch, not even as the faerie, who towers well over him by at least a head, encroaches on his space. The faerie's triangular teeth are bared, and his dark, sleek hair falls to his waist. His clothes are old and filthy, and he wears animal pelts of various colors on his shoulders. Behind him, half a dozen similarly menacing faeries fall into formation, sizing Eoghan and the others up.

"Human." The faerie sniffs the air as he speaks. "What brings you to our doorstep?" The faerie licks his lips as Eoghan's shoulders remain squared, the same warrior's mask he wore inside the prison walls firmly in place.

"Passage to the bottom of the mountain," Eoghan says casually. "We are seeking refuge on the coast."

"Is that so?" A smile curves the faerie's lips, and I watch as the men surrounding Eoghan stiffen. "Perhaps you would like to join us for a meal first."

"No, I think we would prefer it if we continue before the night has frozen the air too much for us to pass. We would hate to inconvenience you with our presence if we were to become stranded at your camp."

"Nonsense." The faerie's voice is smooth yet dangerous. "Allow us to show you just one kindness before you make your way. Then, we will help you on your journey."

There is no question in the faerie's voice. It's clear he isn't going to take no for an answer, and Eoghan knows it. The faeries step aside and beckon our men forward, making quite clear that the invitation is compulsory. Eoghan steps into the camp without a hint of hesitation, and he motions for the others to follow. The faerie leader walks beside him toward the fire at the center of the gathering, the faeries disappearing between the tents.

He was never supposed to enter the camp. He was never supposed to leave our sight. *Damnit, Eoghan, you're going to get yourself killed!* I would like to shout at him and drag him back down the gravel road—back to Báscogar, if I must—but he is beyond my reach, and Bode presses his fingers into my arm to keep me in place.

"Don't," he warns. "If the faeries see you, the whole plan will have been a waste."

"If they get eaten, what's the point?" I counter. "We can't see them. We won't know what's happening."

"Eoghan knows what he's doing. He'll give us the signal," Bode assures. "Trust him. He's never been wrong before."

I settle with an unsatisfied exhalation. *I really hate this whole trust thing,* I complain to myself. *Why is it that Eoghan must always be trusted? What makes him so special?* I close my eyes and reach down the faerie magic. If I can't see him, I want him to know just how stupid I think his whole plan is. I will the magic to send communication down the line, as it had before to Eoghan and the shadow lurker—to the Tine-mallacht fool I am compelled to trust.

I really hate you for this, I will down the magical thread. *This was not part of the plan. I can't even see you. I need to know you're okay, Eoghan Kael. Say something so I know you're still alive.* I wait as the low mumble of the faeries' voices—and those of our men—get lost on the freezing wind. *Eoghan, say something, or else I am leaving this tree and coming to find you. You know just how badly Peadair wanted to eat me. I'm sure these faeries wouldn't last a sec—*

"I'm fine, thank you," Eoghan's voice rises through the camp. So he had heard me. I ease back onto the branch, not at all less unsettled, yet reassured he's still breathing.

We sit and wait and try to listen. The voices remain so low, we cannot distinguish between the faeries and the men. They could be poisoned and incapacitated. The faeries could be eating away at their limbs while they are forced to sit and watch. *Or he could be fine because he said he was fine and you need to trust him.* I swear under my breath at myself, and Bode chuckles beside me.

"This isn't Eoghan's first run-in with the faeries," he muses. "Last year, he helped Gálgalesh negotiate the release of a villager woman from the tribe near Fáintìrean."

"What villager woman?"

Bode shrugs. "It was a friend of Eoghan's. I don't know all the details. I just know he was successful, and the villagers were grateful."

My face heats. A friend of Eoghan's? One he never mentioned before? A woman from the village where he would stay in his cozy cottage and large bed? Why had he risked his own life to negotiate her release? I know he has a hero complex—and is annoyingly loyal in every way—but I don't imagine he would go to such lengths for just anyone. I tug hard on the magic thread, making it hum loudly through my very bones.

What woman did you save last year, Eoghan Kael? Did you bed her in the cottage? Was she one of the girls you danced with at the Fire Offering?

I listen to the low mumbles of conversation. Eoghan offers no response, that bastard. Oh, great savior of women, Eoghan Kael! Jealousy like none I have ever experienced rages through me. Who is she, and why am I so angry about him doing what he could to keep her safe?

Did you drop to your knees before her too? Did she scream your name as I did?

No answer. I groan loudly and stand, jumping from the tree branch to the forest floor. He is going to answer me right now, whether he likes it or not, the gods be damned! Let the stupid faeries *try* and eat me.

Bode scrambles to his feet and jumps down beside me. I am already stomping toward the cluster of tents before he makes it from the tree. Those cursed faeries can all go to the depths of hell, and Eoghan Kael can too. I feel the faerie magic pulse through me like a surge of energy as I enter the perimeter. The faeries have charmed their domain, and their magic is calling to me. I bound forward, hushed, frantic whispers from Bode following close behind. *Where is he?*

"Eoghan Kael! When I speak to you, you will answer me!"

I round the corner, shouting without regard for the danger of the camp or just how appetizing I might be for a group of brutal human-killers. I stop as I see Eoghan and the others in front of me, caught up by their necks, the faeries' long, terrible nails threatening to puncture their throats.

"Kind of busy at the moment," Eoghan wheezes. "But yes, if you must know."

Yes? That Fire Cursed fool! My eyes flick toward the faerie with his hand around Eoghan's neck. *He is going to get himself killed by a bunch of nomad faeries! No! No one is killing Eoghan Kael except me!*

Rage fills me to my core, and I scream as I unleash a torrent of faerie magic. It pushes the faerie leader back, his hand falling from Eoghan's neck. Eoghan takes the opportunity to grab his long sword from his back.

"Yes to which part?" I wield again, and the other faeries fall back a step, giving our men an opportunity to ready themselves.

"All of it." Eoghan raises his sword just in time to block an assault from the faerie leader. His lip ticks up. *Is he amused?* I let out a frustrated scream, and the magic I loose sets one of the tents to my right on fire. "Are you looking for an apology again? I thought we spoke about this already." Eoghan kicks out his leg and pushes the faerie back.

"You are a pig, Eoghan Kael!" A faerie wields against me, but I block it by raising a blue shield.

"I am not. You're just jealous." His blade slashes through the air. He misses the faerie by less than an inch. "I actually don't mind it all that much, though."

"I feel like we are missing something here," River shouts as he catches his own opponent at the knees.

"Stay out of it!" Eoghan and I say in unison, and River mutters something under his breath.

"Just admit that you feel the same as I do every time

another man looks your way because you love me." He smiles as his blade catches the faerie along the arm this time, and Eoghan closes the gap between them. He barrels his elbow into the faerie's face.

"Not today." I flick my dagger past his head and catch an approaching faerie in the neck, taking him down beside Eoghan. Eoghan laughs in earnest as he continues to beat away at the faerie leader.

"You two are meant for each other, you know that?" Trystan Price yells as he struggles with his opponent on the ground. "Both of you are insane!"

I roll my eyes and pull the magic to me before I release it one more time. Bonds wrap around the arms, hands, and necks of the faeries, all except the one Eoghan is fighting. The faerie leader drops back in alarm, and Eoghan brings his blade to the faerie leader's throat.

"I asked nicely for us to cross once already. I will not ask again," he purrs in that low dragon thrum.

"Y-your magic," the faerie stutters beneath Eoghan's blade. "You are human, but your magic is not of your kind..."

"Not all faeries piss me off like you do," I shrug. "Let us through."

The faerie throws his hands up, but Eoghan refuses to drop his sword. I stand at the ready, prepared to wield again. Eoghan motions the others forward as we hold off our attackers, and, one by one, they pass through the camp to the road on the other end. Once all of them have made it outside the camp's borders, Eoghan motions for me to meet him at his side.

"We are leaving. You will not follow us or hunt us. We have earned our safe passage through the mountains."

The faerie nods, and Eoghan sheathes his sword. He takes my hand in his, and we begin to make our way toward the others. Before we reach the perimeter, the faerie clears his throat.

"Woman," he calls out from behind us. "You smell peculiar. May you have mercy on the many who have led you to a fate worse than death." I make to turn around, but Eoghan shakes his head, and I obey. "The Queen of Destruction and Tragedy. Let us hope Donn makes room for us all."

Eoghan pulls me ahead as I wrestle with the words hanging in the frigid air. *The Queen of Destruction and Tragedy.*

I feel sick. Why had he called me that? What had he sensed that had scared him so? We reach the others and carry on down the road in silence once more.

———

WE REACH the bottom of the mountain in the black of night and the coastline at the first signs of charcoal-gray skies signifying morning's arrival. The air is damp and salty and smells of fish. My first breath of sea air fills my lungs, and I wonder how anyone could long for such a smell. It is disgusting at best. We reach a small village of only a handful of houses sitting along a rocky shore. One of the men of our group—whose name I have learned is Klein—knocks on a door. He greets the occupants as they appear on the threshold, speaking in low tones, pointing to the water just beyond the rocks.

"This one is friendly to Gálgalesh. He should grant us permission to use his boat," Eoghan whispers to me.

"You've done this before," I guess from his ease as he watches on.

"Once or twice. There are faster ways to Tinemallacht, though none are especially safe right now."

Klein nods and returns to us as the man retreats into his

home. He approaches Eoghan and I, blowing into his hands for warmth.

"He says we can take it, but in its state, it'll likely fall apart when we reach Merrow Cove."

Eoghan runs a hand through his hair as he thinks.

"We'll stop in Cuanslí then and grab a bigger boat there. There has to be at least one or two ships left in the harbor." Cuanslí, the capital city of the Tonnfórsca territory—Rian's home. It is the main trade harbor between Draíocoinnigh and Oleaíncudd and the heart of all the wealth on the continent, apart from the capital itself. "Best we get moving if we want to make it to Tinemallacht before next spring."

CHAPTER FIVE

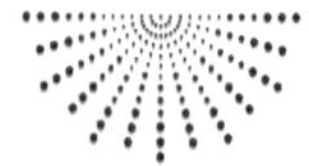

It takes us another three days by boat to sail to Cuanslí, leaving Romiodóg and the eternal winter behind. I do not enjoy sea travel as I thought I might when Rian described his adventures across the trade routes to Oleaíncudd. The motion of the boat makes me ill, and the cramped space leaves little room for privacy as Eoghan pulls back my hair from my face and I empty my stomach over the railing. Perhaps that was the only good thing to come of the coup—to never be dragged for weeks on end to foreign shores.

The evening before we reach Cuanslí, Eoghan comes to find me on deck, a mug of tea in his hand, a spare blanket in his arms. The early spring air is warmer even just slightly south of Romiodóg, but the chill still runs right through my bones.

"We missed you at dinner. Is everything all right?" I ask as he hands me the mug. I have scarcely seen Eoghan at all these past few days besides when I'm ill, or late in the evening when he finally makes his way to bed. He seems distracted by something that has gripped him since we stepped off land, and he hasn't let me in on his thoughts just yet.

"Just going over maps and preparing instructions to be sent ahead once we reach the harbor." He dismisses me with a beat of his hand against the nothingness between us. "We should dock by sunrise if we are lucky and the seas stay calm."

I nod and bring the cup of tea to my lips. "I wonder what it might be like, to finally make it to Tonnfórsca. I have dreamed of it so often, though I'm not sure I have ever been able to picture it just right."

"Have you never seen it?" Eoghan muses. "Not even in a photograph?"

"Never. Rian hoped I might be surprised when I finally arrived. He did, however, tell me the buildings were made of limestone and marble, their roofs almost completely flat. He said the tile work and towering palms make it a paradise for travelers, and the water glistens like diamonds in the sunlight." I close my eyes as I imagine the warmth of the sun on my face after months in the darkness.

"What else did he tell you about the city?" he asks, and I hear the faint annoyance in his voice, as if he would rather not speak of the man we left crumpled on the ground at the prison gates.

"He told me there are opera houses and theaters, that the ships roll into the harbor with sails like giant white clouds that can be seen for miles. He said there are palaces on the hillside that overlook the bay, and at night, they throw parties with light shows on the verandas."

Eoghan's eyes narrow. There is disbelief written across his face, as though I have told him a tall tale more suitable for a child's bedtime than an adult conversation.

"Well, tomorrow, you and I will venture into the city to purchase some lighter clothes and food for the rest of the journey. Even at sea, the heat can become oppressive the closer we travel to Tinemallacht. I want you to stay with me, though. The city can be…tricky to maneuver."

He speaks as though he has been there before, and of course, he had to have been. Unlike me, Eoghan Kael has been everywhere and done everything. I incline my head in agreement, and he smiles weakly at me. His features droop with exhaustion, and I realize he hasn't slept more than a couple of hours in days. How he's standing, I do not know. He plants a kiss on my forehead and then turns back the way he came.

"Eogh?" I call after him. He stops before he disappears into the darkness. "Do you think we will ever see Gálgalesh again?"

"I don't know, Maevie." His voice is sincere and pained, as though he pondered the question himself. "I keep losing people I care about, and I wonder if it's worth it anymore."

"And what have you decided?"

"If you're around, there's nothing more important in the entire world."

He continues his movement again, and I am left alone on the deck once more.

———

"I AM TOLD, if you cut off a faerie's head, it will speak for a week before the magic has run out," a voice croons from the corner of the room. I am in the familiar, dark dungeons of Caisleán Rialú, upon the cold, damp floor, my hands chained to the wall above my head. I am starving and beaten within an inch of my life. Peadair is seated beside me, unconscious. "Is it true that you filthy beasts bleed gold? I'd quite like to test the theory for myself."

That voice. I vaguely remember it from somewhere, though I cannot seem to place it. My head lulls on my shoulder, as if I'm being dragged under as my body gives into the severity of my wounds. Still, they do not let me die. They'll kill Peadair first and make me watch. They have told me so a million times already. I pull at the chains on my arms weakly, and the Faebond cuts into my flesh with a scalding that makes me wince.

"Come now, Gálgalesh. I was told you were smarter than this. Not even you are a match for Faebond."

The man moves into the light, and his rounded stomach draped in elegant garbs of seafoam green bounces as he walks. He is short in stature, with graying-blond hair and a matching beard adorned with three golden ornaments like tassels hanging from a garment. After all the years on the coast and at sea, Bréanainn Doherty cannot wash enough of the salt from his hair to make him look half as regal as his new title of king should demand.

"Tell me how Princess Maeve is alive and why you have hidden her in that prison you so love, and I will let you and your lover go free." Bréanainn kicks at Peadair's still leg stretched out against the stone floor.

"Why would I tell a spineless, pathetic human fool anything at all?" I say back, and Gálgalesh's voice escapes me.

"It does not serve you to protect such a weak waste of a human, Gálgalesh. Be reasonable."

"There is plenty of waste standing in this room." I turn and eye the boy they have decided to call 'prince'. "The woman does not fit the description."

The usurper king rolls his eyes and lets out a sigh. "We will go to call on her. It does not matter if you tell us or not."

"And she will kill you." A smile dances across my face. "My only regret will be not being there to witness her snuffing the life from your eyes."

I spit on the floor, and Bréanainn Doherty motions for his guard to move forward, and then the room falls away to black.

———

I WAKE up just before the sun with Eoghan's arms falling lightly around me, his breathing soft as he dreams. I brush my hair from my face before I kick my feet over the side of the small mattress, planting them silently on the floor. I stand and pick up my clothes at my feet, stepping into my pants and yanking my shirt over my head.

"Where are you going?" Eoghan mumbles, his voice thick with sleep.

"Nowhere. Ignore me. You still have a little more time before we arrive." I brush my hand across his cheek, and he rolls over as his breathing steadies again.

I shuffle through the tiny cabin, one much smaller than even our quarters at the prison. I make my way through the dark interior of the boat as it rocks back and forth against the wind. At the end of the hall is a door leading to the deck. I pass through it. Although we have not docked, we should be close enough to see the lights of the harbor against the lightening sky. Finn has taken the helm to guide us into port, and I smile at him as I approach.

"You're up early," he yawns.

"Bad dreams," I admit. "I thought I might be able to see the city before we arrive. How far out are we?"

Finn inclines his head, and I turn my gaze in the direction of his own. There, sitting at the edge of the fast-approaching bay, rising against the hilly landscape, is Cuanslí. Even at a distance, the hustle of the port city is evident with lights burning brightly in the nearest windows. The stone façades of the buildings are still just shadows in the dark, though they grow lighter with every passing moment. The sun creeps above the hilltop slowly, as though peeking through the night to bring the dawn, and I take in the vast stately homes on the hill, their windows painted with color, blocking out the view of the city below.

"Wow," I whisper mostly to myself. Finn makes a soft,

incredulous sound beside me, and I turn away from the view.

"It is something from a distance—which I think was the plan from the start. I would reserve judgment until we make it into port."

"Why? What's the matter with it? I can't imagine it could be less beautiful up close."

"It's not necessarily the beauty of it that is in question," Finn begins. "It's the purpose."

"Merchant imports? What could be so terrible about merchant imports? Textiles? Food? Wine?"

"Sure, textiles, food, and wine are all fine, but you will find none of them at this port. You'd have to travel to the southern coast of Tonnfórsca for those." My forehead creases as I try to understand. "Cuanslí is interested in one import and one import only."

"And what import is that?"

The boat winds between two ships floating outside of the docks as we pull into the harbor.

"Slaves," Finn replies. His tone is hard and coated with anger.

Our boat settles with a soft thud against the wooden dock, and Finn excuses himself to find Eoghan and the others below. *Slaves.* From my years with Rian, I had always been told his family monopolized imports into the city, but as far as he had said, the contents were products so important to the continent, they had made their wealth within one generation. That wealth only continued to grow until the Dohertys were one of the most affluent families in all of Draíocoinnigh. Had the city become so sinister since the coup that they no longer brought their ships to dock here? What had happened to my kingdom that the slave trade could run so rampant in one of the richest and most beautiful of all our cities?

A man approaches from the dock with a book and pen in his hand to log our entry into port. Eoghan makes his way to the deck as he shoves his arms through the holes of his jacket and approaches me hastily. He stops in front of me, shielding me from view, and pulls my hood over my head.

"Don't let anyone get a good look at you. We will head out into the city once I settle things with the dock attendant." He turns from me, planting himself directly in front of me as the man boards our rickety vessel.

"Sir," the man begins as the others fall in line beside Eoghan, obstructing my vision even more, "I welcome you and your companions to Cuanslí. May I ask what your business in the city might be?"

"We are here to collect supplies. We do not expect to stay longer than the day."

"A day? Is that all? Truly a shame for young men such as yourselves to miss out on the offerings of our city." The man cranes his neck to see around Eoghan's shoulder. Eoghan moves with him, and I tuck in closer to his back. "I would be happy to direct you toward some of the finest auction halls and pleasure houses for you to enjoy. Our courtesans are some of the most beautiful in the kingdom, apart from the king's personal escorts, of course."

"We have no need for such things, thank you." Eoghan's tone is devoid of interest. "One day will do."

The man's smile drops slightly, yet his head bobs in acknowledgement, and he opens the leather-bound book in his hands.

"Name?"

"Donál Togher." Eoghan reaches into his pocket and removes a few gold coins that he places into the attendant's awaiting palm.

"Welcome to Cuanslí, Mr. Togher. I hope you enjoy your time with us."

Eoghan and the man acknowledge one another for a final time, and then we wait in silence while the man disembarks. Once he disappears onto a ship beside us, Eoghan's body softens, and he and the others disband from the defensive wall they built around me.

"What a disgusting place," River says through gritted teeth. "Can you believe how unashamed they are of selling people?"

"What else are they going to say? It's why travelers come to Cuanslí to begin with, isn't it? No reason to beat around the bush." Trystan Price scowls over his shoulder at the dock as he speaks.

I watch as deep creases etch into Eoghan's face. He has been here before, and the city is familiar to him. He seems unsurprised by the mention of its auction halls and pleasure houses, making me wonder if they are not a new development after all and why—if they are so widely regarded—Rian had never mentioned them.

"Ready to explore, Maevie?" Eoghan asks, and his voice pulls me from my thoughts. I look out onto the city as the sun begins to illuminate the cobbled roads along the shoreline and agree. Eoghan turns to the others as he places his hand softly against the small of my back. "Maeve and I are going into the city. Everyone has their tasks to complete. We need food to last us until we reach Tinemallacht and a ship to sail. We will be back before nightfall."

With that, he helps me off the boat and onto the dock. We slide past the dock attendant, who had registered our boat, and onto the long promenade running parallel to the sea. Though it is still much too early for any shops to be open, many of the storefronts are thrown wide in welcome, low lights still burning in their windows and shopkeepers standing near the entrance, waiting for passersby to be enticed by their wares.

"Come and have a look," one woman calls on my right, and I nearly jump out of my skin. "I think I might have something the gentleman would enjoy."

"No, thank you." Eoghan intertwines his fingers with mine and pulls me to himself protectively. I look into the window as we pass. Collars and chains are hung on display. Some are bedazzled with jewels and gold, while others are plain or even barbaric, with spikes on the underside. "Pay no mind," Eoghan whispers to me as I slow to examine them.

"Collars?" I whisper back.

"For the slaves. Many of the wealthy in the city keep one or two as pets and like to display them at parties or while they walk the promenade." As he speaks, a woman passes us with a child, a leather strap around its neck and a matching lead in her hand.

"But they are humans… Why?"

"Because Cuanslí is a city of horrible men who line their pockets with money drenched in blood."

Eoghan leads us down a narrow street rising from the seaside toward the city square. The air smells thick of vinegar and ammonia mixed with a sweet smoke and stale alcohol. Three men lay half-dazed in the gutter, vomit puddled on their shirts and the ground next to them. Square pieces of parchment are strewn across the road in the hundreds, all with numbers written across them.

What a wretched place, I think to myself as we pass the men, the smells of the drug dens and pubs lingering in our nostrils.

Someone exits a door cut into the wall to our left and empties a bucket of brown water into the street. Eoghan navigates calmly away from the rebounding splattering as he continues, his eyes never wandering far from our path.

I take it all in, my mind racing. A few yards ahead, I see a woman and a young girl being loaded into a wagon, sobbing silently into their bound hands as a man kicks them to get them to pick up their pace.

"Hey!" I begin to shout, but Eoghan covers my mouth with his hand.

"He has purchased them. There are laws against interfering with the purchase of slaves here, and I will not allow you to lose your head today. These," he motions to the buildings rising high and obscuring the sunlight, "are what make Cuanslí so infamous to all of Draíocoinnigh and profiteers in Trader's Bay. These are the drug dens and auction halls where slaves are taken when they arrive."

He removes his hand.

"But what will happen to them?" My voice is low as we pass the wagon. The man scowls at us and wipes his nose against the back of his arm.

"I don't know. If they are lucky, they will be sold to a small farm in the countryside, where a farmer and their family will treat them fairly enough."

"And if they are not lucky?" I feel sick to my stomach now. Perhaps I do not want to know.

"If they aren't lucky, they'll stay in Cuanslí."

The road widens in front of us into a large square lined with shops and cafés beginning to open for their morning customers. I take it in as the sun falls warmly on my face for the first time in months. Compared to the filth and darkness of the street we just exited, the square seems so ordinary. There is a tailor on the corner, and a small restaurant with tables and chairs placed just outside the door. A jewelry shop sits at the far end, and a toy shop to my right has wooden tops that spin endlessly on display in the window. How can anyone separate this place from what lies just steps away?

My eyes trail to the center of the square, and I halt my steps. Rising before us in the very center is a bronze statue nearly twenty feet tall of a man with a familiar face staring out in the direction of the bay. Bréanainn Doherty—Rian's father—stands tall as a figure of wonder and strength, staring out toward the darkness, as though surveying his land. My knees quake, and I lean into Eoghan's side. He rubs the back of my hand with his thumb.

"Bréanainn Doherty, the new King of Draíocoinnigh." Ire laces his words as he speaks. "The Doherty family became quite well known nearly fifteen years ago as they transformed the merchant trade in Tonnfórsca. For around a hundred and fifty years, slave trading was largely taboo as the royal family did not themselves buy slaves and many of the aristocrats followed suit. Cuanslí, though still wealthy from textiles and imported goods, had suffered largely with rundown and empty halls and was subsequently overtaken by black market dealers of Ama, heroin, and herb. As a result, many merchants moved their imports to the southern ports of Tonnfórsca, leaving the route open for the taking—at the king's approval, of course.

"Bréanainn came from an unsuccessful merchant family that had largely gone bankrupt. He saw opportunity in the failing city. The story goes, armed with a small armada of merchant ships and no shame, he sailed to Trader's Bay, a hotspot for the slave markets, and cut deals with the slavers promising them half his profits for exclusive rights to their wares…humans, as it were. Being the cunning man he was, he saw the desperation in not only the slavers of Trader's Bay, who had lost out on profits from Draío for generations, but also the city of Cuanslí now struggling to thrive. Even more cunning, when Bréanainn secured the deal at Trader's Bay, he sold his first batch of slaves back in Cuanslí for tenfold what he had arranged with the slavers and pocketed the extra wealth for himself." Eoghan takes in the statue for a moment. "It is said the city began to thrive as he grew his trades, but it was not until a handful of years ago, when he secured exclusive routes by decree of the king, that Cuanslí reached the same affluence it once maintained. They erected this statue in his honor two years ago."

Bile rises thick in my throat, and I drag my hand away from Eoghan's. I turn and race back down the narrow, dark street just a half a dozen paces before leaning against the side of a building and emptying my stomach at my feet. Eoghan follows and places his hand on my back, tracing soft, calming circles as my forehead rests on the cool wall, my hands on my knees.

"I caused it," I breathe. "I fought my father for the trade routes Rian and his father wanted. He had said… I didn't know."

Eoghan shakes his head, and his voice is firm though kind. "You did not do this. You are not to blame."

"But if I hadn't—"

"You did not do this, Maeve. It was Bréanainn Doherty and his son who did this. I would hate to find out what would have happened if you would have actually married the piece of shit." His hand turns warm along my back. It takes him a moment to settle. "Come now. We need to get you some new clothes."

―――――――

WE REACH the dock as the sun rests low on the water. Eoghan and I had gone to the tailor's shop, where Eoghan had helped to pick out linen in light beiges and tans and instructed the tailor to make me a number of items, from linen pants to scarves to save my face from the sand. When he finished his instructions, he asked me to pick out another fabric from a wall of colorful and expensive silks and tulles, and this time, he spoke to the tailor alone while I waited near the door.

We had lunch at a small café, my first meal in any sort of restaurant other than the Golden Wulver Pub. When we returned, the tailor handed him packages of goods wrapped in paper and twine with a smile, and Eoghan handed him a small fortune of gold. As we exited the square, Eoghan stopped at the jewelry shop, leaving me outside, only to reemerge after several long minutes without a word spoken.

The others meet us at the boat, and Eoghan greets them, appraising the crates of goods set along the wooden dock.

"Were you able to find everything?" he asks.

"Everything but an empty ship. These are all filled with slaves who won't be offloaded until well into the night," Bode replies.

My eyes grow wide as I look around the harbor. There had to be a dozen ships docked, all with identical flags of seafoam green hoisted above their decks. These are Rian's ships, filled with humans he cares nothing for. Humans he would sell for gold he greedily kept in vaults to buy palaces and those ridiculous tunics. I think of the two gold coins I had found in the dead faerie's pocket after Peadair tried to kill me, a price placed on a life as though it were nothing more than a disposable product passed between the hands of men. Rage boils to the surface as I lose myself in my thoughts.

"We are taking this ship." I point to the one nearest us that had pulled into port this morning. *Had the passengers on board even been fed since they arrived?* "And we are going to take everyone on board with us."

The men all stare at me with their mouths agape.

"Are you crazy? If we take every slave on that ship, we will starve before we arrive!" one of the men hisses. I step toward him in response, but Eoghan puts himself between us.

"We might not..." Trystan says from where he stands by

our old boat as he takes a drag from something between his fingers. It smells of the sweet herb Cai used to smoke on the castle rooftops in his teen years. He extinguishes it casually. "I watched the crew reload that ship two hours ago to prepare for their next trip to Oleaíncudd. With what we have, we would at least make it to Tinemallacht. It might be a bit of a stretch, but they had to have loaded enough supplies for three weeks. Tinemallacht is a week at most."

Eoghan thinks for a moment as the others watch him curiously. The first man throws his hands into the air in exasperation. "We don't have the time or resources to deal with a ship full of slaves, and you know it, Kael!"

Eoghan glares at the man, and then his eyes soften as he meets mine. "Eoghan, we have to," I nearly beg him. "We cannot leave them here, not if we have the choice."

He is silent for a long moment before he speaks, and I watch his mind work over the idea, more rationally than I have ever been in my entire life. "We are taking the ship and taking everyone onboard. If you have a problem with it, you can stay here."

He takes my hand and leads the way to the ship. The others follow suit, the crates of goods in tow. Where the boat sits docked, a young sailor stands guard on his own in the fading light. He wears wielding cuffs, as so many trained fighters do when they seek to channel their magic for the sake of accuracy, and his hand rests on a sword at his side.

"You think we can get past him?" River asks.

"Doesn't seem like much of a fight," Trystan scoffs. "But who knows how many will come running if he screams?"

"No," I whisper. "I'll take care of him. You get the ship ready." Eoghan looks incredulous as I drop his hand. "This is not a discussion, Eoghan Kael. Go."

"It seems to never be a discussion," he grumbles.

"Are you worried about me, Kael?" I tease.

"Always, Moran," he purrs. He brings his lips to hover over mine. "I'll be right over there, making sure he doesn't lay a finger on you the entire time."

His breath is hot against my face, and there is a moment of intense desire between us before he steps away. I watch as the others creep toward the ship and then walk slowly in the sailor's direction. His eyes raise up to meet mine, though the hood of my cloak casts a dark shadow across my forehead to my nose. He straightens as he takes me in, and I watch as his gaze wanders from my covered face to my chest, and down to my hips. I sigh as I feel the uncomfortable tightness of the traveler's pants on my thighs, but I swing my hips as I close the gap between us. *Let him look. It is better for us if he likes what he sees.*

"Ma'am," he says and tips his head to me. He's younger than I anticipated, perhaps only eighteen.

"Hello." I try to make my voice sound mysterious, though it sounds repulsive in my head. I can almost imagine the cynical smirk Eoghan would give me if he heard it. "I seem to be lost," I continue. "Perhaps you might point me in the right direction?"

I meet him where he stands and pass him, pulling his eyes toward the city's waterfront promenade. He sizes me up again and follows, only one step from my back. I can hear him breathing; I know if my hood was down, I'd feel the faint dampness of his breath on my neck.

"Where were you looking to go?" he asks, as though he cares anything about getting me to my destination and not slipping one of those repulsive collars around my neck.

"Oh," I giggle as I face him and feign bashfulness, twisting my hands. "I think I..." My gaze lingers over the man's shoulder as Eoghan and the others hoist crates over the side of the ship. The man notices my distraction and begins to turn. I grab for his bicep, and his eyes fall to my fingers. "I want to go to one of those houses…the ones where they say I might be able to pay for an evening of…" gods, I make myself sick, "pleasure…"

The sailor chuckles, and I giggle lightly in return as the tension leaves his body. "I'm not sure you will find the sort of pleasure you are looking for in those houses."

His fingers caress mine where I still hold his arm lightly. I squeeze a bit harder as my skin crawls.

"Oh? I'm not so sure about that." Curiosity glows in his eyes, and I close the gap between us before dropping my voice to a low whisper. "Perhaps I might be the pleasure, then."

The sailor swallows hard, and longing washes over his expression. He moves his hand toward my face and pushes my hood to my shoulders. I hold his gaze while he takes me in, his tongue wetting his lips as I part my own in innocent beckoning. He is repulsive—young, yet old enough to know right from wrong and too stupid to care as he transports humans across the sea. He dips his head closer to mine. I flinch, but I do not back away. *Hold his attention until the others finish*, my mind commands. He draws nearer, and I can feel the whisper of his lips against mine.

"Are you finished?" Eoghan muses. I crane my neck around the sailor to find his incredible green-gold eyes staring back at me. His arms are crossed against his chest, one eyebrow cocked upward in question.

"Are you?" I demand, and the sailor's head whips around to Eoghan.

"If you say so." Eoghan shrugs as the sailor stammers wildly, my grip still tight on his arm. "Are you going to take care of him, or should I?"

"I was trying!" The sailor goes for his sword, but I pull the faerie thread, gluing his hand to his side.

"That looked like kissing to me." Eoghan uncrosses his

arms and shakes out his hands. Even with the sailor between us, I can feel the heat. He must be boiling.

I scoff. "I'm sorry! I was just helping!" the sailor shouts.

"Shut up!" I yell back at him and throw my fist into his face. It collides with a twinge of pain that runs through my arm, and he sways back and forth. I hit him again and release his arm as he crumples onto the dock. Eoghan extends his hand to mine; I take it, and he drags me on board.

CHAPTER SIX

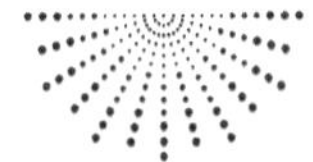

Rian and I stand in the castle hall with Elspeth, one of the maids, as Rian tries his hand at the sign language that is used to communicate with the mute staff who live within the citadel's walls.

"I don't understand what she's saying!" he complains, throwing his hands down angrily.

"She says she doesn't know how to make beds any other way. You will just have to endure the way they make them here." I laugh. "You don't need to be so frustrated. It'll take time to learn, and in the meantime, I'll help you."

"It is ridiculous to have a secret language here." He is red in the face, and I know he will be sour the rest of the day. He is always so awful when he gets like this. His temper is worse than a child's.

"Is it ridiculous, or are you just not any good at it?" I tease. Elspeth signs something to me, and I giggle even more.

"What did she say?" Rian demands as he rounds on Elspeth. "What did you say?" He wags his finger in her face, and she backs away. He catches her arm up tightly in his grip. "Speak, you simpleminded fool! Speak!"

He pulls back his hand and smacks his palm hard across her

cheek. He shakes her by her arm as she clutches her face, her skin turning angry and red. He hauls back his hand and hits her again. I yank him backwards as I shout for him to stop. He releases Elspeth, and she falls to the floor, crawling away over the marble. He takes a step toward her, but I shriek and pull him back, driving the nails of my free hand into his eyes. He cries out in pain and turns toward me as he grabs at my hands.

"Stop!" I shout while he yanks me off him. I've dug my nails so deeply into him, his forearm and face are bleeding, and there is skin beneath my nails. I push him off me. "DO NOT TOUCH ME!"

"You stupid child!" he spits.

"Do not ever treat my staff in such a way," I pant, my teeth clenched and my hair falling into my face.

"She is nothing but a useless maid! I will treat her how I please!"

"Get out."

"Excuse me?" Rian takes a step forward. I hold up my hand to stop his progression.

"Get out," I repeat. "Until you learn to treat others half as well as you expect them to treat you."

His eyes grow wide, and he stares at me for a long moment. I do not move or retreat. He scoffs, anger and embarrassment coloring his expression. Then, he spits onto the floor before he storms off, out of sight.

CHAPTER SEVEN

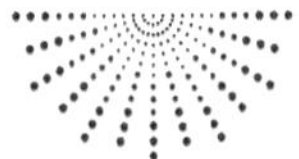

"I no longer believe Tinemallacht exists. It is simply a figment of your imagination, Eoghan Kael."

I pass out bread and fruit to the passengers of the ship, counting them off in my head to make sure they are all fed. There were a dozen women and children aboard the ship when we left Cuanslí nearly a week ago, and there are now thirteen, as one of the women gave birth to a little girl last night. She named her Ayla, and I stayed with them until the early morning hours when Eoghan insisted I get some rest. Eoghan smirks as he listens to my complaints and checks on the children one by one.

"Ah, yes, a figment of my imagination. That sounds right."

He stands while patting one of the small boys on his head. The boy responds by wrapping his arms and legs around Eoghan's own and clinging there as Eoghan crosses the cramped space to me. All the children on board love him. I cannot help but wonder what he might be like as a father to his own. Yearning builds in my chest to give him anything that resembles a normal life, full of love and free of fear and hiding.

"We will be in Tinemallacht tomorrow, and—if my letters have gotten to my father as I hope—they will be expecting us in Bastain by dinner."

"More traveling," I groan. "Remind me never to ask to see the world again."

He brushes my hair behind my ear. "Oh, I don't know. I think green suits you just fine."

I feign laughter and finish passing out the last of our rations to the passengers. Tomorrow, we will depart the ship in Tinemallacht for the first time. Eoghan's home. Cai's home. Under any other circumstance, I might be jittery with anticipation, but as I remember we are still very much wanted in every territory of Draíocoinnigh, I feel a different sort of anxiety settle somewhere in the pit of my stomach.

Eoghan gestures for me to follow him as he carefully pries the young child from his shin, and we bid farewell to our companions. *Maybe I'll stay with them,* I think. *We are so different yet the same in so many ways. Bound against our will and longing for freedom that might never come. Maybe if I stay with them, I won't have to face the rejection of the Tinemallachts when they find I am too much trouble for them after all.*

Eoghan walks back through the quiet belly of the ship, as most of the others have already retired to bed in anticipation of our arrival in the morning. He passes the cabin doors without a word, and I follow until he reaches ours, where he turns the door handle and motions for me to enter. The cabin is dark, quiet. I wave my hand to light the candles on the small dresser that presses up against the edge of the bed. The room is so small, it is a wonder we both fit. Eoghan follows behind as I crawl up onto the mattress to make room for him.

"Are you excited—about tomorrow, I mean?" he asks as

he turns to rummage through a package pushed into the cramped corner of the cabin.

"Nervous, I suppose. I never imagined I'd meet your family, let alone while on the run."

"My family? But not the dragons?" He crouches near the floor.

"Dragons, I can deal with. I survived Gálgalesh, remember?"

He concedes with an inclination of his head, and tears fill my eyes at the thought of Gálgalesh. Where had he gone? Had he tried to make it back to us? Did he flee to Dún? He had told me once before, when I pressed him about his life and his home, that he considered Draío his kingdom now. It had failed him at every turn, yet he still cared for it enough to continue to heal its people and save me. I hope with all I am that he is safe and as far from this kingdom as possible. I wipe my eyes as Eoghan stands and walks toward the bed.

"Well, I think you have nothing to worry about—dragons or otherwise—however," he unwraps a small package slowly, and a gorgeous necklace made of the most delicate chain of gold with a solitary jewel, brilliantly iridescent and colorless like a diamond, comes into view. He lifts it from its resting place in front of my eyes before turning it over so the candle-light catches it, throwing a kaleidoscope of color across the space, "I thought perhaps you might wear this for extra protection, to ward off all evils and single men."

He smirks as my mouth falls open in surprise. I have never been given something so beautiful in my entire life. I reach for it, but Eoghan pulls it away.

"Allow me," he says as he moves to fasten the necklace near the base of my neck. "My princess and my queen," he whispers against my skin. He presses his lips softly below my hairline before he straightens, and our eyes meet.

"It's..." *Perfect*, my mind screams, and I feel a strange

sensation where the jewel lays against my chest. "Warm...?" I bring my hand to the jewel, and a pleasant heat greets my fingertips.

"The stone is impregnated with my dragon fire. That is a piece of the heart from the dragon that shared his fire with me. Dragons transfer their fire when they are about to pass on, and when they do finally succumb to death's call, their hearts turn into a jewel that then belongs to the wielder they have gifted their fire to. I carry a piece in this dagger..." He taps the hilt of a small dagger at his side, and I notice for the first time an iridescent jewel like the one now laying warmly against my chest. "And I have been saving this piece here for...well, for you, I suppose. The jeweler in Cuanslí was skilled in imbuing and helped me lock a bit of my fire into the stone. Don't worry, it's safe."

I drag my fingertips across my neck, and I think I might die from the force of my heart thrumming out of my chest. His dragon fire, his dragon heart. I feel the tears fall against my cheeks in embarrassingly thick streams. He traces his thumbs delicately across my skin as he wipes them away, his cheeks turning pink. Is he bashful now? Eoghan Kael, who has so stolen my shattered soul and repaired it with his love?

"Will you not say anything?" He laughs, breaking the silence of the room. Tears coat the sound of my own laughter as he rubs my chin softly between his thumb and forefinger.

"I don't know what to say." I'm not sure words are enough anymore. I want to give him everything, though nothing feels like it could suffice.

"Say that no matter what happens, it'll be you and me, Maeve. I've watched so many people lose the ones they love to war and greed and stupidity, and I only want you."

"And what if everyone you love hates *me*?" I don't want to think what might happen if he feels he must choose.

"An impossibility. But if they do, they will know where my heart lies, and it will not matter what they think."

"You and me," I promise.

———

Bang! Bang! Bang! Bang! Bang!

The repeated hammering on our door shakes us both awake, and Eoghan rolls over in bed. He grabs the door handle and pulls, his face buried in the pillow and his other arm draped around my back.

"Fuck off!" he grumbles as the door falls open. River greets us with a grin, a bowl of something in his hands. I shuffle under the blankets, covering my bare skin as I will my eyes to stay closed against the light of the corridor. River does not respond; he only remains standing in the doorway, beaming down at us until Eoghan drags his face across his pillow and looks up at him with a tired scowl. "What is it?"

"Good morning to you too," River teases. "I just thought you might like to know we have arrived in Tinemallacht, and our welcome party is waiting to greet you, oh grumpy one."

"What are you talking about? Did my father send someone?" Eoghan wipes his mouth on the back of his hand while I give up on my hopes of more sleep. I bat my eyes open as my head screams in protest. I knew trying to finish the last barrel of ale before we arrived was a terrible idea.

"The understatement of the year." Trystan Price walks past the door in a casual stride. "Good morning, Your Highness. In lovely form, as always."

I groan, and his bark of a laugh makes my head pound. Eoghan pushes himself up to a seat, his arms stretched wide. We should have slept last night instead of exploring the secrets of each other's mouths and the contours of our bodies. I pull the blankets from the bed and wrap them around my chest so I might rise as well. Eoghan looks over at me, exhaustion evident. The last thing I want to do is meet anyone now. Eoghan grabs the wood and thrusts the door shut hard, and River swears angrily from the hallway.

"Give us a minute!"

He stands to find his clothes as well as a pair of tan linen pants and a shirt. He passes them to me, and I drag them on as Eoghan murmurs to himself. What does it feel like for him to be going home? Has he been home since he set foot in Báscogar Prison four years ago? Is he nervous? Excited? Does he wish I was not here with him? I touch the necklace laying against my chest and feel his heat beneath my fingers. *Let them like me*, I pray to the gods. *Don't make him choose.*

When we are finished dressing, Eoghan packs our things in his Tinemallacht pack, and I follow him out the door. His shoulders are squared, his gait quick, as though he is agitated or nervous. I catch up to him, lacing my fingers with his, but he pays me no mind, so I drop my hand to my side. What is the matter?

We reach the deck—the light of the sun is blinding, the heat filling my lungs instantly, making my tongue feel like sandpaper in my mouth. I have never been so hot in my life. I cough, doubling over as I do. Eoghan stops and turns to me. I lift my hand in dismissal, which he ignores.

"A canteen," he demands. One of our men hands him a metal flask. "Easy," he whispers as he lifts it to my lips. "It'll take some getting used to. The air is dry, so your lungs will feel a little parched. Drink." I obey, feeling the cool water calming my throat. "Better?" I nod. "A few hours in Bastain will help acclimate you."

Finn falls into step beside us and studies me to make sure I'm all right. The weather is going to take some getting used to. Even on the hottest days in Golorgleann, it was nothing compared to this. How does anything survive in this place—dragons or otherwise? My smile is unconvincing as I straighten to full height. Finn's ever-appraising stare does not indicate confidence, even as he doesn't speak a word of disapproval or unbelief.

"KAEL!" A voice rises from beyond the ship, and we all stop, eyes shifting to one another. A smile dances across Eoghan's face. "WHY ARE YOU MAKING ME WAIT IN THIS WRETCHED DESERT ALL DAY? TELL THE WOMAN I CAN SENSE HER FROM HERE!"

Gálgalesh! I lock eyes with Eoghan and hurdle toward the side of the ship. Standing below, in the center of a group of men dressed in tan cargo pants and matching short-sleeved shirts, stands Gálgalesh, dressed head-to-toe in lightly colored linen pants and a linen tunic, a wide-brimmed hat on top of his long silver locks. He looks like my mother when she would walk in the garden during the long evenings of the White Night. Still, there he stands, alive and as grumpy as ever.

Eoghan meets me at the railing and looks down toward the crowd. "My gods, what is he wearing?" He shakes his head and rubs between his eyebrows with his thumb and index finger. "Should we go say hi then, or leave him to bake some more?"

Eoghan helps me down onto a makeshift wooden dock, which seems to be more like a dozen enchanted planks keeping our feet dry as we cross into the red Tinemallacht sand. We make our way to the group, and Eoghan greets the men as I rush forward to Gálgalesh. I make to hug him, but he swipes at my hands, and I throw them up in the air out of his reach.

"You look ridiculous." I size him up, his ensemble becoming funnier with each passing glance. "What happened to the powerful and feared Warden of Báscogar?"

"It. Is. Hot! I have lived in Romiodóg for centuries! I feel like I am turning to dust here in this horrible sunlight!"

"Has anyone ever told you whining is a useless waste of breath?" I doubt he could be any angrier with me as I throw the words he has so often spoken to me back at him. I wonder if I might anger him enough that he decides to finally kill me right here in the sand.

"I have no idea why I was ever friends with you. You are a terrible, inconsiderate human. I preferred your brother much more than you in every way."

"I am glad to see you too."

An amused chuckle escapes me as I pat his arm before Eoghan reaches for my hand to bring me to his side. He speaks to a man who I would guess is in his sixties, with hair like Eoghan's but graying slightly at the sides, facial hair, and stunning green eyes. He wears the standard Tinemallacht Tans, a star embroidered on each sleeve of his shirt.

"Maeve, this is my father, General Osian Kael. Father, this is Maeve, my…my Maeve."

Eoghan clears his throat nervously as his father takes me in. I have never been nervous to meet anyone before—not even Rian's father, who cackles like a warbling bird as he laughs. Now, however, I feel as though I cannot breathe. He extends his hand toward me. His grip is much firmer than expected, and it stings my hand a bit.

"Princess." He bows his head ever so slightly toward me.

"Just Maeve," I correct, and he indicates approval.

"Maeve, this is Officer Rhodes and Colonel Hayes. I believe you know their sons, Finn and River." The men lower their gazes respectfully in acknowledgement. "We welcome you to Tinemallacht." Now I see where Eoghan gets his unsettling warrior's mask from. This man has hardly spoken more than two sentences to me, and I feel as though he has the power to lift me up or strike me down. I'm not quite sure which one it might be. "From Eoghan's letter, it seems you have stowaways on board. Officer Rhodes will see to it that they are given care and safe passage to wherever they choose. For now, though, if you and Eoghan are prepared, we need to get back to Bastain. His mother will be furious that we kept her waiting until the afternoon to arrive."

Afternoon? The sun was high in the sky when we retired to our room last night, and sleep came only after long hours of tossing and turning as my body protested in vain. We must have slept the morning away. I wipe my hand across my brow, and Eoghan fixes my scarf to lay loosely against my hair.

"How might we travel to Bastain?"

I retreat toward Gálgalesh, who stands fanning himself. He looks as though he might melt into a puddle at our feet. I survey the desert for any signs of transportation. I see nothing but miles of red sand, like oceans of dry dunes and desolate fields of nothing. There are no wagons or sleighs in sight, and only two camels rest near the water's edge. If we have to travel on foot, I might not make it. The sun has become stifling already. How long might it take to make it to the oasis Cai used to call the jewel of all Draíocoinnigh?

"Must we walk all the way?" I ask as River and Finn join us, shaking the hands of the others and greeting Gálgalesh with a sly smirk.

"Walk? We would combust before we made it halfway," River laughs. "We don't walk through the desert if we can avoid it—luckily, we usually don't have to."

General Osian steps ahead of us, and as he does, something like a tear in the very air opens like a door conjured out of osmosis. Beyond it sits a lush green garden in the center of an open-air courtyard, with a pool of sparkling blue water and tall palm trees casting long shadows as they shield the space from the sun's unrelenting rays. I turn to Eoghan, who just shrugs as though this is not the strangest form of magic to ever be witnessed. Behind him, I watch as Officer Rhodes' eyes gleam and his concentration takes him somewhere beyond our reach.

"Space manipulation," Eoghan says calmly, though I have no understanding of what he means. "Officer Rhodes can manipulate physical space and open passable portals from one location to another. Helpful on the battlefield when needing to make a hasty retreat."

"Helpful when coming home from Báscogar for holidays as well," Finn adds, and I wheel around toward Eoghan.

"Are you telling me we could have been here instantly and did not have to travel for weeks on the Murcean Sea?"

"Of course not. We had no time to slow down and wait in one place long enough for a raven to reach Tinemallacht and alert them of our location." I feel my head wobble back and forth with the phantom motion of the ship. I hope, for Eoghan's sake, that he is being truthful. "But, we're here now, and we don't want to keep Mother waiting. Shall we?"

I look back toward the portal between the desert and Bastain. Gálgalesh and General Osian have already disappeared to the other side, and River and Finn approach easily before stepping over the threshold into the lush green grass. We take a step forward. I reach for Eoghan's hand, wrapping my fingers around it tightly. Just one more step, and I will be in Eoghan's world—in a world so far removed from my own, I wonder if I've made a huge mistake coming here at all. *You made it in Báscogar,* my much-too-rational mind reminds me. *Be brave.* I close my eyes and step forward. Eoghan steps with me, and as we do, a gentle, warm breeze passes across our faces.

I open my eyes, and we stand in the garden, porticos surrounding us on all sides, horseshoe-style archways and brilliantly tiled floors in colored mosaics leading to the interior of the house beyond. The crystal-blue pool at the center of the courtyard is as clear as glass, and tropical flowers line the perimeter. A paradise in the desert.

The others have found their way out of the green haven already. Eoghan places his hand on my shoulder and guides me to the right just as Officer Rhodes steps through the gateway. He nods to us before moving into the house, the portal closing in his wake.

"What about the others?" I ask as none of the other men who accompanied us from Báscogar follow us through.

"They will meet us in Gobaith in a couple of days' time or head to their stations if needed."

"Are we not staying here?"

"Here? No. This is Kael Manor, my parents' home. I want to take you to my home, an—"

There is commotion from somewhere inside, and a young male voice rises in an excited tone. A weak protest rumbles Eoghan's throat, but a smile plays across his lips ever the same. Footsteps, walking at first before picking up pace to a run, echo across the tile floor.

"Eogh!"

A young man no older than me bursts into view and nearly tackles Eoghan as he barrels into him, arms wrapping around Eoghan's center. I take him in: he is within an inch of Eoghan's own height, with the same beautiful features, swirling green-gold eyes, and strongly-built physique. His jaw is slightly broader, his forehead slightly wider, yet there is no doubt they are related. Eoghan pats the man on the back, and a laugh of pure joy escapes him, as though one had longed for this reunion as much as the other. When they finally release one another, they turn their attention to me, broad smiles on their faces.

"Bryn, this is Maeve. Maeve, this is my brother, Bryn." I extend my hand toward him, only to find him catching me up in his arms. I go rigid as he lifts me from my feet in an embrace. "Bryn, calm down! You're going to scare her off!"

Bryn releases me, setting me back down onto the grass as he backs away, appraising me with his eyes. There's no hunger there like so many of the men who have taken me in before, only delight.

"Gods be, she does look just like him," he marvels before extending his hand toward me. "Sorry! Nice to meet you, Maeve. I'd like to say Eoghan has told us all about you, but it was Gálgalesh who filled us in when he arrived. Don't worry, your secret is safe here."

Gálgalesh had told the others about me? An unsettled feeling rises in my stomach as the secret of my identity is laid bare to the world. I wonder if the more people we let in, the closer Rian will get to finding me. Does it really matter anymore, though?

Eoghan continues to hold me in his relentless gaze, as he had that night in Fáintìrean, and my cheeks turn pink in response. Pride and adoration coat his expression, as though he were presenting his brother with a treasure or priceless work of art, instead of a woman with dirt on her face and sand in her hair.

"Where's the twin?" Eoghan asks, though his eyes do not deviate from me.

"Twin?" I say in surprise.

"*His* twin." Bryn inclines his head toward Eoghan. "Out with Sawney. They were tired of waiting for you and decided to go into town. They should be back soon."

I hadn't known Eoghan had any siblings at all, let alone two of them. I realize with a bit of embarrassment that I know very little about Eoghan at all, and he knows so much about me. I'd never thought to ask about his family or his life before coming to Báscogar, apart from what he had freely shared. Maybe I was scared to know, for fear it might make him real to me somehow, not simply the perfect man with the beautiful face who saved me time and time again.

Two more pairs of footsteps approach from inside, and General Osian emerges with a woman so strikingly beautiful, I have to stop and do a double take. Whereas Eoghan resembles the General in mannerisms, and the ways the other Tinemallacht men and women all resemble one another with their tan skin and sun-bleached hair, the woman who stands before us is so stunningly like Eoghan and his brother in every way. Her eyes, not just green but with swirls of gold; her hair, the same shade of brown falling past her collarbones; her jawline; her full lips; the way her brows pull upward in expectancy. He is her spitting image, and as Eoghan leans in and plants a kiss to her cheek, I know it was not General Osian Kael I should have been worried about impressing.

"Eoghan." His mother acknowledges him with a hand on his cheek. "We have been waiting all day."

"Sorry," Eoghan grumbles in quiet reverence. His mother holds up her hand to silence him.

"You must be Maeve." She takes my face in her hands, and her eyes stare into mine before becoming unfocused and milky. "Gálgalesh was right about you..." Her fingers quake against my skin, and I look to Eoghan, who only shrugs before her hands drop to her side and her vision becomes present once again. "Well, lunch is cold by now, but you must eat." She turns from us and walks back toward the house.

"What was that?" I whisper to Eoghan as his father also retreats.

"My parents. Believe me, that went as well as one might hope with them." He places his hand on my back and urges me forward with a gentle push.

———

KAEL MANOR IS a palace in its own right. Although stripped of their ancestral titles, the Kael family maintained their wealth and status within the Tinemallacht borders. Every inch of the space exudes the same sort of opulence Caisleán Rialú had, although it quickly becomes apparent that none of the Kaels care much for riches at all. After lunch, we lounge in a large, airy sitting room on a plush sofa with a much too large fire burning in the hearth—somehow, the heat does not reach us. Dragon fire, as Eoghan had explained. Even in the height of summer, the fire does not burn out. The men kick their boots up onto the short table in front of us, and his mother—Mari—sits cross-legged in an armchair, staring forward, wholly concentrated on something I cannot see.

"Is she all right?" I whisper to Eoghan and Bryn as I lean against Eoghan's chest.

"She's fine," Eoghan chuckles. "Just communicating." I give him a look that says I have no clue what he's talking about. "Mother is a medium. She communicates with the dead—when they have something to say."

"Or when she wanted us to behave as children," Bryn adds, and Eoghan concedes with a small uptick of his lips.

"A medium? Isn't that devious magic? Can anyone really speak to the dead?"

"Depends on who you ask." Eoghan shrugs. "Some will say speaking to the dead is a farce made up by crooks to profit off the hopes of the grieving and desperate. Others swear by it as a means to travel between this world and the land of the dead."

"And what do you say?" I ask as I watch Mari's lips move softly in silence.

"I say she's never been wrong before, and I don't want to test my fate with the dead."

"YOU ABSOLUTE BASTARD!"

I jump at the sound of a female voice in the hall as the

door swings open and bangs against the wall. Mari's eyes flicker back into the present, and she, like everyone else, turns toward the woman standing with her arms crossed tightly against her chest, her brows pulled together in a scowl. Her hair is brown with the standard Tinemallacht highlights. It reaches her shoulders and sweeps across her forehead. Her eyes match the others who take her in from the sofa, unsurprised. Next to her stands a lean woman with ashen blonde hair and blue eyes.

"I waited all morning for you to arrive!" Eoghan scoots off the sofa and rises to meet her. She shoves him roughly, her hand against his chest. "Not all of us have time to sit around waiting for the Great Golden Boy all day! I have things to do while I'm here!"

"What is more important than waiting around to see me?" Eoghan muses. She scoffs loudly in annoyance. "I am your big brother, after all."

"By three minutes! Hardly a record worth noting." Eoghan extends his arms, and she shakes her head stubbornly, but he wraps them around her and drags her to his chest. "Enough!" she complains, pushing at his biceps to let her go. Eoghan releases her and smiles that beautiful smile of his. I notice his eyes sparkle in the same way they do when he looks at me, with a mixture of pride and amusement.

"I see you have not become any less cranky since the last time I saw you, Lo." She throws him a mocking smile, and he turns to the woman at her side. He wraps her in a firm embrace. "Sawney, how you still put up with her is beyond me."

"Love knows no bounds." The blonde's voice is sultry, and I immediately feel scandalized by the heat that forms in my cheeks. I turn my gaze to the corner of the room.

Eoghan's sister rolls her eyes as she rounds the sofa. She drops down into Eoghan's seat without a second glance my way—much too close for anyone's comfort. I turn to Bryn to ask him if he might make room, and as I do, she notices me for the first time.

"Who the fuck are you?" Her nose crinkles in disgust.

"You really are the most unpleasant person on the entire planet, you know that?" Eoghan rounds the sofa to us. "Lowri, this is my girlfriend, Maeve…" A pause of reluctance. "Cai's sister…Princess Maeve Moran."

Lowri's shoulders go rigid, and she stands from the sofa. Fire dances in her eyes as she stares down at me, appraising me for a long moment from head to toe, and then her gaze snaps to Eoghan. She takes an angry step toward him.

"Tell me you didn't." Her voice is a command, but Eoghan stands his ground, remaining silent. "Tell me you didn't," she demands again. The silence is the only confirmation she receives. "Eoghan! You are so…" She lets out a frustrated yell. "STUPID! His sister?"

"I don't think either of us expected—" I begin quietly, but Eoghan cuts in as his sister turns on me, her glare dangerous.

"Maeve, don't speak to her. Lo is just a little emotional right now."

The tension that grips the room at his words is so palpable and heavy, it could be cut with a knife. Lowri's mouth falls open.

"You are shameless and a fool, and Cai would have killed you for this."

"Well, he isn't here, is he, Lo?" He closes the gap between them. He towers over her, yet she does not back away or break his stare. "And I think he might have less of a problem with me dating his sister than you being so rude to her." He reaches his hand to me on the sofa. "We are going to get ready for dinner. I suggest you find your manners before we return."

Eoghan helps me to my feet and leads me from the room.

I'm not sure what I just witnessed or what I can say, but Eoghan's hand turns hot as he squeezes my fingers, and I yelp, causing him to release me.

"Sorry," Eoghan says as he leads the way down the hall. "Lowri is…well, she's Lowri. Don't pay her any attention."

"Is she right, though?" I wonder aloud.

"Of course not." Eoghan opens a door at the far end of the long hall and motions for me to step inside. I enter a large bedroom bathed in sunlight, with mosaic floors and a large bed in the center. The far wall is covered in windows looking out onto a private courtyard, and opposite the bed sits a soaking tub, large enough to hold more than one occupant. Eoghan closes the door behind us and paces toward me, catching me up by the waist. "Lo and Cai have a complicated past, some of it good and some of it not so great. But she loved him—just like the rest of us—and I think she feels like she has a duty to protect him now. Just ignore her. That's what I do."

"But Eoghan, if she thinks Cai would have been angry with us…"

Eoghan brings his lips to mine, kissing me with a passion I have not felt since our last night at the prison, when he pinned me against the wall in the shower room. My lips part in offering to deepen the kiss, and his hands cup my face as his tongue searches my mouth. After what feels like only short, breathless moments—not long enough to savor his taste or the way his smell intoxicates me—he pulls away, his hands still on my cheeks.

"With all due respect to your brother, I do not care anymore if I would have angered him by loving you. Now, can we stop talking, please?"

His lips crash onto mine again, and he pushes me back toward the bed. He pulls his shirt over his head, our mouths only separating for a split second before he kisses me again, moving from my lips to my jaw and down my neck.

"Eoghan," I pant as I push myself up along the mattress.

"If you are thinking of reminding me my family is just down the hall, I am well aware." He unbuttons his pants and drops them to the floor, kicking off his boots as well. "You know, the most amazing thing about me is that I know this very complex magic to silence any space to keep others from listening."

I laugh with a huff, and he smiles as he catches me up again. His hands creep up my back under my linen shirt as he plants kisses against my collarbone.

"Eogh," I moan softly. He pulls my shirt over my head before moving down my chest.

"You were blushing," he whispers against my skin. "In the other room."

Blushing. Yes, I had been, but I was not sure why. Perhaps it was the heat of the fire and the Tinemallacht sun. Eoghan's hand slides past the waistband of my linen pants and teases my entrance softly. *Oh gods, I love the feeling of his hands on me.* I respond by pressing up against his fingers.

"What embarrassed you?" he asks. I shake my head, and his thumb rubs circles around my clit. "Are you really not going to tell me, Mayhem?"

He teases me with just an inch of one finger. I close my eyes and moan as he pulls back and then teases me again. *More, Eoghan Kael!* I bite my lip to keep from protesting his shallow thrusts. He continues to work my clit slowly, keeping the pleasure at bay.

"Sawney." My words betray me, and his eyes flare. He responds by thrusting his finger to the hilt, and I exhale loudly in ecstasy.

"Oh really?" He smiles devilishly as he adds a second finger. "Were you captivated?" His voice deepens with hunger, and he hooks his fingers inside me. My mind fogs as I feel heat rise in my core. His lips press against mine, and he whispers against them, "What could you be thinking about now?"

My cheeks turn crimson as my mind clouds with incoherent thoughts of pleasure and release. Eoghan responds with feverish enthusiasm as he picks up pace, kissing me as I cry out against his mouth. He works me until my head is spinning, and I climax while screaming his name, the sound reverberating off the walls. Eoghan waits until I settle and then kisses me once more before he stands.

"She's a temptress." He walks to the tub and turns on the tap to fill it with crystal clear water. "It takes some getting used to, but remind me to thank her later for that." He eyes me deviously. "Shall we get dressed for dinner?"

CHAPTER EIGHT

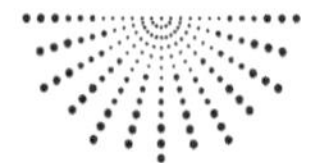

I brush my hands over my skirt nervously as Eoghan and I walk down the long hall to the dining room an hour later. He is dressed in a loose white shirt, left unbuttoned halfway down his chest, and a pair of dress pants in beige. His shoes are a polished light leather, the look completed by the ever-present shadow of stubble on his face. He looks every bit the lost Lord of Tinemallacht, the vision of elegance and power that would have made every head turn at a royal court ball or as he entered Caisleán Rialú for an audience with the king. I would have hidden away to steal a glimpse of him back inside the castle walls. I would have given anything for it. I look down at my own ensemble and feel self-conscious as I wind my fingers into the fabric.

When we had finished bathing in the seclusion of the large, bright room of Eoghan's youth, he had dug another package from his bag, and I recognized it as one from the tailor we visited in Cuanslí. He handed it to me wordlessly, and as I opened it, I could barely comprehend what was inside. In gauzy fabrics of palest pink—the ones I had chosen from the wall of colors in the store—lay a dress more beautiful than I had ever seen. Nothing could even compare. Contrary to Golorgleann fashion that favors high necklines, heavy or opaque fabrics, and long sleeves, the dress was cut to Tinemallacht preferences of light, almost translucent fabrics, bare arms, and tantalizingly low necklines in the front and back.

Eoghan had hardly been able to look away when I finally worked out the strappy pieces. As I take in how exposed I am now, I feel as though I might turn and run back into the room before anyone else sees.

"Have I told you how beautiful you are?" Eoghan whispers as we approach the dining room, where the sound of voices escapes into the hall.

"Only about a thousand times." My fingers touch the stone hung against my chest, and I feel its warmth.

"Well then, make that one thousand and one." He smiles, and my heart flutters a bit in my chest. "Ready yourself for the dragon's den."

He crosses the threshold, and I follow him into the room. He leads us to the table, helping me into a seat next to Gálgalesh who has traded his desert garbs for dress clothes similar to Eoghan's—his shirt a striking, beautiful white against his dark skin and his pants a pale jade. Eoghan takes the empty seat next to me with Bryn at his other side, and I look up to find his sister Lowri seated directly across from me in a scandalous cream dress that makes her skin seem impossibly tan. Sawney sits beside her in a matching dress the color of the desert sand, her fingers interlaced with Lowri's. I divert my eyes to Gálgalesh and busy myself in quiet conversation.

"How are you?" I ask as he takes a drink of silvery wine that dances in the glass.

"The worst of the physical injuries have begun to heal. Scars will remain, but that is all." He places his hand onto the table, and I notice an "F" has been etched into the back of it so deeply, the wound is still covered in a balm to prevent infection from setting in. "As if the ears and teeth were not a good enough indication of my inferiority."

"Gálgalesh," I whisper as my fingers fall lightly to his wrist. "I am so sorry."

"Did they bring back his head?" He takes another drink from his glass without meeting my gaze. I nod and watch as silver lines his eyes, but tears do not escape them. "They burnt the body before I could escape with it. I suppose it's for the best—what good is a body without a head?" His jaw works tightly, and it takes everything in me not to cry. "Did you kill any of them?"

I nod. "A few. I told Drustan Anwyl you would miss his screams before I fed him to the shadow lurker."

I watch his lips curl up into a smile.

"I suppose I will just have to lull myself to sleep with thoughts of his breath leaving him." I feel the faintest touch of his nails against my skin, and I smile back.

Footsteps interrupt us as General Osian and Mari Kael enter the dining room. They take their seats at either end of the table without ceremony, and as they do, the other dinner guests begin to fill their plates with food set out in the middle of the long, horizontal surface. *How very unusual*, I think to myself. All the foods are what one might expect to eat at the castle or at an extravagant party in Draíocoinnigh, yet the Kael family treats the meal as though it's something one might have on any ordinary day. Do the Kaels really live in such luxury always? Gálgalesh elbows me in the side as I watch the others carry on. When he catches my eyes, he indicates for me to serve myself as well.

"Are our numbers still strong?" I hear Eoghan ask as I intercept a conversation.

Lowri scoffs. "You're joking, right? They haven't been this low since the loss of the Second War."

"What about *our* numbers?" he presses as he raises his fork to his mouth.

"Everyone is feeling a bit hopeless, but only a few have wiped their hands of us." General Osian's low drawl is calm and even, his Tinemallacht accent more pronounced than Eoghan's. "Bryn has started helping where he can. It's useful that he does not have a tracker on his magic."

"Not that it's of much help." Bryn stabs at a piece of meat on his plate. I lift my glass to my lips as I listen, and the sweet, sparkling liquid dances on my tongue.

"What's your magic?" I ask, and all turn to me. I wonder if that might be an offensive question to ask. "Sorry." I clear my throat nervously.

"Elemental magic," Bryn answers. His expression is soft, and his response holds no hint of annoyance or offense. "Wind control mostly, though I can suck the air from any room."

"He wields his dragon fire better than any of us," Eoghan adds and pats Bryn's back, causing him to smile weakly. "Most of our magic is advantageous in battle. I can amplify or diminish the force behind a magical attack. Lo has foresight magic and can 'walk' through the past, present, and future—sometimes simultaneously—to see specific outcomes of a chosen event or give insight into the past. She almost always needs a specific target, though, which is sometimes tricky. And Father..." Eoghan points toward where General Osian sits...or sat...?

"Invisibility is always advantageous on the battlefield." I jump at the sound of the General's voice beside me. Gálgalesh swears loudly in surprise and empties his glass while Eoghan and Bryn's shoulders bounce with soft laughter. Lowri, however, scowls, her eyes shooting daggers my way.

"Really nice," she snaps. "Individual magic is to be kept secret if used for battle."

"Lo, who is Maeve going to tell?" Eoghan laughs and tosses his napkin at her. "Relax!"

General Osian takes his seat with the first smile I have seen on his face since I arrived earlier this afternoon. He lifts his fork to take a bite of his meal.

"I won't tell anyone," I promise. Lowri rolls her eyes and exhales loudly, but she doesn't say a word in response. Eoghan continues his questioning, unbothered.

"How has the transition gone since the new sovereign has taken power?"

"Officially? The five territories have welcomed him with open arms and bended knees." The General taps against his plate lightly.

"And unofficially?" I take a small bite as Eoghan speaks— the taste so divine, I nearly lose myself to the sensation of it.

"Unofficially, Tinemallacht has been designated as a breakaway aggressor state, and we have moved all our available men to our northern border. No one from outside the territory—besides the Leader's men—have been let in, with the exception of two who sought refuge in the name of dear Maeve at the time of Gálgalesh's arrival." I incline my head, and Eoghan's eyebrow ticks up in question. "A seamstress with a mouth on her that might just rival Lo's, and an alchemist of whom you are familiar. They are staying in Gobaith with the others."

Tiernan and Dedra are here? They are safe? After all these months hidden away in the prison, I wondered if they would make it out of the city alive at all. I reach for my glass in a daze, and it tips to the side before Eoghan catches it and rights it once again. *I have to see them,* my mind begs. *I have to see them for myself.*

"I like the seamstress, and Tiernan has filled out. Handsome." Lowri gives Eoghan a devious look as she drinks from her glass, and I wonder how Eoghan isn't sweating under the heat he is emitting. He ignores her goading.

"I had worried about what would happen when someone else was crowned. We expected trouble from the Crown, regardless. Now that they know Maeve's alive, we can expect even more."

"We always expect trouble from the Crown," Lowri cuts in. "It's not like the last guy was any good either. The only reason he didn't annihilate us was because we fight better than the rest."

"Yes, but *Cai* was good," Eoghan replies, and Lowri nods in agreement, her glass held between her fingers near her face. "*He* is why we are here, all of us."

The others around the table raise their glasses in salute and then fall silent, only the sound of silverware against china rising among us.

"Eoghan?" I say quietly, and he winds his fingers through mine as he waits for me to continue. "When can we go to Gobaith?"

"When would you like?" he purrs.

"Tomorrow." The word spills from my mouth, and I hear Gálgalesh groan beside me. He must be coming with us, and he is decidedly unhappy about it. I have to see Dedra and Tiernan, though. In my very soul, I need to see them.

"Tomorrow?" Eoghan touches the necklace at my chest before stroking my chin lightly with his thumb. Out of the corner of my eye, I watch Lowri's brows pull together, and I realize everyone is listening to our conversation, some with more interest than others. "I thought you might like a few days in the city to see the gardens and the Falacht River. No?" His eyes soften. "Tomorrow then."

Beside Eoghan, Bryn beams and whoops under his breath as Lowri turns her attention to Sawney in whispered conversation.

"Will you be joining us?" I pull my gaze from Eoghan to address his brother, who looks downright giddy.

"Well, that's where I live, so..." he begins.

"We *all* live in Gobaith—except them." Lowri nods to her parents. "Soldiers live in Gobaith, but it's no place for a *princess.*"

The loathing in Lowri's eyes is so apparent, I feel she would set me on fire if given the opportunity. She spares no bit of kindness for me. I almost think I'd stand a better chance against that deadly mob that tried to tear me apart than I would her. What have I done to make her hate me so much? *Don't let her get to you,* I tell myself. *You're Alana, the woman who braved Báscogar Prison; you don't need to take her shit.*

"Huh." I look up and down the table slowly. "Well, I don't think I see a princess here, and anyway, the Dohertys only have sons. But if I see one, I'll let her know."

Eoghan's expression flares with amusement, and he chuckles as Bryn howls beside him. Lowri's brows pull tightly against her forehead while Sawney gives a sultry smile next to her. I drop my eyes to my plate. Sawney might be harder to look at than Eoghan. General Osian gives me a broad smile and inclines his head respectfully.

"We will prepare for your departure in the morning. For now, let us enjoy our meal together."

———

I CANNOT SLEEP. The sun shines through the windows of the bedroom as Eoghan snores lightly beside me. I lay miserably awake, sticky with my own sweat. Since I first met him, I have not seen him so relaxed, so at home. He had dominated the prison and brought fear to every person who might try to get in his way—but his jaw had always been tight, his shoulders squared, his mind elsewhere. He sleeps so soundly here, I don't want to spoil it with my repugnance of this place.

It'll grow on you, as it had Cai. You'll love it one day, just as he did.

Still, I cannot sleep. I slide from the bed and tiptoe to the door, checking the hall for any sign of life before I make my way through the quiet halls. The house is bright as midday, though utterly deserted, only the sounds of my footsteps thrumming softly against the tile floors as I wander nowhere in particular.

"Woman," a familiar voice calls from the deserted sitting room, and I fall through the doorway to find Gálgalesh lounging in the armchair by the ceaseless fire. "You have the poorest manners I have ever seen, skulking around someone else's home. I would have thought you might have learned something about skulking at the prison."

"You say as you drink their liquor and lounge in their sitting room at all hours of the night." I point to the glass of brown liquid in his hand, and another sails through the air toward me. I take it, amused by his utter audacity.

"This liquor is meant for company," he muses. "And I would not be able to tell you what time it is with that blasted sun shining through the bare windows of this place." So I am not the only one who cannot sleep after all. "You seem to have something on your mind. Will you be telling me, or will you show me some mercy and keep it to yourself?"

I have much more than *something* on my mind. My mind has not stopped racing since the moment Rian appeared in the courtyard all those days ago. *Days.* It has been less than a fortnight, and it feels like months have passed. I have learned so much and traveled so far in the span of a few short days, leaving me with more questions than I have ever received in answers. My whole world seems to have spun on its head, and I cannot grapple with it. I still cannot comprehend why I have been kept in darkness for months on end.

"Why didn't you tell me about Rian and his father?" I take a long sip from my glass while Gálgalesh appraises me. He motions me to sit on the sofa across from him, and I drag myself deeper into the space, sinking down onto the over-stuffed cushions.

"I believed if you would have known, you might have raced back to the Capital to kill him before you were prepared. He would deserve it, though forgive me, I had grown fond of you despite myself. I did not want to see you lose your life at the hands of that repulsive human, or worse —watch you fall back into his arms."

I empty my glass, and Gálgalesh refills it. "I don't think you have to be worried about the latter. I couldn't go back to anyone who killed my family, no matter how I felt about him before."

"Do not be so sure. You might not have had a say. When we learned of the Dohertys taking the throne, I was surprised to find the young man's magic was not widely known. His father's magic is weak at best, as he is only an enchanter, destined to be in a working profession had he not possessed someone else's might to usurp the king. The mystery around Rian's, however, indicates that he possesses power advantageous to be kept hidden. We often think of this as battlefield or devious magic. I could not find anything that would indicate skill in fighting or bravery of any kind, so I began to think perhaps it might be more devious in nature."

"Devious?"

Gálgalesh nods. "Curiously, despite my best efforts, I could not find answers with any of my confidants throughout the five territories. I had about given up when Kael informed me you had shared an interesting tidbit of your own, while out with the Tinemallacht men."

"I realized I didn't know Rian's magic, that he had lied to me for years." Anger reignites within me as I think back to my embarrassment the evening of the hunt. "I had no real information about him. I'm still not sure if I know *anything* about him at all."

"Ah, yes, though it is not what you *knew*, but what you observed that mattered most." He taps the side of his nose with his long finger. "You are not a fool if you do not let your mind get in the way. You mentioned to Kael that you felt as though you were forgetting Rian and not grieving as you should. Curious for a woman in love, would you say? Even now, do you think you would not be devastated to lose Kael?"

"I would burn the entire world down if I did." The thought is terrible enough.

"And would you forget him after just a few short months?"

"Of course not."

"That is because love is not a simple thing to break. I have told you this before. Perhaps love was not what held you to Rian in the first place."

"What then?" I ask, leaning forward in my seat.

"Well, that I do not know, though I feel perhaps it might have everything to do with the magic he wields." He sets his glass down on the table and stands. "Perhaps one day, when we discover it, it might help us to rid ourselves of him for good. For you and for Peadair."

———

"IT'S JUST a short ride through the desert, Gálgalesh. Are you certain you won't join us?"

We stand at the edge of the city, looking out over the vast, red desert. This morning, Eoghan suggested we travel to Gobaith by way of Dune Gliders, rather than the portals that transported us from the coast. The contraption is foreign to me, made of a smooth wooden board with ridges, contours on its underside to help move it through the sand on the desert breeze as if it were on water. To harness the wind, a large white sail rises along a thin mast—a bright contrast against the red-orange sand and endless blue sky.

"No, thank you. I would rather not be made a fool of in dragon territory. I will meet you when you arrive in Gobaith."

Gálgalesh turns and walks away from us, back toward Kael Manor at the far end of the desert oasis. Dragons—had I really forgotten about the dragons? I scan the dunes for signs of life as Eoghan approaches. He fits a pair of goggles over my eyes and pulls my scarf up over my nose and mouth.

"Don't worry, the dragons know the sound of the gliders against the sand. They won't bother us...although a show might be fun!"

He helps me click my boots into the polished wooden board and instructs me on the proper ways to hold the handlebar and steer. As he speaks, Bryn, Lowri, and Sawney all gather nearby to set up their gliders for our journey.

"You'll be fine, darling!" Sawney coos smoothly with a smile. "The first ride is always the best."

"If she can stay upright," Lowri gibes.

"Don't let her get to you. She's just jealous," Eoghan whispers as he hooks a harness around my waist to the mast and checks my glider one last time. The others have no use for harnesses, though I am grateful Eoghan has thought to keep me strapped to the contraption in the very likely event that I fail so miserably, I hurdle myself straight into the sand.

"Of what?" I can't imagine one thing she might be remotely jealous of.

"That I have found another person who might steal my attention. She hated Cai for it for ages. She has never been good at sharing." He plants a kiss on my forehead and then steps away from me, fixing his own goggles over his eyes and clipping into his glider. "Okay, Lo, Sawney, you'll head out first and lead the way," he calls out so the others can hear. "Bryn, Maeve, and I will follow along after. Bryn, let's have some fun—do your thing!"

Bryn beams from ear to ear, his brilliantly white teeth crisp against his tan complexion. He turns his eyes ahead, lifts his scarf over his own face, and for a moment, nothing happens. Then, like a push of a great invisible hand, a gust of wind leads us down the dune as if we are flying across the sand.

I haven't experienced much in my life, but for all I have, this has to be the best. The initial tug of the sails, as if in invitation to become one with the sea of red sand around us, feels as though I have the power to harness the wind myself. With the slightest shift of my weight, I guide the glider to the right and to the left, mimicking Eoghan's movements as I had all those days I watched him train from the shadows of the arena. It's as if I have been granted a pair of giant white wings, gliding over the vast expanse of empty space—as if distance is nothing of concern at all.

Lowri and Sawney glide ahead, jumping over dunes and weaving between the shadows of the rising waves of sand. Eoghan encourages me on and motions for me to follow him as he and Bryn lean into their sails, banking right toward a towering mountain of the softest looking, powdery red. I feel my glider climb with the gust of wind that tugs at my sail with renewed force. We reach the top together, looking out over the barren Tinemallacht desert. Eoghan scans the valley as we ride and then points out ahead to something in the distance.

"There!" he shouts over the howling gale, and for a moment I see nothing. Then, as though bursting forth from the center of the Earth itself, comes the gargantuan beast that gives Tinemallacht its name.

Dragons—one and two at first, then ten, twenty, and fifty more breach the surface in a dance of wings more than twenty feet long. Towers of fire rise to the heavens as far as the eye can see. It is beautiful and terrifying, and I cannot blink for fear of even missing a moment. We glide down the far side of the hill and into the valley below as the dance continues, Eoghan and Bryn guiding us through the immense creatures. There must be thousands here, all welcoming us to their home.

We make it to the gates of Gobaith within the hour, and Eoghan helps me to dismount my glider as the winds die down, bringing the sweltering heat instantly back to drag me down under its tyrannical grip. He takes my goggles, my face pink from the heat and sand, and hands me a canteen of cool water.

"Did you enjoy that?" He removes his own goggles, his eyes glistening with joy.

"Are you joking? I am never traveling any other way again."

He laughs as he fixes my hair and then takes my hand in his own, walking us into the small outpost village. There's not a hint of green vegetation or blue water in this place, only red sand and light-colored houses with flat roofs and canvas awnings to provide shade from the oppressive sun. All around us, Tinemallacht soldiers dart from left to right through the sand in their tan cargo pants and short-sleeved shirts, reminding me of Cai in those last days when he preferred the floor to his bed.

"This is where you live?" I ask as we pass a small shop filled with everyday essentials and a pub overflowing with rowdy, drunken men.

"This is home," Eoghan breathes.

We walk casually down through town, stopping every so often to look in the occasional storefronts or for Eoghan to point out something from his time serving here in the royal military. He turns down a small road paved in wooden planks and half covered in sand. As we walk down it, the sound of the soldiers bustling past falls away. Houses with the same horseshoe archways and dark porticoed fronts line each side, simple yet welcoming, and I take in the intricate carvings across their façades. Fascinating how very different life can be from one territory to the next.

Eoghan turns to the left, stopping at the front of a much bigger home with a low, covered awning and shaded doorstep. He waves his hand to unlock the door, and then he turns the knob and leads us into a cool, dark entry.

"One second," he calls from just ahead and stumbles over something before an orb of warm light illuminates the space. What had I imagined Eoghan Kael's home to look like? Definitely not this. Dark ancient wood furniture, clean light fabrics and rugs, cool tile floors. It's so like the Eoghan I know, all while being so vastly different to the one I had been allowed to see. "It seems as though Bryn has taken the liberty of moving a few things around..." He eyes the space critically.

I walk ahead, taking in the narrow staircase leading upstairs. To the left is an eat-in kitchen, and to the right a relaxed sitting room. The floor tiles have colorful dragons etched across them. Two swords hang over the fireplace, where an eternal flame burns in the hearth, and there are heavy curtains on each of the windows, keeping the sunlight out.

"Does Bryn live here too?" I ask, and he nods.

"Lo and Sawney live across the outpost." His eyes dart nervously from the room to my face. "Do you like it?"

He's asking me if I like his house, as though my approval means anything at all. "I think it's wonderful, Eoghan Kael."

His shoulders relax as a smile envelops his visage. I drape my arms around his neck, drawing near to him as his hands fall to my waist. "Welcome home, Maevie."

"Home?" I pause. I had almost forgotten home could exist for me. I had almost forgotten a life of running was not a life to be lived at all.

"Unless you don't want it..." His voice is unsure again. "We can always find you somewhere else if you prefer."

"I would never dream of it." I rest my head against his chest.

There is a sound behind us, and Bryn enters the house casually, a cookie in his hand. He slides past us to the stairs.

"They've asked to see you," he says as he reaches the first step.

"In a bit," Eoghan responds.

"Gálgalesh insists."

Bryn is halfway to the landing before Eoghan groans.

"Damaris is in that big of a hurry, is he?" Bryn laughs from upstairs.

"Don't be an ass. Áine has made your favorite cookies and everything."

I had nearly forgotten about Tiernan and Dedra. I had half-expected them to be here when we walked through the door, but now, their absence feels nearly heartbreaking, knowing they are so near. Eoghan studies my face and rubs his brow, cursing low under his breath.

"All right." He drops his hands from my waist before

crossing back to the front door, and I scramble to follow him. "Let's get this over with."

He turns the handle, and we step out over the threshold. Wordlessly, he points to our left down a small, covered tile walkway, sand gathering in little piles along it. I walk for about ten paces to the next door before Eoghan stops me.

"Wait here."

All lightness has left his voice, as if something instantly damped his mood. Before I can respond, he enters the house, closing the door behind him. *Wait here?* I think to myself. *Why would I need to wait on the doorstep if they are asking for us?*

He doesn't return for five minutes. I lean against the portico column, and five more minutes pass with only the soft rustle of the awnings lining the street. *This is ridiculous. I'm not waiting here all day!*

I turn the door handle and push the door open quietly into a dark kitchen. The smell of baked goods fills the air. I close the door behind me as a warm wind kicks up outside. This place is smaller than Eoghan's, and off the kitchen sits a compact bedroom, the door pushed open halfway, though no life can be found inside. I take a step deeper inside as muffled voices reach my ears, Eoghan's rising above the rest.

"Let her settle in first!" he barks, and I'm taken aback by the bite in his words.

"And just not tell her?" Tiernan says. The sound of his voice makes my knees shake—tears fill my eyes.

"I didn't say that! Tell her this evening, after she's rested! Do we need to keep piling on information? At this rate—"

"She is a big girl, Eoghan. She can take it." My hand is on the door now. I hesitate.

"Do *not* act as though I don't know who and what she is!" Anger punctuates each syllable.

"Enough," Gálgalesh interjects. "We had our reasons to

wait, but she is here now, and there is no better time to tell her."

I press my hand against the door. It swings open with a loud creak, and all eyes snap toward me. I take in the room, Eoghan and Tiernan standing face-to-face, Eoghan towering over Tiernan with his jaw clenched and his hands flexing dangerously. Gálgalesh stands beside Eoghan, his hand on Eoghan's shoulder, as if restraining him. Dedra, who I had last seen the night I left for the Borderlands, sits on a tiny brown sofa with tears in her eyes and a broad smile on her face as she takes me in. Lowri stands in the corner of the room with a woman I do not recognize—her hair brown with honey colored highlights, slender, beautiful features, and hazel eyes. There's a baby boy in Lowri's arms. He cannot be more than a year and a half at best, with caramel hair and large chocolate eyes that look so familiar, it's as though I have seen them for my entire life.

Eoghan freezes as I walk through the door, his face falling blank with surprise.

"Tell me what?" I ask the room, and it's Lowri who steps forward this time, the baby on her hip, the woman following sheepishly in her wake, murmuring something under her breath.

"Maeve, you know Tiernan Damaris and Dedra Blos." She drags the woman to her side, her arm protectively around her shoulder. "And this is Áine Moran and Theo, Cai's wi—"

The words fade away as my vision spins and my heart races out of my chest. I gasp for air, failing miserably to drag it to my lungs.

"Maeve…" Eoghan's voice sounds far away as he steps toward me, and I reach out to grip his arm, but my legs give way, and the room disappears as I lose all consciousness.

CHAPTER NINE

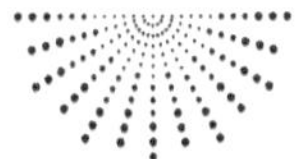

"All I am trying to say, Cai, is that you missed out on the perfect opportunity to decide on a lovely young woman who might become your wife and bear your heir. You could have at least stayed through the third dance instead of sneaking away to the pub with your friends." My mother follows Cai down the hall toward the castle entrance as he pulls his midnight-blue jacket over his tan military attire.

"Because I'm twenty-six now, much too old to be unmarried and uninterested? Was my birthday banquet to honor me or to compel me to fulfill my duty?" The marble floors quake beneath Cai's feet as he strides toward the exit.

"Would it be so wrong if it were? Every suitable family in the kingdom was there last night. Your father placed every eligible woman of worth in front of you for the taking—"

I watch from the shadows as Cai's cheeks go scarlet with rage. He whips around to face her, his eyes filled with frustration. He shoves his hands into hair as though he is fighting the urge to grab the nearest object and throw it down in front of him.

"Suitable. Worthy. Do you hear yourself, Mother? Perhaps you do not mind that Father has handpicked women to parade in front *of me every year since I was seventeen, from families he finds to be pure enough or rich enough or who he believes would salivate at the opportunity for me to fuck their daughters into oblivion until they produce a beautiful brown-eyed boy—but I do not care for it!"*

"Do you so loathe this family that you would turn your nose up to the idea of doing as you were born to do? The fate of the Crown rests in your hands!"

"Then let it be melted down to nothing! I don't care! I am happy in Tinemallacht with the people who matter to me! I am happy to be away from this prison! I am happy to be away from him! He is *a disgusting, tyran—"*

My mother gasps and hauls her hand across Cai's cheek with a loud slap. I still, fighting the urge to burst from my hiding place. Cai takes her in wordlessly as tears stream heavy down her cheeks. This might be the first time she has ever laid a hand on him—or anyone else, for that matter.

"You will leave this castle in two days, and you will not return until you are ready to be a man and do what must be done."

She turns from him and stomps back down the hall, retiring to her rooms. I wait until she has gone, Cai still standing with his fists now clenched at his sides. Then, I move from the shadows toward him.

"Eavesdropping again, Evie?" he says as he stares down the empty hall.

"I never learn anything around here unless I do," I reply as I reach him. "She doesn't mean it, you know—banishing you. She's just angry."

"I don't care if she does. There's nothing left for me in this place anyway."

"What about me?" I ask, almost pleadingly. If Cai leaves and never returns, what will become of me? "You'd come back for me, wouldn't you?"

I listen to his sigh cut through the air. My heart breaks instantly at the sound of his rejection, as though the whole world has rejected me with that single sound. He wouldn't come back, not even for me. He'd leave regardless of who he left behind.

"Come to Tinemallacht with me," he says. "We can leave right now, and we would never have to see this place again. No more King Cashel or Queen Clodah. No more palace walls. You could finally be free. Come...please?"

Thoughts whirl through my mind, making me dizzy. I have always wanted to leave this place and see the world. I've always wanted to be free, to meet people and have a life of my own...but what about my family? What about Rian, who visits me in secret—Rian, whom I love? Would he follow me if I left, or would he wash his hands of me for running away? What if I leave and there's nothing for me outside these walls? Father seems certain there won't be. If I had to come back, would I be able to? Would I survive if I could not return?

"I can't," I finally say. Cai's face falls with disappointment.

"I'm sorry to hear that," he says and shakes his head. "I was hoping you would want a new life away from this castle too." He steps forward and places his lips to my forehead before backing away from me. "I'm late for a meeting. I have to go."

He turns away, leaving me to watch as he disappears out the front door for the last time.

———

"I WARNED you we couldn't tell her like this!"

Eoghan's voice brings me back to consciousness. I feel his warmth radiate through him and heat my skin as he passes his hand gently across my cheek. I recognize the softness of a sofa under me as I slowly come back to the present.

"You keep trying to protect her as though she's some fragile thing. Maybe she doesn't need that." Tiernan is next to me as well. I can tell from the sound of his voice—he is standing, rather than crouched at my side.

"Don't listen to him, Eoghan. I have told him time and time again that he is a careless idiot." Dedra *is* crouching beside me, however. "He is trying to protect her, Tiernan, just as I was when you took her to the Borderlands, and look at how great that turned out!"

"I'm alive, aren't I?" I whisper as my eyes open, and I take in the sight of the three of them staring down at me. Tears well up to the surface at the sight of my long lost friend with her straw-colored mane and giant doe eyes. My heart swells and bursts. Oh, how I've missed them, more than I ever allowed myself to feel. Now, every emotion washes over me like a violent sea.

"At what cost, though?" Dedra reaches to take my hand, but I pull her to me, throwing my arms around her neck. "I didn't know what was happening to you in that horrible prison!"

"I know," I half-laugh against the tears of relief as I hug her. I'm afraid I might break her from holding her so tightly. She doesn't pull away, though, and her tears fall wet onto my shoulder. "I was so scared you would be hurt or killed in the Capital waiting for me. How did you get here?"

I release her before moving to sit up, meeting her eyes.

"Easy." Eoghan places his fingers under my elbow, but he does not stop me.

"Well, the faerie, Gálgalesh, found us as he was escaping the Steel Citadel. He told us we were in danger, that he could take us to safety. I hardly believed him until Tiernan explained he was the one who had taken you to the prison and cared for you. So, we packed up what we could and left, hoping that maybe, he would bring us to you. We arrived here about two weeks ago."

Two weeks. About the same time we left Báscogar. Had Eoghan known Gálgalesh would come here for sanctuary?

Why did Gálgalesh feel Tiernan and Dedra were in trouble? Why do I still feel like I know nothing at all?

I look around the room. It's now empty besides the four of us—Gálgalesh, Lowri and… My head begins to spin as I remember what had been said before I passed out. *Cai's wife and son. Cai has a wife and a son.* I look to Tiernan, who calmly smiles down at me; to Dedra, who pats my hand softly, waiting for me to speak. Finally, I turn to Eoghan—his eyes seem so unsure. He drops his gaze to the floor in front of him.

"Can we have a moment?" I ask as I fix my gaze on him. Dedra nods, her eyes taking us in before she stands. She gestures for Tiernan to leave, and he only begrudgingly obliges before she leans down, her breath warm against my ear.

"Be gentle with him. He seems kind. I would like you to keep him around long enough to tell me about him."

I smile, and she lays a soft peck on my cheek before she straightens and leaves us. When the door falls shut behind her, the room becomes oppressively silent. Eoghan still has not looked up from his feet. I wait for him to speak. Of course, he doesn't offer the first word, so I clear my throat and begin.

"Are you going to tell me what is going on, or am I just going to have to accept that you hid endless secrets?" Silence again. I bristle. "Well, first thing's first: why does your sister believe that woman is Cai's wife?"

"Because she *is* Cai's wife." He plays with his hands in his lap, as though he's attempting to ring them dry.

"And the boy?" He's silent, but a small bow of his head is my confirmation. "When?"

"When what?"

"When did they marry?" I tap my boot against the floor as my knees quake.

"Almost four summers ago."

Four summers ago? Well before my wedding. At least a year before Cai's last birthday banquet, when he had decided to leave the castle behind completely.

"And you knew?" I reach for his chin to coax his gaze toward me. He shakes me off. "Eoghan, look at me. I will not speak to the top of your head." He reluctantly turns his eyes upward to meet mine. His are red and full of sorrow. "You knew?" I ask again.

"Of course I knew."

"Why wouldn't you tell me?" I feel a mixture of anger and disappointment rise through me. If I had dragon fire, the temperature of the room might rise.

"I tried. I thought about it a million times, I just couldn't find the words. Each time you felt as though you had lost him completely, I thought about telling you, but I wasn't sure if it would make you hate him for keeping it from you or hate me for telling you something you might not even believe. I couldn't bear knowing you were angry with him. I needed you to know what they meant to him—know what *you* meant to him—so you might understand why he hid them from you."

"Why did he hide them from me?" I ask, and he shrugs.

"I swear, I don't know. All he ever said was that he could never let your family know they existed. It was essential to him, but he never told me why. It was Cai—he had his reasons for everything, even if he didn't let us in on them."

My heart feels like it's been hit with a hammer and shattered with each new revelation. This time, I'm not sure I have it in me to pick up the pieces. Cai didn't want me to know about his family. He couldn't trust me to know about them. Did he think I would hurt them? Sell them out? Did he think I would tell Father, and he would not approve? How could he have such little faith in us—in me? I would have kept any secret he asked me to keep. I would have done everything in my power to keep them safe, if he only would have allowed me to do so.

"Where did they meet?" I straighten, willing away the tears that fall from my eyes. They do not relent.

"Here in Gobaith. Áine has summoning magic. She can summon anything she pleases, and not just through open space like you can with your faerie magic—through walls and pockets and distance. If she can visualize it, she can get to it. She was in the outpost, making what she could from the parlor magic she knew, robbing soldiers of their pocket gold, when she ran into Cai. She stole his watch from his pants pocket and left, but once she got home, she couldn't stop thinking about him. She decided to return it the next day. She thought he would kill her or have her hand cut off, as is the customary punishment for thieves here. She never imagined that when she arrived at his door, he would tell her he had been thinking about her too and kiss her instead."

My brother—the man who cared so little for love—had fallen for a beautiful thief. Not only that, he had married her and had a son, all without anyone knowing or suspecting a single thing. The Heir of Draíocoinnigh had sired a child who knew nothing of his fate or his title, or of a world inside the castle walls.

"When did they meet?" I ask, and I don't even try to stop the tears now. Eoghan reaches for me as he wipes them away.

"Five, nearly six years ago. After the Battle of Buaeth."

At least as long as I had known Rian. How could he have never told me? The careless bachelor who cared nothing for the women who fawned over him—who preferred to sleep on the floor than in the comforts of his bed in the castle— had done so because he was not a bachelor at all. He was a man in love, a man so devoted to his love, he kept her a secret from the world.

"Does she hate me?" I bite my lip to keep it from quivering. Eoghan brings his hands to cup my face as his brow pulls tightly together.

"What? No, of course not! Why would she hate you?"

"Because I'm the reason he's..." I can't speak the word, not when it means so many lives have been broken because of me.

"Maeve, you listen to me. You are *not* the reason Cai is dead." He brings his forehead to mine.

"Yes, I am!" I sob into his hands. "If it wasn't for me, he would be here with them!"

"You don't know that."

"I do!"

I cry, prying his hands away from my face. I cannot take his pity, as if I hadn't played any part in this. I had begged Cai to return. He refused several times before, but when I became engaged, I insisted, and he did it for me. I sob into my hands, and Dedra pushes through the door, Tiernan following behind. I stand from the sofa, crossing the small room to her. I throw my arms around her and cry into her chest as she rubs circles softly along my back. Eoghan turns to Tiernan, his face hard and furious.

"Are you happy now?" he snaps.

"I didn't do anything!" Tiernan bites back, and Eoghan crosses the room this time, his footsteps landing hard against the tile.

"Both of you, out!" Dedra shouts. Both men stop in alarm, their eyes finding her as she pats my hair. "OUT!" she says again, and one of her hands flies through the air toward the door. "Do not make me enchant those pillows to chase you out of this room!"

The men grumble under their breath while they retreat into the small kitchen. Dedra waits until they have left and guides me back to a seat. She gently detaches me to examine my face, wiping my wet eyes with her palms.

"Come on, baby," she coaxes. "Settle down."

"He keeps everything from me." My voice breaks as I try to stifle my tears. "He didn't tell me about Cai, and he could have."

"I know," Dedra agrees, "but he wasn't the only one who could have told you. Tiernan knew too, you know. And the faerie with the bad attitude." I laugh, and she smirks. "He can't shoulder all the blame. He might have just been doing what he thought would keep you safe."

"But he has so many secrets!"

"So does Tiernan. He does his runs and sells contraband right under my nose; still, he tells me nothing about it. He won't even tell me why he was so worried about seeing Eoghan, and I've been pressing him since we got here. Men are complicated. Do you believe he is good?"

"Of course I do. It's the only thing in this world I do know for sure."

"And will he keep you safe?"

I nod.

"Then trust all his secrets will come to light at the right time." She sweeps my fallen hair away from my face. "You must love him." Her smile widens, and my cheeks flush pink.

"How can you tell?"

"Because, even while you're mad at him, you still look at him as though he holds your whole world in his hand." *Oh gods, how embarrassing.* I fall back into the cushions and cover my face with my hands. "It's okay. He loves you too."

"Oh, really?" I sigh and rub my fingertips across my forehead. "And how do you know this, Dedra the Wise?"

"Because no man fights another man so fiercely to protect a woman's heart unless theirs is tied to it. From what I saw, his very breath depends on yours."

I laugh from my stomach now and hit her with one of the pillows propped up on the couch. She laughs back, unabashed.

———

Eoghan, Lowri, and the others leave me, Tiernan, and Dedra to ourselves for the rest of the afternoon. It feels like coming home. Dedra tells me of the moment Tiernan returned without me, how she almost beat him black and blue when he told her he had sent me to Báscogar.

"She cried for a week!" Tiernan grumbles, and Dedra admonishes him with a slap on his arm.

"You would have cried too if you were stuck with only Tiernan Damaris for months on end! I thought about joining you at that horrible prison rather than listening to his grumbling or complete arrogance."

I tell them about my time at Báscogar and my training with Gálgalesh; how he had been concerned at my lack of common magic, about the blood bond—much to Dedra's dismay. I tell them about how he had taught me to spar. I tell them about Peadair and the attack in the forest near Fáintìrean, how Eoghan had found me and saved me, how Gálgalesh paired us together after our return to the camp. I leave out no details—though I spare Tiernan any stories of our return to the cottage. We speak about every last trivial point and inconsequential moment of my time away. About Kruz. About Gálgalesh leaving and Drustan Anwyl. The dungeon. The bargain with the shadow lurker. Eoghan melting the Faebond to get to me. About Rian and how I discovered he was not dead at all—and finally, our escape.

"Wow," Tiernan says as I finish. "Gálgalesh told us nothing of your time at Báscogar—except that you were not dead. If I would have known..."

"Would you have come to save me from Eoghan Kael?" I eye him, and he rolls his eyes.

"I would have never sent you in the first place."

I bat the air between us with my hand. "I needed Báscogar. It was the best thing you could have done for me." I pat his shoulder once. "Thank you, Tiernan Damaris, for sending me to my death so I could learn how to live." Dedra scoffs reproachfully, and I chuckle lightly as I lift a glass of water from the small side table. "Although," I pause as a question passes through my mind, "you were both at the coup, weren't you?"

"Unfortunately," Tiernan says, and Dedra winces.

"You knew Rian had not been killed along with Cai and my parents. Why did you not tell me he was alive?"

Tiernan shrugs helplessly. "We weren't sure what had happened to him until his father was crowned. We thought maybe the members of the coup had killed him before they dragged the rest of you out onto the platform."

"But..." I think back to the day, as they tied me to the post and Rian whispered to me. "He was next to me on the platform. He spoke to me before they untied the others." Tiernan and Dedra look to each other, confusion etched across their features. "He was next to me on the platform!" I insist again. I *know* I spoke to him before he was taken away.

"Maeve, Rian was not on the platform on that day," Dedra insists.

"Yes, he was!" How did they not see him? "Who was beside me on the platform then?"

"Cai was on your right," Tiernan says, and I remember the weight of Cai's head lulling against my shoulder. "And Oli Raven was on your left, though he wasn't a prisoner. He left as the killings began."

Oli Raven? No, Oli Raven could not have been next to me on the platform. I had spoken to Rian. I know I had spoken to Rian. Tiernan stands and brushes his hands against his pants to flatten the creases, and I hardly register his next words. Dedra says something back to him, though I don't catch it, and she stands as well. Tiernan looks down at me expectantly for a long moment.

"What?" I ask, shaking my head.

"I said it's getting late. We should eat something," he replies and reaches out to help me up.

"I need to find Eoghan," I say.

"I think he went to train across the outpost," Tiernan begins. I rush past him and out of the door, both he and Dedra calling after me. I cross the kitchen of the small desert house and make it to the front entrance as Áine peeks her head from the bedroom on the right.

"Where do they train?" I ask.

She appraises me before she clears her throat. "Go down the road to the main square. You should find them there. They like to spar with the others in the open." Her voice is soft, matching the delicate beauty of her features.

"Thank you," I say as I grab the door handle and exit onto the quiet, wood-planked road.

The winds have picked up, and a thin veil of sand hangs in the air around the outpost. I pull my scarf up over my nose and mouth and head down the street at nearly a run. I need to find Eoghan. He did not lie to me that day of the hunt when he told me about Rian concealing his magic. I can trust him now. I can trust him *always*, even with his secrets. I turn at the end of the road as the square comes into view, hazy through the mist of sand. I pick up my pace, covering my eyes at a gust of wind.

I reach the square, and there he is, shirtless in the oppressive heat, shaking sand from his hair as he circles Lowri in a deadly dance. Sparring—he is sparring his sister. Not mildly or with any sort of hesitation, but as though she is one of the opponents in the training arena I had watched him batter and bruise time and time again. She meets his ferocity in stride, the perfect match to his powerful strikes. He moves, she counters. He punches, she hits back twice as hard. I pause as they continue to brutalize one another. Lowri takes him down at the knees, driving a dagger through the air to his throat. His breath is heavy as I have never seen it in all of the times I have watched him spar. He stares up at her, searching for an advantage. Finally, he places his hand to the dirt and taps out.

I rush forward as he rises, laughing and brushing the sand from his knees. Lowri backs away, sheathing her dagger before wiping sweat from her brow. He catches me out of the corner of his eye as I break through the crowd, and he turns as I barrel toward him.

"Hey!" he begins before he notes the look on my face and catches me in his arms. "What's wrong?" He releases me just enough to take me in. "What happened?"

"Is there magic that can mask the wielder's appearance or voice?" I pant. Concern washes over his face.

"What? Maeve, what's happened?" he demands again.

"Just answer me!" I shout. The others in the square turn their attention our way now. Lowri steps toward us curiously, listening in. "Is there magic that can mask the wielder's appearance or voice?"

Eoghan thinks for a moment. He turns to Lowri, who shrugs. "I don't know. Maybe...? Why?"

"Could Rian wield such magic?"

Gálgalesh steps forward from the group of onlookers. I hadn't noticed him there before. He crosses to us and looks down at me, his expression like stone.

"No, he could not, but there are some who can. Come, let us go inside so I can tell you what I learned in the Capital."

CHAPTER TEN

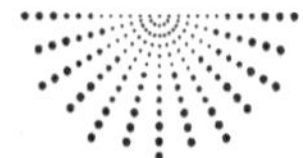

"Gálgalesh." Eoghan's voice is strained as he grips my arm like he is holding me back.

"Not here," Gálgalesh responds. "Come."

He starts back toward the house, across the outpost square and up the small street. Lowri retrieves Eoghan's shirt and canteen and shoves them into his hands. With an exasperated sigh, he motions for us to follow Gálgalesh's lead. We make it back to Eoghan's door before Gálgalesh slows his pace. He has not turned around once to even confirm we are with him at all. The door swings open of its own accord as he steps over the threshold, familiar with the space. We follow, and he leads us into the dark, cool sitting room, wordlessly commanding us to take a seat.

"Would someone please tell me what the hell is going on?" Eoghan pulls his shirt over his head. He refuses to sit, instead choosing to stand protectively at my side. Gálgalesh's eyes fall on me in silent question.

"On the day of the coup, when we were taken from the castle, we were tied to a platform in the front garden. I had not initially known where we were, because those who had taken me captive obscured my vision, but when they tied my hands to the post, Rian spoke to me. I knew he was there with me until they untied the others, and then I was left alone." I feel sick just thinking about it. "I was certain he had been killed, just as the others were. How could he be taken prisoner and not be? What purpose would that serve? When I saw him at Báscogar, I couldn't understand what had happened. Everyone seemed to know he was alive except for me—but he had been there that day. It didn't make sense."

Eoghan starts to speak, but Gálgalesh holds up his hand to silence him and indicates for me to continue.

"I asked Tiernan why he hadn't told me Rian was alive after he witnessed the coup and saw him survive when the others had not. He seemed confused by the question, and when I pressed him again, he said Rian had not been on the platform at all—that Sir Oli Raven had. How could that be? I heard him speak to me—he was there on the platform! Why would Tiernan see Sir Oli Raven when it was Rian beside me?"

Gálgalesh's lips pull into a thin line, yet he doesn't answer me. Instead, he turns to Lowri.

"Bring Damaris here," he commands, and without a word, Lowri exits the room. I listen as the front door opens and shuts behind her. Gálgalesh walks to the hearth, where the eternal flame of dragon fire burns. He runs his hand in front of it before pulling back his palm to examine his skin. "Dragon fire is curious. It burns what it chooses and leaves the rest alone. I wonder where the heat hides, though… Kael?"

Eoghan, deep in thought of his own with lines of worry etched across his face, shakes his head. "Sorry?"

"The heat," Gálgalesh says again. "Where does the heat hide from this fire here? Why does it burn in constant glow day and night and never warms the room?"

"Are you asking me about dragon fire?" Eoghan gibes, and I feel the same sense of ridicule rise up in me as well. What does it matter if the dragon fire burns hot or if it doesn't? What does this have to do with anything at all? Why is he not answering me?

"Yes." Gálgalesh is undeterred, staring at Eoghan, waiting patiently for him to continue. I look between the faerie and Eoghan, who stands dumbfounded by the question; then, after a moment, he speaks.

"Dragon fire burns at the dragon's—or wielder's—discretion. It can burn that which the dragon feels is worthy of being burned and leave the rest unharmed. Usually, a dragon will only burn that which is evil in its sight. Wielders are generally taught the same."

"And the heat? Where is it now?" Gálgalesh points to the fire.

"It remains with the dragon."

I cannot take it anymore. I cannot take one more second of useless conversation about dragons and fire and heat, as though it means anything at all! As though we do not have enough heat in this sun-drenched desert already! He's avoiding me, avoiding giving me answers, instead trying to make me forget I asked the question. He doesn't want me to know. He is hiding yet another important piece of information from me, and I cannot take it anymore! I'm done with being treated as though I don't need or deserve to know anything.

I stand, but as I do, the sound of the door opening makes me pause. Two sets of footsteps cross the short distance to the sitting room, and Lowri reappears with Tiernan at her side. Gálgalesh turns and motions toward the sofa, and I feel a heavy, invisible weight on my shoulder, pushing me back down toward the cushions.

"Now that the feallwr has joined us, perhaps he can tell us once again what he saw during the coup."

"I wish you would stop calling me that," Tiernan grumbles, and Gálgalesh's eyes sparkle with a satisfaction that tells me not even with his dying breath will he absolve Tiernan of his indignation. A subtle, almost imperceptible smirk plays across Eoghan's lips. "On the day of the coup, a large group of men and women stormed the city gates, shouting for the death of the king. They flooded the streets, marching toward the Steel Citadel, armed with daggers and clubs. It didn't take long to realize the coup was coordinated and well-timed. The crowd reached the gates of the castle and forced them down while the organizers erected a wooden platform outside the front entrance. At first, the men from the military station in the city rushed to help the guards secure the Citadel—but several turned on us when the king was dragged out onto the dais. He was the first, followed by the queen, Cai—who they had brutalized from what I could see —and then Maeve."

"And the fiancé?" Gálgalesh asks, and that familiar sound from deep in Eoghan's chest fills the room.

"I never saw him. We thought perhaps he had been killed inside the castle trying to protect Maeve, or maybe he had fled when word of the mob reached him. We didn't suspect anything."

"Maeve said you mentioned Oli Raven was on the platform as well. Was he being held captive as the others?"

"Not that I'm aware of. He was seated next to Maeve, but when the others were brought to the front, he stood and walked back into the castle alone."

"And you watched the others as they were killed? Are you certain of it? Could any of them have survived as she did?" Lowri speaks and points toward me. My chest instantly fills with a hope I had never let myself have before, only to be dashed much too quickly with the shake of Tiernan's head.

"None of them survived. The king was the first to be killed. I watched as the crowd dismembered him. The queen died before the crowd rushed across the stage. Cai..." He pauses, and the whole room swallows back collective tears. "He fought as much as he could, but in the end, there was no way he could have survived."

They were all dead, just as I heard it happen that day. None of them had survived—no one except me, and that was only due to obvious lack of care on the murderers' part. I had heard it, but Tiernan had been forced to stand there and watch as the life left their eyes. I can hardly imagine it. I rise from the sofa and cross the short distance to him, winding my arms around his neck in a tight embrace. Gálgalesh inclines his head solemnly, and a weight drags Eoghan's shoulders down, making him seem smaller somehow. Angry tears rage in Lowri's eyes as she wipes away the trail of them that has escaped down to her jaw.

"In the wake of the new king, there has been a resurgence of highdruí activity within the castle. Since King Fergal's ascent to the throne nearly two hundred years ago, the high-druí have played little part, publicly, in the ruling of the king-dom. It is said this was due to the Moran family's lack of care for the gods, though the druí colonies in Gálamáistir and throughout the kingdom were given stay and their temples left unbothered by the king as a show of good will. That is, with the exception of the temples in Tinemallacht honoring the goddess Brigid."

"Dragons burned every temple in the territory down ages ago and all highdruí with them," Lowri offers.

"Ah, yes indeed. Dragons are untrusting of most, yet as Eoghan has so rightfully explained, they do not use their fire to harm unless they have deemed their target evil in their sight. I have always found dragon magic endlessly intriguing, even if a bit mundane." Lowri huffs her displeasure, and the room's temperature rises before Gálgalesh continues. "When I arrived in the Capital, I was surprised by the druí presence that had become so overwhelming, it seemed they had even made their way into the inner workings of the king's court. This only confirmed my worst fear—someone inside the prison had surmised your identity and made your existence known to the usurpers."

"Druí Whelan?" Eoghan asks.

"He had been curious about Maeve after he had seen her properly for the first time in my office before my final supply run. It seems he had been in contact with someone who had the king's ear."

"What does this have to do with Oli Raven being on the platform during the coup?"

"No human wielder, in their own power, has been known to shift their appearance or voice at will. That is considered black sorcery wielded within the cults of the wielder communities, most famously within the druí colonies of Tinemallacht. The highdruí of these cults credit their patron gods and goddesses for this exceptionally dark magic, and I would even agree that it is not this world that has produced such evil. Woman, are you aware of when Oli Raven came to be your father's emissary?"

I shrug. "Long before I can remember, perhaps even before I was born."

"Sir Oli Raven took up his post just after the druí temples of Brigid in Tinemallacht were burned to the ground." The room goes still. "I would venture a guess that Oli Raven was indeed seated beside you on the platform that day. I do not pretend to know why, but I have a feeling it has to do with his new position as the King's Hand."

Sir Oli Raven was seated next to me on the platform.

Somehow, he had spoken to me and made himself appear to be Rian. Why? If the intent was simply to kill me, why go through all the trouble? What purpose would it serve to deceive me?

Eoghan crosses from the far side of the room to the rest of us, and I realize my arms are still draped over Tiernan's shoulders. I drop them to my sides and take a step back, closer to Eoghan. I feel his warmth envelop me as he places his hand on the small of my back softly, and I lean longingly into his touch. I've had about as much as I can handle today; any more information, and I might lose my mind completely.

"Sir Oli Raven," I say to the room, almost to myself. "He experimented on me. He knew my weaknesses and fears—perhaps more than anyone else. Now that they know I'm alive, I'm sure they will send him after me."

"I won't let him near you." Eoghan's deep growl is so full of ire, I tense as he speaks. "I'll kill him before he has the chance."

"Be that as it may, it would be best we be mindful when speaking with anyone outside of this room. If the new Sovereign has black magic on his side, we do not know who we can trust." He reaches me with sympathetic eyes, his gaze locked with mine. "Enough for today. Let us give Eoghan and Maeve their privacy. They have much to discuss, and if they do not, I fear Maeve might start throwing daggers. Her aim is surprisingly good for such a truly insufferable human. I would bet on Eoghan losing an eye this time."

I smile despite myself, and they all make their exit. Eoghan wraps his arm around my waist softly, dragging me to him, his chest against my back. My head is pounding, and I'm not sure what might be worse: to never know anything at all, or to learn so much, you can never trust anyone again. Gálgalesh had kept information from me, and now he cannot seem to stop supplying it. At least, though, he's speaking. Eoghan had tried to protect me by telling me nothing, had not thought I could handle any information at all. He saw me as too weak, too stupid, too emotional—too much of a liability to let me in on his plans. Will he ever trust me enough to tell me things before I find out from someone else?

I disentangle myself from him and take a step toward the door, putting space between us. His touch feels less comforting now, more like a tool he utilizes to keep me from challenging him or wondering what he's up to. He leans back on his heels, taken aback by my aversion to his touch.

"Is something the matter, Maeve?"

"I think I need some time alone." His shoulders stiffen at my words.

"What have I done now?" He does not reach for me, but his hands flex uncomfortably at his sides.

"What haven't you done?" I snap despite myself. "You've hidden everything from me, Eoghan. From the moment I met you, you've been keeping secrets from me. You promised me no more secrets, and there's a new one every time I turn around. How can I trust a word you say? I just need space to think."

"I didn't hide anything from you to hurt you. You have to believe that."

"I don't know what I can believe anymore. I feel as though every moment we have spent together has been some elaborate game to see just how much I'll believe, just how far I'll follow you blindly. Do I even know you, Eoghan? Can I say you've shown me enough of you for what we have to be real? Or have I fallen for the idea of who I believe you to be? I can't love a lie. I need to be able to believe you."

I reach for the chain hanging warm against my chest and

unclasp it. I hold it slack in my hand and reach for Eoghan's. He flinches at my touch.

"Don't." His voice comes out as the softest plea, but I place the necklace into his palm anyway.

"For now," I assure him, though maybe I am just trying to appease my own broken heart. "Just until I figure out anything at all."

He's silent, his eyes wide, as though everything in him has shattered with my words. I can't stand to look at him. His beautiful green and gold eyes that once held nothing for me but scorn are now silver with grief. *Just leave,* I tell myself. *Just walk out the door before you reconsider.* I take a step, my boots feeling as heavy as lead, and I leave him standing in the room. Unsure of where to go next, yet unwilling to stay here, I continue to the door, nearly stumbling over the threshold as I exit. I lean forward with my hands against my knees, and my breathing fails me. Heavy pants heave my chest up and down as I listen for the sound of Eoghan rushing to find me, to fight for me. He doesn't come.

"Harsh." Lowri leans against the outside wall, her arms crossed against her chest. "I find that he bleeds just as easily with the blade—but I suspect you're looking to leave lasting scars."

Why does it have to be her? "What do you want? I would have thought you'd be happy to have him rid of me."

"Sure I would…but we both know that isn't the case." She pushes herself to stand and steps into the desert sun. "Come on. You'll stay with us tonight. Tomorrow, you start training with me. No one else I love is going to die on account of you."

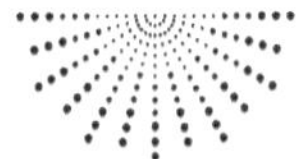

CHAPTER ELEVEN

"Protect your face unless you want it to be black and blue!"

I fall back into the sand, and Lowri drives her fist into my jaw so hard, my ears ring. We have been sparring together for six days, and I'm starting to think Eoghan was the easier of my opponents. She winds back and barrels down toward me again. This time, I block her with my forearm and roll; she loses her balance and falls into the sand. She's quick to recover, and I scramble into a crouch as we circle each other.

"Nice one!" Bryn shouts from the outer perimeter of our makeshift sparring ring, where he has been every morning since the one after I left Eoghan alone in that sitting room. "You could talk to him, you know. He'd like that."

Lowri lunges forward to catch my leg, but I drive my elbow into her arm, and she lets go with a frustrated growl. I continue to circle, watching her hands, knowing she won't miss the next time she strikes.

"I don't have anything to say to him," I shout to Bryn as I lunge forward this time, narrowly missing Lowri as she masterfully steps to the right. "Is that why you're here? Does he send you to spy on me?"

"Of course not." Bryn plays lazily in the sand, creating tiny dust devils that swirl around in front of him. I'm distracted as one whizzes past us, and Lowri takes the opportunity to spring toward me, pulling me into a barrel roll and pinning me to the ground.

"Stop distracting her!" she calls to her brother as she presses her boot into my stomach. "She's pathetic without your warbling." She looks down and releases me, gesturing for me to rise again. I'm panting for breath now. It's so hot. My lungs feel as though they have turned to dust in my chest. "Get your act together, *princess*, or you won't last a day outside of this outpost."

"Don't call me that." I clench my teeth as I ready myself again.

"Oh, I'm sorry, I forgot you don't like that title. You prefer to be called a royal pain in the ass."

"I really hate you," I snap and throw everything I can into my next attempt to bring Lowri down into the sand. I take out her legs from underneath her as I haul all my weight into her chest, knocking the air out of her as she hits the ground. I hold her there with my elbow into her stomach. She tries to throw her fist into my unprotected face, but I throw up a blue shield of magic, her hand rebounding off it back toward her.

"He's miserable and he's lonely, Maeve. I've never seen him like this. Maybe if you would just come by, just for an hour..."

"He's not even in Gobaith, Bryn! Knock it off!" There's a small trickle of blood running from Lowri's nose where she clocked herself with her fist.

"Eoghan's not here?"

I straighten, forgetting I'm in the middle of a sparring

match with Lugh—the god of war—in living form. Lowri takes the opportunity to shove me off her onto my back, unsheathing a dagger from her side and dragging it across my exposed collarbone, the Tinemallacht mark of a winning match. Blood trickles up to the surface, signifying my defeat.

"No, he's not, and you're dead if I was an actual opponent." She stands and walks away from me to Bryn, who hands her a canteen. "You don't expect him to sit around crying over you all day, do you? He's a soldier, first and foremost, not just your doting boyfriend. We are in the middle of a war, if you haven't noticed—and we unfortunately don't even know the half of it yet. Eoghan, Rhodes, and Hayes are important to the cause. Everyone here but you is important to the cause, and that means they need to figure out what we are going to do next. Maybe if you would stop being such a selfish brat, you might be able to help too."

"I thought you didn't want me near him," I scoff as I approach Bryn; he hands me a towel and a canteen as well.

"Absolutely, I don't. I would love for you to fuck off forever and go back to where you came from, but I know that's not going to happen. You'll end up getting us all killed because you have the biggest target in the kingdom on your back while we are all tasked with making sure you don't die." *Go back to where you came from.* I remember Eoghan whispering those words to me after we had sparred for the first time, as if I was a burden just being alive. "Do you even care that he'd die for you? I still can't believe you stood there, just watching that asshole of an ex-fiancé of yours with big doe eyes, as if you would do anything to be with *him*—jump from the second story corridor into his arms—even though *he* murdered your family like animals for slaughter."

"How do you...?" I drop my canteen, and the cold water spills out into the sand.

"He's my twin. Do you think he tells me nothing?" Lowri

taunts, and then, as if realization washes over the three of us simultaneously, amusement leaves her face, and she hesitates for an agonizingly long moment. Then, she continues, her tone softer by the slimmest margin. "Gálgalesh wanted you to meet him in the outpost library after we were finished. Dinner is at eight. Don't be late, or Sawney will have a fit and think I ran you off."

She caps her canteen and pushes past me, her elbow ramming into my side as she leaves the center of the square. Bryn watches her disappear into one of the outpost buildings and then dives for my canteen. He brushes the sand from it then hands it to me, but I'm not thirsty anymore. My blood runs cold despite the heat.

"She didn't mean it," he says softly. "She's always been mean to everyone, but she doesn't mean it. Not really."

"Yes, she does." I throw the towel over my shoulder and shake my head. "It's fine. I deserve it. She's just protecting Eoghan. I'd do the same if it were Cai."

"Speaking of." Bryn pushes his hand out in front of him, and a gust of wind intercepts an oncoming cloud of sand to divert it. "Have you thought about visiting Áine and Theo?"

"No." I watch as two soldiers pass through the square and eye me with interest. I smile at them weakly, and their lips pull up at the sides as they grow taller in their boots. "I don't know how I could bear it, not with knowing that he—" I pause and then change the subject. "Anyway, Gálgalesh will be furious if I'm late." I indicate toward the library. "You coming?"

A broad smile brightens Bryn's already-warm features, and we set off to continue my faerie magic lessons. We cross the outpost square, and the sun beats down heavily upon us from its stationary position in the sky. I still don't understand how it seems to never move here. It is always overhead, bearing down on the land, as if its only task is to dry out the desert. It has done a fantastic job of it, save for Bastain, which is the only place in the whole territory where the river flows freely above the sand. Still, the vast land from west to east really does seem to be cursed by heat, if not dragons themselves.

"Where is Eoghan?" I ask before we reach the library door. Bryn shrugs.

"Across the territory, I suspect, meeting with the others. I'm just the little brother, not the twin. He tells me nothing if he can avoid it."

We walk into the library to find Gálgalesh hunched over a stack of parchment on a small desk between the stacks. It reminds me so much of the days in his office at Báscogar, and I can't help but feel a tinge of pain and longing deep in my chest. I had been miserable then, absolutely hopeless in the endless winter of Romiodóg, but my mind was lighter, not weighed down with the burden of truth that has now stolen my every waking thought. I set my canteen on the wooden table behind him. He doesn't look up as he pushes a stack of parchment through the air toward me. It lands like a command in front of me.

"Morning," I say as I pull a chair back to sit. Bryn joins me and shuffles through the parchment, captivated by the faerie incantations, choosing one he would most like to watch me master this time. Gálgalesh waves his hand in greeting. "What is so interesting that you cannot spare one hello?"

"Your brother," he says and lifts the parchment from his desk. "Old letters he had written to myself and others. He kept a copy of every correspondence he ever wrote, whether he ultimately sent it or not. He is more intelligent than any other human I have ever met."

"Are there any to me?" I watch his head bounce in confirmation, and another stack of parchment lands in front of me.

"Practice first. You are to learn each of those spells by the end of the week. It is necessary for your training to move faster now, in case anyone decides to show up to kill you."

"Pleasant," I mumble as Bryn passes a lone page to me. I scan it, my eyebrow raised at one side. "Lifesaving charms... Well, yes, this, I will definitely need, you know, if I want to save my own life. You're becoming old, Gálgalesh. You haven't even thought of anything clever to name these."

"Perhaps you will need to save someone else," Bryn suggests, and Gálgalesh's faint hum of a response indicates approval. "Try the first one."

I review the symbols and sequences of the first incantation. It seems simple enough, similar to the blue shield I mastered back at the prison months ago. I tug on the faerie thread and lean into its response, sending a command down the line. Nothing happens. I look down at the parchment and check the sequence before trying again. Still nothing. I look at Bryn, who tilts his head to the side curiously, waiting for a spark of light or some sound to make the magic known. I try once more...and get the same result.

"Gálgalesh, this spell must be wrong. Nothing is happening."

Gálgalesh looses a heavy sigh of annoyance and stands from his desk. He walks back toward us, taking the parchment between his long fingers to look it over.

"Stand," he commands, and I obey. "Do this again, as it is written."

I tug the thread and send the command down the line. The results are the same. I look up at Gálgalesh and raise my shoulders. As I do, he places his hand on my chest and pushes me hard, shoving me off of my feet and onto my back. I fall and hit something not quite firm enough to be the ground beneath me. A familiar sensation. I look over my shoulder and see I am hovering above the floor.

"Some magic you must trust, even if it stays hidden from

you. Well done. It would have been a shame if you smashed your head into the tile. Keep working."

———

I CONTINUE to work through the stack of spells—each one ranging from fall breaking to moving from one side of the room to the other in the blink of an eye. By the afternoon, I am exhausted, and the thread of my faerie magic feels weak and depleted. Gálgalesh assesses me before taking the stack of parchment from me.

"You are excused for the day. The feallwr is hiding around that corner," he points to the far side of the stacks, "waiting for you to finish."

I hear a loud exhale, and Tiernan emerges with Dedra in tow. "I was not hiding, I was being polite!" They make their way to us and greet Bryn before Dedra throws her arms around my waist. "We just thought maybe you wanted to go to the pub with us. You know, a bit of normalcy. You don't have to train all the time while you're here. You can actually have fun too."

"We can make up for all the times I wouldn't let you out of the house in Gairdín," Dedra adds. "We haven't seen you at all since you arrived. We just thought maybe..."

"Sure." I wave my hand in the air casually. There isn't much else to do at the outpost besides train and drink anyway. "Bryn, will you join us?"

He agrees, and I say goodbye to Gálgalesh before Dedra drags me to the door. The hot rush of wind from the outside greets us as we step into the sun. Tiernan's arm hangs lazily around my shoulder in a platonic gesture of affection, his other playing with the dagger holster at his side. Dedra clings to my hand, as though she's willing me to stay beside her—as if she is worried I will disappear again as I had all those months ago. We cross the square about half the distance to the pub, and as we do, Eoghan, River, Finn, Sullivan, and three more men I don't recognize approach from the outpost gate.

I pause. Since the day we arrived, I have not seen Eoghan. Three mornings ago, I heard him in Lowri's kitchen, his low purr of a voice cracking softly as he spoke, but I pretended to be asleep until he finally relented his pleas and left. Now, with him just feet from me, my heart beats wildly in my chest, and it takes everything in me not to reach out my hand for his. He slows as he notices us, and the others match his cadence, staying just behind. He stops in front of me when he reaches us in the middle of the square.

"Hi." His eyes brighten as he looks down at me. His scent fills the air, and his towering figure casts a long shadow over me. I refuse to meet his gaze. If I do, I might break, and I can't break, not until he stops keeping secrets from me—and that day might never come. "What have you...I mean, how have you been?"

"Fine, I suppose." Dedra shakes my arm, and when I look to her, she mouths something. I only catch 'invite him' from the rush of soundless words. I shake my head and move my gaze from my feet to his chest, then back again. "You?"

"I'm..." He pauses. This conversation feels too intimate for so many spectators. "Fine. Where are you off to?"

"The pub," Dedra interrupts excitedly. "Would you join us?" Eoghan opens his mouth to respond, but I cut in before he has the chance.

"Eoghan's obviously busy. He'll have to join us some other time." I need to get away from him before I forget why I'm angry in the first place. I need to be as far away from Eoghan Kael as possible. "Finn, River, Arran, good to see you." I finally meet his gaze. "Kael."

As though I have punched him square in the face, his

eyebrows pull together in an expression of pain and shock. Tiernan clears his throat, and the sound cuts through the silence like a knife before he guides us around Eoghan and the others, who stand dumbfounded in the center of the square. *You idiot,* I admonish. *Why would you do that to him? Even if you are angry with him, that was cruel.* I look back over my shoulder to see him standing like stone in the place we had left him, staring at us as we leave. River leans in to speak to him, but he throws up his hand and leaves the others as he marches toward the library entrance—disappearing through it as we make it to the pub.

———

EIGHT O'CLOCK IN THE EVENING, I stumble through the door of Lowri and Sawney's desert home at the edge of the outpost. The room smells of chicken tagine and spicy grains, the customary foods of Tinemallacht. I lose my balance and fall back into the wall with a crash as I try to kick out of my boots. Lowri whips around the corner at the sound. Her face scrunches into a scowl, and her bare feet pad against the tile floor as she stomps toward me. She pushes me down onto a low bench by the door, where she starts to untie my laces.

"You're drunk," she chastises as she sets the first boot aside. "Ugh, you reek of liquor. What did you do, drink the pub dry?"

"Maybe," I giggle as Sawney joins us with a cool, damp towel that she pats softly against my face. "Bryn told me I drink like a Tinemallacht."

"Bryn is an idiot and twenty years old." Lowri dislodges the second boot from my foot, then straightens.

"I'm twenty too! What is so wrong with being twenty? What is so wrong with being young?"

"Nothing," Sawney coos, and my cheeks grow pink at the

sound of her voice. I smile up at her, leaning my head back against the cool, brick wall.

"You're pretty," I mumble. My outstretched finger passes to Lowri. "You're pretty too… You're mean, though, so I don't like you." Sawney laughs, and Lowri doesn't react, allowing her annoyed silence to speak for itself. "Eoghan's pretty." I gasp. "No! Eoghan is beautiful—but he doesn't tell me anything, so I can't even look at his beautiful, dumb face anymore."

"What makes you think you are entitled to know anything?" Lowri motions to Sawney, and they each grab one of my arms and lift me to my feet. I sway as they drag me between them, my arms draped over their shoulders. "Don't you have secrets?"

"Nooo, I do not." The room is spinning as they move me toward the kitchen.

"You're a liar. Everyone has secrets, and they are allowed to keep them—even if it's inconvenient for you." They set me down into a chair, and Lowri lowers herself to meet my gaze. "Listen, even though I doubt you will remember any of what I say tomorrow: Eoghan is going to have secrets, whether to keep you safe or just because he wants to sometimes. Your brother had secrets, even from us, even from Áine, and that was okay. He told us and you—whether you believe it or not—what we all needed to know, and we could trust him for that. Regardless of my understanding as to why, Eoghan loves you, and you are hurting him for your own pride. Not because he has done anything wrong, but because you think you are the only one allowed to play the game of secrets and love and life."

"I don't have secrets," I say again as my face heats.

"Oh really?" She points to my chest, where this morning, she had sliced her dagger across my flesh. Nothing remains, not even a scratch. "Whatever you say." She lifts an eyebrow and retreats to her own chair, Sawney in tow. "Eat," she commands, and the room falls silent.

————

I AM BACK in the Romiodóg mountains, my legs flying fast beneath me through the snow. I am running from something—what is it? I have no clue, but everything in me says to keep going. The howling of the wind through the trees has me pausing, surveying the forest around me. I see nothing except the pitch-black, starless night as the white snow falls in torrents to the ground. It is up to my knees now, and if I don't move soon, I'll be trapped.

I carry on through the white powder, and up ahead, I see a clearing. I need to get there. I just need to get there. I reach the tree line and stop dead as I see Peadair and three others circling someone, hunger in their eyes. Me. Realization washes over me then: it is the night Peadair took me from my bed. I am a spectator as that horrible scene plays out before my very eyes. The one man lunges for me, and I dig my teeth into his hand. I can taste the blood— metallic and warm—on my tongue, and I nearly gag as I watch on. Heat drives up through me, the same anger from that night boiling to the surface. I want them dead. I want them all dead. The faerie draws near, and I steal his blade, plunging it into his chest as I take him down. Over and over, I bring the blade to his heart until he dies beneath me. Peadair stops and holds out his hand to halt the other man's advance, fear and disbelief in his eyes. They step back toward my vantage point in the trees and begin to run away into the night.

"Demon woman!" the man hisses under his breath as they pass.

"Death," Peadair breathes. "Bringer of death."

He overtakes the other man and leaves him far behind in the snow. I turn away from the scene as I watch my chest heave against the icy air in my lungs, knowing I survived and will soon make the nearly impossible journey toward Fáintìrean, toward Eoghan.

Relief charges through my veins...but then a pang of panic rises again. I am not the only one watching. I turn and gasp as the faerie leader from the camp near the Romiodóg coast stands over me, so close, I can feel his breath on my face. I try to run, but my legs hold firm, and his mouth widens into a terrifying grin of triangular, razor-sharp teeth.

"My queen," he growls, and his words fill me with terrible promise.

I wake with a jolt. My head pounds as light shines through the thin brown curtains. I shield my eyes from the relentless sun. There is a watch on the bedside table that Bryn has given me to help distinguish the hours of the Tinemallacht day. I reach for it and sigh. It's not even midnight. I roll over, and the low moans and whispers of Lowri and Sawney in the next room remind me of where I am. I rub my face tiredly, wishing for nothing but the comfort of Eoghan's arms. I bury myself into my pillow as tears fall heavily against the fabric. *What have I done?* I sob, and my head spins nauseatingly in circles. *Go find Eoghan,* I beg my legs that are too heavy to move. *Find Eoghan and tell him you're sorry.* The roof sways, and my stomach rises into my throat. I lean over to the table beside the bed, where a round ornamental bowl sits just for show, and vomit into it. Tears stream heavy down my face, longing and regret tearing an Eoghan-sized hole right through me. Relief comes only when the world drifts away, and I once again succumb to sleep.

CHAPTER TWELVE

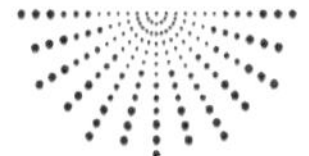

I shake my head into my pillow as the room comes into view, though a veil of sleep still hangs over me, my body aching and my mouth tasting vile of sick. The curtains do nothing except mute the intensity of the sun shining through them. It's still too bright, and I groan as I roll over onto my back.

"How's the head?"

Eoghan is seated in a small armchair near my bedside. He is in pajama bottoms and a sleeveless undershirt that exposes the muscles of his arms—taut and impossibly golden from the endless sun. I swallow and wince. I move to sit, and Eoghan shifts in his seat, as though tempted to reach for me, before deciding against it. His fingers flex against the wooden arms as he adjusts awkwardly and remains where he is.

"What time is it?" I reach for the watch and give up when I find it's too far away. Eoghan chuckles softly to himself.

"Still early. Almost four." That explains the pajamas. "Lo says you've been out since dinner. Face-planted into your plate, as she so eloquently put it."

"Is that why you're here? She called you over to laugh at my drunkenness?" There is a glass of water where the ornamental bowl had sat on the side table, and I extend my hand toward it before Eoghan rises and offers it to me. The fingers of his free hand graze my hair with the softest, almost imperceptible touch.

"No, she didn't. Curiously, I was lying in bed a few hours ago—staring at the ceiling and finding no rest—and your voice began to echo so loudly through my mind, it was almost as if you were screaming at me from somewhere in my room. Well, sobbing, actually. I thought you were in trouble, so I came to find you asleep. Don't worry, I won't stay. I just had to make sure you were all right before I left."

I take an endless drink from the glass and empty it. Eoghan reaches out for it and replaces it on the table.

"How did you hear my voice? I didn't try to call you." I remember very little of the evening, and even still, I cannot remember trying to call Eoghan to me. His face falls as I speak. For the first time since I have known him, the temperature drops in the room.

"Oh, well, maybe I made it up in my head." He straightens and makes his way to the door. "I should go. Like I said, I only stayed to make sure you were all right. I'll make sure Lo lets you sleep in today. There's no way you can spar in the state you're in."

Eoghan reaches for the doorknob and turns it slowly, savoring his last moments in the room with me. I want him to stay. The only thing that feels right is for him to be near me. If he walks out that door, when will I get another chance to tell him I'm sorry?

"Eogh?" My throat burns from the lingering effects of the vomit, and his name comes out in a sort of rasp. He pauses and turns to face me. His eyes are soft, and I can tell now as the light peeks through a small sliver of the curtains and onto his face that there are darkened circles under them from lack of sleep. Has he slept at all this past week—or, like me, has he found himself tossing and turning until morning greets him once again? I drop my gaze to my lap as my own eyes begin to feel heavy and threaten to release a torrent of emotion at any given moment. "Thank you."

I hear him sigh as his expectations are dashed like a campfire in a downpour. He shakes his head slowly from side to side and rubs his lips together, fighting whatever he is trying so hard to keep hidden beneath.

"You're welcome, Maevie." His hand finds the handle once more, and he exits the room, pulling the door closed softly behind him. I hear him take one step and another, and then his footsteps disappear as he heads back home.

———

"Why didn't you go after him?" Dedra scolds me as she sits on the end of the bed in Lowri's spare bedroom.

"Because she is a stupid woman with no common sense," Lowri shouts from the sitting room. Her fists collide with a heavy sandbag hung in the doorway.

There is a storm passing through the outpost, and all residents have been ordered to stay inside, forcing me, Lowri, Sawney, and Dedra to spend the afternoon together in the small quarters. It has been awkward at best, with not-so-subtle jabs at my intelligence and snide, hate-filled remarks about how I might be better off standing out in the storm, letting my lungs fill with sand. Nevertheless, Dedra and Lowri seem to get along surprisingly well.

"I tried after I woke again this morning—Eoghan and Bryn weren't home."

Tried would be an understatement. I had pounded my fist against the front door for twenty minutes, shouting Eoghan's name, until Gálgalesh dragged it open and ordered me to leave.

"He won't be home for a week." Lowri walks to the doorway and leans against the frame. Horrible as she might be, she never ceases to be beautiful, even as sweat dampens her hair and her cheeks glow red with heat.

"A week? Where did he go that would take him away for a week?"

"To Tonnfórsca. He's trying to figure out why your ex-fiancé organized the coup against your family and if it had anything to do with what Cai was preparing us for."

"Isn't that dangerous?" Dedra asks, and Lowri shrugs.

"It's Eoghan. Try telling him anything is too dangerous and see if he'll listen."

She pushes off the doorframe and disappears back down the hall. Eoghan has gone to find out why Rian killed my family—tried to kill me. Tonnfórsca has always been a stronghold of the Crown, with spies and aristocrats hoping to benefit from bending the king's ear, and Eoghan is wanted throughout the Kingdom. It would be a death sentence if he was caught. We had received a raven to the outpost just yesterday that announced the bounty laid upon our heads, with an ultimatum from the new king, hoping to compel our deliverance to him. It stated that I—the lost princess—had survived and joined forces with famed Tinemallacht warrior Eoghan Kael to seek retribution against the 'Liberator of Draíocoinnigh'. One hundred thousand gold coins had been promised for our return to the capital city. Upon receipt, General Osian had sent an unequivocal denial of the king's demands and moved more of his men to the border in antici-pation of retaliation from the Crown. Eoghan risking his life to go to Tonnfórsca is like him walking himself right up to the castle gates.

I throw the pillow from my lap, and it falls from the bed

onto the floor with a soft thud. "I should have asked him to stay. Maybe he wouldn't have gone in the first place."

"I ask Tiernan not to go on his secret runs, and he never listens to me." Dedra shrugs. "Men will do what they want if they think it is the best thing for them to do…especially if it will make you worried about them. He is probably smug just thinking about how worried you will be while he's gone."

"Doubtful."

Lowri and Sawney round the corner into the bedroom once again as I speak, a small package in each of their hands.

"Stop worrying about him. He's fine." Lowri nearly tosses the package into my lap. I place my finger underneath the flap and pry it open curiously. It is filled with provisions commonly found throughout Draío, used during the time of the month when the moon peaks in its cycle and all women of child-bearing age bleed. Sawney hands me another with tonics used to relieve the headaches and symptoms common for the first few days of each bleeding cycle. "It's hard to tell here with the constant sun, but the moon is peaking in its cycle, and Sawney thought you might not have anything prepared."

I look down at the contents. Of course. I had spent so many months as the only woman in a prison full of men, I had nearly forgotten women *should* bleed at the height of the moon's passing. I had not even thought about what anyone might say if I did not. For years, I had badgered my mother and maids for tonics and provisions I would hide or discard so no one would be the wiser. The castle floorboards hide millions of secrets from my years in solitude. Now, how could I have forgotten the normal passing of womanhood?

"What's the matter?" Lowri examines me as I sit in silent contemplation for too many long moments.

"Nothing's the matter. Thank you." I push the packages away from me on the bed.

"Give us a minute." Lowri's eyes penetrate me as she addresses Sawney and Dedra. Without question, Sawney takes Dedra's hand, guiding her to the door, making casual conversation about plans for supper. Dedra opens her mouth to speak, but I wrestle up my best, easy smile and motion for her to leave. Slowly, they exit together, and I tug at my magic, pulling the door closed behind them. "How far along are you? Does my brother know? Are there no contraceptive tonics in the prison? I would guess Gálgalesh could make one without much trouble…"

"I'm not pregnant," I say, and Lowri raises a cynical eyebrow.

"Why did you become so pale at the sight of these, then?" She points to the packages beside me. She doesn't buy a word of what I am saying. Her eyes trail to my stomach, searching for any sign of a young life there.

"Because I…" Anyone but her. Let me tell anyone but *her*. "Because I…" She doesn't stop staring at me, as though I'm the biggest idiot she has ever seen. Gods be damned, fine! "Because I do not bleed. I cannot bear children. I cannot bear anything except my own name, and now even that feels impossible."

I scowl at her and wait for the torrent of ridicule to begin. I wait for her to tell me I do not deserve her brother, that I am a waste of his time, that she will kill me for taking yet another thing away from him. However, those words do not come. Nothing passes her lips besides a small quiver that she bites back as her eyes finally soften for the first time.

"Does Eoghan know?" I shake my head. The one person I can never tell is Eoghan, not when he deserves a life so much better than anything I can give him. "Secrets," she says. "Secrets to keep others safe, or for burdens we aren't yet ready to share." She picks up the packages and shoves them into one of the empty dresser drawers. "They are stupid anyway. I don't know why the gods insist on making us suffer."

"Children or bleeds?" I ask with a short, ridiculous laugh, and Lowri matches me with one of her own.

"Both, I suppose." She turns back and pats my hands in my lap. "He doesn't have to know yet, but don't be afraid to tell him. He won't care. Like I said before, regardless of whether I understand it, he loves you, and he will love you just the same if you can't bear children."

"Watch out, Lowri. You're walking the line of actually being nice to me." She smiles, in earnest this time, and shakes her head as she walks to the door.

"Fuck off, princess," she says as she turns the handle.

"That's better," I laugh and watch her exit the room.

"It is a game of stealth, although I have given the others permission to stab you if you fail." Gálgalesh is standing in the center of the outpost square in his ridiculous oversized hat and airy desert garbs—I can hardly look at him without laughing. Around the square, Lowri, River, Finn, and Tiernan are placed at opposite corners, their backs to the center. Each has a dagger sheathed at their right side and one in their hand with the blade dulled, brightly-colored paint glistening against the steel surface. "You will make your way to them and unsheathe their daggers before they can mark you. When you have unarmed all four opponents successfully, you will be done for the day."

"Is that it?" I shade my eyes from the sun with my arm. "That doesn't seem too hard."

"I would not be so sure about that. Are you aware of the magic your opponents wield?"

I look across the square and realize only half of them

have shared such information with me, and only one of them willingly. Maybe this will be harder than I thought.

"Ah, see, you are not as foolish as you once were, woman. So often we know nothing about our opponents other than what we can surmise from seeing them across the battlefield. In your case, your opponent, the heir to the Draíocoinnigh throne, knows everything about you—or, at least, he believes he does—and you know nothing of worth about him. You cannot rely on your knowledge to give you the advantage. You cannot study him enough to beat him, so you have to be skilled and have confidence in yourself. Do you understand?"

Absolutely not. I nod anyway.

"Good. Now, ready yourself, and let's begin."

I assess my opponents in the square, hoping to choose the easiest first. I had seen the way River and Finn moved through the snow, no match for a tiny rabbit. Tiernan, though a skilled alchemist, is certainly not someone I would consider quick on his feet. That just leaves Lowri, who I have found can be formidable from all my time sparring with her over the past two weeks.

"Woman! What are you waiting for? Get on with it!"

Right. *It's not about them, Maeve. It's about you and your ability to best them.* I decide on Tiernan first and wake the faerie magic as I concentrate on his back.

The sensation of bending the space between one object and another is like none I have ever experienced. It's as if the air around me begins to swirl and whirl, dragging me through it with a heavy tug at my center before dropping me through nothingness to my destination. The landing is always the difficult part, as I constantly lose my footing and stumble ridiculously, or I end up falling flat on my back. Gálgalesh never has such problems and constantly reminds me of such during our lessons.

Just get close enough to reach his dagger, I think and send the sequence down the line. The swirling starts, and I feel the tug near my stomach, then the sensation of weightless falling all within a blink of an eye. Time slows in this place of magic and space. I see Tiernan come into view as my feet hit the ground behind him. I reach out to grip his dagger, and then...he catches me. As soon as my feet collide with the back of his heels, he wheels around and pegs me in the arm with a dash of blue against my skin.

"Damnit!" I laugh as Tiernan grabs my other arm to steady me so I don't fall.

"A bit close." Gálgalesh clicks his tongue. "I have never tried landing on top of anyone before, but I would say that is probably not the best tactic—although, if you are going for the element of surprise, you would definitely succeed. Try again."

I feel an invisible hand on my chest push me back into the center of the square. *All right, someone new this time.* I choose Finn, who stands quietly near the small shop that sells fruit imported from somewhere much further away, somewhere green. I concentrate on a spot just a few feet from him, keeping far enough away this time that I will hopefully just be in arm's reach. I lay the incantation down the line, and then I am moving across the square...but when I land, exactly where I had hoped to, Finn is gone. I wheel around on the spot, casting my gaze across the square. I spot him standing right in the middle, where I had just been. He smiles, and within the blink of an eye, he is in front of me, flicking green paint from his dagger onto my shirt.

"Speed?" I breathe.

"Most advantageous to General Kael's ranks...and lucky, too. It is a rare magic to wield in any kingdom or on any continent."

"You've never seemed fast before!"

Finn shrugs his shoulders innocently. "Never needed to be."

Gálgalesh pushes me back into the center of the square, and everyone resets. I look to Lowri and shake my head. Not yet. I take in River, who stands across from Finn about one hundred yards to the left. I concentrate again and make the jump toward him. This time, I end up a whole fifty feet short of his position.

"What the hell!" I shriek. He turns to face me and waves. I look toward Finn to see where I went wrong. I landed exactly where I thought I needed to be.

"Stay there!" he shouts and jogs over to me. He runs his blade in bright pink across my unmarked arm.

"How did you do that?" I pant in disbelief, bested for a third time.

"Amazing how easily people will trust their eyes." He winks.

"Illusion magic is some of the most bothersome magic humans can wield. Though River cannot replicate his appearance like some illusionist wielders can, he can appear to be closer or further to his opponent—whatever might suit his advantage." Gálgalesh grumbles something under his breath I don't catch, and River laughs in return. "Again, woman."

I walk to the center of the square this time, trying to buy myself a few lingering moments before choosing another opponent. If I choose Lowri now, she will know I'm coming, and she's quick. But I can't leave her forever either. I settle on trying my hand at Tiernan again on the opposite side of the outpost. *I'll make a double jump*, I decide. *I'll jump to Tiernan and then to her, and I'll catch her before she suspects.* I ease my mind and concentrate on my two intentions. I need to keep Tiernan in my sight first, then switch directions as soon as I land. If I concentrate on them both, the magic will tear me in two—or so Gálgalesh said. I set my mind on Tiernan, and I inhale deeply before I reach for the magic. I'm pulled through the expanse between us. I land with only a little wobble and immediately find Lowri in my mind. I throw the sequence down the line again, and I jump, only to find myself staring directly into her green-gold eyes. She smirks as she taps her blade, soaked in orange, on each of my cheeks.

"One more jump might have confused me," she says. "Plus, you exhale too loudly when the magic releases you. I could hear you from a mile away." The others agree with a laugh.

We continue to train for countless more hours until my skin is red from the sun and we are all too tired to go on. I never best anyone—with the exception of Tiernan, who I expect let me win when Dedra called for him to occupy her back at the house when the afternoon dragged on. I look down at my paint-covered body, a display of complete incompetence, and also joy as the ache in my stomach reminds me that I haven't laughed so much in years. Gálgalesh makes his way to my side and examines me as the others collect their canteens before they head back inside.

"That went better than I expected," he says. "I lied when I said your opponent's magic did not matter, but you took it in stride."

"You knew I could not best them," I say. He smirks down at me from under his enormous hat.

"You can best them, just not yet. I simply need you to not be afraid to try. We will work on the rest in time. For now—" He looks toward the outpost gates and points a long finger. I follow his gaze to see Eoghan walking through them alone, a slight limp in his step. "I think there is something more important that needs your attention."

Gálgalesh retreats to the library as Eoghan beats forward into the square. He stares down at his shoes, muttering to himself in hushed tones. Something has agitated him, and his brows pull together as he takes pained strides across the sand. I don't move as he closes the distance between us. One hundred yards, ninety, eighty, seventy... He is nearly fifty yards away when he raises his eyes from the ground. He halts as they meet me, alone, painted like a kaleidoscope of colors in front of him.

"Maeve? What are you doing out here, and why are you covered in paint?" he breathes—his voice gravelly and hoarse.

I do not answer. I have been waiting a week for him to walk through these gates. I feel my legs move underneath me, hauling me forward at a run as he stands like stone, unsure of what to do—but I do. I throw my arms around his neck as I reach him and press my lips to his. His arms wrap around my waist instinctively, hoisting me to him as my hands snake into his hair. I do not let him go. I will not let him go. Not this time, not ever again.

It is only when I cannot breathe that I finally pull away.

"Are you still angry with me?" he pants.

"No." My breath comes in heavy draws, and I watch as his eyes soften. "Just don't leave like that again. I've been worried sick about you."

"I was fine, only in minor danger the entire time." He smiles, but I watch as it changes to a wince when he shifts his weight to one side. I release him and plant my feet back into the sand.

"You're not fine! What's wrong?" I demand.

"Nothing. I sprained my ankle as I was making a run for it in Trader's Bay."

Trader's Bay? He was across the sea in Oleaíncudd?

"I was told you were in Tonnfórsca, not Trader's Bay!"

"I was in Tonnfórsca with Bryn and Officer Rhodes. What we found led us to Oleaíncudd. We had to make a quick escape when slave traders discovered we had led them around for days with no interest in a sale."

"The others? Are they all right?" My heart sinks at the thought of Bryn being in danger in Trader's Bay.

"They're fine, just resting in Bastain. Bryn will ride back tonight." He laces his fingers around my waist and pulls me near. "Now, will you explain what the fuck is going on here? Why the colors?"

"Training with Gálgalesh. I'll tell you later. Tell me what you found that took you to Oleaíncudd."

"Later." He flicks my chin softly. "Take me home first, before my ankle gives way."

CHAPTER THIRTEEN

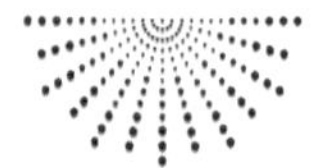

I position myself at Eoghan's side and sling his arm over my shoulder to lead him up the street. He attempts to bear the weight on his leg to no avail, and I feel him lean into my side, my boots sinking down further into the sand with the weight. He's hurt, more than he will ever let on. We make it to the small road up to his house, and he squeezes my shoulder, compelling me to stop. When I halt our stride, he releases his hold to slump against one of the awning poles outside the first house.

"You're hurt and you aren't telling me," I complain as he wipes the back of his hand against his forehead. I didn't realize I was so out of breath, but my words come as breathless pants. Eoghan sighs and reaches for the hem of his shirt. He lifts it, revealing a gash in his side, stitched together crudely with some sticky, clear substance. My fingers hover over it, unsure of where to land. "Eoghan!"

"I *do* have a sprained ankle," he assures me, as though I might be worried about that now. "And I *was* running to get away at Trader's Bay. This," he points to his side, and his face contorts in discomfort from the movement, "was a gift from your ex's fleet commander, before I broke his neck."

"You didn't!" I gasp. He only shrugs, as though he has said nothing more alarming than a comment about the weather. "Why?"

"We were in Trader's Bay for four days, gathering the information we could. On the final morning, six ships pulled into port bearing the Doherty flag. I watched as women and children lined up on the docks—dozens of them, their wrists bound by Faebond—and I remembered how it made you sick to think you might have helped that bastard in some way. I thought about the slaves on the boat we stole from the harbor in Cuanslí, and I couldn't bear it. I couldn't bear the thought of any more of them crossing the sea. So, we ended our discussions with the slaver we had been meeting with— not a moment too soon, honestly, as I was about to break his neck. Bryn and Officer Rhodes helped the slaves escape, and I burned their fleet for good measure. Needless to say, the gold in His Majesty's pockets might be a little light for the time being."

He had risked his life to free the slaves because he could not bear the thought of me or anyone else being harmed by Rian and his father. He had burned their ships to ash in the harbor and had been injured because of it. I could kiss him. I could fling myself into his arms and drag him to bed for how my heart thrums in my chest. I assess him, his shoulder pressed up against the awning as though it keeps him upright... Well, maybe not to bed in this state. I take his face in my hands to kiss him softly, tenderly. Tears stream in thick tracks down to my chin as I think of how much I missed him, of how easily I could have lost him. His lips move from my lips to my cheeks, kissing away my tears as they fall before he pulls away reluctantly, passing his fingers across my jaw.

"So I just have to put myself in danger to get you to stop being angry with me. Got it." He laughs, his green eyes smoldering with desire. Such a typical man, Eoghan Kael.

"You caught me on an emotional day."

He looks up and scours the bright sky, casting his arm across his face to shield his eyes from the sun.

"Is that what it is? Eh, bound to happen, I suppose." He pushes off the awning and straightens. "Well, before your emotions take us on another dangerous journey I might not survive, I think I can finish the walk back to the house."

We reach his door and step inside the cool, darkened room. I haven't been here since the day we arrived at the outpost, and I hesitate for a moment on the threshold. Going inside means I have forgiven him. *Have I?* I wonder to myself. *With no discussion or resolution? With secrets still between us? Can I forgive him?* He eyes me curiously as he drops his familiar pack on a low bench in the entryway and begins to unlace his boots with difficulty. *He set those ships on fire for you. He came to you when you wanted only him. He gave you the space you asked for...and Lo is right—you have secrets too.*

I take a step inside and watch as he struggles, his brows pulled together. I push his hand away from his boots and motion for him to sit instead. He nearly died for me; the least I can do is help him take off his shoes. He groans as he leans back against the wall, as though there is no part of him that doesn't ache with fatigue or injury. I crouch down in front of him and take his laces in my hands.

"You don't have to do that," he protests. His fingers entwine in my hair softly, his movements slow and lacking energy, yet an electric current passes through me, begging for his hands to search more of me.

"Shut up, Eoghan." I pull the first boot away from his injured ankle, and he inhales sharply. With the most tender touch, I massage it, remembering how he had done so for me when my injuries from Peadair's attack were still so new. "The Lord of Tinemallacht gets some special treatment, doesn't he?"

I release his first foot and set it gingerly against the tile before unlacing his next boot, which he has already loosened halfway.

"Technically, if the title still stood, that would be my father," he laughs through tired sighs as his eyes fall shut. I remove his boot and begin to massage this side.

"Fine, Mr. Technical. What about King of Draíocoinnigh, then?"

I feel him go still in my hands, and I pause my movement to look up into his face. His eyes have flown open, and he is staring down at me. His brows knit together, crinkling above the bridge of his nose, and he straightens in his seat. I set down his foot on the floor as I watch him. His eyes don't glimmer now the way they had—neither with fire nor tears, only concern as he takes me in.

"Is that what you want, Maeve? To be Queen of Draío-coinnigh?"

I slide between his legs on the floor and bring my hands to rest on his thighs. I take a moment to run my fingers up and down the muscles there, his pants lightly coated with sand as everything is here in the desert. He leans toward me, captivated by my touch, and I rest my head against his left leg, staring up at him through my eyelashes.

"When I kill Rian and his father, it would be mine, wouldn't it? Would I not be the queen regardless?"

"You could be anything you want. What is it that you want?" His fingers run lightly through my red locks as he speaks, and I plant kisses against his arm softly.

"I want you, Eoghan."

"You already have me, Maevie. Forever."

"I want us to have everything—to show them they can't

destroy us no matter how hard they try." My hands glide up toward his belt, and he grabs my wrist softly. He traces slow circles against my skin with his thumb, and a shiver runs through me. He extends my arm to bring my palm to his lips, and he presses them to it, working his way to where my pulse beats wildly at my wrist.

"Does that require a crown?" he whispers, and my mind goes blank as his breath falls warm against my skin. A crown, a palace, this whole world—I'd give him everything if he required it. Right now, all I can think to give him is me.

"Would anyone in their right mind refuse it if given the chance?"

Eoghan shrugs and presses his lips against my skin again. The heat rises in the room, as though we are walking on the sun itself—even in these thin linen clothes, I just might melt into a puddle on the floor.

"Well, there are more important things to accept. This house is a palace enough for me. You are already my queen, and I have enough jewels for you to bathe in without the Crown of King Fergal. Maybe instead, you will simply choose to accept me, accept happiness, and a couple of daughters…or sons, if the gods so wish, to chase around the desert. Or Fáintìrean. Or anywhere you so choose."

I feel my heart sink in my chest. "Eogh—" I begin, but he hushes me with almost a whisper from his lips.

"Not now, Maeve. Don't worry, not now. I'm more than happy like this."

He kisses down my arm once again and then drops it back into his lap softly before settling against the wall. I'm not sure what to say. I don't know if I have ever thought of a family with anyone besides Rian, and even then, I knew it would not be a family in the true sense of the word. Eoghan has a vision for our lives—will he still want me if I can't promise to give it to him? Will he settle for less if I ask him to? Am I willing to settle for life here in the desert for him? What of the Crown—my birthright?

"We should eat or something." I stand and brush out my pant legs. My arms are dashed in pinks, blues, greens, and orange, and I remember for the first time since we arrived that my clothes are stained with color. "Can you stand?" Eoghan lifts himself to his feet from the bench with a low groan. I nod and turn toward the kitchen. Then, I pause. I have only seen the entryway and sitting room of his house. Would it be presumptuous to make myself at home?

"The kitchen is that way," he whispers in my ear, "but the bedroom is up there." I watch as his fingers pass in front of my face to point up the stairs. "I could find the strength in me to suffer up to the next floor if you so choose..."

I roll my eyes and bat his hand away. "I'm making you a meal, Kael, and then I'm showering."

"If you insist." Eoghan brings his teeth to graze my ear and then rests his arm over my shoulder. "This way then."

He leads me in slow steps into the kitchen. The room is filled with more light than the others from a glass door that leads out onto a small courtyard. The counters and cabinets sit against the far wall, with a long table in the middle of the room surrounded by more than a dozen chairs. I drop Eoghan into one before crossing to the stove. I pull a pan from a hook above the burners and set it down in front of me, and then I stare at it endlessly. Eoghan chuckles softly, and I do my best to ignore him. The kitchen falls silent for many more long minutes. This time, he clears his throat.

"Yes?" I ask in a hollow tone as I keep my eyes glued to the stove, willing something, anything, to happen.

"Is something the matter?" His voice is coated with amusement, and the sound makes me blush.

"I've never cooked anything before. I don't know what to do." I had only ever been in a kitchen a handful of times, and the only time I paid any attention at all was when Eoghan cooked our final meal at Báscogar. I hardly remember anything that happened while he spoke. The food could have appeared out of thin air for all I knew.

"Would you like me to do it?" He begins to rise, but I wheel around and shoot him an admonishing glare. He raises his hands in surrender as he slides back down in his seat. I look around the room, desperate for anything at all, and see a basket of flatbreads, apples, and a jar of honey sitting at the far end of the counter. I pull them toward me through the air and guide them to the table. Then, I make my way to Eoghan's chair, reach down to his belt, and loosen one of his daggers. I hold it out in front of him, eyebrows raised in question. "No, it's clean. I didn't stab anyone with that partic-ular blade."

I summon a towel from the counter anyway and wipe it. Then, I pick up an apple and begin to peel it in one long, curling strand. Eoghan's gaze remains captivated until I finish. I tear one of the flatbreads from the basket in half and recall a plate from the cabinet. I drizzle honey over the top before shoving the plate across the tabletop to him. With a smug grin of satisfaction, I wipe the blade clean then reach down along his thigh and place it slowly back into its sheath. I watch his throat bob and his breath catch as my fingers linger.

"A meal." I sink into the chair next to him. He smirks as he purrs his thanks and begins to eat.

WE'VE SAT at this table for hours. We haven't spoken for hours. Our lips have found their way to each other several times, but that has done nothing to fill the chasm of things we cannot say. The paint has certainly ruined my clothes now, dried and cracked with my smiles or when my brows pull together. We should move. We should leave this kitchen and find something else to do, but neither of us wants to be the first to rise. Neither of us wants to be the first to do anything—for fear of bringing us together or tearing us apart.

Eoghan clears his throat. I thought he had fallen asleep when his eyes shut five minutes ago. Now, they trace the ceiling, and I follow them to intricate carvings laid out all across the expanse of the room.

"You can have secrets, Eoghan," I whisper through the silence. "Everyone has secrets. I'm just so angry about always being the last to know. I want you to trust me enough to tell me things, in time."

Eoghan nods and continues to study the ceiling. "Tiernan and Lowri," Eoghan begins. "Tiernan was never stationed with us in Gobaith. He was recommended for the alchemist post in Gairdín by Cai before graduation from the military academy and took up his position right away. We were happy for him, even if it meant the three of us would not be together. He was still assigned to create weapons for our unit and visited as often as he could. He was sent to the outpost during the Battle of Buaeth, though. I'm not sure how much Cai told you about that day, but it was a miracle we won against the Iranndairians. The king liked to paint it as an overwhelming victory, though in truth, we were hanging by a thread. The only reason we didn't retreat at all was because Lo had foreseen victory."

Eoghan pauses, and I remain silent as I wait. At first, I don't think he will continue as he traces the etchings in the ceiling with his eyes. Only when the silence becomes too pregnant with expectation does he finally relent.

"*All* magic has limitations. That's the problem with humans believing they can be gods simply because they are more powerful than the rest. Magic is not perfect, and that is the beauty of it—well, perhaps not on the battlefield. When Lo sees the future, sometimes, she only sees the outcome and not the circumstances that lead to it. We should have asked more questions, had her scry. We should have been sure of everything that day before we walked into battle, but we were young and confident and knew we would win. None of the generals or the king gave a shit about us to begin with. We were disposable to them, no better than any squadron of enlisted grunts—maybe even worse when our egos got in the way."

His gaze falls to the table. He plays with my fingers against the wood surface. I feel his own quake ever so slightly. "Tiernan had created heat-sensitive bombs that would detonate at our command should we raise the temperature of the sand as the Iranndairians advanced over our borders. Simple, as our fire wielders were positioned at the front of the ranks. Lo had volunteered to set the bombs on her own that day, and we trusted Tiernan's work beyond any other weapons we had. But we didn't anticipate that the Iranndairians would strike in the early morning hours as Lo was setting the last of the traps. She had scrambled to finish, panicking as she heard the first riders approach the border through the canyon paths and—well, Tiernan had forgotten to account for the touch of a scared Fire Cursed Warrior.

"One of Tiernan's bombs detonated in Lowri's hand. She fell at the border, and we assumed she was dead—and really, she should have been, if not for a wicked little vial of blood hanging on Cai's belt."

"My blood," I whisper. I remember the vials packed into crates and shipped off to Tinemallacht week after week to keep Cai alive. Eoghan nods.

"The only time it was ever used. Cai wouldn't have touched the damn stuff. We burned every crate he ever received, except one or two vials he would carry just for show, but I had, in my desperation, begged him for it. He obliged only that once. When the battle ended, Tiernan left, returning to Gairdín without a goodbye or even a visit to Lo's sickbed. Not one word of apology from him after all these years. It's as if he didn't care he had nearly killed her. He never cares for anything or anyone, though—no one but himself."

I interlace my fingers with Eoghan's against the cool wood. Cai had told me almost nothing of the Battle of Buaeth, except that it had been bloodier and more difficult than expected when they had arrived. Eoghan had almost lost his sister, and Cai had used his to save her. Why hadn't he told me of it before?

"Lowri seems to have forgiven Tiernan, though. Perhaps if she can—"

"Lo doesn't remember what happened that day, only that she woke on the battlefield after we had won. I didn't have the heart to tell her, and Cai thought it best to just let her believe in the victory of the battle, but wouldn't anyone have at least apologized?"

"I don't know, Eogh." I don't have the experience to form the words of comfort he seeks. I push up from my chair and straddle his lap, lowering myself onto his warm thighs. He takes my face into his hands.

"Thank you for saving her life, even if you didn't know it."

He brings his lips to mine, and I melt into his kiss. His tongue sneaks gently into my mouth as he deepens our embrace, and I lean into him as I kiss him with all I have. He moves to my jaw and down my neck, and my eyes roll back as I feel his tongue trace down to my collarbone. Everything about him is like a drug. From the soft primal sounds he makes as he pleasures me to the touch of his fingers against my skin, I never want him to stop. I'd rather die.

He tugs the hem of my shirt and pulls it over my head, giving him freedom to roam over my breasts. My hands fist his hair as his mouth covers every exposed inch. He flicks his tongue across my nipples one at a time, and I gasp as they tighten with his breath. I roll my head back and whimper softly in response, reaching between us and running my hand against him. I feel him grow hard at my touch. I unbutton his pants slowly, a soft popping of the buttons punctuating each heavy breath we take in unison, and sneak my hand under the waistband of his underwear.

"Mayhem," he whispers against my skin in that purr that makes me ache in my center. I feel the heat between us grow. "I'm not sure I could get you to the bedroom in this state."

His teeth graze me as my fingers wrap about his cock. He lets out a whisper of a moan that ignites something inside me. I want him now, right here, on the floor, anywhere and any way he pleases. I need him desperately, as though his pleasure is paramount to my own. I rub my thumb against the tip of him, and he responds with renewed heat as he grows harder in my hand. I feel one of his large, calloused hands slide beneath the linen fabric of my pants and find my clit as his mouth works its way to my lips once more. I shudder at his touch, and a desperate whine escapes me. I had forgotten how good his fingers could feel. He hasn't been this close to me since he made me come at Kael Manor, which had been the most erotic moment of my life.

"Eoghan," I beg as my hand strokes him. His skin is soft against my grip, but I feel him strain as I run a finger against the backside of his cock. I hear him choke back a groan of pleasure and frustration as his own fingers pass lightly over my entrance, making me press up against him in response.

"Do you know how much I missed you?" he whispers as

his lips pull away from mine. "All the incredible, delectable parts of you." He slides his finger inside me, and I nearly scream as my pent up desire rushes to the surface. "I missed how you felt around me," he thrusts his finger slowly and then draws it back, "how you taste." Again, to his last knuckle this time. "I missed whispering how much I love you in your ear as you come. I can feel how much you missed me too, Mayhem, as you run down my palm."

I can't take it anymore. I release my grip, and he growls low in protest as I stand, his finger sliding out of me. I shove my hands past my waistband and roll the remainder of my clothes to the floor. Eoghan responds by hoisting himself from his chair and pushing his pants from his hips to his ankles, where he kicks out of them easily. Then, he reaches to pull me to him, but I press my hand to his chest and shake my head.

"Can you stand?" He nods slowly, his stare making the room feel stifling. "I want you like this." I turn away from him and lean over the table, stepping my legs apart as I hear him exhale behind me.

"Fuck," is all that escapes his lips. The growing heat of his body presses in on me as he steps forward, taking my hips in his hands. "Didn't I tell you, Maevie, that I would be happy to take you anywhere you pleased?" His voice is a sensual drawl as I feel the head of his cock against me.

"And what if I want to take *you*?" I shoot back, and his laugh vibrates through him. He lines himself up—I am soaking by now—and slides inside me easily. I cry out against the table's surface.

"Don't," Eoghan pulls back and then thrusts back in, making my body lunge forward, "tease with empty promises." One of his hands holds my hip still while the other glides featherlight over my skin, and I gasp at the intensity of the touch. "I might make you keep your word."

My body is on fire now. He picks up his pace with a steady rhythm that keeps my thighs pounding repeatedly into the table. His fingers run up the back of my neck and into my hair as he pushes in to the hilt, stretching me as he grinds his hips into me. I'm so close to my climax, my vision beginning to blur as I feel him pull away again and thrust back into me.

"Have you been thinking about me all those nights alone at Lo and Sawney's?" He fists my hair gently, lifting my head with a soft tug. "I know there hasn't been a second I haven't thought about you, about how good you might taste on my tongue or how much I'd like to feel your lips around my cock." He pulses inside me as he speaks.

"Eogh!" I cry out, and my gods, I've never felt so overwhelmed with need. He leans over my body, bringing his mouth to my ear.

"My princess and my queen," he whispers as he reaches for my clit, and I tighten around him, bringing his climax to the surface with mine. He continues long and steady strokes until my body stills and he comes back down, breathing heavy pants. He helps me rise from the table, our skin sticky with sweat as he wraps his arms around me. I lift my chin, and my lips meet his.

"Let's get you to bed," I whisper, and the lingering pain seems to disappear from his eyes as he scoops me into his arms to take me upstairs.

CHAPTER FOURTEEN

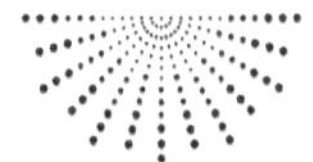

Eoghan's chest is warm and bare, and my cheek heats against his skin as I draw circles lightly across his stomach. My hair is wet from the shower that lasted an eternity with my body pressed against the cool stone, Eoghan finding his strength to kneel before me as he had all those months ago. To our credit, we had spared a moment to clean and bandage his wounds, though my expertise is not that of a field medic or healer of any kind. *It'll do for tonight, though*, I reason as I pass my fingers over the stark-white bandage. I still can't decipher the time in the sun's endless rays, but Eoghan's curtains blot out the light much more fully than Lowri's had, and the world is quiet outside, save for the sound of the howling desert wind that began to blow more forcefully when Bryn finally made it back to the outpost this evening.

"We should sleep." Eoghan yawns. "We have an important meeting in the morning."

"Am I actually going to get to join you this time?" I ask. "You won't leave me to warm myself beside the fire while you get to have all the fun?"

"It's warm enough without a fire," Eoghan mutters. "No, I think it's time you join us, whether Gálgalesh agrees or not. Besides, after we're finished, I thought it might be nice if we went to visit Áine and Theo. I heard you haven't been since we arrived in Gobaith."

I hadn't been able to bring myself to visit them, not with the weight of Cai's loss hanging over us like a black cloud. I'm not sure how I am going to bear it, seeing Cai in his child's eyes.

"Eogh, I don't know..."

"Come on, Maeve. Áine wants to meet you properly this time and introduce you to Theo. I promise, it'll be fine, maybe even enjoyable—and if it's not, just say the word, and we'll come right back home." He punctuates the last word as he runs his fingers up and down my back, reminding me I'm welcome here. I belong here, with him. "Do it for Cai?"

Damnit. How can I refuse that? I exhale in defeat, dreading the morning's fast approach. "Fine. For Cai." Eoghan smiles into my hair and kisses my head. "Did you visit often while you were at Báscogar?" I knew he could leave the prison any time he wanted, but I never imagined he had left the Romiodóg mountains.

"Only twice before the coup: once when Áine and Cai had their marriage and entwining ceremony, and once when Theo was born. I stayed for about a week both times, and I only made it back to Bastain once. Before the coup, Cai would visit Fáintìrean often to meet with Gálgalesh and the others—hence why he needed the village cottage, though I'm not sure he would have wanted it back now that we've spent time alone there." A devious smirk dances across his lips. "Sometimes, I would think about coming home for holidays or because I just missed the sun, like River, Finn, and Sullivan did, but I knew Cai had me there for a reason. After Cai's death, I only made it back once, on the day I received a raven from my father explaining what'd happened."

"And Cai's son, Theo—you know him?"

"As anyone can know a baby, yes." Amusement coats his words. "He has his eyes, you know, brown saucers that take up half his face, and that same brown hair all you Morans seem to have. Well," he runs his fingers through mine, "not anymore, I suppose."

"I'm scared to meet him. I think I might begin to miss Cai even more, and I might not be able to bear it," I admit so self-ishly, I surprise myself. "I miss him so much, I can hardly stand it already."

"I know," Eoghan says without any sort of judgment. "Just try, though, Maeve. Maybe you'll find you like having a family again."

A family—I'd hardly had one to begin with. Eoghan seems to believe that's something we could and should have. He believes it's something he would want with me. I've never been so sure of something as he is of his relentless desire to build a life here and include me into a piece of it somehow. *Take care of Rian, and then you can give him everything.* I close my eyes and listen to his heartbeat, resolved that our family will be complete, even if I must burn the world down to make it so.

———

"GÁLGALESH and the others will be here in a minute." Eoghan sits next to me at the long table in the middle of the kitchen, River and Finn across the table from us. It feels like we're at Báscogar again, though the food has improved and the unending chill that had ran through my body day and night has been replaced with constant sticky sweat on the back of my neck.

We're waiting for the Leader's men to arrive so Eoghan can tell us what he found on he and Bryn's secret trip to Tonnfórsca and Trader's Bay. Bryn stayed in bed for most of the morning but has finally decided to join us, his hair sticking up on one side, clad only in his underwear. He is strikingly like Eoghan in so many ways, and I divert my eyes as I notice his toned arms and muscular chest are strikingly similar as well. My cheeks turn pink while River snorts a laugh.

"Mixed company!" River shouts. Bryn turns to face us, not an ounce of embarrassment in his eyes. He shrugs and sits at the end of the table, reaching his long arm to pick at the food laid out. "Kael men..."

The front door creaks, and we hear the sound of boots on tile as Gálgalesh and the others enter. They cross into the kitchen and take their seats at the table. Gálgalesh settles in at the far end as the rest of the empty seats fill with numerous faces, some I recognize, such as Trystan Price and Bode, and others I only know in passing across the outpost.

"The others are on their way." Gálgalesh folds his hands against the tabletop as the familiar mask of the Warden of Báscogar falls into place. His features are like stone—his expression emotionless and unyielding. This meeting is important, and although so much has long been kept from me, today, I'll be able to hear the truth.

The front door creaks open again, and Lowri enters with a group of men, mostly Tinemallacht warriors, Tiernan following behind. I watch out of the corner of my eye as Eoghan's shoulders square while the room fills with members of the Leader's personal army. Each chair is occupied, meaning several men must stand along the walls and in the dark corners of the kitchen. I reach for Eoghan's hand, but he pushes my fingers away softly. Right now, I'm not

Maeve, Eoghan's lover. I'm about to earn my place among the ranks as a valuable member of the Resistance.

"Kael," a man with a towering frame and broad shoulders speaks from the door. "You've called us all here. Do you have news to report—besides you becoming Enemy Number One in the kingdom, of course?"

"Technically, Enemy Number Two," Gálgalesh cuts in as General Osian Kael, Officer Rhodes, and Colonel Hayes join us. "Enemy Number One is a far more wicked beast than Kael in every way."

Gálgalesh lifts his chin in my direction, and it takes everything in me not to drop my eyes like a bashful doe. Eoghan sits taller in his seat as an almost imperceptible smirk lightens his features. The others in the room eye me with interest, and Lowri stares off into the far corner, as though bored with the conversation.

"I've called you here because Bryn, Officer Rhodes, and I have just returned from gathering information in the other territories and in Trader's Bay. Just over a week ago, we left for Tonnfórsca, hoping to find out more about why Bréanainn Doherty and his son decided to organize a coup and take the throne. We found little the first days. In fact, no one could tell us how the coup had begun or the Dohertys' part in it. Even more curiously, no one could recall how Doherty himself had come to be in Tonnfórsca, prior to Bréanainn Doherty's seemingly sudden rise to wealth and power, trading slaves in Cuanslí. All that could be agreed upon was that less than two decades ago, ships with green flags emblazoned with the Doherty crest began to roll into port from Trader's Bay."

"Was his family not from Cuanslí?" Trystan Price asks and Eoghan continues as if he hadn't heard the question.

"Our contacts helped when they could, but the Doherty trail ran dry just prior to the resurgence of the slave trade.

We couldn't find anyone who had known them personally, so we decided to go to Trader's Bay to learn about the deal Doherty had brokered to begin his trade."

Eoghan rubs the back of his neck as he speaks. I watch him stifle a wince as he lifts his arm, yet his warrior's façade doesn't break. "The slavers in Oleaíncudd were generally untrusting at best, dangerous at worst. Doherty is their most profitable partner. They benefit from his protection, so they offered very little on the subject. While Officer Rhodes and I were busy trying to earn the slavers' trust, Bryn spent his days with the scribes at the library in the center of town, trying to find any information he could on Bréanainn Doherty or the Doherty line. We almost gave up—the slavers wouldn't talk unless we made purchases, and the scribes seemed like a dead end until—"

Eoghan pauses and looks to Bryn, whose head rests on his palms as he dozes silently at the end of the table. Eoghan kicks him with his boot to wake him.

"Sorry," he yawns. "Can't sleep in the darkness."

"What did you find in Oleaíncudd?" I ask.

"Oh, it was sort of by accident. I had the scribes looking for the Doherty name, and they led me to a history of King Fergal's reign. I scanned through it, not sure why they'd led me to it, and I found that the Oleaíncudd histories of the ascension of King Fergal to the throne didn't match ours here in Draío. Our histories teach us that the last royal line died out, and there was a tournament to crown the new king. Fergal, from a family of no status or name, beat out every noble family for the Crown. In Oleaíncudd, the scribes described a massacre on the Night of the Great Darkness—a night when a darkness caused by black magic passed across the kingdom so thick, no one could see through it. It said Fergal had entered Caisleán Rialú, hidden from sight, and slit each royal's throat. Before the darkness cleared, he had murdered the entire staff and the court. Then, he took the castle and the throne and, in an act of what was only described as the approval of the gods themselves, the kingdom bowed down to him in fealty. No one tried to challenge his rule."

"What does any of this have to do with the bastard who killed Cai?" a man says as he leans up against the counter in deep greens and browns, with a much-too-heavy cloak draped around his shoulders. I notice the armholes in the garment, used to keep the cloak in place during unpredictable gusts of wind, and realize he's traveled to this meeting from Gálamáistir. His arms are crossed at his chest, and I feel his impatience rise, along with the others in the room.

"It wouldn't have anything to do with him at all, if not for a single name." Eoghan reaches into his pocket and pulls out a folded piece of parchment. He tosses it into the center of the table, and quick hands from every side reach for it. It soars away from their grasp and into Gálgalesh's long, awaiting fingers. "The scribes note that on the night of the massacre, one of the princes wasn't in the castle. In fact, he wasn't in Draíocoinnigh at all. Errol Doherty, the youngest Prince of Draíocoinnigh, was on a quiet trip to Oleaíncudd to procure a wife. Being the fifth son in the Doherty family line, he was not entitled to a bride from one of the noble families. He had traveled across the sea, and in that time, he had become—unbeknownst to anyone in the whole of Draío, including King Fergal—the sole survivor. Fearful of the fight that might occur to take back the throne, the scribes' records show he settled in secret, living in relative poverty with a woman from Trader's Bay. It wasn't until his great-great-great grandson, Bréanainn, made his first journey east across the Murcean Sea at nineteen that anyone from the Doherty line stepped foot in Draío again."

Eoghan finishes, and the room falls silent. Gálgalesh's brow furrows as he looks over the parchment in his hand; then, he passes it to General Kael. Rian always had a fascination with the castle and the capital city. He always knew so much about the foundation of the kingdom and the history of the earliest battles for the continent that were seldom taught by my tutors. 'Old, useless history,' they would say, instead teaching stories of the great, valiant king who saved the kingdom from collapse—the powerful warrior king who ruled by the hand of the gods.

"Are you telling me," Lowri interjects, "that those fucks killed Cai because they thought they had a right to a throne they lost and were too scared to take back almost two hundred years ago?"

"That's what it seems." Eoghan's voice is steely, firm, devoid of any emotion. His eyes move to mine in silent question, asking if I'm all right. I can't be entirely sure, but I nod anyway as my palms grow slick with sweat. I turn away from him as voices rise around the room.

"How long does a claim to the throne stand? I'm no fan of the kings of my lifetime, but surely, there would be no challenge to the throne after that long."

"Regardless of claim, usurpation can happen. If the cause is due to the original usurper's carelessness, the matter is still the same." Gálgalesh leans back in his chair, and my mind races with unanswered questions.

"They didn't successfully kill me. Does that mean they didn't successfully usurp my family?"

"Doherty has already been crowned and supported by the Five—Four Seats. Do you wish to challenge their authority to the throne, knowing that, by your family's own laws, a woman like you has no claim to the title of sovereign?"

"No," Eoghan speaks before I have the chance. My head whips in his direction. "No, it's not about who will wear the crown next. It's about what the Dohertys did to wear it now. Perhaps Cai learned about Bréanainn Doherty and was preparing us before we ran out of time. Now, maybe our goal is to fight for Cai's honor in death."

"But why would Cai have hidden such a thing from me? Had I known, I could've stopped Rian from gaining access to the castle and our family long before the coup."

"Secrets always have their reasons." Lowri's eyes shine bright with angry fire, and unlike Eoghan, she has no problem with letting it loose.

"But what's the point of a secret if it doesn't protect? I don't accept that Cai knew. I don't accept that he wouldn't have told me."

Gálgalesh raises his hand, and the room falls silent. "Regardless, we now must decide how we use this information to our advantage. The king and his men have become aggressors at the border. Two in our ranks are wanted for treason—surely all of us by association, if not by name. Our top priority is to keep ourselves safe, and as we do, we'll continue to gather information as to how the Dohertys assembled their coup under our very noses." He rises, and the others seated at the table go with him. "For now, return to your posts. We'll contact you if anything changes."

Rian's family had been on the throne, and it had been taken from them. He and his father had somehow blamed mine for the deeds of a man we never met. I think back to Kruz Lanzo, who had been so willing to take my life as payment for the injustice of my father's punishment. What made us worthy to be the debtors of someone else's sins?

The room begins to clear out, and I hardly notice. Eoghan's gentle touch shakes me back to the present.

"Thank you." I wait until it's only Gálgalesh, Finn, River, and Bryn who remain before I lean back into his arms, and I feel his muscles relax as the warrior in him falls away.

He blinks. "Why are you thanking me?"

"Because you let me into the room. You didn't hide any information from me—even if it means me knowing Rian is going to do everything in his power to kill me."

"He's not going to kill you. I'd kill him before he even had the chance to try." His hands grow warm against my skin.

"I know he won't be able to hurt me, but I also know he will try. I needed to know that—to know I'm not safe until he's dead. I needed to know why he had come after us, if even just to be sure I hadn't caused it myself."

"You could never have caused it. That coward used you to get to your family. Nothing you could have done would have changed his plans."

I know Eoghan's right, but my stomach still turns uneasily knowing I had a part to play. I was the weak link Rian manipulated for his own gain. A woman used by a man to get what he needed. My skin crawls at the thought, and I almost pull away from Eoghan's touch, not wanting to mar him with my filth. Knowingly, his hands grow warm—but not hot—against my skin.

"Don't worry about him. He's not here, and he'll never hurt you again." He pulls me harder into his chest.

The room is empty now, silent except for our breathing. He can't protect me forever. No matter how much he loves me, this angry hole in my chest—this burning that tells me I can't stop until every last person at the coup that day pays for what they did—will not heal, will not cease. I don't know how I can ever make him understand that until Rian is dead and that crown rests in my palms, there is only hurt.

———

MY FINGERS DANCE anxiously as we stand in front of Áine Moran's door. We've been in this spot nearly fifteen minutes, and still, I can't bring myself to move. Eoghan is patient—much more so than I've ever been with him—but his patience is wearing thin.

"What's the worst that could happen?" he muses. "You survived my scorn when you first met me, and I am definitely much scarier than Áine."

"That's different." I trace the lines in the wood with my eyes.

"How so? You were convinced I'd kill you."

"I also wanted to kiss you from the moment I met you."

Eoghan laughs. "You wanted to kiss me, and yet, you never once tried. I had to do all the kissing from the start." He places his hand behind my elbow. "You're being ridiculous." I begin to retort as he pushes the door and rolls his eyes. "You made a deal with a shadow lurker, and you're afraid of a baby. Come on."

We enter the house, and Eoghan walks me to the small sitting room, only releasing me when everyone turns to greet us. The room is filled with familiar faces: Tiernan and Dedra lounge on the sofa in each other's arms. Bryn, Finn, and River play a Tinemallacht gambling game with a set of dice in the far corner, a stack of gold coins between them. Lowri sits in an armchair, bouncing baby Theo on her knee. Notably, Áine is nowhere in sight.

Eoghan steps away from me and holds out his hands to Lo, who lifts the baby up into his arms. He cradles him as if it were his second language, as if it were no more spectacular than breathing. The baby nestles into Eoghan's shoulder, and Eoghan's large hand rubs small, affectionate circles along his tiny back. Eoghan coos softly to him as he crosses the room to me, and I fight every urge to retreat. Whatever was left of the Tinemallacht warrior in Eoghan's eyes has left. Instead, an expression so tender, so unguarded, so full of love drenches his perfect face—the look of a man who holds everything he's ever wanted. He cradles the little boy and turns him to face me. I nearly sob as I take in the sweetest brown eyes and rosy cheeks I've ever laid my eyes on.

"Maevie, meet Theodore Conri Moran."

I reach out, and Eoghan passes baby Theo as my heart begins to melt in my chest. I've never seen anything or anyone so perfect in my life. Not the stars in Romiodóg, the Golorgleann fields in the morning light, not even Eoghan can compare to the sight of him, so much like Cai in every way imaginable. The world falls away in an instant, and the war that has been raging for the last eight months—the endless burning in my heart—subsides as I take him in. This time, I don't have the strength to hold back the tears.

"Maeve, are you all right?" Bryn asks, his voice far away from me, drowned out by the rapid pounding in my chest.

"She's fine," Eoghan assures. He's enraptured by the sight of us, his eyes never leaving me.

The door behind me pushes open, and I tuck Theo into me as I turn to find Áine standing just steps away.

"He likes you," is all she says, her smile gentle and her eyes as warm as the Tinemallacht sun.

Without a second thought, I close the gap between us and wrap an arm around her neck in the tightest embrace. I feel her tears fall softly onto my shoulder as her arms envelop me. We cry together in an empty room—a very full room— and my soul begins to mend with each passing tear.

Time creeps away from us unnoticed as we embrace, and when we finally break apart, Áine takes my face into her hands and kisses me on the forehead.

"Welcome, Maeve, to our home—your home, if you so choose."

Her voice is like velvet. She smiles, and the whole room lightens. There's no denying why she captivated Cai so completely. In her eyes, there's the promise of hope and none of the bitterness I thought I'd find. Where Cai burned with passion and strength, she is his perfect match of mild calm, the sister I was never given a chance to know until now.

"Before we forget, Eoghan tells me today is a special day." I know nothing of it and raise an eyebrow in confusion. Áine summons, and as if appearing out of thin air, a cake settled on top of a large tray appears in her hand. Almond, cooked to a perfect gold, still warm from the oven. "Your birthday?"

My birthday? My birthday falls in the middle of spring just before the White Night settles in upon Golorgleann. Has it really been so long since I left the Capital?

Eoghan says, "The fifth of Beltané, isn't it?"

"How did you know?" I'd never spoken of my birthday to him, hadn't even given it a thought. He simply shakes his head. "Thank you."

The room bursts into song, and for the first time in nearly a year, I feel as though I am finally home.

"Evie." The door creaks open, and I pull my blankets up over my head. "Where ancient oaks whisper secrets of old, in meadows where myths and legends are told."

"Cai! I'm sleeping!" I protest, but I hear his shoes slide toward the bed.

"May the spirits of Draío sing bright and gay, a joyous tune for your birthday!"

He yanks back the covers to reveal him standing over me, a single piece of cake balanced on a golden platter in his hand. He feigns surprise, and I crinkle my nose at him in annoyance. It's much too early for cake or singing or any merriment at all. The sun hasn't even begun to peek through the castle windows.

He sets the plate down on the bedside table and then jumps on top of the bed, hands outstretched, shaking me wildly as I scream with laughter.

"HAPPY BIRTHDAY!" he shouts, and I place my finger against my lips to silence him. "No! Let's wake the castle, little sister! You only turn twelve once!"

"What's so great about being twelve?"

I have never had a proper birthday celebration before. Father and Mother would never allow it—opting only for a day free of lessons and a lone package left at my door. Yet, on the fifth of Beltané every year, Cai wakes me in the same fashion—loudly and before the world awakens. He's twenty now, and I thought he might forget this time.

"Every year you are my sister is a reason to celebrate!" He shakes me once more. "Besides, after this year, I'll be off on my duties as heir to the stupid Draío throne, and who knows if I'll get to celebrate with you on your birthday again?"

He slides backwards off the mattress, pulling my arms as he goes. I stand, in my long nightdress and bare feet, and stretch my mouth into a wide yawn. He picks up the plate from the nightstand before motioning for me to follow him out of the door.

"Must we?" I whine as we traverse the deserted halls of the castle, up the spiral staircases toward the upper-most floors.

"Just humor me one more time, Evie." He laughs as he continues, and I sigh as my feet find the cold stone. We make it to the top landing with the lowest ceiling in Caisleán Rialú, and he mumbles an incantation that unlocks the hidden trap door overhead. It swings open, and a small ladder appears. "After you, Princess."

He bows playfully, and I ascend onto the castle roof. The lights of the narrow Gairdín streets greet us as we burst into the night, the first signs of morning on the horizon. This is, without a doubt, the greatest view from the castle. I find our hidden blanket—a dirty scrap of cloth from birthdays passed—and lay it down across the steel before taking a seat. Cai settles in beside me and hands me the plate of cake, a buttery almond confection he always compels the cooks to make. I take it from him and shovel a piece into my mouth.

"To another year of you," he whispers. We watch the sun glow orange and pink as it rises. The city awakens slowly, unaware of our presence amongst them. "Happy birthday."

———

WE SPEND hours celebrating and laughing in the small sitting room. I do not relent my hold of Theo, who naps quietly in my arms as I lie on the floor against Eoghan's chest. We've eaten our fill of cake, played games, and shared stories until our voices are weak. There is an air of contentedness that hangs over the room.

"Come with me," Eoghan whispers after everyone goes silent.

"Where?" I ask with an air of wonder in my voice as Theo stirs slightly.

"A surprise."

Eoghan motions to Áine, who gently pries Theo from my arms. I only protest a little before Eoghan wiggles out from underneath me and pulls me to my feet.

"We'll be back in the morning," he says to the others. They nod absentmindedly, and I wonder if they even remember we're here now. He interlaces his fingers with mine and walks me out the front door. "Before we leave..." He pulls the dragon heart necklace from his pocket and holds it between us. He unhooks the clasp, taking one side of the chain in each hand and fastening it around my neck. "It killed me knowing you weren't wearing it." I feel the heat—his fire—warm against my skin. "And one more thing."

He reaches into his pocket once more, and this time, a silk scarf in reds and golds emerges. He motions for me to turn around, and I stare at him with my eyebrow cocked. He smirks, and without a word, he spins his finger in a circle once more. I do as instructed, giving him my back. He places the soft silk over my eyes and ties it gently at the back. I can't see anything except for a shadow of sunlight that only makes the darkness more golden and slightly pink.

"Is this necessary?"

"Yes. I don't want you to guess where we're going." Eoghan is enjoying every moment of this. As if I could guess where anything might be in this sand-covered barren. "Stop whining and trust me. It'll only be a few minutes; Officer Rhodes is going to transport us there. I won't keep you blindfolded forever."

I exhale and hold out my hand. "Fine, but I better not run into anything, Eoghan Kael, or so help me—"

He grabs my fingers and tugs me forward. Without sight, my senses are heightened. I can identify the smells of breads, soups, and roasts. I can hear the whisper of sand against the buildings as the wind picks up around us. I can feel the calluses rough on Eoghan's palms from his years of training with a heavy sword. Cai always wanted me to find a man with calloused hands, the sign of hard work and sacrifice, distinguishing men from boys. I wonder how he might feel knowing my choice now. I run my thumb softly against the back of Eoghan's hand, and he gives me a gentle, reassuring squeeze.

We continue forward, and I hear voices pass us, speaking to Eoghan quietly in greeting or question. He answers stiffly, as he would anyone at Báscogar prison. How different he is when he speaks to me, as though the only time he's himself is in the quiet hours in each other's embrace.

He begins to slow, and I hear Officer Rhodes's familiar timbre ask if we're ready to leave. There is no audible response from Eoghan, but after a moment, he urges me forward. The low sounds and smells of the outpost fade away, and then the scarf is removed from my eyes to reveal nothing but red sand for as far as the eye can see in every direction and the solitary mouth of an enormous cave.

"Where are we?" I ask.

"The Caves of Fortún, north of Bastain."

Right. The Caves of Fortún…whatever that is.

"And why are we here?"

"You'll see."

Eoghan wanders forward, and I wait until he disappears into the darkness before I follow him. It's pitch black, and the air is moist, so unlike the rest of the Tinemallacht desert. Built into the cave wall is a torch held permanently in an ornate cradle carved into the shape of a dragon. Eoghan lifts his hands and wields his dragon fire so a dozen more torches light along either side of the cave down a sandy, sloping passageway. Eoghan waits until the light extends beyond our view, and then he begins our descent.

We walk down the winding passageway, and the air grows heavy and damp. It is still warm, much too warm for the dark, and the walk becomes steep as we turn the next corner. My boots slide dangerously against the sand, and Eoghan reaches out to grab my arm, keeping me upright. I steady, and he tucks me close to his side.

"Almost there," he assures.

We walk for two or three more quiet minutes, and suddenly, the already enormous passageway opens up before us. I pause as the room comes into view: a chamber so vast, it must stretch for miles under the surface of the desert. At the cavern floor, a lush pool of iridescent water glimmers and runs into the underground river, fresh water over red rocks. Across the floors and along every inch of the cave are gemstones in every color, hundreds of thousands of them, sitting in piles towering high like mountains of technicolor. I have never seen more wealth in my life, and I doubt I would ever find any to compare it to in all of Draíocoinnigh. Not even in the castle vaults had such wealth existed. My father would have lost his mind with jealousy. Finally, most extraordinary of all, I take in no less than fifteen dragons resting on various overhanging stone shelves above the cavern floor.

"As legend goes," Eoghan's voice is a reverent, velvety hum, "the dragons of Tinemallacht have lived for centuries in the Barrens, long before the rivers dried up with the unrelenting heat of the sun. When the first humans came to the continent, the dragons would only allow the bravest of men into their lands—the ones who could handle the harshness of the desert and the oftentimes fierce tempers of the dragons. Dragons live for only one hundred and forty years, just longer than humans themselves, but they breed often, and their numbers are endless. As each dragon dies, so does the dragon's magic, each as rare to the dragon itself as the gemstone of their heart." Eoghan points to the jewels spread out before us.

"As the dragons came to trust the first settlers of the land, they offered the human wielders a gift. At the end of a dragon's life, the dragon will transfer its magic to a man—or a woman—to extend the life of the magic nearly two-fold. In return, the humans gain the riches of the dragon hearts, the greatest secret of our land, and extended health and strength to the wielder of dragon fire. Dragon fire, the gift of our dragon protectors, is given at the tender age of five in the Fire Rite ceremony. It takes about a year to settle into the wielder's genetic makeup. At thirteen, we have our first wielding with a ceremony, a tattooing, and a feast. That is, unless your name is Cai Moran, who had his Fire Rite and Wielding in two years' time."

"Cai? Cai wielded dragon fire?"

Eoghan nods. "The only non-Tinemallacht-born wielder

since the original settlers. The dragons rarely take to anyone, especially foreigners, yet they recognized Cai as one of their own."

Cai's tattoo had been hand-tipped into his skin, given to him as a mark of the fire he wielded when he became one of the Tinemallacht Fire Cursed. No wonder he never came back to Gairdín. He had found home so completely here.

"And what happens to the magic when the human wielder passes away?"

"It passes back to the gods, and the wielder's heart becomes that of the dragons. We bring them here to this cave to be protected and to honor the dead."

"So the fire isn't a curse at all?"

"Well, if the fire doesn't take, it can be deadly—but dragons are picky, and their magic rarely fails, perhaps only once every few decades or so. The magic is a gift from the dragons who protected the first brave settlers. It is the mark of our people and the mark of our home."

The mark of their people. The only mark of my people I've ever received was a mark on my life. Even then, I have never belonged to a chosen people. Not like Eoghan. Not like Cai.

"Would you like to go for a ride?" Eoghan says, and I still. His face glows multicolored from the jewels refracted in the low light of the cave, and his eyes shine with promise. "On a dragon, I mean."

My mouth must have fallen open in surprise, because his lips curl up in amusement, and he rubs my chin softly with his thumb.

"Is it safe? I've always heard dragons are unapproachable."

"If you were Bréanainn Doherty, I wouldn't suggest trying to take a ride on a dragon's back. However, you're with Eoghan Kael, the Dragon of Báscogar, as you said. I think you will be fine."

My cheeks grow hot with embarrassment. I don't remember calling him that out loud.

"You talk in your sleep, Maevie." He leans in and kisses my lips. His tongue passes into my mouth with tender, passionate hunger. "Just wait until I show you what this dragon can actually do."

Warmth rises in my abdomen, and I almost whimper when he pulls away. He unsheathes his blade from his side and lifts it to the light. It creates a long, glimmering beam against the wall, and one dragon lounging fifteen feet above us turns its head. Eoghan twists the blade back and forth, catching the light, and a shiver shakes the dragon's body. It stands, stretching its wings wide. I gasp as it bounds into the air and soars around the cave, from one side to the next. Eoghan replaces his blade and wraps his fingers around my biceps, pulling me back with him as he steps into the passageway. The dragon lands in front of us, its massive head settling about a foot away. Eoghan pats its nose, and it exhales, filling the passageway with heat and steam.

"Reach out your hand so she can smell you before we fly."

I reach my fingers out hesitantly. Each time the dragon breathes or sniffs the air, I flinch, but Eoghan places his hand on my back and encourages me forward. The dragon lifts her nose and presses it firmly against my palm. The scaly, rough skin is wet, almost hot to the touch. My entire hand is not even the size of one of its nostrils. The dragon sniffs and nuzzles against my fingers, then drops her head in a soft nod. Eoghan smiles and pulls me around her front legs. We reach her side as Eoghan places his hands on my hips, lifting me up onto her back before seating himself behind me. His hands fall to rest against my thighs, holding me in place.

"Hold on," he whispers, and with a soft click of his tongue, the dragon begins to ascend with great speed.

The walls of the tunnel flash by as streaks of light, and I

close my eyes as the motion makes my stomach churn. The dragon picks up pace as it weaves through the tunnel, and I pull my knees in to hang on. I feel the dragon tuck its wings closer, and then suddenly, they expand. My body is thrown back against Eoghan with a heavy jolt, and the feeling of fresh, dry air begins to whip around us. I open my eyes. The cave has fallen away, the ground far below our feet. We're flying through the Tinemallacht sunshine, over the barren dunes of the endless sea of sand.

The sound of the dragon's wings beating steadily through the air and the rushing wind fill my ears. I run my hand against the dragon's hide and feel the bumpy surface of scales as hard as stone. Eoghan wraps his arms around my waist, pulling me to himself, his body relaxed and his breaths easy. I lean my head back against his chest as the dragon banks right, bringing valleys and mountains of red into view. Far off, I can spot a small outpost like Gobaith, with tiny square buildings and horseshoe archways lining the terraced dirt roads. Further still, I see small dots of white racing across the sand as gliders make their way across the empty Barrens.

"Tinemallacht, as far as the eye can see," Eoghan whispers in my ear. "That way," he points ahead, "is how I went to Gálamáistir. It took a week on foot to transport my gear by myself through the desert. I camped in tents at night when I needed to rest. It's a rite of passage for warriors to cross the desert alone."

"I'm sure Cai did that too," I muse with an almost drunken contentment as I run my fingers along Eoghan's jaw.

"He wouldn't have lasted a day," he laughs. "Only the bravest warriors do it." He extends his arm to our left. "Only a few minutes north, by dragon, is the Golorgleann border. I saw the Golorgleann flower fields for the first time from a dragon's back when I was fifteen and couldn't believe anywhere could be so colorful."

"Golorgleann?" My hand rises to his hair, and I run my fingers through it softly. "Would you take me to see it?"

Eoghan is quiet. I look up at him, his brows pulled tightly together in contemplation. He's worried.

"Please, Eoghan?" I ask again, and I press my lips to his jaw softly. "Just once?"

"I don't know, Maeve..."

I graze my teeth lightly over his ear, and he shudders against me.

"It's my birthday," I remind him with a whisper. "Please?"

He sighs, and I feel his right thigh tighten against the dragon's back to coax it to change direction. It yields to him, and we begin to fly north toward the capital territory.

He tightens his hold on my waist just slightly as the Golorgleann night comes into view, and we fly toward the Tinemallacht crossing checkpoint. It is a spectacular chasm as the magic divides the desert from the copious valley—the night from the day. Darkness falls like a veil of black, and the sand recedes at the separation of the two territories. The border remains still, silent, boring even. Eoghan leans over against the wing and surveys the quiet barracks of the Tinemallacht stronghold.

"That's strange..." The dragon beats the air as it skims low over the checkpoint. "There's supposed to be fighting on the border." As he speaks, a red spear of light flies through the air from the Golorgleann side.

"Shit!" Eoghan yells as he pushes me down against the dragon's back, and the light streaks past my head. Shouting rises from the border as Tinemallacht warriors burst out from beneath the sand, sending their own streaks of magic into the darkness. "Hold on!"

Eoghan wills the dragon to turn, but she's slow to

respond. Another spear of red sails just past her left claw. He shouts out in frustration and commands again. This time, she turns as we cross into the night. Her body wheels back toward the Tinemallacht border, and Eoghan grips me hard as the force of her sharp shift in direction threatens to throw me from the dragon's back. Thankfully, she straightens out and heads back toward the Tinemallacht side—

Neither of us see the attack before it collides heavily with the dragon's stomach. With the Tinemallacht border just within reach, red flashes as blinding as lightning around us, and the screeching of the dragon's pained cries fill the air. She's been hit—targeted by a wielder at the station below— and we are going to crash. The dragon jolts hard on impact, and we're thrown from its back, deep into the night.

CHAPTER FIFTEEN

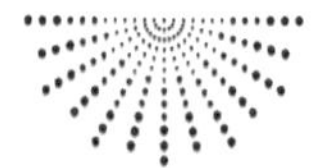

"MAEVE!"

Eoghan's voice pierces through the night. We are falling, plunging through the sky toward the ground. The dragon's lifeless body barrels to the Earth some half a mile away, closer to the border. She's been shot through the heart by a royal soldier standing directly beneath her. We had no hope of stopping it, and now, we're racing toward our own deaths in the starless, Golorgleann night.

Eoghan reaches for me, but his fingers miss me as he careens into the darkness. We're going to collide with the ground, and the impact might well kill us. If it doesn't, our injuries will give us no chance of escaping to Tinemallacht. *You have to save Eoghan!* my brain screams, jolting me into action. I wake the magic inside me, and it rings in my ears so loudly, I can barely hear the rush of wind as I fall. *I need something to stop his fall.* I send a hurried combination of symbols down the line as the ground rushes up to meet us, and I pray to the gods the magic has granted my request.

"Oof!" I hear Eoghan grunt as he collides with the invisible protective barrier just feet from the ground. *Oh, thank you!* I cry. He's safe—bruised, perhaps, but that will probably be the worst of it…

I'm still falling.

Crash!

My body collides with the Earth at full speed, and I scream out as my bones crack and break. The sound is sickening, and I feel the throes of pain grip me from my skull to my feet. *This will kill me. This has to kill me.* My vision blurs and goes black for what I assume is a few long moments, and then I'm back—alive and gasping for air.

"Maeve!" My magic has released Eoghan, and he meets the ground with only a light thud before he jumps to his feet. He races toward me and skids across the grass to my side. "Maeve, gods, what the hell did you do?" He looks me over, his eyes wide.

"I'm fine." My bones cry out like they're set alight, but the familiar jolt of magic coursing through me indicates my body's healing. I begin to wiggle my fingers and toes before I rise to a seat.

"I see that, but *how*? You should be dead! And why the fuck would you save me and not yourself?"

"You can't heal."

I roll my head from one side to another, loosening my stiff neck. I had almost forgotten how the pain lingers for days, even after all signs of injury have gone. I'll be sore tomorrow, but Eoghan will be alive.

"You shouldn't be able to either, Maeve!" He presses in on me, his face mere inches from mine. "How long have you known?"

"Since we got to Fáintìrean. One of the prisoners caught me with a blade as we were escaping. When we reached the cottage, all signs of the attack were gone."

"And you kept that from me?" He's livid, and I feel his anger rise like a wildfire around us.

From a short ways off, the sound of soldiers shouting to one another and the rustling of foliage in the field around us grows louder. We're the two most wanted people in the kingdom, and if we don't move now, we will have offered ourselves up on a shining, dragon-shaped platter. I take hold of Eoghan's arm and hoist myself to my feet. The sharp pain of freshly-healed breaks radiates through my legs, but I ignore it, instead looking around the dark field where we've landed. A small shed sits not far from us.

"Now is not the time to compare secrets, Eogh. We need to get to that shed and figure out how the hell we are going to get out of here."

He swears under his breath, and his eyes scan the darkness behind us. They're nearly on top of us now. Eoghan grabs my hand and crouches as he runs toward the shed.

"I would have told you something like that!" he admonishes as he leads me through the tall grass, his eyes adjusting much more quickly than mine. I still feel blinded by the sudden plunge from the sunlight directly overhead into the blackest night.

"No, you wouldn't!" I hiss back. "You tell me nothing!"

We reach the shed, and Eoghan shakes the door handle. It doesn't budge. I wait, expecting him to mumble an incantation of common magic under his breath as Tiernan had to unlock his brother's barn. Instead, he rams his foot into the wood with a loud crack, and the door gives way. Eoghan nearly launches me into the shed before following, throwing his back against the door to jam it shut. There's no way the Golorgleann fighters didn't hear us. The force of Eoghan's boots might have been heard clear to Gairdín.

"Why didn't you just unlock the door?" I huff. Soldiers close in outside.

"I—" Footsteps cross in front of the shed, and Eoghan pauses as they pass. "I can't wield outside of Tinemallacht right now. I have a tracker on my magic—all the men in the royal military do, unless they're not officially enlisted, like Bryn. I haven't been able to since we left the prison and the king started looking for us."

I freeze. Eoghan can't wield. He hasn't since our escape. Even when they were trapped by those damn faeries, he hadn't used his magic to free them, because he knew it would lead Rian to us. And. He. Didn't. Tell. Me.

"More secrets?" I raise my voice, and he casts an angry glare my way before he notices the silencing charm I've thrown up around us.

"This is less of a secret than just a lack of knowledge on your part."

Someone presses in on the door, and Eoghan digs his boots into the dirt to hold it in place. I race forward and throw my own weight against it.

"That's not fair! You should have told me!"

"*You* should have told me your magic came back!"

The door is shaking beneath the force of the men outside as they attempt to push it out of the way. They know we're in this shed, and in a few moments, they're going to blast us out of here the way they blasted that dragon out of the sky.

"Eoghan, now is not the time. We need to get out of here before they decide to take this place down." I reach for my daggers, and as I do, I realize they're not strapped to my thighs. I have no weapons whatsoever. I look Eoghan up and down and see he only has two daggers of his own.

"I'm thinking!" he shouts. He tests the dragon fire in his hand, and it grows stifling in the shed. Then, he adjusts the magic somehow and the fire burns cooler.

The men outside ram the door, and it takes Eoghan's arm across my front to keep me from falling face first onto the ground. We're out of time. I close my eyes and summon the faerie magic, but before I can wield, Eoghan slams his hand against the wall, and my eyes fly open.

"Don't wield! Rian thinks you have no magic. He can't know you do now. I have an idea… You aren't going to like it, though."

"I'm all ears," I pant.

"I'm going to set the shed on fire."

I blanch. "Like hell you are! There's no way I'm going to burn to death here on my birthday!"

"It won't burn you." He wields in his hand and presses it against my chest—the fire is cool to the touch. "Dragon fire burns only what the wielder wants it to. I'm going to burn the shed and give us a chance to run for the border. Do you trust me?"

Do I even have a choice? If we stay here, these soldiers are going to kill us—it's not a matter of if, but when.

"Fine!" I snap and take a deep breath as the wood smolders and catches fire. It builds up around us in columns of flame and smoke, and Eoghan pulls my scarf up around my mouth and nose as the building burns red and angry. Still, it stays cool, the heat only rising no more than Eoghan's own body temperature as he controls the dragon fire around us. The wood falls away to create a door-shaped hole in the shed wall, and the rest of the structure remains intact. The men fall back as angry tongues of blazing hot death lash out toward them on Eoghan's command, and we wait in the center of it all until they've cleared our exit.

"Ready?" Eoghan shouts over the crackling, roaring flames. He reaches out, and the flames die down enough to clear a path for us to run through. "Go!" he commands, and I dash through the door into the dark flower fields, tall stalks rising at all sides. Eoghan pushes forward just behind me, and, with one last wielding, he unleashes the fire, letting it burn out of control.

We run as fast as we can, the faint light of the Tinemallacht border straight ahead not more than a quarter-mile. *We will make it*, I assure myself, though I can hear voices catching up to us from behind.

Eoghan urges me on as I struggle to keep his pace. I'm slowing him down. He won't make it if he sticks with me. My legs ache as I give it everything I've got—still, I'm not fast enough.

Woosh! A rush like a cyclone flies past us and takes out at least half of the men who followed us into the fields. I pause, and Eoghan slows beside me as the flower stalks susurrate ahead of us, heavy footsteps approaching through the darkness.

"Are you done trying to die out here?" Lowri's voice rises from somewhere ahead, and a moment later, she and River burst into view. She's carrying Eoghan's sword, her own strapped to her back, and she tosses it to him before taking hers in her hands. "What the fuck were you thinking?"

Eoghan pushes me past them and then spins around in one fluid motion to face the royal soldiers. A blur of a dark mass slows as it approaches. Finn has come to save us too.

"I wasn't. I was flying." Eoghan raises his sword to block the first soldier's blade and knocks it away with deft precision.

"Idiot!" Lowri drives her blade into another soldier's stomach. "If I hadn't asked where you had gone, I never would have seen you fall out of the sky." A soldier rams into River's side, and I begin to wield, but Lowri slams her elbow into my gut, knocking the wind out of me and driving me to the ground. "No!"

I cough and wheeze against the ground as Eoghan slices one man's head clear off his body. They whirl and stab in perfect unison, and it's not until the last soldier falls into the darkness that they cease their battle dance.

"Thank you," Eoghan finally says with one panting exhale, and Lowri replaces her sword on her back.

"Come on. Officer Rhodes is waiting at the border. Dad's going to be furious."

Lowri, Finn, and River all begin to head back toward the Tinemallacht border checkpoint, leaving Eoghan and I behind. He walks over to me, my ass planted firmly in the dirt, battered and sore, though unharmed. He reaches his hand out to help me up. His lips press into a flat line as I stand, his gaze distant. His pride is hurt, but worse than that, he's angry. The same anger that had overtaken his features when Kruz Lanzo had attacked me is written all over his face now. He pulls me close to his side and presses his lips to my temple before we follow the others back home.

CHAPTER SIXTEEN

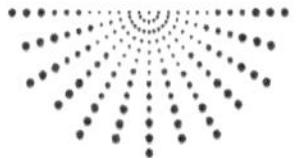

"How could you be so stupid?"

General Osian Kael's voice rises from the sitting room. The door was left slightly ajar when he stormed in ten minutes prior and demanded Eoghan, alone, follow him into the dark room. The shouting began as soon as they crossed the threshold.

I sit on the bench in the entryway and listen as Lowri, Finn, and River enter the house. Finn and River slide wordlessly into the room while Lowri remains in the entryway, glowering at me.

"I made a mistake. I didn't think there'd be—" Eoghan's voice is tired, and his father cuts in with renewed anger.

"You didn't think! No, why would you ever think flying over a war zone would be dangerous? It's not as if your lover has started a war with the Crown! Now, we have a dead dragon *and* a destroyed border stronghold!"

There had indeed been both when we crossed back over into Tinemallacht. The dragon had suffered catastrophic injuries, dumping gallons of blood across the border before falling directly on top of the Tinemallacht checkpoint, largely flattening most of the outpost buildings. It killed two soldiers and injured at least a dozen more; the border would be weakened, if not a complete loss, for the foreseeable future.

"It was your idea, wasn't it?" Lowri's voice is gravelly and austere. I don't answer her, and she steps forward until she's uncomfortably close. "Just because you have no sense in that pretty little head of yours doesn't mean that you have the right to ruin his. You pull something like that again, I'll take you out into the desert and kill you myself."

She shoves my shoulder hard as she passes and walks into the sitting room, closing the door behind her. I hadn't known what was going on at the border or that Rian's men were actively trying to cross it to arrest me and Eoghan—they've been trying to cross and overtake the territory since the Tinemallacht refusal to recognize the Doherty claim. I hadn't known Eoghan would be largely defenseless if something were to happen, or that I wouldn't be allowed to wield. I didn't know, and now people are dead because of it.

I wait by the door until it opens again, and General Kael marches past me without a single glance in my direction. River, Finn, and Lowri follow him, exiting through the front door. Eoghan's the last to emerge. He limps with each step, his injuries from Oleaíncudd still new. I can't read anything except anger and shame in his expression—the temperature of the room rises, the silence agonizing. My eyes scan him, from his Tans covered in dirt to the hole in his knee. His dragon scale leather jacket has a barren space on the shoulder that stands out like a sore thumb. I hadn't noticed anything there before, but now, its absence is blaring.

I stand from the bench to meet him. He holds up his hands, halting me before I get too close. The heat from his body makes sweat bead across my skin, even at a distance.

"I'm leaving for a few days to help clean up the border

checkpoint. You stay here and train with Gálgalesh and Bryn while I'm gone." His words are flat, and he barely looks at me as he speaks.

"I'm sorry," I breathe, and he tenses. "It was just an accident. I didn't know—"

"No, Maeve, you don't know. You don't know what's going on outside of these walls. You don't know they've taken captive and interrogated every single person outside this territory who has known us. You don't know they've targeted my entire family. You don't know!"

Rage boils in my veins. "Well, then tell me! You tell me nothing—I know nothing unless I pry or find out from someone else! How am I ever going to be of any use at all if you don't talk to me?"

"I am trying to keep you safe! You will be useful if you stay alive."

"So that's it then? Stay here? Stay alive? I'm not Áine. I'm not going to stay at home while everyone risks their lives! Gods be damned, Eoghan!"

"Don't!" Eoghan's face turns red with frustration; he's burning so hot now, I have to retreat a few paces to keep from feeling as though my skin will burst into flames. "I didn't say that! I didn't say you had to stay home—!"

"You did!"

"That's not what I meant, Maeve! Of course, that's not what I meant. I just don't want to see you die because of my stupidity."

Bang! Bang! Bang! A heavy hand meets the front door in a clamorous rhapsody, demanding our attention. Eoghan groans and rolls his eyes as he crosses to answer it. A woman about Eoghan's age, with long, sandy hair braided down her back and loose wavy tresses framing her face, stands on the threshold. She wears the Tinemallacht Tans, signifying she serves in the Tinemallacht army, and she is trim while maintaining just a touch of curves.

"Time to go, Eogh." Her gaze is soft when she looks at him, familiar even.

"Or my own stupidity, right?" I scoff and storm toward the stairs. I hear Eoghan begin to call after me, but I ignore him, hoping he will fuck right off and not follow me. I reach the room and slam the door shut behind me.

I cannot stand him. He's perfectly fine letting another woman in—letting another woman risk her life, but not me? Does he think I'm so inept, I can't be of any use? Or perhaps he just prefers anyone else's company over the whining, selfish princess. All it takes is for one woman to arrive at the door for him to jump at the opportunity to run off and be rid of me for days on end.

I scream, and the dresser topples over with a loud bang against the tile floor. Footsteps from the hall warn of Bryn's approach a moment before he charges into the room.

"Maeve?" He steps forward, and I scream again. He stumbles back against the wall in surprise. "Maeve…"

Eoghan rushes up the stairs—his boots thunderous as he bounds across the landing—and pushes past Bryn into the room. He crosses to me without slowing even as I attempt, and fail, to wield a barrier of blue between us. He dips his shoulder and throws me over it. Then, he turns back out of the room and down the stairs. He takes the entryway in long strides exiting the house, his breathing deep, angry inhales, and a low growl loosing from somewhere in his chest. *What the hell does he think he's doing?* I pound my fists against his back.

"Let me go, Eoghan!" I scream as he makes his way down the road toward the outpost square.

"No." Eoghan's voice is hard and firm. I haven't heard him sound so frightening since last fall.

He walks through the open square, past a group of men sparring and laughing in the sand, and doesn't stop until he reaches the outpost gates. I hit him again, and he drops me hard onto my ass. "Stop shouting in my head when I can't shout back!"

He stands over me, his eyes wild with fury.

"I didn't—" I begin.

"Yes, you did! I don't prefer Dex's company to yours, but yes, if you would stop acting like a child, maybe you would be a bit more pleasant to be around!" I open my mouth to speak, but he points his finger toward me, and I hesitate. "I don't think you are inept, and I *don't* want you to stay in the house! I want you to live until we can kill that bastard sea boy together. I would love *nothing more* than to kill him. Just thinking about him makes me go blind with anger!" He takes a step forward, and I slide backward in the sand. "You keep punishing me as if I deserve your wrath when all I've done is try to keep you safe! WHEN, MAEVE? When will you finally decide I'm not like him? When will you decide you can trust me?"

My breath comes in heavy pants as his glare burns a hole right through me. "W-w-what's wrong with your jacket?" I stammer and point to the vacant sleeve.

"Fuck my jacket!" He rips it from his shoulders and throws it onto the ground. "Answer me, Moran! When will you decide to trust me? Ever? Am I going to pay for the rest of my life with you?" He drops to his knees and crawls toward me through the sand, placing his hands on either side of me. "Or are we going to finish this here?"

"What's wrong with your jacket?" I ask again, unrelenting. He shakes his head, and I smack him across his face. He stiffens, his expression feral. "Who's Dex?"

"A friend." I smack him again. "A good friend."

"One who knows you the way those women in Fáintìrean do?"

"Yes."

Bastard. Fury boils up inside my chest, and I grab him by his shirt, heaving him into a forward roll in the sand. We tumble over each other, and then I shove his back against the ground, pinning him with all my weight and bringing my fist down into his jaw. I probably won't leave a mark, but it feels good anyway.

"Your jacket?" I ask again.

"Not until you decide I'm not your enemy." I draw my dagger I only just replaced on my thigh and hold it against his neck. He leans in, and I watch as a drop of blood beads along the blade. "I. Trust. You." He wraps his fingers around mine, holding my hand firm. "When will you trust me?"

He'd let me kill him, just to prove he's given me all of himself. He's fully at my mercy, and as I look down in the sand, I see his daggers are discarded, relenting to my will. My hand loosens, and he lets me go. I drop the dagger from his neck. He lies back in the sand, his chest heaving softly.

"I trust you." That's all I say. I roll off him and onto the sand, lying next to him.

"Now that wasn't so hard, was it?" he breathes as he reaches for his jacket. "I was demoted to Captain for dereliction of duty. Instead of protecting you, I chose to put you in danger. They took my insignia from me to remind me of my failure." He shakes the sand off as he lifts the jacket and pulls it around my shoulders. "And *that* is what's wrong with my jacket, Mayhem. Now, are you going to trust me enough to stay and train with Gálgalesh, or must I take you with me and Dex to preserve my own honor?"

I push up from the sand, and he follows me to my feet. I tug on the thread of magic and send his awaiting glider soaring through the air. It lands in the sand in front of him.

"I'm keeping the jacket." I remark over my shoulder as I turn to walk back through the gates.

"Looks good on you. Don't tell your boyfriend, though. He's a jealous dragon," he purrs, and I gesture toward him as I keep walking. I hear his boots clip into his glider as he laughs, and I disappear into the outpost.

I HATE IT HERE. I don't like the heat of the desert or the sand creeping into every inch of space. There are no gardens in Gobaith, and though the houses and buildings are spectacular and ancient, there's little to do beyond sparring and drinking in the pub. I suppose the military is little more than a prison in many ways. There are always rules as to where one can go and what they can do.

I spend the morning in the library with Gálgalesh and Bryn as I practice new faerie spells and enchantments— much to Bryn's continual amusement. Gálgalesh still pours over the letters on sun-bleached parchment and refuses to let me see them. Instead, he points to the stack of those addressed to me. I've read them a thousand times, and they make my heart ache endlessly. I can't understand why Cai had chosen this place over his life in Gairdín; though as I read his words, I can sense the happiness he kept hidden as new light is shone on his life in the desert.

At lunch, Bryn and I head to Áine's house, where she's prepared too much food for us to eat. She doesn't speak much, retiring to her room, where she naps quietly in the darkness. Theo, however, is endlessly entertaining as he simply babbles incoherently throughout the afternoon, only one or two odd words making the least bit of sense. I have trouble not staring at him in awe of all his perfect features or playing with his tiny fingers and toes. There's something so beautiful about him, and he's the only thing I truly love about the desert—I'm not sure even Eoghan can compare anymore.

The evening rolls on quietly as we leave the small abode just after dinner has finished. The sun still shines, and I look at the watch Bryn has given me to see if the day has really passed at all.

"Maeve?" Bryn says beside me.

"Hm?"

"Would you like to go watch the sunset with me?"

I almost laugh out loud. I don't know much of anything—that has been made abundantly clear—but I know for certain the sun does not set in Tinemallacht.

"What are you talking about?" I lean against the exterior wall between Áine and Eoghan's homes and scrutinize Bryn—no humor fills his expression.

"I was going to take a ride out to the nearest dunes and watch the sunset. I thought maybe you were tired of sitting around a boring outpost too."

"What sunset?" I do laugh now, but his eyes remain earnest.

"Let's get our goggles, and I'll show you."

———

If anything can be considered fun in the desert, the gliders are the most fun I've ever had. Tinemallachts know how to travel, and though I've heard the airships of Gálamáistir are awe-inspiring, I struggle to believe they could be anywhere near as freeing as surfing across the red sand, guided by Bryn's wielding propelling us forward on the wind.

We reach the top of a dune ridge, the sand so soft that my feet sink down into it as if it were banks of snow. Bryn conjures up a blanket and pulls forth two bottles of ale from the pocket of his leather jacket, offering one to me. I take it with a nod of thanks. I find a seat in the sand, and he follows me down. The sun is still unfathomably high in the sky, and I point toward it with one critical, outstretched arm.

"I hate to tell you this, but the sun is still firmly in the sky." Bryn chuckles softly beside me.

"You northerners are all the same. You want the dramatic sunsets; that's why the White Night seems so long to you. The sun sets everyday here too, though, when the gods give us relief from the heat. Even in the dead of the summer, we're gifted that."

"I don't believe in the gods and their gifts," I say as I lean back on my elbows. Eoghan's jacket nearly swallows me up, but much to my surprise, it's not as hot as I imagined it would be.

"No? Well then, how do you explain that?"

He points toward the empty expanse of the valley below, and I watch as dragons begin to rise in clusters, as though they were sleeping together in a nest. They shake their wings out and lift their heads as they awaken on the surface of the sand like they were simply summoned there by some sort of magic, moving about, sliding on their stomachs, their four legs outstretched. Some blow puffs of fire lazily in front of them while others take to their hind legs, the youngest dragons finding each other, running circles around their parents in what looks like a game of tag.

"How incredible," I whisper, captivated by the hundreds of winged beasts below.

"Most days, the dragons dive below the sand for water, as the Falacht River flows freely there, but when the sun sets and the temperature drops ever so slightly—imperceptibly to most humans—the gods bring them to the surface to play and race and hunt and fill the desert with their majesty."

I watch as the dragons awaken and their movements become more agile. Some fly low, their claws skimming the sand, while others roll onto their backs and sun their bellies. The steady movement of the dragons makes the sand itself seem alive, churning as the dragons—some red, some orange, some brown, others dark green or blue—bring the barrens to life. I study them for long minutes, forgetting everything besides what it feels like to be in the presence of such power —mighty and dangerous, yet a beautiful and wonderful mystery.

"You're unhappy here, aren't you?" Bryn finally says.

"No, I'm not unhappy here." I'm not sure if it's a lie or not myself. "It's just not my home. It's so different here. I'm not used to it yet."

"You've lived in a castle your whole life. You're allowed to hate it here." Bryn nudges my shoulder. "I've never been anywhere else, only when Eoghan took me with him to Tonnfórsca and Oleaíncudd after I begged. Even then, I had to threaten to volunteer on the border in order to get him to agree to take me."

"I thought you were a soldier like the rest of them. Are you not allowed to fight?"

"I am…sort of. But I'm the youngest, and after the Third War Against Iranndair, when Lo was injured, Eoghan's always demanded I stay home. I wasn't even allowed to join the academy or the Leader's men. I'm the glorified canteen boy for the rest of them."

"Maybe he just worries about you. He cares for you so much, you know."

"He cares about you too. He'd rather die than see you hurt…or even miserable."

"It's called love," I laugh. "I know he cares, sometimes too much, but that's Eoghan."

Bryn nods. "Sounds like Cai and Áine. He was always protective of her—he was even afraid to take her to the Capital; but now that he's gone, I think a part of her died with him. They say that hearts become one after the entwining ceremony, so I guess we all should've expected it. She's sad all the time now. I can't imagine how that feels."

"I wonder if all of it is worth it—the entwining, I mean." I finish my bottle of ale and set it down next to me in the sand.

"Would you not bind yourself to Eoghan?" I shrug.

"Would you?" I ask.

"Not to Eoghan," he teases. "But with Ovidia, I would."

"Are you in love, Bryn?" I lean forward and nudge him. His cheeks grow pink with embarrassment. "Where is she? Have I seen her in the outpost?"

"No." He hides his face in his knees, and the dragons purr in a symphony of sound from the valley below. "She lives in Iranndair. I met her on the border when I was first sent on patrol. She's forbidden in every way—being in love with an Iranndairian is next to being in love with a dragon, maybe worse—but one day, whether I have to leave Draío or bring her here, I'm going to be entwined with her." I can't help but smile. He sounds so much like Eoghan in the quiet hours of the night when he whispers his love to me. "Don't tell anyone."

"Your secret's safe with me."

I link my arm around his bicep and pull him toward me. We watch as the dragons continue their song and dance until the valley quiets, and we head back to the outpost for the night.

CHAPTER SEVENTEEN

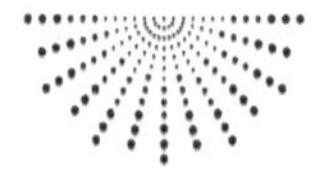

Two days later, I'm standing in the square, once again covered in paint. It's less this time, as it only covers my shoulders in four streaks, plus my chest in one thin line. I've bested Tiernan and River now. Finn is nearly impossible to match, though, and Lowri takes great pleasure in besting me —she often takes the opportunity to knock me to the ground or kick the shit out of me in some way.

Gálgalesh monitors us from beneath a large canopy he has ordered erected in the square as the sun grows hotter with each passing day. He shouts out orders like a queen from her throne as he lounges lazily with a canteen in his hand. The summer months are drawing near, and I'm not sure how he—or I—will stand it when the sun peaks in just a few months' time. He might just melt, even now. I walk over to his tiny oasis and steal the canteen from him.

"Have I told you how ridiculous you are?" I bring the metal to my lips and drain it. I hand it back to him. His expression is aghast as he stares back at me, empty canteen in his hand.

"Have I told you just how much I would like to feed you

to the dragons? Perhaps Peadair should have had his way with you—at least then, I could be inside." I crinkle my nose at him and settle at his feet. "We are done here for today. I think if we continue, Lowri will run an actual blade through you. Kael has asked us to meet him in the lower barracks when we finish. Collect your things, and we will head there together."

I lean against Gálgalesh's leg, and he shakes me off admonishingly. For all the time I've spent with him, he really is so stubborn to refuse my friendship. I sigh in defeat and summon my towel and daggers from the center of the square, sheathing them to my sides. It's amazing how easily the magic comes now, so much like common magic to normal human wielders. I hardly have to think about wielding anymore.

I rise, and Gálgalesh joins me to set off toward the abandoned lower barracks at the north end of the outpost. I've only explored the expanse of the small settlement once or twice, though I learned from one of the soldiers that the outpost was practically abandoned when the Dohertys took the throne and the Tinemallacht borders were secured. Most of the soldiers in Gobaith were from other territories, stationed here to fight for the Royal Army, mostly officers or specialized fighters who trained at the military academy. Tinemallacht couldn't keep them here and risk being accused of taking hostages when they became a breakaway state. So, the soldiers were ordered to the border, where they were forced—many against their will—to leave. The lower barracks have remained empty since.

"How have you been?" I ask as we walk.

"I have seen you daily since you arrived here, woman." His gaze stays fixed ahead.

"I know. I just meant—"

"I know what you meant," he says, and I can hear agitation in his voice. "I am..." He pauses as his eburnean colored eyes glisten silver around the edges. "I am lonely. Peadair was my lover for centuries. It seems wrong to be without him now."

"You had been separated before, hadn't you? When you were first imprisoned?"

"We were, but at least then, I knew he was alive, and I would see him again one day. Now, with Peadair dead and the finality of it all, it seems as though a hole has been carved right through the very center of me, a missing piece I will never have back again."

Sadness overwhelms me. My mind wanders to Eoghan and how desperately I need him—how awful it feels to spend just a day apart—and I haven't even known him a year. What must it be like to spend hundreds of years with another, only for them to be taken from you? I'm not sure I could bear it.

"Do you think you might ever love again?" I wonder aloud.

"No. Peadair was my first and last partner. It is enough to know I loved once, even if this sorrow threatens to drive me mad."

Gálgalesh leads us through the entrance of the brick barracks building lined with tall, rounded archways and colorful tile floors. It could be more temple than barracks, though that could be said of all the architecture in Tinemallacht. Elaborate carvings adorn the walls and rounded, smooth granite pillars rise toward the heavens, holding the painted ceiling aloft. At the center of the barracks, there's a riad garden bathed in light, speckled with purple and green fruit trees that wouldn't survive without a careful, persistent hand and a bit of magic.

Finally, we reach a small, windowless room. The door is cracked halfway, and I see a small orb of low light dance across the walls. Gálgalesh gestures for me to step inside, and as I push the door away, Eoghan is there to greet us.

"What's this?"

I take a hesitant step toward him. The room is bright, and cabinets line the walls on every side, holding tonics and potions swirling with life inside their vials. In the center of the room is a metal chair, and my mouth goes dry as I take it in. Other than the absence of leather straps, the chair and the room are so very like Sir Oli Raven's dungeon at Caisleán Rialú.

"Healer's quarters." Eoghan moves aside to make room for me to sit in the chair, but I remain standing as my hands tremble slightly at my sides.

"Kael has shared a few curious details about your accident at the border, woman." Gálgalesh pushes me down into the seat as he passes me and heads to a drawer, which opens as he approaches. "Why have you kept such a secret from us? Your healing magic returning is nothing short of a gift from the gods."

"I..." I can't think in this room. "I didn't know what it might mean or if it could be a manifestation of the faerie magic as it grew stronger."

Gálgalesh digs into the contents of the drawer with his back to us. Eoghan studies my expression as I blanch. I feel my heart trying to escape my chest in desperation to get away from this place, and my breathing becomes heavy, rapid gasps.

"Are you all right, Maevie?" Eoghan asks. The blood rushes like a stampede in my ears, and I barely register the timbre of his voice. Gálgalesh turns to face us. In his hand, he holds a long, very sharp needle—one I recognize from my weekly visits to the secret depths of the castle.

"No!" I scream and jump from the chair. Eoghan rushes

forward and catches me up in his arms, pulling me to him. Gálgalesh's hand falls to his side. "No, no, no, no, no!"

My body convulses at the sight of the weapons of my torment, and my mind races with horrible memories I try to blink back. They do not relent—the sound of my own phantom screams make my head ache.

"Be calm, woman. Your magic manifesting once again is curious. No one has ever documented such an occurrence in all written history. I do not understand it or what it means. Your blood has also smelled peculiar several times since you arrived at Báscogar, and I cannot place it. Kael and I were hoping you might allow me to—"

"Do not touch me!" I shout. I want to run. I want to run as far away as I can from this place, yet my legs feel as though they might give way at any moment.

"Woman, what is the matter with you?" Gálgalesh demands. I push against Eoghan's arms to release me. He doesn't loosen his grip. "Gods be!"

Gálgalesh stills, and his eyes become milky. I feel a tug on the magic from somewhere far away as if it is pulling me from my own mind into the abyss. The room begins to fade to black as my memories rush to me with greater clarity now, as if I'm watching them play out as a spectator rather than the subject of attention. Memory after memory, from my first at the tender age of three to my last on the evening before my wedding, arise in perfect, high-speed intervals. Pleading, begging, crying fills the air—and pain fills my senses like a flood, Sir Oli Raven's face smiling devilishly over me.

"Come now, Maeve. Do not be scared," Sir Oli Raven coos as he straps my tiny toddler arms to the metal chair. "Just a small prick now and a bit of blood."

"Will it hurt?" my tiny voice asks.

"Oh, well maybe just a bit..." Sir Oli Raven's lips turn up at the sides.

The image changes, and my ten year old self cradles my arm to my chest. I've fallen from a tree in the garden, and my bone has healed wrong, a painful lump protruding from my wrist. Sir Oli Raven steps forward and passes his long fingers over it.

"Stupid girl." He grabs hold of my hand and forearm and snaps it with enough force to leave me breathless before the screaming begins.

The scene washes away again, and I am seventeen. This time, he breaks me simply to see if anything at all might kill me.

Finally, the light of the room grows more yellow and sinister. Twenty year old me sits strapped to the chair in the figure-hugging golden dress I wore to dinner the night before my wedding. Sir Oli Raven has ordered a double batch of vials this time, and my head sinks to my shoulder as my vision darkens around the edges. Too much blood has been taken, and even with the life-giving magic coursing through me, I feel so weak, I am sure I'll pass out at any moment. Rian stands in the corner of the dungeon room, his sleeves rolled up to his elbows, his back leaned up against the wall.

"Make sure there's enough in case things go awry," he says as my eyelids grow so heavy, I can barely keep them open. The room fades to black, and when I come to again, I am in my bed, Rian on top of me, buried inside me as he grunts and moans out his pleasure. My head aches, and I can still feel where the needle had pierced my arm. "Mine," he whispers, and I roll my head back against the pillow with no strength to fight anymore. My eyes go closed as he continues into the late hours of the night.

The memories slow, and the cries become less shrill in my ears as the darkness begins to lift around me, bringing the room and Eoghan back into view. I'm laying limply in his arms, and his face is pale with worry. Gálgalesh's eyes refocus to find me just feet away. He drops the needle to the floor with a hollow clang of metal to tile.

"What the fuck was that?!" Eoghan shouts. Gálgalesh only continues to gape at me. "Is anyone going to tell me what's going on?"

"Woman." Gálgalesh's expression is soft now. "I am so sorry." He kicks the discarded instrument away and passes to the door. "Kael, take her out into the garden," he commands, bitterness dripping from his words. Eoghan follows as he helps me to stand and supports my unsteady legs.

We reach the warm sunshine, and Gálgalesh summons an ancient wooden bench with orange rounded cushions. I lower myself down to a seat. Gálgalesh himself remains standing and paces in front of me, rubbing his chin between his thumb and index finger.

"We will never take Maeve back into that room. Not ever. Do you understand?" Gálgalesh waits for Eoghan to answer. Eoghan holds his palms up in surrender. Gálgalesh kneels in front of me. "I am not here to harm you. Kael is not here to harm you. I would like to test your blood to see how your magic has manifested, but not against your will."

He runs his long fingers softly against my cheek, and it's too personal, too kind. My eyes fill with tears, and I don't know if I should hold them back to spare them both of my wailing or let them fall. I'm not sure I'll have a choice if Gálgalesh continues to look at me with such pity and under-standing.

"If I offer you a vial, will you fill it for me?" he asks. "Just a cut on your hand will do. I do not need much."

He doesn't reach for my arm, doesn't try to touch me beyond the gentle caress of his fingertips on my face. He doesn't offer to let Eoghan in either, and as he stands quietly next to me, I know it's my choice. They are secrets I need to share, but they're not anyone else's to tell.

I hold out my palm to him, and he reaches into his pocket, where he finds a small glass vial shaped like a teardrop. He uncorks it before offering it to me. I take it from him and then unsheathe my dagger at my side. *Just a cut. Just one tiny cut.* I drag the blade against my palm, and blood rushes thick to the surface. I place the vial to the river of crimson trickling down my hand and catch enough to pool at the bottom of the glass. The three of us watch as the laceration seals itself without leaving even a mark behind. I hand the vial back to Gálgalesh, and he smells it before he replaces the cork.

"Thank you." His voice is little more than a whisper as I replace my blade at my side. "Your blood smells normal now. When you were in the forest with Kruz Lanzo, it had smelled different—dangerous."

"When we were crossing the Romiodóg mountains, the faerie leader we encountered mentioned she smelled peculiar." Eoghan's eyes are glued to my blood-stained palm. He reaches into his pocket and pulls out a rag that he hands to me.

"In the Golden Wulver Pub, that shadow lurker—Sonja—told me I smelled of death..." *But not as the sick smell of death... You bask in it.* Her words ring in my mind.

"That was the night I met you. You caused quite a scene, trying to stab the shadow lurker with your dinner knife. You were angry or frightened then, weren't you?" I nod. I had been frightened from the moment she approached our table, and the anger—well, that hadn't ceased since I'd awoken in the tunnels of Gairdín after the coup. "What about when you met the faerie leader—were you frightened or angry then?"

Eoghan boffs. "Was she? She set a tent on fire as she stormed the camp." He glows with amusement, and my cheeks burn red with equal amounts of embarrassment.

"Hmm..." Gálgalesh stares at the ground, deep in thought. "Do you lose control of your wielding when you are angry or frightened?"

The question is almost laughable. Only a few days ago, I had destroyed a dresser and had nearly thrown Bryn through a wall in my anger, and I had not even tried to wield. When I had attempted to throw the barrier up between Eoghan and I as he stormed into the room, I'd been unable to make it hold, although it's one of the spells I mastered long ago with little trouble at all.

"Yes."

"She's also communicating with me when her emotions are high, and she doesn't know she's done it. Her voice will shout in my mind, yet she claims she wasn't speaking to me. It's a bit fucking maddening, if I'm honest."

"Peadair loved to shriek at me through our magic. It was endlessly tiresome." Gálgalesh smiles playfully at the thought. "I wonder if perhaps your magic has re-manifested through your anger or strong negative emotions such as fear. As your healing magic is your individual gift, it would affect any common or other magic you possess and could make wielding more difficult or more powerful. Perhaps if we anger you and collect a sample, I would be able to examine it against your 'normal' sample, as it were, and see if the composition is different in any way."

"Well, if you want to make me mad, Eoghan has plenty of practice." My eyes darken, and he challenges me with a sensual smirk that almost makes me melt.

"A lover's quarrel will not cause the sort of emotional distress necessary for your magic to respond."

"You underestimate Maeve's temper, Gálgalesh." Eoghan's eyes are like fire, and I almost forget why we're here in the abandoned barracks in the first place.

"I should have never demanded you two work together. It was a lapse of judgement I continue to pay for each and every day." Eoghan steps closer to me, his fingers grazing my cheek. "If

I shall be needing her to smell of lust and sex as she does now, I will call upon you, Kael. In the meantime, I will test the existing sample to understand the new magic better. Now, it is blistering in this horrid sun, and I tire of watching you two give each other amorous looks each moment of the day. I am leaving."

Gálgalesh says nothing more as he walks back through the empty barracks, leaving us in the silence of the garden. What really is there to say? My magic has manifested, magic no one ever understood to begin with, yet it was coveted and made my life worthwhile to protect. Now that it's back, will that make a difference to anyone here? Will General Osian demand my blood as my father demanded it? Will Eoghan desire it for himself? Will they drain me and experiment on me too?

I stand from the wooden bench and turn to leave. Eoghan catches my arm. I flinch. He drops his hand and steps back respectfully, and my shoulders relax as I take in his unguarded expression. There's no greed or hunger in his eyes like when Rian ran his fingers through my hair and it danced with magic light. Eoghan looks at me as he had the first moment we'd truly met, as we sat at the end of that oversized bed in Fáintìrean and he began to unveil his secrets to me.

He doesn't push, doesn't ask questions. He simply steps away, giving me room to continue as he follows behind, careful not to stand too close. I have so much I still haven't told him, as though my secrets are meant to be kept—that they might spare us both heartache. If I don't speak them out loud, his rejection might never come. He doesn't ask, as though he doesn't want to know, as though he already knows it'll tear us apart if he hears it all from me.

He follows me back to the house, and the silence continues for the rest of the day.

———

"A PRETTY LITTLE THING INDEED!*" Bréanainn Doherty appraises me with his eyes as Rian nearly drags me into the room. I feel exposed, although fully clothed, as if I am a prized farm animal up for auction. "Your Majesty, she is radiant."*

My father nods, not at all pleased by the situation. He still hasn't spoken to me since he was told of the engagement. "The wedding will be at the castle, and it will be a private affair. You and your wife will be the only attendees from outside Caisleán Rialú's walls."

"Sire." Bréanainn Doherty bows his head respectfully towards the floor. "I have many wives, as you know..."

"Your son's mother, then." Bréanainn Doherty shrugs, as if he cannot place her. A sigh escapes my father's lips. "You may bring one wife of your choosing, and that is all."

"And what of your son? The Heir? Will he not be joining us on this blessed day?"

Bréanainn Doherty's grin makes my skin crawl. He is a man of the sea, and his rosy cheeks and brambly beard with medallions hanging from it, as if treasures from the far off lands, make him seem a dirty pirate at best. No wonder my father prefers the company of Rian at every meeting.

"He will not be attending." My father stiffens at the mention of my brother.

"What? Of course he will!" There is absolutely no way I'm letting this fight between my father and Cai get in the way of him being here for my wedding. "He will be here."

"Delightful! He is something of legend, your brother. It would be a shame to miss him." Doherty is almost giddy. "Now," he continues, and I watch my father close his eyes in exasperation. Mother would have been preferable to him now. She is much more hospitable. "I wonder if the rumors are true. I have heard this one," he points to me, "has a magic no one else in the kingdom possesses.

Is it why we have been forbidden from meeting her for so long? Is it true she heals from all injury?"

"Her magic is for me to know and you to not be concerned about."

My father grabs my arm roughly and makes to leave. He tires of this conversation, and my own discomfort is evident. Bréanainn Doherty clears his throat.

"Such secrets could break the marriage agreement between our families. I would hate to disgrace you in such a way, and although the reasons for the withdrawal of the proposal would be kept quiet, I could not guarantee rumors would not start in its wake. I would hate for the kingdom to believe dearest Maeve was unfaithful to her betrothed—or even that the king is untrustworthy to his people. I cannot imagine that would sit well with the people of Draío, especially since they have no solid proof their princess, in fact, exists. It will be difficult enough to inform them that the wedding will not be a public event."

My father tightens his grip on my arm as he glares down at Rian and his father. He is seething with anger, and his nails dig painfully into my skin. I attempt to pull free of him, but I wince as my shoulder cries out from the forcefulness of his grip. Finally, he relents and pulls forth the elaborate knife he carries ceremoniously at his side. The ancient blade glistens in the sunlight cascading through the windows, and Bréanainn Doherty's eyes glimmer as he takes it in. Oh gods, no, please! I yank my arm away from him, though his grip is like steel. He brings the blade to the crook of my elbow, and I feel the tearing of flesh as he drags it down to my wrist.

I'm not sure when I'd started screaming. Eoghan shakes me awake, a hand on either of my shoulders. My eyes snap open as my chest heaves in frantic gasps. I can't breathe. All I can feel is the pain radiating through my arm and the blood that poured from me onto the marble floor. I'm going to be sick. I push Eoghan's hands from my shoulders and race from the bed into the hall, to the bathroom where I throw myself down against the tile floor. Eoghan follows me in, crouching low beside me, rubbing soft circles against my back with the flat of his hand.

"You're all right, Maevie," he whispers as I heave and empty my stomach into the porcelain basin.

"Eoghan, I—" I'm sick again. Eoghan hushes me with quiet, calm sounds that match the slow, easy pace of his gentle caress.

"Before the Battle of Buaeth, I was sent to another battle on the eastern coast of the territory, where Iranndair was attempting to cross into Tinemallacht by way of the sea. We got caught in a bit of a mess there, our numbers too few and the Iranndairians much too proficient at fighting on the water. We were captured and taken to their base—Muertmarch, a death camp they had taken Draío prisoners to since the First War. They gave us no food, rancid water, and beat us for information about our battle plan. I remember thinking I might never be free again, nearly wishing for death to come before I suffered too long.

"About three weeks after we were taken, as we were living off desert rats and water that tasted of dragon piss, we found a tunnel used by the Iranndairians to transport supplies from their base in Lindoval to the camp. We couldn't believe it, they had left the whole fucking thing unguarded. We followed it and fought our way out when their men caught up to us, just as our forces approached on a rescue mission." He laughs in a sort of sad, understated way that's meant to hide the pain in his voice. "We got out that day, all thirty of us. We went back to fight and, well, you know the rest; but there were nights—there still are nights—when my mind goes back to that place, and it feels as it had when I thought I might not survive. Sometimes, I wonder if I even did. I wonder if I'll ever stop going back there and reliving what they did to us."

I roll over to face him, and he brushes my hair from my face with knowing gentleness. I want to tell him everything, for him to see the broken parts of me he might never be able to fix. I want him to know why he shouldn't love me the way he does—even though I need him to, more than I can explain.

"Sir Oli Raven used to experiment on me at my father's direction. He used to cut me up, drain me of my lifeblood, and take what was not his for research or pleasure or whatever he saw fit." Eoghan's hands ball into fists as his temperature rises. He takes a breath and wills them to soften again, remaining silent as he listens. "My father used to break me in his anger and watch as I healed, as if the pain meant nothing and my bones were made only to display his power and his rage. This arm," I hold out my right arm, and his tender touch passes along my skin, "was broken more than a dozen times on the evening Iranndair invaded on the eastern coast of Tinemallacht. I was fourteen."

His fingers slip from me, and his eyes meet mine, his mouth agape.

"Rian enjoyed watching as Oli Raven strapped me to the metal chair in his dungeon and filled his vials with my blood. He'd muse about its value, as though he could sell it to the highest bidder. He never cared that it made my body so weak I could barely stand, or that my head ached for hours as my magic tried to replenish itself. He only saw *it* was precious, not that I might be. I was used for their amusement and their benefit, and now I can't stop thinking about it, about how broken and worthless I am. Now that my magic's back, what does that make me? Valuable again? Another experiment?"

Eoghan wraps his arm around my waist, dragging me to him. He settles to a seat on the floor. His bare thighs are warm against my skin, and the feeling of his fingertips is so intense, it's as though I can feel every fiber of my being when he touches me. It's an electric, spiritual experience as his hands pass over every inch of me, and I feel for a moment that he has the power to stitch all my shattered pieces back together with the delicate way he moves, in reverence or tribute—like Gálgalesh spreading the ashes against the altar of the praying tree.

The bathroom is silent for an eternity as he holds me, trembling as he touches me but unable to keep the delicate, calming caresses at bay. I don't want to be the porcelain doll he cradles and tries not to break. I want to be the iron pulled from the Earth that's forged into his blade—unyielding and strong, a companion to the power that courses through him.

Finally, he takes my face in his hands and brings my forehead to his, forcing me to meet his gaze.

"Maeve Moran, you listen to me." His voice breaks as he speaks. "You are not broken, and you are *not* worthless. You mean more to me than anything or anyone in this whole kingdom, this entire world, has ever meant. Like I said that first night in the cottage at Fáintìrean, you are *everything*, and I will *never* let another person hurt you again. I'll kill them all for what they've done. I'm just sorry I couldn't stop them before now."

I struggle to find words as I force the tears away. "When Gálgalesh suggested experimenting..."

"Fuck Gálgalesh's experiments." His voice is a fierce growl. "I don't care what your magic can do beyond keeping you safe."

"But Eoghan, I'm broken." I have to tell him everything. I have to make him see that he won't want me, not like this. "I'm broken, and I can't give you what you want or what you need."

"You're not, Maeve." He holds me tighter as he speaks. "I

don't care about any of that. I don't care that you can or can't heal or how valuable your blood is. You are the only thing that I need."

"No, Eogh, you don't understand!"

"I do, and I don't care about any of it, Maevie."

His tone is so confident and sure... How could he know? How could he ever understand?

I open my mouth to speak again, but his hand falls from my cheek and to my stomach. His touch feels like a death sentence. I open my mouth to protest, but he shakes his head, his green eyes holding me, making the silence feel unbearable. I want to scream. I want to hit him and throw him from the room. I want him to stop touching me, as if some promise lays in a womb that doesn't exist.

I grab at his fingers, but he shakes his head. I can't hold the tears at bay anymore. I break completely, and my tears fall against his cheeks as I sob.

"I know, Maeve, and I don't care," he says firmly in almost a whisper and then drops his hand. "I had my suspicions the moment the moon first peaked at Báscogar when you arrived, and it was confirmed last week when you were the only woman in the outpost who could stand to roll out of bed. It doesn't matter to me."

"But you will care. What about your daughters? The ones you want to chase around the desert?"

"Maeve, I don't care about that." I begin to speak, and I falter when his beautiful green eyes make me come undone again. "I only said those things because you had refused to tell me your secrets. I didn't want you to feel as though I had suspected—or worse, that I had not and had no interest in a life with you. Do you want to stay with me? Will you marry me and allow me to love you as long as I live?" How can he not care? How can he still look at me as though I'm the only thing he can see? "Maeve," he wipes the tears away as he always does, "answer me. Do you want to stay with me? Will you allow me the honor of loving you? If not, I need to know."

"I…" I stammer. His eyes remain soft as he waits for me to speak. He's always so patient, so slow to anger, so kind. He brushes another tear from my cheek. "Yes," I breathe finally, as if I'm a bird being set free for the first time.

"Then that's all I need. *You* are all I need. You and you alone." He kisses my cheeks as he pulls me in close to his chest, and I wrap my legs around his waist. I weave my hands into his hair as he kisses my jaw and down my neck in unhurried affection. Then, he pulls away. "I have to show you something."

Without untangling me from him, he stands from the floor and carries me out of the bathroom, down the stairs, and to a small closet under the stairwell. He coaxes me from his arms, and my bare feet find the cool tile floor. When I'm standing firmly upright, he digs into the bottom of the tiny hidden storage space. He reemerges holding a small wooden crate with at least a dozen glass vials glowing crimson in the dull light.

"This arrived just after Cai left for Gairdín that last time. He never used them; he hated even the thought of them, and we would burn them in the courtyard each time they arrived. This is the last one. Why don't we burn them together and release the memory of what those bastards did to the gods?"

The last of it—the last bit of the torture and the pain. The last bit of the magic that existed before the coup; before I died and became something new completely. I am no longer a naïve child who had never gone beyond the castle walls, who thought love meant pain and tears. I am strong, I survived, and Eoghan saved me.

He takes my hand and leads me out into a small courtyard bathed in light, and in the quiet of the night, we set that crate on fire, watching it burn until the last trace of what I was disappears forever, engulfed in the dragon's healing flame.

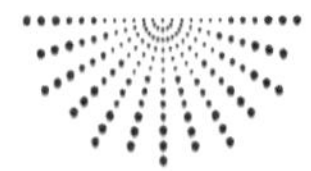

The bedsheets rustle as I bury my face in the pillows and pull the blankets over my head. We didn't get back to bed until the fire had finally burned out just before three in the morning. We couldn't have slept more than a couple of hours. My eyelids feel heavy, burning with exhaustion. The mattress sags next to me, and then footsteps tap quietly against the tile floor, and I know Eoghan is awake.

"Mmm," I groan in protest.

"Go back to sleep," Eoghan whispers from the side of the bed as the metal of his belt buckle tings softly. "It's still too early."

"Where are you going?" My voice is heavy with sleep.

"There's been an attack on an outpost near the Gálamáistir border, and they need fighters. Lo, Finn, River, and I are heading there now. Bryn and Sullivan will stay in Gobaith with you. Spend the day with Dedra, and I'll be back later."

He leans down and kisses my hair.

There's been an attack, no doubt from Rian and his men. There had been attacks nearly every day since we arrived in Tinemallacht, along with continued demands for me and

Eoghan to be handed over. From what I've gathered, though, Gálgalesh's whereabouts are still unknown. A miracle from the gods—if they exist. Had Rian known Gálgalesh too was here, I doubt he would do anything short of obliterate each and every man, woman, and child to get his hands on us.

"I'll come with you."

I rub my eyes and sit up from my pillow. I don't wait for him to agree before I begin to find my clothes and pull them on.

"You're exhausted," he says. I ignore him. "Wait." He turns to the dresser and opens a drawer. He digs around inside and then hands me a set of Tinemallacht Tans, the desert fighting pants and shirt commonly worn by the Fire Cursed soldiers. "Wear these."

The Tans are my size and brand new. He had known he would be taking me with him to fight and had prepared for the certainty of it. I strip off the linen pants and shirt I had haphazardly pulled on and replace them with the clothes that match Eoghan's. He nods as I finish and then takes my daggers and their holsters from my nightstand. He kneels in front of me and wraps the straps around my thigh.

"These can be tricky with the pants." He pulls the leather until it holds firm, though not too tightly, to my leg. He secures the buckle and moves on to the next one. "I'm not sure what we're walking into, so I need you to promise me you'll stay back if I ask." He secures the second holster to my thigh and then places the daggers into their sheaths. "I won't ask you to stay here, but please, let me keep you safe."

I nod. He knows asking me is a losing battle anyway; at least he isn't fighting me this time. He runs his hands against my thighs once and then rises. He grabs his own daggers, plenty more than I carry myself, and his sword, holstering them all before he makes for the hall. I follow him out of the room and down the stairs, where Finn and River wait in the entryway. Surprise fills their expressions when they see me. Wisely, however, they say nothing as Eoghan closes the gap between them.

"Where's Lo?" he asks.

"Waiting for us at the gate. My father is coming with us." Finn's voice is more serious than usual, and I realize I've never seen any of them as soldiers before. "It's bad, Eogh."

Finn gives a quiet glance my way, and Eoghan is silent for a long moment before he shakes his head and Finn nods.

"Let's get going then."

We leave the house and walk down the silent, deserted road toward the outpost gates. I can barely keep up with the three men, their long strides taking me nearly twice as many steps to match. As we cross the square, the air is flat, not a single bit of breeze passing through. The temperature, even this early in the morning, is stifling. I see Bryn and Lowri standing together, waiting for us just past the outpost boundary.

"What's she doing here?" Lowri snaps as we reach them.

"She's coming with us. I don't want to hear about it; we don't have time."

Eoghan greets Officer Rhodes with a silent gesture. I've only ever heard Finn's dad speak once or twice, and it seems as though once again conversation will be limited to gestures and stares.

"You're an idiot, Eogh." Lowri glowers down at me.

"And you're acting like a bitch. Let's get the fuck out of here before Bellrúg is overrun."

Lowri seethes. If looks could kill, we would all fall dead in the sand for the way her eyes glow with hate and fire. I wonder if she'll ever stop looking at me that way—as though I am the most dangerous thing to them all—or if she'll hate me until the sun finally sets in Tinemallacht forever.

Officer Rhodes opens a portal, and bloodcurdling

screams meet our ears. Lowri, Finn, and River step through and disappear from sight. Eoghan places his hand on my back.

"We're being dropped off outside the outpost. If it's too bad, I'll send you back through to Bryn."

"No." I take a step toward the portal and grip the hilt of my daggers to keep my hands from shaking. "I'm staying."

Eoghan sighs and then nudges me forward. We step through together, and instantly, the sky is darker, and it takes a moment for my eyes to adjust. Bellrúg sits so close to the Gálamáistir border, it's almost not in Tinemallacht at all. The early morning sun just starting to rise in the other territories shines dimly, leaving a sort of haze over the scene. But the screams—they are louder now that we've left Gobaith, if that's even possible.

The outpost of Bellrúg, sits not far off at the bottom of the small sand dune we've been dropped off on. It's larger than Gobaith and less of a military training camp. From what I can see, shops line the square, and houses reach to the border, where the imposing forest of Gálamáistir rises like a natural barrier. On the other side, buried in the trees, is a border checkpoint from which a continual volley is shot across the sky. Each time they land, the screams reignite with vigor. There's no fire, however, and no sounds of cannon blasts or streaks of light through the sky.

"What's happening?" I ask as I take in the scene and cover my ears to quiet the screams.

"Lo?" Eoghan asks. Lowri remains silent, her body frozen as she looks out along the valley to Bellrúg. He sighs in frustration, reaching toward her and pulling what looks like a spyglass from her hands. He places it to his eye. "You have got to be fucking kidding me!"

"What?"

I yank the spyglass from him and aim it toward the

outpost. Chaos erupts in the streets, people running for cover as glass orbs of some kind fall heavily from the sky, crashing down and breaking open, spraying a purple liquid in every direction. I watch as some of the orbs hit civilians dead on; they scream out in pain and fall to the ground, writhing as their skin boils and burns. Others are doused with the rebounding splashes of potion as they crash in unrelenting streams—and they, too, fall.

"What is that?"

"Acid rain," Eoghan bites. "Its use has been absolutely forbidden since the First War. It never stops burning. You can't wash it away. The victim will burn endlessly until their body finally gives up…or their mind does, and they take their own life."

The spyglass falls into the sand beside me. What sort of monster burns innocent civilians to death? How could anyone be so cruel?

Lowri's hands are shaking, and she hasn't said a word. Finn and River swear under their breaths as the cries from below continue.

"What do we do?" Eoghan's words are directed at Officer Rhodes this time.

"You try to slow the volley as much as you can from here. Any closer, and they'll be able to track you. Finn and River, you get inside the outpost and try to get as many civilians out to this dune. Lo and I will try to reach the border and take out their numbers."

Everyone agrees, but I feel utterly useless. There's nothing for me to do besides sit and watch. Finn and River race down the hill together, and Officer Rhodes opens a portal somewhere within the darkness of the trees. Lowri unsheathes a sword from her back—the twin to Eoghan's own—and pushes herself through the portal. Officer Rhodes follows before it closes behind them.

"What can I do?" I ask. My stomach feels sick from the shouts of the men and women below, and I almost collapse as I hear a child cry out for its mother so loudly, it's as though they are crying out for the gods themselves.

"Keep me focused. Watch for anyone approaching."

Eoghan throws out his hands to wield, and I watch as the cascading volley slows its descent, though it does not cease. We all know Eoghan alone can't make it stop. Cai could have redirected them, but Eoghan can only slow them. We need something more.

Another volley crashes into the houses in the residential quarters, away from the square. Lights flash in the windows as residents race from their homes, screaming and crying or carrying their loved ones from the wreckage as they too burn endlessly. Somewhere in the chaos, River and Finn are trying to dodge the oncoming barrage and get the civilians to our position. Only one or two have made it out of the gates since we arrived, running past us out into the Barrens for safety.

"Eogh, let me help!" I shout over the chaos of crashing glass and wailing cries.

He shakes his head, not breaking his gaze from the attack. "You can't wield! What if they see you? They'll tell Rian about the faerie magic!"

"Do we have a choice? Everyone is going to die if we don't do something!"

"I'm not going to risk it. I can stop this."

The next volley is comprised of nearly two hundred orbs soaring through the air, and Eoghan is breathless as he hits them with every bit of magic he has. He's not built to wield against so many opponents coming from every direction. A handful would certainly be manageable, a few dozen would create little challenge for his magic, but two hundred sepa-rate attacks is impossible for any single wielder to match. He slows nearly half as the others race through unaffected and crash into Bellrúg with such force, lamp posts and storefront porticos are demolished on impact.

"Let me help you," I demand again, and he groans his exasperation. He doesn't have the energy to fight me anymore.

Think, Maeve! I demand and wrestle with anything I can do to help. The skies need to be protected. If we can't stop the barrage from coming, we need to keep it from hitting the outpost. My mind races to the blue shield I'd become so good at erecting while at Báscogar, and I remember how I would throw up my daggers then shield my face as they barreled back down toward me. I've never made a shield so large before, but now seems like the perfect time to test it out. I reach for the faerie magic, and it's already humming, ready to wield. I concentrate on the outpost below and send the command down the line. An eruption of blue falls like a canopy over the settlement and covers at least ninety percent of it, but the outlining perimeter of the outpost is still exposed. I urge the magic to expand, but I have nothing left to give.

"That's all I can do," I breathe and hold my concentration as we watch the orbs crash and disintegrate against the shield.

"It's great, Maevie. You're great." Eoghan pants as he continues to wield. "We need to get as many people out as we can before you drop that shield."

Shit, he's right. If the shield falls, no one will be able to escape the downpour of deadly potion and broken glass. I hadn't thought of that when I erected it.

"On it." I will the shield to hold true while I send my voice down the one-way communication line of faerie magic. *I'll hold the shield as long as I can. Get everyone to the dunes, NOW!*

I can't tell if my message made it to Finn or River, but we wait, growing in exhaustion with each passing breath. Then, like rushes of small waves at the seashore, clusters of people begin to race out of the outpost gates in steady streams, some helping the screaming wounded, and others thankfully unharmed. We count as fifty, one hundred, two hundred, five hundred rush toward us on the dunes.

Then, out of the corner of my eye in the growing light of day, red and blue bolts of light jet across the wooded compound of the Gálamáistir border checkpoint, another and another as the rush of civilians slows. Light flashes, and we watch as the bolt only makes it feet from its wielder and then rebounds off a shining blade of a long sword. Down the wielder falls. Eoghan lets out a soft, tired laugh as we watch the battle play out in streaks of light ricocheting in all directions before being extinguished entirely. The response comes as the volleys of acid rain slow and, finally, cease.

Shouting rises from the border, and within moments, Lowri and Officer Rhodes race through a new portal, falling into the dunes as it snaps shut on the incoming royal soldiers. They're breathless, on their hands and knees in the sand.

"Good job," Officer Rhodes gasps in heavy pants. "Is everyone out?"

My eyes dart toward the Bellrúg gates at the same time as the others, and we gasp in unison as our eyes meet the last two figures exiting the outpost. Eoghan is on his feet, racing down the hill before I can process what's happening. Lowri screams profanities and then points to the far end of the outpost, where the blue light of the shield illuminates the perimeter walls. Royal soldiers round the top, making their way toward us.

"Drop the shield!" Lowri shouts.

"What about Eoghan?"

"He'll be fine! He'll be clear of it! Drop it now!"

I relent. The blue shield disappears from overhead, and

like the roar of a waterfall, acid falls from the sky and across the settlement in torrential sheets. Screaming renews from below, this time from the soldiers who had been unlucky enough to clear the wall. The others shout orders of retreat into the forest.

Lowri, Officer Rhodes, and I stand and race down the soft dune to Eoghan. He's stopped halfway down, where he caught up to Finn, standing winded and battered. River lies in the red sand, writhing and screaming in pain.

"We were clearing out one of the housing blocks when an orb crashed through the awning where River stood. It caught him square in the face and ran down his chest." Finn's eyes are downcast while Eoghan's are smoldering with rage. "It spared his shoulders and arms because of his dragon leather, but..."

I look down, and I nearly lose my footing. River's face is red and mutilated. The acid has burned the skin, leaving angry, open wounds. He reaches to cup his eyes, which are no doubt burned as well. Though his leather jacket seems untouched, his shirt has melted away, and his chest has welts and burns where the acid has reached.

"Get him and everyone else to the medic camp near the sea," Eoghan orders, and Officer Rhodes wields to open a portal in front of us. Lowri stands as she shouts orders to the civilians around us.

"Eogh." Finn's voice is low. "The seal on the vials...they were inscribed with 'TD'."

Eoghan's glare turns lethal, and his teeth clench as his skin boils.

"Are you sure?" he bites out, and Finn nods his head.

I've never seen Eoghan so angry. He storms off, helping others toward the portal in feverish, forceful demands. There's no longer even a semblance of softness in his features; all that remains is a brutal warrior ready to kill.

I fall into the sand beside River and hush him quietly as the dunes empty. We all know what this means. The healers at the medic camp won't be able to help River or many of the others. The best we can hope for is that they won't suffer longer than necessary. I take his hand timidly in my own and fight back everything inside me that wants to curse the gods for what they've done. River, the man who barreled through my door at the prison to get a good look at me, to offer me friendship in a place where nothing but violence and death existed, the man who had helped save me without question simply because Eoghan loved me…and that was enough of a reason for him. I pat his hand as he chokes back his pain.

"Maeve," he whispers, his voice only a rasp from the acid that has burned through his throat.

"Shh, River," I beg. He tries again to speak.

"Maeve, my princess. For you, we fight and gladly die."

Tears stream down my cheeks as Lowri approaches and helps Finn lift River from the sand. They walk him through the portal, and Officer Rhodes closes it behind them.

"Let's go, Maevie," Eoghan says from somewhere beside me, and I turn, my vision blurred with tears. He places his hand gently around my elbow and helps me up—together, we walk back to the quiet gates of Gobaith.

CHAPTER NINETEEN

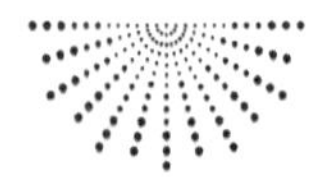

Dear Evie,

Thank you for your letter. I miss you more than I could miss anyone in the world. I'm happy to hear you're enjoying the planning of your wedding, though I've always thought it would be torture to have Mother help plan anything so extravagant. You are braver than I'll ever be.

I'm sorry to have to let you down once again, but I will not be attending your wedding ceremony. I fear traveling to the Capital now might be the end of me—I'm not sure I'd survive it. I'm not sure either of us would—and now, I think I might actually have good reason to stay alive a bit longer. You'll never forgive me for it, I know. Just please trust me when I say it's for both of our goods that I stay here for now until I can figure out what to do next.

I have so much to tell you, Evie, about life and love and the meaning of it all. Please forgive me, and promise me you'll come to Tinemallacht one day so we can be united again. Then, I can finally tell you the truth about everything. Until we meet again, if ever you are in trouble, find Tiernan Damaris. He's the only one in Gairdin you can trust.

Loving you always,
Cai

UNSENT CORRESPONDENCE

If I ever thought Eoghan was capable of murder, the look on his face would confirm it. I can't bear to look at him for the terror his quiet rage brings forth, bubbling just under the surface, waiting for the moment to strike. He doesn't speak, barely even breathes, his inhalations and exhalations coming heavy and deep. If I touch him, will he lose all the control he is fighting to keep? I watch his hands clench and flex, and the low smoldering fire dances across his palms as I take a step to my right, creating the smallest gap between us.

Eoghan passes through the gates of Gobaith and up toward the house. I race forward to keep up, but there is such determination in his stride, I can only hope to follow along behind him. Bryn is in the square, working through his early morning exercises, and he stops as he spots us approaching. Had it only been a little more than an hour since we'd left? Bryn bounds forward to meet us before he registers Eoghan's glare and moves out of his path.

"What's happened?" he asks as he falls in step at my side.

"It was terrible." I can't bring myself to elaborate as I try to catch my breath and keep pace.

"Lo?"

"She's fine." Eoghan pays us no mind as he starts up the wood-planked road. "Eogh, slow down," I beg. He ignores me completely and passes our front door. Instead, he turns to Áine's, throwing it open with a bang as he steps over the threshold. "Eoghan! What are you—"

He raises his hand to silence me. He doesn't even turn to look at me, his eyes darting through the house as Áine peeks out of her bedroom door, her hair disheveled and her eyes heavy with sleep.

"Where is he?" he demands in a deep, guttural growl.

"Who?" Gálgalesh appears from a second bedroom off the kitchen, his long hair braided down his back, wearing a pair of dark brown pajamas.

"The fucking alchemist! Where is Damaris?"

The door opens to the small sitting room, and Dedra and Tiernan crane their necks from just beyond. Tiernan places his glasses against the bridge of his nose and stretches his arms. He moves forward into the kitchen at the sight of us, his feet bare against the tile.

"Don't you have any manners at all, Kael? Do you not know what time it is?"

Tiernan yawns as Eoghan crashes into him, grabbing him around the neck and pushing him against the wall with such force, the house shakes. Dedra shrieks, Áine throws her hand over her mouth as she gasps, Gálgalesh swears loudly, and

Bryn and I race toward them, pulling at Eoghan's arm. His grip remains around Tiernan's neck.

"ACID RAIN?" Eoghan bellows, spit flying from his mouth and landing on Tiernan's face. "ACID RAIN? THAT'S WHAT YOU'VE BEEN WORKING ON IN THE CAPITAL FOR YEARS ON END? AN ILLEGAL WEAPON OF DESTRUCTION?"

I still, my hands gripping Eoghan's scalding biceps. Finn had told Eoghan the seal on the vials of the acid potions were inscribed with 'TD'. Tiernan had made the weapons used against the outpost at Bellrúg. He had aided—knowingly or not—in the killing of countless innocents. Bile rises in my throat at the thought, and Tiernan's eyes grow wider at each of Eoghan's words.

"What happened?" Tiernan rasps, and Eoghan slams him against the wall again.

"WHAT HAPPENED? PEOPLE DIED, YOU TRAI-TOROUS BASTARD!"

"Eoghan!" I pull on his arm, but he ignores me, his skin burning my own.

"DID YOU MAKE DOHERTY AND HIS FATHER A STOCKPILE BEFORE YOU CAME HERE SO HE COULD TRY TO KILL US ALL? ACID RAIN IS ILLEGAL, DAMARIS!"

"I know!" Tiernan beats at Eoghan's arm. Eoghan has him by at least fifty pounds and doesn't ease his grip. "I didn't..." He gasps for breath. "I didn't make it for Doherty."

"THEN WHY THE FUCK IS YOUR NAME ON THEIR WEAPONS?"

"I made it for her father!" Tiernan points in my direction. This time, I actually might be sick. My head begins to spin, and blood rushes in my ears. "Now let me go so I can explain!"

Eoghan growls angrily and then drops his hand from

Tiernan's throat. Tiernan sinks toward the floor, his hands on his knees as he sucks in long, difficult breaths. Áine rushes forward and, with an admonishing look toward Eoghan, hands Tiernan a glass of water, which he accepts with a gruff word of thanks. Eoghan's still furious beyond recognition; all the same, he relents, placing his hands in the air before reaching for mine and grabbing it so tightly, I almost pull away in shock. He eases. As Tiernan stands, I pull Eoghan back a pace to put some distance between them.

"Start speaking now, before I kill you right here, Damaris."

"We have been manufacturing acid rain for the past four years. It's pretty much all we've been making at the Capital's base. There's a stockpile of the stuff, about a million vials of it at least, down in the vaults. We were supposed to begin shipping it here in the spring."

"Why? Why would we need it?" Eoghan's hand is hot around my own, and I tap him softly. He looks down and exhales, the heat dissipating slightly.

"Because," Tiernan's eyes close for a long moment as he breathes in and out, "King Cashel was going to order an invasion of Iranndair by the Tinemallachts and an invasion of Dún by Romiodóg soldiers this year. He wanted complete control of the continent, even if that meant using all the weapons at our disposal."

Eoghan takes a step forward, and I pull him back toward me. Bryn steps up and places himself at both men's sides so he might be able to intervene if a fight were to break out between them again.

"Why did you agree? You *knew* what you were creating and what it's capable of, and you still made it."

"What was I to do? I'm a soldier just like you! I have orders!"

"You say 'no'! You refuse, and then you come to Tinemallacht, where we could protect you! You have some sort of honor! But, of course, you have none, and now your name is stamped all over the weapons killing us!"

Tiernan lets out a frustrated groan. He's angry now, and his expression matches the deadly one on Eoghan's face. He moves toward us this time and closes the gap between them. He's just shorter than Eoghan by less than a handful of inches, but in his anger, you might be forgiven for thinking they were the same height. Bryn begins to step in before Eoghan shakes him off; he releases my hand and gently pushes me out of the way.

"Do you have *any* idea why I was in the Capital in the first place? Of course not. No, Eoghan Kael can't comprehend a soldier could have any other job than to throw themselves into battle. There's no greater honor than being in the fight, is there?" Eoghan's fists ball at his sides. He doesn't move, doesn't speak. "Cai ordered me to the Capital to find out which potions and tonics Sir Oli Raven was creating. I was to stay there at *all* costs until he got the information he could, and only then was I allowed to leave."

"He wouldn't order you to make acid rain. He wouldn't have wanted you to do that."

"He ordered me to do *anything* to stay there and get the information he needed because it was important to the cause! You talk about honor as if you hiding away in Báscogar, playing with swords all day, trying to learn how to fight without your magic, is more honorable than anything else we were ordered to do. *Everyone* has sacrificed, Kael. For him…and now for her. Some of us had to sacrifice our very souls for this."

Eoghan's rage does not cease. He does not relent his stance over Tiernan or his piercing glare. For just an instant, though, I watch as something flashes through his eyes.

Shame? Guilt? It disappears as quickly as it comes, but for a moment, it finds its way through the solid stone of his anger.

"Now your sacrifice is being used to kill innocent civilians," he growls. "Was it worth it?"

"I don't know. I guess if we ever figure out what Cai was up to, it might be. All I know is, I'd rather have to live with what I did than have to live with the regret if I'd never done it."

"I'll remind you of that when it's your family dying out there, Damaris."

Eoghan turns and shoves his hand through his hair as he storms out of the house, leaving the rest of us standing in silence in his wake. Tiernan's shoulders begin to sink, the fight that held him so tall to face Eoghan vanishing now.

"What happened, woman? Who have we lost?" Gálgalesh asks.

"River. He's at the medic camp by the sea," I say, and the whole room gasps.

Tiernan sinks back against the wall to the floor, his hands falling over his face and his shoulders heaving in silent sobs. Dedra crosses the threshold and sits beside him on the kitchen floor. I hadn't ever realized or thought River and Finn might be friends of Tiernan's as well. I hadn't thought that perhaps they too had spent time with him, gotten to know him beyond these few weeks we'd been in Tinemallacht, but of course they had. They were all fighting on the same side, following the Leader. They had to have known each other, spent time together, fought together, shared meals at the same table. Where I could count the amount of meaningful friendships I had throughout my life on one hand, I can't begin to know what friendships these men had shared with one another, bonded by their trust in the one they had thought might save them from something they could not even comprehend.

I turn and quietly walk out the front door onto the street, still silent as the morning passes slowly and the residents of the outpost only just begin to wake. *I need to find Eoghan. I need to make sure he's okay.* I walk toward the center of the outpost, only to find, when I reach the bottom of the road, that it's empty. *Perhaps he's gone to where River lived.* I hadn't ever been to River's home in Gobaith. As a single, enlisted soldier, I'm sure he lived in the upper barracks, away from the small, quiet streets of officers and their families. I cross down the furthest road above the rest of the settlement and make my way to the large building where most of the Fire Cursed soldiers live.

My footsteps echo across the tile in the large, open expanse of the hall as I push the barrack's door away and enter. Not a single soldier walks through the open chamber, identical to the lower barracks I had visited yesterday with Gálgalesh and Eoghan. The marble columns tower around me to the painted ceilings depicting dragons and battles in colors that awaken the senses. I weave through small clusters of wooden couches with cushions in blues and greens, where soldiers might relax after a long day in the sun and recant stories of valor in triumphant tones.

I continue to the quiet halls where the boarders sleep, so much like the prison, I can almost feel the phantom chill of the snow and wind. Here, the oppression is different—one the Tinemallachts so often choose, to be anything in this world that sees them as nothing. A life of duty here brings honor to one's family and name, so it's worth the price, worth living in these bare halls and tiny dorms. It would've been easy for River to transition to a life at Báscogar from this place.

Eoghan isn't here, I finally decide as I reach the end of the long passageway. I lean against the wall and sink down to the floor. If it hadn't been for me, Rian's men would have never attacked Bellrúg. Those people wouldn't have died if I wouldn't have come here. How many have already lost their lives on account of me? Am I worth their sacrifice, or is Eoghan simply protecting me in vain? Surely, I'm not worth this.

"What are you doing here, Mayhem?"

Eoghan stands halfway down the corridor, his hands in his pockets, years of ceaseless, quiet rage still clouding his beautiful features.

"Looking for you." I move to meet him. He takes a step backward, and his mask betrays him with the faintest quiver of his lower lip.

"I'm terrible company at the moment."

He's asking you to walk away. Don't. I take a timid step, my boots sounding like thunder in the empty hall. He flinches, his body rigid. I take another, and he holds up his hand to stop my forward progression toward him. I ignore his silent demand. I want to hold him, want to tear that warrior's mask away from him so he can feel. I want to share his pain, and then I want to take it away from him forever.

"You're not angry with Tiernan." I'm only steps from him now, and I can feel his anger grow at the name.

"Of course I'm angry with Tiernan. If he hadn't done what he did—"

"Then, my father would've compelled someone else to, Tiernan would be dead, and Rian would still have all the weapons he needed to do what he did. We *both* know Rian was the one who did this to River and those people in Bellrúg." The toes of my boots touch his as I stop in front of him. I've never seen him so undone before. He grasps on to every bit of control he has in him as he keeps his hands at his sides. "You're not angry with Tiernan for this—you're angry with Tiernan because he was in Gairdín when Cai died, and he wasn't able to stop it. You're angry with Tiernan because of

Lowri. Every time Tiernan doesn't stop bad things from happening, you blame him. It isn't his fault, Eogh. You could never have stopped it either. You have to forgive him—for Lowri and for Cai *and* for this."

Eoghan cracks, his hands trembling. Pain, sadness, and fear flood to the surface like a tidal wave. What had he carried for all this time? What had he felt? Had he ever let it come to the surface in anything other than fury? Had he spent quiet moments in his freezing room at Báscogar, allowing the tears to fall where they may, or had he raised his sword and fist in the arena, driving the pain so far away, he forgot what sadness had felt like? Had he—like me—become numb to anything beyond the desire to blame someone, anyone, for the hole torn into his heart?

I reach for him, and he leans away from my touch. My fingers pause for a moment in the space between us as I find his gaze, willing him back to me. I try again, and the muscles in his jaw flinch, though he does not back away this time as my hand touches his cheek.

"Forgive him, Eoghan. Please."

He shakes his head.

"I don't know if I can." His voice breaks. My fingers slide up into his hair, and I hold him to me, not letting him turn away.

"I'm here because of Tiernan. I would have never met you if he would not have saved me and sent me to train with *you*. He is not your enemy. He is not mine. He is one of us, and if we're going to survive this and finish what Cai started, we need him. Please, Eogh."

As if the world comes crashing down around us, Eoghan releases his pain and sorrow for the first time. He falls to his knees and grips my legs as he sobs, the sound of his tears echoing through the halls. He cries until the legs of my pants are drenched—until the sound of his sobs brings me to my own knees and my tears fall anew. Eoghan, always so strong and sure, is weak and trembling in my arms. The weight of this war, of the losses we share and will share until the end, falls heavy on our shoulders.

It's not until the ceaseless tears dry up that Eoghan nods into my chest, and we rise together to find Tiernan and head to the medic camp by the sea.

CHAPTER TWENTY

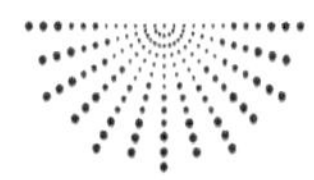

Dear Evie,

Thank you for your letter. I certainly miss you more than words could ever say. I will be happy to attend your wedding on the twenty-third of Lúnasa; of course, I would never miss it.

Please don't tell Father of my arrival, as I'll be staying at the military base in the Capital. I will, however, be attending your wedding supper and the ceremony before I return to Tinemallacht.

Perhaps you can slip away in one last rebellious act and meet us at the base for a pre-wedding celebration of our own.

Be safe. I love you endlessly.

-Cai

———

The medic camp is filled at every corner with wounded and dying Tinemallacht men and women. It seems the children succumbed to their injuries first, their cries only echoing in our souls now as we lean over the sickbeds, applying Iaslium Gum to the burns that will never cease their searing.

Eoghan crouches by the bed of a woman, her hands burned beyond saving, though the medics are fairly confident it will only be her hands she'll lose, rather than her life. He runs his fingers softly across her forehead while whispering comforts just between them, and I register the gold wielding cuffs still attached to his wrists. I hadn't noticed them before today. Now, I can't remember a moment since we've been here that he hasn't been wearing them. How many times has he left the outpost for battle since we arrived in Tinemallacht? How much sorrow has he witnessed?

I pass through the tent to the next, where the more critically injured lie in near silence, apart from low moans and choking cries. River is here, at the far side of the tent, Lowri at his side. She hasn't left, hasn't even moved since their arrival; instead, she chooses to hold River's hand day and night. I step quietly to his side and crouch beside him, taking his free hand.

"How is he?" I ask.

Lowri's eyes are red and swollen, and her usual glare is replaced by a look of such hopelessness, I can almost feel my own tears begin to well.

"He can't hear you anymore. He's almost gone." She squeezes his hand, and I feel the lightest response of his own —almost a whisper of pressure against my fingers. "I warned him." Her words are wet with tears. "I told him if he came with us, he wouldn't be coming back. I told him, and he didn't care. He said, 'we make our own luck, Lo', as if I hadn't seen the burns and heard the screams. They never listen."

River begins to cough with a strained gurgle that makes me ill. Lowri picks up a damp cloth and pats it against his disfigured throat to ease the heat and irritation as the acid continues to burn clear through. River had known he would lose his life, and still, he didn't care. He had run willingly into Bellrúg to save the others. I can't comprehend such bravery. I lift his hand to my mouth and kiss it softly.

And what of Lowri? She'd warned him of his fate, had asked him not to come, and yet, he still had. How she can bear it, I'll never know.

Eoghan and Tiernan cross the tent and crouch on either side of River as Lowri and I move aside to make room. Tiernan's tired eyes take River in. His hands are covered in Iaslium Gum, his brow sweaty from the stifling heat of the tents. He pulls a cloth from his pocket and wipes his palms clean while shaking his head solemnly.

"The Iaslium Gum won't heal any of his burns. The impact was too dead on. Nothing can take the burning away. If he hadn't been drenched in the acid, it might've been able to ease the pain to a manageable degree, but not like this. I'm sorry." His eyes meet River's face, and he whispers again, "I'm sorry."

Eoghan's shoulders sag as the last bit of hope leaves him. He pats River's hand and then rips a small ribbon of a patch off his own shoulder and holds it to River's sleeve.

"Where's Dedra?" He looks around, and Lowri stands.

"I'll get her." She walks out of the tent to find Dedra, who had followed Finn to get some much-needed sea air.

"It's a patch of valor," Eoghan explains. "Enlisted men aren't eligible to receive them—only officers in the Royal Army who've studied at the academy."

Tiernan examines his own dark brown jacket, long and heavy, the alchemists' regalia. He yanks at his blue ribbon on his shoulder and tears it from his sleeve, then places it next to Eoghan's. Dedra reenters the tent to kneel next to Eoghan at River's side. Wordlessly, she takes out a spool of thread and a needle from her pocket, getting to work adhering the patches to River's dragon leather jacket.

"Come with me, Maevie," Eoghan whispers as Dedra finishes and River's breathing stills to finality.

I can't stand to be here anymore with the wounded and the dying. I can't stand to listen to their cries for one more moment. Eoghan's pinky brushes mine in a featherlight motion that reminds me he's here, he's still alive, and although pain and suffering and loss has marred us today, I'm still here too.

We leave the tent. Eoghan's gaze is distant, and I know his thoughts are anywhere but with me. I almost feel selfish for wishing they were. He walks us across the red sand of the medic camp as healers rush past us with tonics and tools to cut and suture. We reach another canvas tent, the flaps closed to block the desert wind, and Eoghan urges me forward. I hesitate, unwilling to witness more heartache. He motions again in an understanding yet persistent sort of way, and I dip my head as I relent and step through.

What I find is not the injured and dying, and the relentless cries of suffering don't meet my ears. Instead, standing around the empty tent are at least two dozen faces I have never seen before. Finn, Arran Sullivan, Trystan Price, Bode, and the other men who traveled with us to Tinemallacht from Báscogar, as well as Gálgalesh, all stand in the cramped space, chatting amongst the others in quiet, solemn voices. Everyone's faces are downcast, disheartened, full of worry, but as we join them, their expressions change, almost like hope has been reignited within them once more.

Eoghan places his hand on the small of my back and urges me into the center of the group. Every eye in the tent follows me, and I feel self-conscious.

"Maeve, it's time you meet the Leader's men."

———

WE RETURN to Gobaith when the day turns to evening, and the heaviness of the camps gives way to the fatigue of our bodies. I can barely stand. I can't remember the last time I had a proper sleep of more than a couple of hours. Eoghan walks me into the house and guides me to the sitting room, where he helps me to the sofa. I yawn and lean my head against the arm.

"You need to eat something before you sleep."

"Ever my protector," I tease as my eyes fall shut.

"Always."

I hear his boots against the floor as he heads to the kitchen, and I settle into the soft cushions. Sleep, the glorious calm that calls us to rest and dream. What I wouldn't do to sleep. I feel my boots hit the floor as my feet fall from the sofa, and my eyes snap open for a moment, then fall closed again.

I had met a cohort of men and women today at the medic camp who I will be unlikely to ever forget. Solace, Ravine, Thatcher, and Bardot are all iron smiths from Romiodóg, who specialize in nearly indestructible weaponry, most notably the twin long swords Eoghan and Lowri carry. St. James, Monroe, and Huxley first met Eoghan, Tiernan, and Cai at the military academy, where they were learning to fly airships for the Gálamáistir units and now run a flight unit in secret within the territory. Ashbluff, Wix, Gannon, Katz, and Fleet are all skilled in espionage and concealment. Chevalier, Fotos, Ford, Landry, Luna, MacCrimmon, Edris, Agha, and Dagon—all had served with my brother and still serve his cause in the wake of his death.

I can't comprehend that these men and women are

just the tip of what Cai started. They are only the leaders and commanders of his men, more numerous than I have been able to witness—and they are good. Every one of them in that room was genuine, honorable, the sort of individual I would trust with my life. Still, it begs the question: why had Cai needed them? To what ends would he need spies and iron smiths and airship pilots? What did he know? Why did he keep his secrets so close, none of them knew anything beyond the tasks they were given to complete?

Eoghan returns with a bowl of Sunfire Grain and vegetables, a common desert dish consisting of a crop from the fields of the far east, herbs, and ale simmered in a large pot until the grains become tender. He carries a glass of water with him and sits in front of me on the low table. He coaxes me to rise from the arm of the sofa and hands me the bowl. I take it from his hands and inhale the scent.

"Eat, and then I'll get you to bed before I leave." Eoghan takes a sip of the cool water before offering it to me. I shake my head, and he places it on the table beside him.

"Where are you going?" I lift the fork to my mouth, even though I have no desire for food. He watches me with interest.

"To Bastain to discuss what happened today. I'll be back before you wake in the morning, I promise."

"Eoghan, you need rest. When was the last time you had a proper night's sleep? You can't just keep going—"

"I'll be fine, Maevie. We can stay in bed the whole day tomorrow, if you desire."

He gives me a promising smirk that sends heat through my core and brings life to my tired mind, but his eyes are weary, and his shoulders sag with fatigue. How many times had he been called away in the night without me knowing? Had he slept at all this week? He's exhausted and, without proper rest, I'm not sure how much longer he'll be able to function.

"You need to sleep, Eogh. Can we go in the morning? I'll go with you." He shakes his head as he yawns into his fist.

"No, I have to leave tonight. There's a meeting with the Generals in an hour."

In an hour, he might be splayed out on the floor.

"Then go and stay there for the night. Bryn and I can ride into Bastain in the morning, and I'll meet you there before you wake."

"Are you sure?" He cocks one of his eyebrows in question.

"Yes. I'm a big girl. I can take on the dragons of the Barrens without you. Go; don't keep them waiting. I'll finish here and head to bed. You don't have to wait for me."

Eoghan appraises me before he rises from his seat on the table's edge. He leans in and kisses my hair softly, his fingers caressing my throat seductively with a featherlight touch, and I close my eyes. We stay captivated by one another for much longer than our exhausted minds can bear. Then, he stands to full height and exits the room.

I listen to his footsteps walk through the entryway and out the front door, and I fall back into the cushions of the sofa. I place the bowl of untouched food onto the table, and my eyes fall shut before I can find the strength to unlace my boots or walk myself up the stairs to the bedroom.

I'M WALKING down a familiar dark corridor lit only by torchlight and the faint gray of the eternal night sky visible through the open archways of the corridor leading to the eastern wing of boarding accommodations. Báscogar Prison. A chill wind whips past me as I walk, and my black cloak clings to my body.

I have received correspondence I've been waiting over a month for, and still, I know nothing of what I'm to make of it. It lends no answers to any of my questions, and my mind races with even more as I make my way to room 264.

I walk swiftly past a group of prisoners I know want nothing more than to kill me. They do not trust faeries, and although I'm their warden, they do not trust me either, though they do not dare attempt it. Somehow, they know the magic coursing through my veins has no master, that it could flatten them with not so much as the lifting of my pinky if I so chose—even in these tyrannous walls. I walk on, giving away not a hint of my discomfort as I pass. Only one human has ever tried to kill me here, and they met their end long before I will ever reach mine.

I turn down the passageway lined with boarding dormitories for the residents of the prison. I once lived down this hall, confined to a diminutive room of bare walls and thin blankets. I hated it. Though this prison is not as oppressive as the dungeon cells under the Steel Citadel or in Oleaíncudd and Dún, no being—human or otherwise—is made to live in such isolation, fearful of death at every hour. Not even locks are fitted on the wretched doors.

I stop in front of room 264 and raise my fist to the wood. Eoghan Kael cracks the door open, his shirt discarded and a sword at his side, the tip of the blade resting against the stone floor.

"Gálgalesh?"

His voice is smooth and questioning as he takes me in, finding the parchment in my hand. I point into the room, and he moves aside to let me in. I step over the threshold, closing the door, and hand Kael the letter I just received. He sits down upon the edge of the small bed covered in a blanket emblazoned with the Tinemallacht crest and reads it through.

"This makes no sense. Why would he fear for his life when attending the wedding of his sister? Will it not be a public affair?"

"I have heard rumors the king will allow for no one except the family to attend the wedding. Why does the prince still refuse to tell us plainly about the threat he has discovered? He speaks in code as

if we somehow understand it. I cannot continue without further information, Kael. He is taking too long. How can he ask me to funnel food and supplies to his men in the Borderlands on each of my supply runs and think no one will notice? It has been nearly four years. He must tell us now what we are facing!"

"He has his reasons. He always does."

"But he must tell us why! He is asking for a dozen more men to find sanctuary here. I cannot harbor a dozen more men without reason."

"Then tell him no. I can't help you. I know only as much as you do."

"That is a lie, Kael, and we both know it! What did he tell you last time he was in Fáintìrean—when he pulled you aside after our meeting with the men?"

I round on Eoghan, and he backs away, the sword still held cautiously in his hand. He has no quarrel with faeries, but his lack of magic in this place keeps him on constant edge.

"He said nothing of interest, just that the answer to everything is in his words. Since he tells us nothing of consequence, however, and speaks in codes we don't know, it's just useless—"

Long fingers wrap around my biceps to shake me awake, and I gasp as my eyes fly open. I take in the sitting room sofa, the endless dragon fire crackling in the hearth in front of me. Then, my vision is obscured by a tall, familiar, dark-skinned figure, bent into my line of sight, his triangular teeth inches from my face.

"Why were you foraying into my dreams?" Gálgalesh snarls with a dangerous glare. I attempt to pull my arms free of his grip.

"Y-y-your dream?" I stammer as sleep still holds me.

"Yes, woman. I sensed your magic—our shared magic— within my dream. Why were you there?"

"I..." *What was I doing in that dream? A memory of Gálgalesh's, surely—and one I know nothing about.* "I wasn't aware I had done so," I admit, and he sighs as his fury eases and he loosens his grip on my arm.

"Have you done so before?" he asks.

"I'm not sure… When I was traveling from Báscogar, I had a dream about you in the Caisleán Rialú dungeons…but that was the only time that felt close to this. I was you in the dream."

Gálgalesh lets go of my arm fully now and backs away from me, just enough to ease the tension in my shoulders.

"Our magic must have somehow become entangled. I will work on a remedy for it in the morning. I am sorry to wake you." He turns to leave.

"Wait," I say, and he pauses. "In your dream, why did Cai say he was fearful to attend my wedding? Did he know what Rian and his father were planning?"

Gálgalesh shrugs in an almost defeated motion I've never seen from him before. So rarely does he not have a single answer.

"We never found out. That was the last correspondence we received before the coup, and I still have not decoded his letters."

"And what of his journals? What did they say?"

"Journals?" Gálgalesh's expression is one of utter confusion.

"Cai kept journals his entire life. I never knew him to be without one, even when he would visit from Tinemallacht. Perhaps his journals might have some answers."

"Perhaps…" Gálgalesh turns as his gaze grows distant in thought. "Goodnight, woman."

"Goodnight," I sigh, and as soon as my head hits the cushions, I fall back into a dreamless sleep.

———

Bryn and I leave early to surf across the red sands of the desert to Bastain. I don't think the feeling of riding the gliders will ever become anything less than a wonder. Perhaps I'll ask Bryn to ride with me out into the Barrens on our way back to Gobaith, just for some extra time out on the sand.

We make it to the oasis on an impressive tail wind in less than an hour and park our gliders at the entrance to the city with the others. I count six lined up near the storage building, waiting to be cleaned and put away. Eoghan's glider, a longboard with the Tinemallacht crest prominently displayed on its sails, catches my eye. I remove my goggles and scarf from my face and shake off the dust before I follow Bryn toward Kael Manor. I have yet to explore the city of lush green gardens and palaces along the Falacht's shores, but even still, everything about it feels more like a traditional city than the outpost ever will.

Bryn and I reach the Kael's front garden, and I pause as a line of men and women winds from the front door to the road. Some are anxiously wringing their hands in front of them while others are quietly weeping; still, others smile broadly, excited as they chat with their neighbors. My brows pull together as I study them, and Bryn meets me, placing his hand lightly on the center of my back, urging me toward the house.

"Mother is speaking to the dead today," he explains as we cross the vibrant tile threshold into the cool palace bathed in sunlight. The entryway takes my breath away, with the intricate painted ceilings and dragons carved into the columns. "People travel from every corner of Tinemallacht when she speaks to the dead to communicate with their loved ones or find closure in some way. They'll be lined up for the next week until the dead decide they've had enough."

"Do you really believe she can speak with the dead? I was

always told mediums were cons who stole money from the simple-minded."

Bryn laughs. "You should try it sometime for yourself, Maeve. You might be surprised."

"Are you saying I can speak to anyone who's died?"

We round the corner to a silent, long hallway I remember leads to the bedrooms.

"No, you can request to speak to anyone you like, but the dead must decide to answer. Sometimes, they just don't want to speak to the living." Bryn points down the far end of the hall. "I imagine Eoghan is still asleep, if you'd like to see him. If he's too boring, come find me, and we can explore until everyone wakes up."

I thank him and then turn away to head down the quiet hall. I reach the familiar door of ancient walnut covered in ornate engravings. I push it open slowly and peek inside, Eoghan's face buried into his pillows, the muscles in his back laid bare, the blankets gathered at his waist. I take a timid step into the bright room, the large tub at the far end and a pile of Eoghan's clothes discarded on the floor. I unlace my boots and step out of them before I cross to the bed.

"Eogh," I whisper as I crouch beside him and run my fingers through his hair. I love to watch him sleep, especially here in Tinemallacht, where the worry lines across his forehead soften and his jaw unclenches as he dreams. He groans quietly into his pillow and turns his face toward the sound of my voice.

"Why are you not in bed?" he purrs, his eyes still closed.

"I've just ridden across the desert. I'll get sand between the sheets."

That primal sound of longing from deep in his chest sends chills down my spine and heat deep in my abdomen as he reaches out his arm and hooks it around my waist. He pulls me roughly onto the mattress and up against his side, nuzzling tiredly into my hair.

"You do realize I'm a Tinemallacht Fire Cursed, right? Do you think I'm unfamiliar with sand in my sheets?"

"Talk about your old girlfriends one more time, Eoghan Kael…"

His laugh is deep, and he kisses my temple. "You're so jealous, Mayhem. I don't see any of them here with me now. Do you?"

The heat from his body and the smell of sandalwood, bergamot, and cedar embers is intoxicating. It's been weeks since he's held me in his arms in the playful way that makes me want him endlessly, weeks since we haven't fought or confessed or wept. His lips find my cheek and kiss down my jaw, his eyes still closed. My gods, I've missed him, missed the quiet moments when he would wrap his arms around me and I'd know I was his and I was safe. Even the short time we allowed ourselves at the prison was enough to make me crave his desire, his passion, his love. My cheeks grow hot and as crimson as my hair when his eyes finally open, and he takes me in with those resplendent green and gold swirls of color.

"Hello, beautiful Mayhem," he whispers. "It's nice to see I can still make you blush."

He kisses me deeply, passionately, as his hands wrap around me and pull me under him. My lips part, and his tongue finds its way inside my mouth. My hands run along his back and down his ass, and now he's blushing, warm and red rising up along his neck and cheeks. I kiss him until I am breathless and then pull away.

"Your meeting?" I pant. He shakes his head, planting kisses across my skin.

"Not right now." He grabs the hem of my tan shirt and pulls it up and over my head, throwing it onto the floor. "I don't want to talk about yesterday, or this war, or *your* exes as I have you here with me."

He turns his attention back to the exposed parts of me and steals the breath from my very lungs.

"I had a dream last night…"

"Mmm?" Eoghan's mouth makes its way down my skin with a passion he hasn't had since before we left Báscogar.

"I was Gálgalesh, and I brought a letter to you at your room in the prison from Cai—"

He raises to meet my gaze, a stern look of displeasure on his face. "I want no mention of *your brother* as I pleasure you, Mayhem. I want no talk of *my* brother or *my* sister or Gálgalesh or Damaris or Dedra or anyone else. The only name I want to hear come from your lips is mine when you're coming for me in this bed. Have I made myself clear?"

My breath catches in my throat, and I nearly have to squeeze my thighs together to keep them from falling open for him. I bite my lip and nod, and he smiles as his eyes fill with a promise of pleasure. He grabs me by the hips and lifts me higher up against the headboard before he continues his slow, determined procession to the waistband of my cargo pants.

"Now that we have that settled, tell me about your magic. Have you figured out a way for me to communicate back to you, or will I just have to settle with hearing your sweet little voice in my head?"

He unbuttons my pants and pulls them down to my knees in one, easy tug. Then, he hooks the side of my underwear and teasingly runs his finger along it. I feel like I'm on fire. My whole body is electrified at his touch.

"What do you mean?" I nearly come undone when he pulls the band down to meet my Tans. His lips trail along my pelvis as I feel the warmth of his breath on my skin, and he smiles against me.

"Well, maybe when you're training in the square, I want to tell you how delicious you look." I feel his tongue trail against my center. "And all the things I want to do to you when I get you alone."

"Oh gods," I breathe.

"How I can't stop thinking about that night in the kitchen when you finally came back to me. I hadn't slept when you were gone. I can't sleep without you near me. I can't think of anything except you."

"You were sleeping when I got here, Kael." He smiles again.

"A technicality." He spreads my legs wider. "I knew you were on your way to me." I feel his tongue stroke and then work its way inside me. I grip the sheets of the bed as he passes a finger over my swollen clit.

He works me, a finger sliding in to meet his tongue, and my vision narrows as stars dance in my eyes. He's steady, measured, driving me to madness at his touch. My chest rises and falls almost frantically as I fight every urge to beg for more. I bite my lower lip as he strokes me with a second finger, bringing his tongue to work my clit in lazy licks and flicks.

"Do you want me as much as I want you, Mayhem?"

I feel him hook his fingers inside me, and I let out a cry of pleasure.

"You have me," I whisper through my moans. His steady rhythm deepens, thrusting to his knuckles.

"And you have me forever, Maevie." My hands fall into his hair as he stretches me, making me want all of him inside me. There will never be enough of him for me to have my fill. "I'd give up every single thing in this world for you."

My hips rock as I try to drive his thrusts harder and deeper, and he keeps his pace, his tongue matching the rhythm of his hand. A current of pleasure runs up my spine, and my body shivers. I can't stifle the sounds of my desire as I gasp for more, asking him to continue. He's encouraged by my cries and brings me to the edge of my orgasm before holding it at bay, teasing me until I whimper with need.

"Eoghan…" My thighs tremble with the anticipation of release, the pleasure near maddening.

"See; doesn't it sound great as you gasp and beg?" With that, he thrusts with hard, deft determination as his lips wrap around my clit, and I sink down into the depths of my ecstasy. My fists ball up in his hair as I am thrown over the edge again and again, electricity rushing through me like lightning. I can't stop the rush that comes over me. I can't stop the utter chaos in my brain as my screams reverberate off the walls of the room. He does not cease his eager strokes and greedy mouth. He knows what he wants, and he takes it with ease. My orgasm stretches like a ceaseless current on a powerful sea.

Eoghan grabs my hips to steady me. I hadn't even realized I was trembling violently beneath him, but he doesn't relent, keeping the fire in my mind burning out of control.

"Beautiful," he coaxes as I finally calm, gasping for air. "You're so beautiful." He sits up with a smile across his lips. "Well, I guess you've made your presence known."

I look around the room, and for the first time, I realize where we are. I cover my eyes with my hands and shake my head, humiliation washing over me.

"Oh gods," I moan as he pulls my underwear back up my thighs and works on my cargo pants.

"What's wrong?" He laughs. "You should be proud. I've never forgotten to silence a room before."

I roll over into the pillow and hide my embarrassment. Eoghan moves off the bed and to a small sink in the corner of the room. He picks up his toothbrush with smug satisfaction and brushes his teeth as he lazily leans against the wall.

Once he's finished, he saunters back over to the bed and climbs over me, planting kisses across my exposed shoulders.

"Mayhem…" His lips are next to my ear. "I need you to come to a meeting with me today, and I'm going to need you to listen to me when we're there. If I ask you to leave, I want you to leave and come right back to this room. Will you do that?"

"What's the meeting?" I ask, not wanting the presence of his body to leave me.

"An envoy is coming from the Capital to meet and discuss terms and demands. They're still ordering we be turned over to the sovereign, but I'll burn this kingdom to the ground before I let that happen."

He massages my back softly as he speaks, and I shudder at his touch, nearly wrecked by the lingering desire still heating me to my core.

"Will Rian be with them?" I ask, and his hands falter.

"Do you want him to be?" There's something simmering underneath his words in a dangerous, quiet way that tells me he might kill Rian on sight.

"I'd like nothing more than to never see him again, unless it's to take his final breaths from him, but I just wonder if they might try to send him to reason with me."

"If he does come, will you leave the meeting if I ask?" Eoghan's fingers begin trailing over my skin again.

"I trust you to keep me safe." I reach for his arm and pull him to me. I kiss his lips lightly, and he groans with lust before he continues.

"Good, because I don't want you across the Falacht from him, let alone a table."

"Jealous dragon," I whisper and kiss him again. "Who else will be at the meeting?"

"Well, my father, of course. Lo, Finn, and a few other generals from the Tinemallacht command." I roll over to face him, his chest still exposed and his underwear only covering the most scandalous parts of him. "I want you to wear the Tinemallacht Tans in the meeting to show you're one of us, that we're ready to fight if necessary to keep it that way. Although…" he runs his fingers through my hair, "there is a tiara somewhere around here, and more jewels than the other four territories put together possess. Perhaps we show them our princess lives."

Princess. He doesn't use the title often, and when he does, it's usually not warmly. There's nothing about me in this place that is anything remotely like the princess I was, and until I have Rian's head and the Crown of Fergal to place upon my own, I want nothing of it. I crinkle my nose in disgust.

"I'll wear the Tans, but I want you at my side, to show them the warrior who has stolen my heart."

"And the one who will break their necks if they get close to you ever again."

"I love you," I whisper.

"You are the very thing that I live for. I am intoxicated by you, enthralled with everything you are, utterly destroyed by my need for you."

He presses his lips to mine once more and then rolls off the bed. He walks over to a closet and drags open the doors, pulling out fresh Tans. When he's finished, he walks back to the bed and places his fingers softly against my throat in that way that makes me melt into him.

"And if I didn't make it abundantly clear, I love you too, Mayhem."

CHAPTER TWENTY-ONE

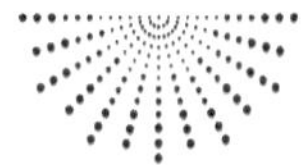

We sit at a long wooden table at the military base just outside Bastain's limits. The room is stifling with so many Fire Cursed hotheads in one place. Eoghan sits beside me, his hand protectively against my thigh. His breathing is so deep and audible, I can hear it even over the pounding of my own rapid heart. To my right, Finn sits with his chair close enough to crowd me, his father seated on his other side next to Colonel Hayes—River's father. To Eoghan's left, Lowri, General Kael, and Lieutenant-General Adlani have fallen into place, Lo and Eoghan both sporting twin blades strapped to their backs.

I fidget in my seat uncomfortably, and Eoghan runs his thumb against my thigh, the knot in my stomach easing ever-so-slightly as we wait for the envoy. My hands feel clammy, pressed together in my lap, and I fight the urge to fan myself against the heat of the room.

"It'll be fine, Maevie," Eoghan says quietly.

I want to believe him. I want to believe the situation is under control and everyone in this room will be all right, but what if Rian does walk through that door? Eoghan will kill him on sight, and then he'll be executed for violence during peace negotiations. Even with the Tinemallacht borders closed and their designation as a breakaway territory, they would still abide by the rules of conduct and honor. I'm not sure how I might restrain him if it were to happen—even if I'd secretly revel in watching him tear Rian apart. Still, there is absolutely no way I'm losing him like I've lost everyone else.

"No one will speak until we are told what the Capital wants from this meeting," General Osian Kael commands. "Finn, if their demands become threatening or dangerous in any way, Eoghan will give you orders to take Maeve back into the city to Kael Manor. I do not want her to set foot outside the manor walls until I have made sure the envoy has crossed back over the Golorgleann border. Is that clear?"

Finn nods his understanding, and I feel his own hand tap my knee reassuringly. It's an intimate touch, though in his eyes, I see only friendship.

"I'd like to stay for the entire meeting, if possible," I say to the room—mostly to Eoghan as he straightens in his seat.

"If the danger is minimal," General Kael replies.

Tough nut, your father, I whisper down the thread of magic and watch Eoghan's lips tug up on the right side, a devious smile of amusement and secret knowing. *I wonder what you might be thinking now that you could be sharing, if only I was better at my magic.* His eyebrows pull up in silent intrigue, and I can almost see all the thoughts racing through his mind. *I keep thinking about the way it felt when your fingers were deep inside—*

Eoghan grips my thigh hard and covers his mouth with his free hand. He clears his throat loudly, as if he's trying to drown out my voice so the others can't hear. Lowri looks at him curiously, his face red with embarrassment. He waves her off and takes a sip of water. I smile to myself and lean back against the chair in smug satisfaction.

"Whatever you two are doing, knock it off!" Lowri hisses to us, and Eoghan and I laugh in earnest now, our shoulders shaking. Finn smirks and shakes his head in silent mirth.

"Fuck off," Eoghan says in a quiet chuckle, and all four of us—including Lowri—burst into a fit of laughter. His father turns our way, eyeing us with a stoic expression. We all pause and straighten, the smiles falling away.

The minutes tick down in silence as we continue to wait for the envoy to arrive. Perhaps they decided against it, finding it too dangerous to travel to the Tinemallacht capital. *Maybe*, I think, *they'll decide to leave us alone completely*. Even I'm not naïve enough to believe that might ever happen. Rian will hunt us until we're dead—or until his last breath is taken from him.

The door is pushed open with a loud creak, and a soldier in Tinemallacht Tans enters.

"They are here, General," he says to Eoghan's father, who inclines his head in understanding.

"Send them in."

The soldier bows respectfully to the table and then exits the meeting hall again, only for numerous sets of footsteps to replace his own mere moments later. All our heads turn to the right in unison as six highdruí in long, brown robes and white cinctures tied around their waists enter the room. Their feet are bare or covered in thin, moleskin shoes, uncomfortable for traversing the hot desert sands. We watch them file in and take their seats at either end of the table, leaving space directly in front of me and Eoghan. Then, once they're seated, the sound of metal soles against the tile echoes through the room.

My hands begin to tremble in my lap, and my mouth goes dry as Sir Oli Raven enters, finding a seat directly across from me at the table. I feel sick—utterly ill as the blood rushes from my face. His eyes lock on me, and his lips curl into a smile. He takes me in properly for the first time since the morning of the coup.

Finding Eoghan's fingers, I squeeze them with everything I have, trying to keep the tears welling up in my eyes at bay. That terrifying face, with his pale skin and graying beard. His cheekbones are so high, they are nearly in his eyes, just below the puffy, black bags of his lower eyelids.

"Maeve." Sir Oli Raven's voice sends a chill down my spine. "You have certainly changed. I did warn you cutting your beautiful hair might have that effect."

Eoghan lets out a dangerous sound under his breath that the whole room recognizes as a warning of violence.

"I imagine you shared that information with the men who shaved every bit of it off of my head and tried to kill me," I spit, the words like venom on my tongue.

Sir Oli Raven's smile only grows wider as I speak. "I do not have the faintest idea what you are talking about, child."

Eoghan's body heat rises to a fever pitch. I hold his hand against my thigh, keeping him in his seat. General Kael coughs twice with purpose, and Sir Oli Raven's eyes finally leave mine to face him for the first time.

"Let us get to the point. Why are you here?"

"Well, General Kael, to put it quite simply, to secure the fugitives who belong to the Crown for their treason against the Sovereign."

"And not to discuss the indiscriminate bombing of an illegal substance on the Bellrúg outpost?"

"Certainly not." Sir Oli Raven and the highdruí shake their heads in unison. "It was not an indiscriminate bombing at all. Our information from credible sources stated the fugitives were hiding at the Bellrúg outpost near the Gálamáistir border. We were only doing as is our right: flush them out of the outpost and bring them under our authority."

"That's ridiculous!" I exclaim. "We were nowhere near—" Eoghan squeezes my knee under the table, and out of the corner of my eye, I see him shake his head just a minute degree.

"So, from your information, you believed the lady, Princess Maeve, and the Tinemallacht Captain, Eoghan Kael, were in Bellrúg, and you used illegal means to flush them out?" General Kael asks.

"General," Sir Oli Raven's voice makes me want to scream in disgust, "the weapons commissioned have been authorized by King Bréanainn to be used on those found guilty of treason." Eoghan clears his throat angrily. "Innocent bystanders injured in such a mission are the responsibility of the spineless traitors who have hidden themselves among civilians. There is nothing the king could have done to mitigate such an outcome."

I want nothing more than to beat my fist into Sir Oli Raven until he is dead. I want him to bleed. I want him to suffer. I want him to beg for me to end him. Lowri cuts in before my mind has even formed coherent sentences beyond the rage enveloping me.

"Innocent bystanders... You tried to kill everyone in the outpost, you snake. There are rules to war, but of course, you wouldn't know that as you kill without any regard. By the Draío Codes of Conduct, we could flay you and nail you to posts in the Barrens for the dragons to feed on for what you've done."

"Ah, Lieutenant-Colonel Lowri Kael, is it?" Sir Oli Raven's voice is as smooth as the poison that swirls around vials in the castle dungeons.

"Commandant," she corrects. She places her clasped fists on the table, her gold wielding cuffs glistening in the light.

She leans in with a quiet strength that makes me nervous. I watch as several of the highdruí slide back in their seats to distance themselves.

"Commandant." He smirks. "Such a shame your father has not recognized your ability and promoted you yet. Well, at least you are of higher rank than your twin, the Captain." I feel Eoghan's muscles tense in his arms. "By the Draío Codes of Conduct, all deserters of Báscogar prison are freed from their sentence if they successfully return to their home territories upon escape."

"Eoghan is from Tinemallacht—" I begin, but Sir Oli Raven continues.

"He is. You, however, dearest Maeve, are not. Your home territory is Golorgleann, and your failure to return has made you a wanted woman."

Eoghan lets out an angry laugh that bites like a wolf's snarl. "You cannot be serious? Well, you and your Codes of Conduct can go fuck yourselves, because Maeve was never a prisoner at Báscogar. Where she goes is none of your concern."

Sir Oli Raven holds up his hand dismissively, and the calm on his face makes me want to vomit.

"Regardless of the name entered into the prison rolls, Maeve assumed the identity of the slave girl, Alana Moran—"

"Who does not exist!" I cry out.

"—therefore, she is responsible for her sentence."

Eoghan slams his hands down onto the table, and I notice one of my daggers is held tightly in his grip. I watch his fingers flex and ball into fists as he breathes in deep.

"So you're here to demand Maeve, who had no sentence except for the death sentence you placed on her head, and myself, who successfully escaped and returned to my home territory—for what? Because that jackass slave trader is angry he didn't succeed in killing his bride on his wedding day? Where is he, anyway? He sends you with his demands because he's scared to face me?"

"Actually, we care nothing about you, *Captain*. We are here to secure the fugitives, Maeve Moran and the faerie, Gálgalesh Devenallt. Based on the events at Bellrúg yesterday and the intervention of faerie magic used to stop us from securing the fugitives, we have proof you are harboring the faerie wanted in each of Draío's five territories."

The table goes silent. I had wielded the faerie magic, and when I had, Eoghan was worried the witnesses would tell Rian of it—and he was right, but they had not suspected it of me. Instead, we had led them right to Gálgalesh.

It's Finn's voice that breaks through the taciturnity this time.

"Tinemallacht has seceded from Draíocoinnigh. We do not recognize your calls for fugitives, and we will not release any, wanted or otherwise, to your king. Our princess and the faerie are citizens of Tinemallacht as long as they seek refuge here."

Sir Oli Raven's lips turn toward the ground dramatically without an ounce of sincerity behind them. Finn's fingers brush like a whisper over my knee—calming me, protecting me.

"That is disappointing. I can assure you, I seek not to harm Maeve in any way, only to return her, as is ordered by the king. What he decides to do in light of her escape from Báscogar, the killing of a number of the king's guards and the honorable Drustan Anwyl, and the breach of her marriage contract through clearly disloyal acts with the Captain here —which warrant beheading of the betrothed and the lover— well, that is not up to me."

"I think trying to kill Maeve on her wedding day breached their marriage contract long before I met her."

Eoghan's eyes darken. "But by all means, please send your prince to come discuss the matter with me personally."

I can't seem to breathe. I'm going to pass out right here at this table.

"The prince has a right to his property, Captain Kael. Even the right to kill her, if he so chooses. I imagine you do not heal as you used to, Maeve." He pauses, watching my expression with interest. "The prince might enjoy breaking you now that you can bleed freely."

My mind fills with horrible images of Rian and the times when his pleasure meant my pain. I push back from my seat as Eoghan and Finn rise in unison, fire dancing across their palms, the promise of death in their eyes. General Kael and the other men stand too, quiet rage boiling just below the surface. I rush toward the door, but Lowri is quick and catches me up in her arms before pulling me to her chest. She holds me, her hands gripping me to keep me upright.

"Stop it," she demands as the room grows quiet and she traps us in the sphere of her silencing charm. "Do not leave. Do not cry. This is the man who harmed you, isn't it?" I nod into her shirt. "Do not let him see you as weak. You are one of us, and Tinemallachts don't run. He can't hurt you here. Now, stand."

I feel the heat of her hands against my arms, and her firm grip guides me as my knees find the strength to hold me. I stand, and as I do, the sounds of the room come racing back to meet us. Lowri turns to face the table, her hand wrapped around my waist in assurance.

"I said, you can get the fuck out. This meeting is over," I hear Eoghan say. He is leaning so far over the table, he's nearly on the other side. General Kael raises his hands to the room.

"Lieutenant-General Adlani, Colonel Hayes, and Officer Rhodes will accompany me to see you find your way back to

Gairdín." The other men's shoulders square at the command. "Captain Kael, you and Corporal Rhodes have your orders. On our leave." Eoghan's nod is little more than the slightest motion of his head. His eyes do not break their lethal glare.

The General and his men watch the six highdruí and Sir Oli Raven file out before following in their wake. Eoghan, Finn, Lowri, and I are left in the meeting chamber. As the door falls shut, Lowri finally releases me from her protective grip.

"Fuck!" Eoghan slams his fist into the table and then buries his hands into his hair.

"It's fine," Lowri assures, though her tone is grim. "They got nothing from us. They will get nothing from us."

"But they know about Gálgalesh," I say as I find Eoghan's scalding arm and wrap my own around his waist. He cools just enough to not burn me at his touch.

"At least they don't know about you," Finn cuts in. "We can deal with it."

Eoghan sighs and presses his lips to my hair. "Lo, get Maeve to the Manor. Finn and I are stationed on the border to make sure none of those idiots come back. Wait for me in Bastain before you head back to the outpost."

CHAPTER TWENTY-TWO

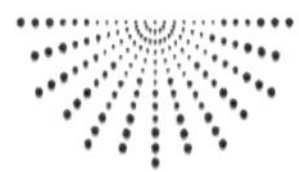

I've been at Kael Manor for nearly a week. Lowri had taken me back to the manor house and ordered me to stay inside while Eoghan and Finn made their way to the border. The fighting started just an hour after Sir Oli Raven and the others boarded an airship headed back to Golorgleann. The bombardments only worsened in the following days at every outpost and checkpoint near the border.

I can't seem to sleep without nightmares of Eoghan falling to the sword and Finn meeting the same fate as River. My mind becomes a battlefield of my worst fears as I wait day-in and day-out for news, lying in bed, wishing to be anywhere besides this manor house, with its brightly colored floors and walls lined with windows. I think about all Eoghan has to protect here. Not just me—his family, Gálgalesh, Sawney, Dedra, even Áine and Theo. My little life seems like nothing in comparison to all those he's fighting to keep.

Bryn left us yesterday morning, called back to the outpost to prepare for patrol on the southern border with Iranndair. I miss him immensely. He's the only person I have to speak to in this house, as Lowri and Mari Kael seem to either despise my company or not notice me at all.

Now, though, it's quiet, as the evening hours have arrived and the never-ending line of visitors has been turned away for the night, as the dead have finally refused to speak. I sit at the table with Lowri, Sawney, and Mari while the sounds of scraping spoons against ornate bowls fills the room. We dress in our formal gowns, though no one joins us for supper, and I think the formality of it is ridiculous. The gauzy dress in palest pink nearly exposes my breasts and scarcely covers any other parts of me. Tonight, Lowri is dressed in the brightest of red, and Sawney dons white, making her look like an angel with her darkened skin—keeping hold of my gaze for much too long.

"Maeve?" Sawney's voice rouses me from my thoughts. "Have you and Eoghan decided when you might have the ceremony?"

My brows pull together in confusion. "I'm sorry, the what?"

"The entwining ceremony, Maeve." Sawney laughs lightly, making my head spin with a desire I don't understand. "You wear his dragon heart around your neck, don't you? Have you chosen when your ceremony might be?"

My hands reach for the jewel simmering ever-warm against my skin, and I realize a lovely pink gemstone lays low on a long chain between Sawney's breasts. I divert my eyes, and I watch her smile broaden along her lips.

"They aren't having a ceremony, Sawney." Lowri's hand hasn't left Sawney's upper thigh all night as her fingers trail along Sawney's exposed skin. "Eoghan would never."

"I wouldn't be so sure, Lo," Sawney coos with such a hunger, it makes me wonder what she might sound like when Lowri's hand trails further beneath her skirts. I blink furiously, trying to clear my mind. *What is wrong with you,*

Maeve? "Eoghan's destined for an entwining ceremony. After Seren completed hers last year, I imagine he is ready to find someone of his own as well."

"It'll pass." Lowri lifts her spoon to her lips. "Eoghan's never been interested in it to begin with."

Seren? Who the hell is Seren, and why did her entwining ceremony matter to Eoghan? I place my spoon down into my bowl and look over at Mari, who's mumbling to herself in that unnerving way she so often does, her eyes milky and distant. I turn my gaze back to Sawney and Lowri, the latter not caring a bit about my existence, apart from her annoyance that I continue to breathe.

"Who…is Seren?" I ask, and Lowri rolls her eyes.

"Here we go…" she mumbles under her breath. Sawney admonishes her, her brows pulling together in a scowl before answering.

"Seren was a friend of Eoghan's. They were close in childhood until just after the Battle of Buaeth. Everyone believed they would be entwined one day, but Eoghan never asked her, so she finally moved on. She and Finn had been close as well, though she ended up entwining with a man named Ellis Lago last year. Such a shame; I would have thought if not Eogh, at least Finn might have a shot."

"That's because Eogh and Finn share everything." Lowri takes a drink from her glass and raises an eyebrow at me. Her eyes scan my body as if in question. "I heard Eoghan hated fucking her." My cheeks grow hot at the crudeness of the conversation. I eye Mari again, and Lowri scoffs. "She's not listening," she continues. "He tried everything, but she was too much of a…*princess*, I'm told."

"Stop that." Sawney takes Lowri's face in her hands and compels her to meet her gaze. "You're just being cruel. This is going to be your sister soon. Be happy for Eogh and Maeve." Lowri mumbles something between the two of them, and

Sawney laughs. "I think Maeve's a beautiful match for him." Her eyes fall on me, and Lowri looks in turn. I feel uncomfortably exposed now, and my hand passes across my chest nervously.

"I'm not denying she's beautiful," Lowri sighs. "But you're dangerous, Maeve. I'll kill you if anything happens to Eogh because of you and that ex-fiancé of yours."

"Leave her, Lo. Not another word, not unless you want to invite her to join us after dinner."

Sawney's voice is like silk, and if I didn't have a burning desire to touch her before, I have to fight everything in me not to reach out for her now. Lowri's hand disappears beneath the white of Sawney's dress for a moment and then reemerges. She straightens her own and then goes back to drinking her wine in silence. The room quiets, and the sound of scraping spoons fills the space once again.

Caisleán Rialú glistens like a diamond held up to the light as the sun's rays fall low through the windows. Not even the beauty of this place can distract me from my pacing as I wait in the entry hall like a child awaiting gifts on their birthday. He is coming. They informed me of it thirty minutes ago, when he requested entry at the city walls of Gairdín. I couldn't help but race to the door, not even completely dressed, to meet him.

It's been weeks since I've seen him, since his anger boiled over and he stomped out of the front gates. I thought he might never return, yet now, as my bare feet walk back and forth across the marble, I know he will, and I'll be able to hold him in my arms.

But where is he? Why is he taking so long to reach the castle gates? Was he not here to see me at all?

The loud, metallic clanging of the fortress walls gives me pause, and I catch my breath as I count the boot steps on gravel to the entrance of the castle. The feet stop just short of the castle doors, and with a deafening sound, they swing open toward me.

Eoghan Kael stands on the threshold in his Tinemallacht Tans and his dragon leather jacket. His expression is tired, his lips a hard line.

"You came back." I rush to him, tripping over my dressing gown and stumbling into his arms. He catches me in his soft grip, though there's no relief in his expression as I throw myself around him. I press my lips to his, but he pulls away quickly.

"Maeve," he begins, his voice matching the exhaustion in his eyes, "don't."

"But I've missed you..." His fingers are so lightly settled on my hips, it feels as if he decided on the touch as the only suitable place-ment for his hands. What's wrong with him? I've thrown myself into his arms, and he shies away from me as if I'm repulsive to him. "What's happening?"

"How can you not understand what you've done?"

"What I've done is what was needed so we could be together and safe."

"Not like this, Maeve."

"Why?" I demand as Dedra enters from the grand staircase. She pauses, and Eoghan motions for her to leave. She doesn't budge. "I'm the queen, am I not? And you're my king! We answer to no one!"

"At what cost, Maeve?"

Eoghan unlaces my arms from his neck and releases them in front of me. Red. Bright red blood drips from my palms onto the floor, pooling and puddling as it flows up to the surface like the Falacht River from the depths of the Tinemallacht sand. I wipe my palms against my dressing gown, painting myself in crimson, and when I look at them again, the blood remains. I wipe and wipe again, over and over, and still to no avail. My feet are covered in it, and it floods around me to my ankles, then my knees.

"Eoghan, help me!" I beg as the blood reaches my chest.

"I don't think I can anymore, Maeve."

The pool is at my neck now, and I reach out a red-coated hand to Eoghan. He simply shakes his head and turns away, walking out of the doors toward the castle gates.

"Eoghan!" I choke as I slip under. Eoghan reaches the gate, turns to look at me one final time, and then, he's gone.

I wake up panting for air in Eoghan's bright room at Kael Manor. I had fallen asleep in my dinner gown, the skirts tangled around me from my tossing and turning. I need to get out of here. I need to be anywhere, anywhere at all, besides stuck in this house, waiting for Eoghan to return. I push off the bed and look around the room. My Tans and linen clothes have been taken by the housekeepers to be washed. All I have is my underwear and this ridiculously scandalous dress. It'll have to do. I march to the door and throw it open, heading down the hall. The house is quiet; it's much too late for anyone to be awake. I pass three doors on the left-hand side and stop at the fourth. I knock. No answer. I knock again and wait. No one responds. They can't be so asleep that they haven't heard the raps on the door. I groan and roll my eyes before pushing the door open.

Lowri is positioned between Sawney's legs on the bed, her face buried deep into her pelvis, one of Sawney's knees draped over her shoulder. The room is silent—a silencing charm thrown up around them to the threshold. I take a step inside the room, and the familiar coo of Sawney's voice echoes in a moan against the walls. I pause for just a second, unsure now what I was doing, and then I take another step toward the bed.

The sound of my feet against the bare floors stirs them, and Lowri lifts her head from Sawney's center, her eyes coated in a sex-addled haze.

"Oh, fuck. Don't tell me you've decided you want to join us?" Lowri laughs. "Eogh won't approve if I'm in the room."

"No." I shake my head and divert my eyes as Lowri lays back on the bed, exposing them both completely. "I had a nightmare…"

Ridiculous, Maeve. Utterly ridiculous. But it's all I can think to say, as my brain has decided to refuse to work at all. Sawney straightens the sheet and throws it over her and Lowri before patting the bed beside her.

"Come, Maeve," she whispers to me, and Lowri huffs audibly in annoyance. "Don't be shy. It's fine."

I walk timidly to the bed, my brain slowly registering what I've interrupted without the head-spinning desire for it to continue. Sawney grabs my hand and pulls me to her on the mattress, running her hands through my unkempt hair and down my shoulders. Her hands pass lightly over the gauzy fabric covering my breasts and I forget to breathe.

"So, we're really going to comfort a grown woman with a nightmare?" Lowri doesn't bother to cover herself. She takes a long drink of water from a glass perched on the bedside table.

"Shh, Lo. We have all the time in the world. What's bothering you, Maeve?"

"I can't stay here anymore. I need to get out of here. I need to leave this house. I'm going mad thinking about the fighting every day."

"No," Lowri interjects. "Out of the question. It isn't safe, and you know it. I can't let you leave until Eoghan gets back —no matter how much I'd like to be rid of you. What happens if you get hurt?"

"I'm not looking to leave Bastain, just this house! I just need fresh air."

"No."

She will never understand. She's spent her life in this place. She doesn't know how it feels to be trapped here. She'd be happy to make me suffer, not caring how I feel—just as

Eoghan seems to not care. Whatever the Tinemallachts feel is right goes, regardless of what I have to say. I groan in exasperation. Sawney hushes me as she plays with my necklace against my chest. She hums a soft sort of lullaby that feels like a tonic on my brain, and I sink back against her as her touch sends shivers down my spine.

"Look, I hate being here as much as anyone else, but Eoghan said no, and that means no. I trust him. We're staying here until he returns. Now, please, go fuck off back to your room and get some sleep. Maybe he'll be back in the morning."

Sawney presses her lips to my temple before releasing me, and I stand. I walk to the door quietly, my feet against the tiles the only sound.

"I'm sorry." I turn, only to find that Lowri has already taken up her spot between Sawney's legs once again.

"Not at all." Sawney smiles and waves as I leave.

I can't believe I'm stuck here! I walk back down the hallway toward Eoghan's room. I refuse to wait another minute in this stupid house. I refuse to sit alone like the helpless princess while Eoghan is out fighting. I refuse to be held by these walls, even if it is dangerous. Even if Eoghan ordered us all to stay put. Even if it's for the best, I refuse. I tug on the thread of magic, and it awakens.

Eoghan, I whisper down the line. *If you can hear me, I'm leaving. I just need fresh air. I'll come back, I promise. I'll be safe.*

I'm not sure how far the magic can reach, but I send out the message and then turn toward the front of the house. I walk through the kitchen into the dining room before crossing into the entryway to the front door. I reach for the handle, drawing it open toward me. I wait a minute, then two, and when I'm certain no one is coming to stop me, I step out into the sunlight.

I don't have a clue where I'm going; all I know is that

Bastain is beautiful in the silent hours of the night. Green palm trees and colorful vegetation line the roads. Pools of crystal clear water glisten in the sunlight, and small dragons gather, eating from feeding bowls left out as tribute just for them. I walk down the deserted streets, making lefts and rights indiscriminately, as though I'll ever be able to find my way back. I follow the lines of houses, each grander and more luxurious than anything in Gobaith could ever claim to be, and I hear the soft sound of rushing water as I approach the banks of the Falacht River.

My mind quiets and calms as I make it to the water's edge. I crouch down before it, my bare feet in the warm sand, the gauzy fabric of the dress trailing behind me. I run my hand across the surface. The water is so cool, it takes all my will not to dive in and swim. I savor the feeling of it against my fingertips. Then, I hear someone move behind me.

"Maeve?" I turn and stand as Finn steps out onto the sandy shore. "What are you doing outside at this hour?"

"Finn? What are *you* doing here? I thought you were with Eoghan at the border."

"I was," he says. "We just got back. I thought I saw you walking alone along the road, so I followed you." He motions. "Come with me, and I'll take you to Eoghan."

Something about him seems different somehow—whether fatigue from days of fighting or something else entirely, I can't be sure. He begins to walk away from the river and back up the street. I pause for just a moment and watch him leave. Curious… His gait is labored as he walks. Has he been injured? He stops and turns, urging me to follow him again with one of his beautiful, easy smiles.

This time, I take a step forward and follow as he leads me back through the houses easily, unraveling the labyrinth I've woven for myself. We walk in silence through the streets, the sunlight still unwelcoming and hot against my exposed skin.

We pass the road I recognize as the one that leads to Kael Manor, and I pause.

"Finn?" He turns and looks at me quizzically. "Are we not going back to the house?"

"No," he laughs. "This way."

He continues to the edge of the city, where the trees begin to fall away and the houses are scarce. Not far off, I can see the military base at the edge of the Barrens, where we met the Capital delegation days ago. Finn stops near a shed where gliders are kept.

"He's in there, storing our gliders. Go ahead; he wants to see you."

I look back at him and he smiles, waiting for me to continue without him. I step forward to the shed.

"Eogh," I say as I grab the door. It's dark and quiet inside. "Eoghan?"

I pull at the handle, and as I do, I feel a piercing pain rush through the back of my head before my knees buckle, and everything around me goes black.

CHAPTER TWENTY-THREE

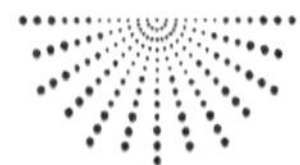

P ain radiates through my skull before my vision comes back slowly, one sliver of light at a time. I groan and try to reach for my head—only to realize I can't move my arms. I try again, and the edge of something metallic cuts into my wrist, blood trickling over my skin.

Blinking back the haze of sleep still threatening to drag me under, the room comes into view—a military-issued camp tent used at outposts and checkpoints throughout Draíocoinnigh. Each territory has their own in the prominent color of their landscape. This one is a deep forest green, so I would guess I am somewhere in Gálamáistir, days away from Bastain. In the corner, a wooden table draws my attention, crude tools of silver spread across the top. The chair beneath me is made of metal, similar to the one in the castle dungeons, and my stomach churns uneasily at the sight of it. On my wrists are cuffs of Faebond attached to the arms of the chair, binding me, trapping me. I'm not even sure how I got here and for how long I've been held captive. All I remember is Finn Rhodes. He was the last face I saw before something came down with a crushing force onto my head and the world disappeared.

"You are awake," an unmistakably familiar voice that makes my skin crawl says from somewhere behind me. "Are you hungry, Maeve?" Sir Oli Raven steps into my line of sight, and my head lulls to the side, my body weakened by the effects of the Faebond. He holds up a piece of cake that smells of almonds. "Your favorite, as I remember."

I shake my head lamely, but he ignores me and forks a bite into my mouth. There's a bitter aftertaste to it, and all at once, the sweet, heady smell of Angel's Trumpet fills my senses. I try to spit it out, but Sir Oli Raven covers my mouth with his hand and runs his fingers against my throat, forcing me to swallow. When I finally succumb, he releases me. I cough and gag while he simply looks up at the ceiling, as though even the canvas of the tent is less repulsive than I.

"Where's Finn?" I ask.

"Oh, Corporal Rhodes? Back in Tinemallacht with your Captain of the Fire Cursed." Finn and Eoghan hadn't been in Bastain at all. I had been deceived, and I fell for it so easily. "It is hard to believe how dimwitted enlisted men can be. It was all too easy to get him to speak at that meeting, to get a feel for his cadence and mannerisms. He looked at you so fondly, I was starting to think two of them loved you until he stood with Captain Kael. That's when I realized he cared for *him*. They cannot be brothers, but the protective nature was all the same. It made me believe he might be close enough to fool you both."

"Did you hurt him?" My head becomes more clouded by the moment, and I'm sure whatever was in the cake will take hold at any time, even as my thoughts escape me like puffs of smoke.

"No." He seems thoroughly uninterested now. "I have no time to harm people who mean nothing to me. I simply needed to sneak back into Tinemallacht and wait for you to leave the General's sanctuary. I will say, you stayed hidden for longer than I had bet. You do so hate to be caged."

I try to find the magic thread in my mind, but it's lost in the darkness as the Faebond grips me, glowing green against my skin. *He's going to kill me,* I reason. *There's nothing I can do about it. He is going to kill me.*

"Rian sent you then, to bring me back to him?" He is gathering instruments from his wooden table now—each a common torture device of my youth.

"He sent me to kill you. He wanted to break you himself for all the trouble you put him through, though he did not care enough to make the journey. To be frank, I believe your filth of a boyfriend frightens him a bit more than me." He turns back toward me, a long knife in his hand, and tremors of terror rush through me wildly against the metal arms of the chair. "I see you remember this—a favorite of mine."

I pull at the bonds on my wrists and try to kick my legs toward him, but those are secured as well. He takes a step toward me, and his eyes are bright with amusement. He's enjoying watching me squirm and try to free myself. He's always loved it when I screamed and cried and begged for mercy. He draws nearer to me, and the Faebond cuts deep into my skin, my wrists stinging and burning as blood flows freely from them.

"Now, now, Maeve, I will not kill you yet, not when I can have my fun." He's directly in front of me now, and he runs the blade against my skin in slow, teasing motions. "I was told by our men at the border that you fell from a dragon's back without so much as a scratch—right into the checkpoint. I will admit, you do surprise me. I had assumed perhaps your magic could re-manifest itself, but I was not sure when and in what form. Magic can be fickle, after all. It seems to continue to succumb to Faebond, as all magic does, however, which is really quite unfortunate for you."

He grips my hair that has grown nearly to my shoulders now and examines it, so utterly crimson like the blood rushing from my wrists, so unlike the caramel hair that fell close to my waist when I used to be strapped to this chair in that dark dungeon. He never used Faebond back then, even when he would cut into my skin. He enjoyed watching it heal seconds later. I was needed then, and so my survival was important, even when the pain was of no consequence. This, I realize, is what it feels like to be hated and hunted. My life is so much fuller now, the Faebond so much more necessary in so many ways he cannot even begin to know—but he doesn't need me, so he will gladly kill me.

"Why is it red?" he asks almost to himself. "Why do the stars not still dance in it?" He brings his blade below my chin. "Rian Doherty did not specify how quickly he intended me to kill you, and for that, I am thankful. I would much like to examine you more thoroughly before that wick of your life is snuffed out. Do not worry—I will give you time to heal. And in the evenings, the men of the camp will be happy to see all you have been sharing with that Fire Cursed Captain."

The effects of the laced cake begin to take hold, and I feel myself slipping, my muscles relaxing of their own accord, though the room stays in view. He's paralyzing me. He's making me unable to fight him.

"Don't." I almost choke on my tongue as my mouth goes dry.

"Don't what, Maeve? Come now." He runs his blade across the bare skin of my chest, the pink dress from dinner still the only thing I wear. He runs it still lower as it passes down my stomach. "This time, it will hurt."

And my screams fill the tent as he pierces my skin.

———

"Evie," Cai whispers to me.

I can hear the men outside laughing and shouting—the clinking of steins as they toast one another. They've been reveling over dinner for at least the past hour and becoming more drunk as the minutes pass. One or two have already stumbled in through the canvas tent door to ogle at the half-naked woman in the pink dress. I am so fucking tired. I have no more energy to keep me awake, even if it means these men will have their way with me when I finally succumb to the fatigue. My head rolls to the side heavily against my exposed shoulder, the skin hot with fever.

"Evie," Cai coaxes again. "Come now, wake up."

I turn my eyes toward the sound of his voice, and I see him, standing over my bed in Caisleán Rialú years ago, his hands pushed deep into his pockets. I'm no more than nine— pale and clammy. I'd been playing in the garden, picking flowers, trying to decipher which the chefs would dice and place in our suppers. I had chosen poorly and had been bedridden for days.

I reach toward the scene, but my limbs no longer answer to my command, not since the last round of poison was shoved down my throat.

"Cai..." My voice is only just a rasp and mimics younger me lying across the way in my sickbed.

"Just hallucinations, of course." He places his lips to my forehead and crouches into my line of sight. "I'm sure you remember what Nanny once said about Angel's Trumpet: 'It starts with a dry mouth, then shooting stars in your eyes. Before you know it, you're paralyzed.' A bit of a mess you're in, sweet sister mine."

My eyes flicker open, and the tent comes into view again. The soldiers' revelry hits a fever-pitch, and I feel drool trickle down to my chin. I try to move, but it's only my mind that stirs, and my eyes become heavy once again.

"No, Maeve, you don't know."

I'm back in Eoghan's desert home, and he stands over me, anger and frustration pulling his features into a tight line across his face.

"You don't know what's going on outside of these walls. You don't know they've taken captive and interrogated every single person outside this territory who has known us. You don't know they've targeted my entire family. You don't know!"

"Well, then tell me! You tell me nothing—I know nothing unless I pry or find out from someone else! How am I ever going to be of any use at all if you don't talk to me?"

"I am trying to keep you safe! You will be useful if you stay alive."

There's a rustling outside of the tent, and I try to lift my head as I hear Oli Raven's chilling voice just beyond. I'm slipping away now, and I beg for the darkness to pull me under, if only to be rid of him for good.

Cai is back, holding my wrists as fresh blood runs from my fingertips to the floor. The wounds have healed, but not as quickly as they had the last time. Cai's home from the Academy and found me crawling from the dungeons after Oli Raven had left me strapped to his chair of torment. He'd been called away—too soon to clear away the evidence of his experiments. My vision blurs as it had that day, and my head feels dizzy from the loss of blood.

"He's going to kill—" I watch as my heaving breath silences my cracking words. "He's going to kill me."

"Yes, he'll try...but you've been here before, haven't you? Hundreds of times. Even when death didn't come. You felt it —your body nearly yielding to the pain as it was broken and bleeding."

His thumbs smear the tracks of blood on my arms as he speaks, and my younger self sobs tears I don't have the strength to let free now.

This is when he leaves me, I recall. *When he walked out of the door and demanded answers, and instead, my father sent him back to the Academy. If he leaves now...*

"It was different then," I call out this time. My head feels like lead as I try to lift it. "I could heal."

"And still you can. You just have to keep fighting until you're freed. You have to hold on through the pain until someone comes for you."

His lips don't move with his words, and I'm certain I imagined it. Still, I need him. I need him to stay here with me. I need to alter the memory to keep him here—keep anyone here while I take my last breath.

"What if no one ever does? What if no one can find me?"

There are boots against the dirt outside, and Cai turns toward the hall he disappeared down the last time this scene played out. I count at least five sets, growing closer with each step.

"Stay alive, Evie," Cai commands.

"Is that an order from the Leader?" I almost scoff, if not for the fatigue.

"If you want it to be. Stay alive and then kill every last one of them."

I swear, I heard him say it, though he hadn't, wouldn't, couldn't have. Cai draws his hands from his pockets and taps on the doorframe as he passes to the exit, and the younger me races after him.

"Cai, no!" she begs. "Don't tell father!"

She passes the small wooden table, so much like the one filled with Oli Raven's metal tools he has used over and again these past...hours or days I've been strapped to this cold chair of death. The crown of King Fergal appears upon the wooden surface, glistening even in the darkness of the room, beckoning me to it. I want it—no, I need it, and I will not yield until every one of them is dead and I've been crowned queen. Heat rises inside me.

The tent door rustles, and as the memory fades, a group of men in deep forest green regalia enter, greed and hunger inscribed across their features.

———

I DON'T KNOW what day it is, or the time, but the sun is rising outside. There was a steady stream of soldiers last night who came to see the lost princess—some to touch, some to watch, some who wanted both. Sir Oli Raven had waited until I was nearly catatonic before he released the Faebond from my arms so my body could heal…and then he bound me again.

Every time I would begin to move and fight, as weak as the bonds might have made me, he would shove some more of the rancid cake into my mouth. The thought of it makes me ill now. How poetic—the only simple pleasure of my life being used to bring me to the precipice of my death. At least when I die here, the smell of it will leave me forever.

Sir Oli Raven enters the tent, his clothes fresh and his hair still damp from his bath. My pink dress Eoghan bought me is now covered in sticky red blood from the bodice to the skirts—though there's little left of the skirt at all. The men tore at it as they took me through the night, like animals tearing at their prey's dead carcass while they feed.

"Shall we continue?" He takes a metal bucket from the wooden table and sets it on the ground under my arm. "I have none of my usual instruments here for collecting your blood, so I suppose I will just have to open your veins and let you bleed."

If I could feel anything in my nearly immobile body,

anger would be boiling over the surface. How I loathe him. He takes a strip of cloth from his pocket and ties it tightly around my upper arm, making my veins rise to the surface in a familiar way.

"You know, Maeve." He runs his knife wetly across a stone to sharpen it. It is a small, much more precise dagger than he likes to use. "I first set foot in the Barrens of Tine-mallacht over a hundred years ago, when I became highdruí to the goddess Brigid. Before that, I lived not far from this tent here, studying with the druí as their experimenter and charged with human sacrifice to the gods."

"So the same crusty old bastard, even after all these years." I try to catch my breath, each one feeling like a challenge now.

"Funny, dear. I had asked the gods to bring me a sacrifice worthy of my talents, a sacrifice that could give and give and give endlessly. It was not until you were born that I knew they had finally answered my pleas."

He brings the blade to the bend of my elbow on my right arm and finds his favorite vein. He cuts, and as he does, blood pours from me, and pain like a rush of fire has me biting clear through my lip while tears stream down my cheeks.

"You were the perfect sacrifice. I have always enjoyed the cries of the weak as their final breaths left them, and yours that never cease were always music to my ears. I could take from you what the gods demanded and then take it again the next day. And you were wonderful each time."

His eyes roll back into his skull, and he groans out in ecstasy. Bile rises in my throat as I watch him salivate. Highdruí take no wives—they deprive themselves of all bodily pleasures. Sir Oli Raven doesn't need any of it. He gets his pleasure with each slice of his blade.

I watch as the bucket begins to fill, and I feel my body

sink into the chair. My head aches and spins like a whirling top. If I had the strength, I would want nothing more than to kill him, but I'm not sure I have it in me anymore. I'm not even sure I'll survive this time.

Somewhere in the distance, I hear the faint shouting of a soldier. I can't make out what he's saying, save for the frantic tone of his voice. Sir Oli Raven's eyes focus, and he looks over his shoulder, then back at the blood.

"Excellent, Maeve. Perfection."

Something smells off in the tent as I struggle to keep my eyes open, something like violence—something that makes my heart settle in a way that tells me the danger is not my own. I try to place it, but my brain is nowhere near functioning now.

The shouts of the men outside the tent grow louder, though I'm rapidly slipping away from awareness.

"By gods, what is going on?"

Sir Oli Raven's gaze shoots to attention as one of the soldiers rushes into the tent, screaming as blood pours from him. Sir Oli Raven jumps back in surprise, knocking into my legs, and my eyes fly open as the soldier falls to the dirt floor. His eyes are gouged out of his head, and blood streams down his face. I can't pinpoint one singular mortal wound, though it looks like rows of razor sharp teeth and nails have shredded his skin from his neck and clear down his torso. The shouts become louder, and the sound of stampeding feet and the metal of swords join the cacophony. I gasp as one, two, three soldiers stumble backward through the tent entrance, only to be pulled a moment later by their legs back to where they came.

"Damnit to Donn!" Sir Oli Raven dashes across the tent to retrieve a long sword from the far corner. He holds it haphazardly, as though he has never wielded anything so large and powerful before. I'm sure that's true—he prefers kitchen knives and scalpels to anything that might be used in a fair fight.

There's a clash like thunder from somewhere outside that shakes the tent, then another, closer now, moving at a hurried and determined pace. Again, the blade crashes, and the sound rushes through my body like a wave of electricity. *Boom!* The tent is filled with the roaring sound of the attack, and bodies fall with suppressed thuds on the dirt as Eoghan pushes through the tent entrance.

His eyes are a blaze of rage and fire, and the tent fills with heat as I take him in. His sword is bloody, his forehead damp with sweat, and his golden cuffs radiate with power. His chest heaves heavily, suppressing just enough of his anger to keep him from becoming the beast within.

"Look, Maeve. Your Captain has arrived."

Sir Oli Raven attempts to tease, but his hands betray him as Eoghan takes a step toward him, and his fingers tremble on the hilt of the long sword. He lifts the blade in front of him with an unmethodical swipe through the air. Eoghan's faster. He swings his blade with so much power, Sir Oli Raven's breaks in two as it falls from his hands. Eoghan steps forward again, and Sir Oli Raven backs up toward the side of the canvas tent—and as he does, the entrance flies open once more, bringing Finn Rhodes and Gálgalesh into view.

"Help Maeve." Eoghan doesn't take his eyes off Sir Oli Raven as the others cross to the center of the room. Finn reaches for the Faebond cuffs, but as he does, the smell of the tent rises again.

"Stop! Don't touch them!" I warn, and I swing my gaze to Gálgalesh, who is examining the crimson rivers rushing from my arm.

"I'll do it. Go help Kael," he says and begins to unlock the bonds with his magic.

Eoghan has Sir Oli Raven pressed into the side of the

tent, nearly blocking him completely. Finn rushes to his side, but Eoghan holds up his hand to stop him.

"Not him. He's mine for what he's done to her." His words are a snarl as he places his blade between them. "For how you mutilated her." He drives the sword deep into Sir Oli Raven's abdomen, a gasp falling from the Experimenter's lips. "For how you used her." Eoghan turns the blade over. "For how you took her innocence and her trust." He shoves the blade in deeper. "And I want you to know, as your life leaves you in this tent, that you did not kill her, but I was never going to stop until I killed you."

Eoghan drives his sword upwards, gutting Sir Oli Raven before he pulls it from him, and the man of my lifelong misery falls to the ground.

Gálgalesh finishes with the bonds around my wrists and unties the leather straps around my ankles. With a welcome rush of power, I feel the gash on my arm close and the blood stop flowing. I stand uneasily, and Eoghan rushes to me, taking my face in his hands and bringing his lips to mine.

"Kael!" Gálgalesh interjects. "Do not touch her!"

"It's fine." Eoghan lifts his lips just a whisper from mine, still cradling me softly with his fingertips. I back away from him. "Maeve?"

"The blood. It smells of—" I begin, but I'm interrupted by the terrible sound of crunching gravel. I jump back as Sir Oli Raven drags himself across the floor.

Eoghan pushes me behind him and raises his blade. Sir Oli Raven—his organs sliding sickeningly across the floor in his wake—reaches for the bucket of my blood, and it spills into the dirt at our feet. Eoghan, Finn, and I fall back as an invisible hand pushes us away from the rush of red like a flood that coats the floor. Sir Oli Raven pants as he hauls the bucket toward himself and sticks out his tongue, running it along the bloody rim.

It is my worst nightmare coming to life. I have never seen the vials of my blood used before, but as his mouth reaches the rim, his body begins to heal.

"Eogh," I say. He grabs my clean left arm, pulling me as close as I'll allow him.

Sir Oli Raven rises to his feet as his body pulls itself together, the wounds from Eoghan's sword closing as if they had never been there in the first place. It's as though I am looking straight into the eyes of death itself, towering over us with a greedy grin upon his face. I quake, and Eoghan's hand grips me tighter as Sir Oli Raven steps forward.

"Clever words, Captain, but it seems you might have forgotten just who your little princess—"

He falters, and his eyes grow wide as something begins to stir within his chest. It's a terrifying sight. Something wrestles around under his tunic, and he brings his hand to his chest. Then, as he opens his mouth to speak, a white foam bubbles up from inside him and pours out past his lips. He gurgles and chokes as the restlessness of his chest continues down the whole of his body, his eyes bulging wildly from their sockets. He tries to step forward, and his feet turn to lead beneath him. He falls to his knees, his body convulsing as his hands scratch at his throat in a desperate plea. Eoghan yanks me back as Sir Oli Raven reaches for us—but then, the Experimenter's hands fall to the ground along with the rest of him, and the choking stops.

Everyone is still as we stare at where Sir Oli Raven lies dead at our feet.

CHAPTER TWENTY-FOUR

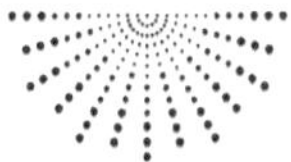

"Do not touch her," Gálgalesh says, his eyes transfixed on Sir Oli Raven's unmoving body.

Eoghan keeps my left hand firmly in his. He's not letting me go. He doesn't care what might happen to him.

"What just happened?" Finn's face is pale, and he looks as though he might be sick.

"Maeve's magic has manifested itself as protection. Sir Oli Raven has now learned what it means to meet death made flesh."

I blanch at Gálgalesh's words. *Death.* I want nothing of it. *But what of him dying? Was that not the most satisfying moment of your life?* My mind betrays me with the thought. There's no denying the sight of Sir Oli Raven gasping and choking on the ground was beyond satisfying. It was retribution, and I felt it sing to my very core.

"A canteen?" I ask. "On that table there? And a rag?"

Finn crosses to the wooden table and searches, coming back with a few clean rags and a bottle of druí wine.

"This is all that's there." He holds them out to me.

"Fine. It'll do." I take the wine, soaking the rags before I begin to wipe the blood from my arms. The wine leaves sticky purple droplets behind, but still, I wipe at each exposed part of my skin and down my legs. I try not to wince at the thought of the endless night when the soldiers made their way into the tent.

Once I make sure I've gotten all of it off me, I throw the empty bottle and the rags onto the ground. I step out of the remains of my dress, and Eoghan sets them all aflame. Then, as naked as the moment of my birth, I throw my arms around him, and he drags me to him, my legs locking around his waist.

"Why would you leave the house?" His voice isn't angry, only drenched in worry.

"I couldn't stand it anymore." I don't care that Finn and Gálgalesh watch on in surprise at my nakedness. I don't care about anything except Eoghan being here with me.

"One day, you are going to get yourself into a lot of trouble, and I won't be able to save you. Then what will I do? If you hadn't told me you were leaving, it would have been days before I got back to Bastain, and we might not have been able to find you."

"I'm sorry," I cry into his shoulder.

"How long were you kept in Faebond?" Gálgalesh finds a blanket in one of Sir Oli Raven's wooden trunks and passes it to Eoghan, who wraps it tightly around me.

"Most of the time. He laced a cake with Angel's Trumpet that paralyzed me, and then after, he..." I pause. "When I was to the point he thought I might not survive, he would release the cuffs and allow me to heal."

Eoghan examines me under the blanket for any physical signs of injury that would never show once the magic has done its job. I push his hand away when it reaches my thigh —wincing as the phantom bruises still sting—and his brows pull together, full of concern. I stare back at him wordlessly, and rage fills him again.

"That would explain how I was able to locate you. Through our blood bond, I can enter your memories and thoughts; it is almost as though I am looking through your eyes when I do. I would hate to do so on a regular basis, since you are constantly pining over Kael, but I thought in this case, it might be the only way. I could not seem to find your magic in my searching; it was as though you had disappeared completely. Then, just for a few fleeting moments, you emerged, and I was able to surmise your approximate location."

"Well, thank you," I say.

Eoghan's eyes are like fire on me now, and I divert my own from his gaze. One of his hands remains on me, supporting me in his arms. He brings the other to my chin and compels me to look at him.

"Who touched you?" His voice is shaking with fury. "Besides him." He kicks Sir Oli Raven's head with his boot.

"Some of the soldiers from the outpost, about a dozen of them."

He places his hands tenderly on me and peels me from his body, placing my bare feet gingerly onto the dirt. He grabs both sides of the blanket to pull it around me like a cocoon and then grabs his sword. He turns to Finn.

"How many of those soldiers did you leave alive in that outpost building?"

"About ten, maybe." Finn unsheathes a blade for each hand.

"Wait here, Maevie."

Eoghan storms from the tent, and Finn follows. I make to leave as well, but Gálgalesh places his hand out to block my way.

"No. Let him finish this. And cover your ears."

Nothing could stop the screams of the men once Eoghan got his hands on them. Piercing and terror-struck, their cries fill the forest as the resounding slashes of Eoghan's blade strike them down one-by-one. By the time he's finished, even the birds are silent with fear.

Eoghan walks back into the tent, his boots and blade covered in blood and his face a steely calm. He extends his hand to me and pulls me to him.

"Let Officer Rhodes know we're ready now."

———

WE ARRIVE BACK at Kael Manor to General Osian Kael, Lowri, Tiernan, and Bryn waiting for us in the courtyard. I drag the blanket further around my shoulders as their eyes take me in. Lowri steps forward first, but Eoghan lifts his blade between them, and she holds her palms out in surrender.

"Do not get near her," he nearly snarls.

At the sound of his anger, Sawney exits the house and crosses the grass, pushing past the others to me. She wraps her arms tightly around my shoulders. With a sigh that sounds like relief, Eoghan releases me into her hands.

"Take her to get cleaned up, Sawney," he says in a much gentler tone. "The rest of you, in the sitting room. *Now.*"

Sawney guides me down the hall toward Eoghan's room. She pushes open the door and settles me at the edge of the bed, where my Tans and linen clothes sit folded in a neat pile, as if I'm a child being called in from a day of play. With the gentlest expression, she crosses to the tub to bring the taps to life.

"We were so worried, Maeve," she says as she empties a jar of fragrant soap into the water, bubbles coating the surface. "Eoghan arrived only about an hour after you left our room, and he was shouting about you leaving. He was so angry. We looked everywhere for you, but when we realized you were gone…I've never seen him so upset. I thought he might burn this house to the ground with Lo in it."

"I'm sorry." I'm not sure what else I can say. Eoghan had sworn he would let the world burn for me, and in his fury, he almost had—in my stupidity. "I shouldn't have left."

Sawney makes her way back to me and then leads me to the tub. She takes the blanket from my shoulders before she helps me step into the oversized bath as the water still fills around me. Once I settle to a seat, she leans me back against the side and wets a cloth she pats along my cheeks and forehead. Had she been a healer in years past? She moves with such gentleness, it's as though caring for the weak and the injured is as second nature to her as breathing.

"No, you shouldn't have, but it was a mistake, and that's all."

We sit in silence as the tub fills, and she turns off the tap. Then, she begins to wipe the wine from my skin. I close my eyes, exhausted, calmed by her soft touch.

"What did they do to you?" She takes a small cup and pours water over my hair before lathering her hands with soap and working her fingers along my scalp. "You don't have to answer."

I wouldn't have the words to tell her even if I'd tried. How does one explain what it feels like to be brought to death's gate over and over and beg for relief, but it never comes? It's almost ridiculous to think I might be sitting here, Sawney's hands in my hair, as if my blood hadn't spilled enough to kill me…minutes ago? Hours?

She finishes with my bath after scrubbing every inch of me clean and then helps me out of the tub again, throwing a towel over me. My hair drips along my back, and I feel heat from her hands begin to pull out the moisture. She picks up a brush and detangles my crimson locks with slow, gentle passes.

"I didn't know you were one of the Fire Cursed," I say, and she laughs softly.

"I'm not, but Lo would find that endlessly amusing. I'm from Oleaíncudd, brought on a slave ship to a brothel in Cuanslí when I was fifteen. I'm a temptress, so I wield the magic of seduction—well, I wield nothing at all. It's a part of me just as I imagine your healing magic is a part of you. I was there until I was nineteen, when Lo found me. She had been passing through to a military camp just a bit inland in Tonn-fórsca, and she noticed the men coming in and out of the pleasure halls and drug dens, abusing women and leaving them half-naked in the alleyways, battered in dark corners. She walked into the pleasure hall I had called home for the past four years, and she killed them, all the men and women who had paid for and benefitted from our services. Then, she sent the tempters and temptresses here to this house, where we were given our freedom. Most chose to find their own ways and crossed over the border into Iranndair, but when Lo arrived back here, I knew I loved her from the moment I saw her, and I stayed."

Sawney had been a slave in a brothel in Cuanslí, no doubt a victim of Bréanainn Doherty. Lowri had saved her, just as Eoghan had saved me time and time again. She sets down the brush and places her hands on my shoulders as she passes her fingers across my skin with a seductive tenderness. She releases me and reaches for my Tans.

"The heat is from the entwining. In Tinemallact entwin-ings, some of the heat of the dragon fire is gifted, in any way the Fire Cursed chooses. I noticed Eoghan has already placed his into your necklace. My hands have always been cold since I was a child, and Lo chose to warm them."

What a remarkably thoughtful gift—so simple, yet

endlessly romantic. I've only once had the opportunity to experience Lowri's tenderness, and it seems everyone is afforded many more chances than I've ever been given. Still, the love she feels for Sawney is so evident, it might rival anything Eoghan and I feel for each other.

"Sawney?" I question aloud, and her hands trace my skin once again as she waits for me to continue. "How does Lowri stand it—with you—I mean..."

I don't find the words to finish my thought. Sawney chuckles softly, though, as if she understands. "How does she stand that every person in the world feels drawn to me because of my magic?" I nod sheepishly. "She doesn't mind it. She understands I can't control what my magic makes others feel, but she knows what we have isn't simply a ruse. I love her, and she loves me, endlessly. That's all we need."

"And how do you stand it?" I'm not sure I ever could.

"After years of being desired, I have allowed it to become only flattery, as one might feel when someone compliments their hair or their outfit. I can always tell when someone is particularly drawn to me—even you, Maeve. Sometimes, it's the desire to be close and seek friendship. Other times, it's arousal. I sometimes wonder if that has to do with how much I feel for that person as well. Magic doesn't let us in on its secrets." My cheeks turn pink at the thought, and she smiles. "Do not be embarrassed. I know you can't control how you feel, and I'm more than thankful for the kindness in your eyes." I wonder if kindness is the right word for it.

"And Eoghan? Has he ever...?" My gods, I can't believe I even ask.

"No. He is the only person I have ever met—human or otherwise—who has not shown a bit of interest in me beyond familial love and kindness. He's a man of purest heart and deepest affection...and he loves you eternally, Maeve."

I shudder despite myself. The night before comes

crashing through my mind, of being taken and used and marred forever. I get dressed slowly, and Sawney waits patiently for me. When I finish, she moves from the bed and motions for me to lie down. Then, she places a woven blanket in warm desert colors over me. She crouches next to me and passes her fingers against my cheek.

"Sleep. I'll let Eoghan know you're resting." She straightens and turns back toward the door. "I'm glad you're safe, my princess."

———

THE FEELING of gentle arms around me nudges me awake. I try to roll over, but a set of lips against the back of my neck and the smell of Eoghan envelops me.

"It's just me," he whispers as he nuzzles close. His hair is wet, and I pass my hand over his bare thigh, only a small pair of underwear high on his legs. "I thought I lost you, Maeve."

His voice is full of sorrow, though none of his anger remains.

"I'm sorry."

"No, *I'm sorry*. I'm sorry I left you here. I'm never leaving you again."

"You had to go. You—"

He cuts me off. "No, Maeve. Nothing in the world makes sense if you're not right here in my arms, safe. I don't care about my orders or this war. They can take everything away from me, as long as I can keep you."

I face him, his expression full of remorse. His hands stay clear of any sensitive places, falling only upon my waist and back. He's fearful I've been hurt—that he might hurt me now. I run my hands up his chest, his collarbone, to his neck, where they settle over his warm skin.

"I love you. I'm never leaving you again." His eyes are so utterly captivating. "Were you hard on her?"

I don't have to elaborate. He knows exactly who I'm speaking of.

"She's lucky I let her live."

"Don't be so angry with her. It was my fault. I barged into her room and demanded to leave, but she told me no and asked me to go back to bed. She couldn't have stopped me."

His fingertips dance along my spine.

"I don't want to have to speak to you through my mother," he grumbles, and I can't help myself—I laugh out loud at the thought.

"I wouldn't answer. I think it's all a hoax to begin with."

His expression cracks, and his laugh lightens his face. "Stubborn Mayhem." His fingers shake as they reach my hair, and he closes his fist around it, tugging just enough to bring my lips closer to his.

"Jealous Dragon."

CHAPTER TWENTY-FIVE

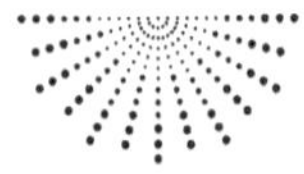

We do not stay another night in Bastain. With Sir Oli Raven's death and the slaughter of nearly fifty royal soldiers, the Capital had renewed its attacks on the Tinemallacht border with as much force as they could muster. The territory, which had been under constant siege for months since Bréanainn Doherty took the throne, is now threatened to the brink of collapse.

"The forces will hold," General Osian Kael concludes.

"Call in the Leader's men. They are ready to desert their posts and help us fight."

Lowri and Eoghan pace in perfect unison back and forth across the room. Bryn stands against the wall next to me, his hands tucked in close against his chest. He traveled without rest to be here from the Iranndairian border when he heard I'd gone missing. His eyes seem weary as he fights off sleep. Gálgalesh stands with the other Tinemallacht officers, including Tiernan, overlooking battle plans strewn across the table. Finn has already left to meet Sullivan in Gobaith.

"We do not need to call them yet, Commandant." General

Kael's tone is always so hard to read. I never know if it is quiet anger or apathy beneath his words.

Lowri nearly growls. "Yes. We. Do. Look around! Entire outposts are being wiped out! The border will fall, and then that fat bastard of a king will be at *your* doorstep to behead you and take over!"

"Easy," Eoghan warns, and Lowri nearly screams in exasperation.

"We have lost one outpost, but as tragic as any loss might be, it gives no indication the border will fall. You will all make your way back to your stations as ordered, and we *will* hold off these attacks."

"I'm not going back to the border." Eoghan's voice is anything but timid, and as his father's eyes fall upon him, he rises to his full, six-foot three-inches in height, and his shoulders square. "I'm taking leave in Gobaith."

"Captain Kael, what reason do you have to take leave? Dereliction of duties, as you well know, would be cause for yet another demotion in rank."

"To prepare for his marriage and entwining ceremony."

I step forward, and all eyes in the room fall on me. I have no idea what I'm doing or if Eoghan had ever planned on such a thing at all, but I've learned enough about Tinemallacht traditions—especially entwinings—from soldiers in the outpost square to know that leave is given to any soldier for a month before his planned marriage and for a month after, regardless of station circumstances. Maybe in that month, we can figure out what the hell we are going to do.

Lowri scoffs loudly, and the others remain silent as their gazes pass between me and Eoghan.

"Maeve…" Eoghan starts.

He's confused. Of course he is. Beyond discussions in the silent hours of the evening, fielding topics of far off plans, we have never spoken of marriage. It always seemed so taboo.

It's only been ten months since I had been preparing to marry Rian Doherty in that very empty room of Caisleán Rialú, only eight since I had met Eoghan in the cold passageway between our tiny quarters at Báscogar. To think, he would want such a thing now… I had to be mad for suggesting it.

I eye him pleadingly as the inquisitive stares of the others make me wish I was able to wield invisibility like General Kael. I watch as Eoghan swallows hard, and then he clears his throat as he gives me a subtle nod.

"To prepare for my marriage and entwining ceremony."

General Kael, for once, displays something I can read. This time, he's the one confused.

"You never told us…" he says, and his General's façade cracks ever so slightly as he takes in his son. "We thought you would choose not to, given the state of things and how deeply Áine's loss has affected her." Eoghan doesn't speak; he barely even breathes. "Very well. You will take leave in Gobaith—unless Commandant Kael is right and the borders fall. Commandant, Lieutenant, you will report to the northern and southern borders, respectively, after two days leave in Gobaith. Now, pack up and head out. I want to see gliders on the sand within the hour."

Everyone nods in agreement as General Kael and the other officers leave the room. Tiernan makes his way to me before he exits.

"I'm glad you're all right," he whispers between the two of us. "I'll let *you* tell Dedra. She's going to demand she sew you a dress herself." He smiles and winks at me as Eoghan approaches. Tiernan turns. "Kael, congratulations."

Eoghan nods once, his jaw tightly set, and Tiernan pats my arm before disappearing through the door. There's something lingering on Eoghan's lips, and Bryn begins to back away from us. Eogh opens his mouth to speak just as Lowri rounds on us. He pauses at the sound of her voice.

"Could you be any more idiotic? They're going to kill you when they find out you aren't getting married, and *you*," she turns to Eoghan, "you're going to get demoted for this, *again*! You'll be lucky if Bryn isn't higher ranked by the time our father is finished with you!"

"Who says we *aren't* getting married?" Eoghan pushes her away lightly with one hand. "Maeve said we are, and we are."

"I think it's brilliant!" Bryn beams, and I can't help but feel sick at the thought of letting him down. The look in Eoghan's eyes warns me of the colossal mess I've caused.

"Shut up, Bryn!" Lowri barks then softens immediately when she takes in the downcast expression on his face. "Let's go pack and leave the two lovebirds alone."

Bryn follows Lowri from the room, and as soon as the door closes, leaving us alone, Eoghan sags against the wall and exhales loudly.

"I'm sorry. I just didn't know what to do! I know you wanted to stay in Gobaith for me, and I just thought—" I feel like I've used all my breath to apologize lately, but what did I think? That I could just say it, and it wouldn't mean anything to him at all?

"Maeve," he says, his head in his hands and his fingers in his hair. "Do you want to marry me?"

Yes, you idiot! my brain screams. My mouth goes dry in an act of betrayal. *Just say yes, Maeve.* But what if that isn't what he wants—not now at least? Maybe all his talk of our future is just that—talk of the *future*, ages from now?

"I haven't thought about it," I finally say.

Liar. Eoghan's hands drop to his sides, and he taps his foot behind him on the wall, his eyes turned from me. Is that disappointment on his face? I thought he would be relieved.

After all, he hadn't seemed ecstatic about the idea a few moments ago.

"Well, you have a month to decide. I won't hold you to it, if you choose otherwise. I already told you, I don't care about my ranks or what they want to take away from me, as long as I can keep you safe."

He doesn't move toward me or embrace me as he always does. There's no soft kiss from him in the way that makes me feel safe or the passionate touch of his hands. He simply pushes himself upright and indicates to the door before walking away and leaving me to stand alone in the large meeting hall.

Lowri is right—I couldn't be any more of an idiot if I tried. What was I waiting for? What was I going to find that is better than Eoghan Kael? I want nothing if it's not him. *Then what holds you back?* I wonder to myself. *The fear he might also try to kill you?* No, not Eoghan. Never Eoghan.

By the time I finally pluck up the courage to face him again and walk back to his room, my rucksack is packed and sitting on the bed. His is gone completely, along with him. Bryn leans against the edge of the tub as I enter—clearly, he's been waiting for me.

"He said to ride back to Gobaith with you. He needed to leave right away."

Of course he did. He needed to be as far away from me and my stupidity as possible. What an absolute mess I always seem to get myself into.

I pick up the rucksack from the bed and swing it over my shoulder before we set off for the Barrens.

————

"Let's stop here for some supper!" Bryn shouts from his glider over the rush of wind.

There is an outpost halfway between Bastain and Gobaith, only a couple kilometers south. Bryn suggested we take the long way, as the dragons fill the valleys in the evenings and he feared navigating between them might prove challenging for a novice rider. We pull up to the gates of the most minuscule outpost—if you can call it an outpost at all—with one pub near the entrance and a handful of houses within its walls, and park our gliders in the sand just outside. Bryn removes his goggles and unclips his boots.

"I'm starving." He sighs and throws his arm around my shoulder. "And this is the best pub in Tinemallacht."

Wonderful. The best pub in Tinemallacht sits out in the absolute middle of nowhere. I'm starting to believe my brother might have been a lunatic. What had drawn him to this place at all, besides his service orders? He could have lived in any of the five territories, and yet he chose to pour sand from his boots each day, as if this place were some sort of nirvana?

Bryn urges me through the gates and to the pub entrance, where he pulls open the door, standing aside for me to step inside. The place is dark, and the temperature is nearly half of that outside. Only small torches burn in holders on the walls, and the low light casts long shadows across the room. The tables are nearly completely empty besides one or two soldiers in their Tans, seated together playing cards. Bryn walks to the bar and takes a seat on one of the tall stools. A slender woman with long brown hair pulled up into a loose bun approaches from the other side of the counter. Her skin is dark and smooth, and she is resplendent. Her eyes are a light brown and dazzle with life, though the long hours behind the bar are evident from her wrinkled apron and the soft glow on her face.

"Bryn!" she greets him with a noticeable Tinemallacht accent, taking his hands in her own and squeezing them gently. "It's been a while since you passed through. You just missed your siblings and Sawney. Heading back from Bastain as well?"

Eoghan had been here? So he hadn't had to rush back to Gobaith after all.

"Hi, Seren." *Seren?* Oh my gods, this day just keeps getting worse... "Yes, heading to Gobaith for a few days leave. I'll be back through in a couple days on my way to the southern border, though. Maybe I'll stop by."

Seren nods with one of the most genuine smiles I have ever seen and then turns her attention to me. "Who's your friend, Bryn?"

If the gods were good, they would turn me into ash right this moment and I wouldn't have to sit here in my embarrassment any longer. Please, please, please, let me leave. I debate the merits of running straight back out the door.

"This is Maeve, Eoghan's—"

"Oh my gods, you're the one." Her mouth falls open, and so does mine. What one? The one who made an ass of herself over and over again? Perhaps the news of me had spread fast, even to the smallest outpost to ever exist. "You're the princess—Cai's sister." Of course, everyone in Tinemallacht knew my brother probably better than I ever had. "You're the one Eoghan spoke about."

I feel my cheeks heat, and I'm suddenly glad for the darkness of the room.

"What did he say about me?" I ask, even though I'm not so sure I want to know.

"Only that you and he are going to marry and that he loves you endlessly. Lowri did say..." She pauses, and this time, I know I don't want to know. "I should have recognized the dragon heart on your chain when you walked in. His is the most recognizable one in Tinemallacht, bigger than all the others by at least two sizes. Not that size matters but..."

She smiles, and I notice one on her bracelet in amethyst. "But you're Cai's sister, aren't you?"

"I take it you knew him."

Sadness fills her face. "Everyone in Tinemallacht knew him, and to know him was to love him. He and Ellis—my husband—were very close. They all fought together, Cai and Ellis and Eoghan." Her thoughts become distant, and she takes a moment to fill two glasses of ale for us before she continues. "We last saw him the night before he traveled to the Capital. He and Áine had brought Theo with them, strapped to a pack on his chest as they surfed the sand from Gobaith, if you can believe it. That was Cai for you, though. He had wanted to meet with Ellis. In fact…" She rummages under the counter a moment and pulls out a leather-bound book. She looks it over once and passes it to me. "He left this with Ellis that night and asked us to keep it safe for him. I thought it might be a journal of some kind—the writing is his, but it's unreadable. Perhaps you'd like it? To remember him by?"

Cai had kept journals all his life, all of which were unreadable to anyone except himself. They were mostly filled with his thoughts on women and the military or the foods he secretly hated. I deciphered one as a child, only to find it was filled with dirty jokes he'd been told by the castle staff. Why had he left this one to Ellis?

"Thank you," I say and open my rucksack to place it inside. Seren watches me for a long moment, taking me in. There's no hostility in her expression. Despite what I'd been told of her and Eoghan, she doesn't look at me with anything but kindness, which makes me feel all the more ridiculous for the jealousy brewing so strongly in my gut.

"Well then. Supper?"

———

WITHIN THE HOUR, after several glasses of ale and too much food that tasted of heaven, Bryn and I leave the pub and Seren behind to complete the second half of the journey to Gobaith. My body feels tired and my head feels drunk. I wonder if I'll ever learn my lesson and not drink myself blind. We weave through the dunes, Bryn guiding us lazily on the wind, and we reach Gobaith as the dragons dance across the sand near the gates.

Bryn laughs loudly at something he hasn't told me out loud as he pushes me up the street, his hands flat against my back. I lean against him, resisting his command and laughing as he stumbles and very nearly falls. He must be more drunk than I am—and we must look a sight, two of the youngest people in the whole outpost laughing and playing in the dusty road.

We reach Eoghan and Bryn's house, and I push open the door loudly before pulling Bryn over the threshold. This time, he almost completely tumbles to the ground and catches himself on the wall. He howls with laughter, and it's not until I help him rise and brace him while he toes off his boots that I see Eoghan leaning in the doorway between the entry hall and the kitchen.

"Go to bed, Bryn," I giggle. He salutes me and dashes toward the stairs, his socks slipping on the tiles. Eoghan watches him as he makes it to the landing and collides with his bedroom door on the way inside.

"Seren's pub, I take it?"

I nod. "He's drank too much."

"And what about you, Mayhem?" There's a hint of amusement in his voice, but he's sober, and his words are clear—unlike my own stupid words every minute of the day.

"I drank less." It was true, though that means next to nothing. "Tell me, Eoghan Kael, why is your dragon heart so big?"

Eoghan laughs. "Some might think that's a crude question."

"Why?" I ask again. "Are you just bigger than all the other men?" I lean against the wall for support as I unlace my boots. He watches my hands, no doubt debating whether he should help.

"Am I the biggest man you've ever seen?" he asks, and a knot fills my abdomen.

"The biggest ego, yes." Another laugh. "Seren quite likes the size of you." This time, the amusement leaves him. He rubs his temples and sighs heavily.

"She does not." I step out of my boots. I feel so small as I approach him, my toes against the cool tile. "She has the dragon heart she desired."

"She's quite pretty, though. Beautiful, even," I press. He watches my lips as I speak.

"She is."

There is no hunger in his words. *Eoghan hated fucking her.* Lowri's remarks ring in my mind, though I can't tell if they ring true. My blood boils bitterly at the thought that he might have enjoyed her, craved her once as he seems to crave me now. Had his tongue, his fingers, all of him pleasured her ceaselessly throughout the night?

"Was she one of your many conquests?" His jaw tightens. "Or was she more than that?" Silence. "Did you offer her *your* dragon heart?"

Deep creases appear between his eyebrows. "You know I didn't, Maeve. You're just looking for a reason to fight, and I don't want to continue to fight with you. I'll fight for you, but I am done fighting with you."

My toes touch his as I stand in front of him. He towers over me in a way that used to scare me—a way that should scare me after what he did this morning, after all the lives he took to save mine. He doesn't scare me anymore, though. Instead, I think I scare him.

"Did I anger you?" I ask.

"No, of course not."

Still, his hands remain in his pockets. He's hesitant to touch me. Maybe he will always be now that my blood reeks of poison and my body is damaged beyond the existence of scars.

"You left without me."

"I needed to clear my head."

He's holding something back, I know he is. He doesn't want to tell me what's wrong…even if I already know. I've backed him into a corner, caged him like a beast caught on the hunt. He feels trapped now, and he's too good to say otherwise.

"Why?" I press.

"Because it's all I could do not to head straight to Gairdín and finish the job by killing that blond bastard. When I got to Bastain and found out you were missing, all I could think was that I would never stop until I found you. If you were harmed, there would be nowhere those men could run that would be far enough to escape me."

"And now that I'm safe?" I'll never get over the way his voice reverberates in his chest and brings goosebumps to my skin.

"I still want to kill him. I want to be rid of him so we can finally move on, so I don't have to worry you won't be here when I come home. But I know when the time comes, you'll be the one to do it—not me."

"You left so you *didn't* kill Rian?"

"I'm still hanging by a thread. Forgive me if I disappear in the night and bring back his head for you the next morning."

Something about his protectiveness sends electric currents through my body.

"I'm sorry about this evening. I wasn't thinking."

"Are you apologizing because you think I was unhappy with you announcing we are getting married, or are you apologizing because you don't have any interest in marrying me at all? If it's the former, there's no need. I've known you were the end of my life as I knew it from the moment I met you. It was never a matter of if, just of when." His hands leave his pockets to grip the front of my shirt and pull me close. I gasp softly as heat grows between my thighs. "And to answer your question, my dragon heart is the biggest because my *dragon* is the biggest dragon in the history of Tinemallacht. And it's yours, since day one. So stop trying to find a reason to hate Seren and shout at me."

He lets me go. I feel lightheaded and flush with color. He smirks, and I realize he's enjoying teasing me. *That bastard.* I take a step away and swing my rucksack from my back. As I do, I remember what Seren had given me at the pub. I reach my hand inside the canvas and find the leather-bound book of Cai's writings.

"What's this?" Eoghan examines the book without touching it.

"Seren gave it to me," I explain. "She said Cai left it with Ellis the night before he left for Gairdín for safekeeping. I haven't opened it, but she says it's unreadable… I imagine it had to be important if he hid it before he left, right?"

Eoghan takes it from my hands and examines it, flipping through the pages and pausing to read the contents. His brows furrow as curiosity and frustration mingle in his eyes. It's the same expression I saw through Gálgalesh's perspective as I entered his dream. He doesn't know a damn thing about it. I could've handed him any old tome, and he would've been more familiar. Then, he closes the book and, without a single word, pushes past me toward the door.

"Put your boots on, Maevie. We're leaving. Now."

CHAPTER TWENTY-SIX

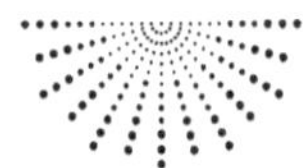

"Where are we going?" I struggle to keep Eoghan's pace as he crosses the outpost square in long, hurried strides, the leather book still held firmly in his grip.

"Kildar." He clears the gates and finds our gliders by the shed, waiting to be cleaned.

"Where?" I pull my goggles back up to my face.

"An unofficial base to the East. Can you ride?"

"Wha—I…" I stammer.

He places his hand behind my elbow and pulls me toward him as he drops my glider to the sand and grabs his own.

"Clip in there." He points to a spot on the board in front of my left boot. I do as he instructs. "And there." He points to my right and holds the glider steady as I step on. Then, he clips his boots in on the outside of my own. His body is pressed against my back, his arms wrapped around me, hands gripping the handlebar. "Feel free to sleep if you get tired."

He pushes off the low slope at the outpost gates, and we head out into the Barrens. The Tinemallacht night has its firm grip on the desert as it calls the beasts to the surface of the sand. Eoghan weaves through them back and forth as we head toward the expanse of land known to be nearly completely uninhabited. There are no outposts to rest, not even one small oasis to hide from the heat of the ever-present sun. Only the best Fire Cursed warriors have braved traveling across it to the eastern seaboard, and some never make it.

"Are we traveling all the way to the coast?" I ask, and Eoghan reaches one hand from the glider to fix my scarf that's fallen from my hair.

"No, we'll be at Kildar by the morning." I nod, my head lulling lightly against his shoulder as my eyes become heavy. "Sleep, Maevie. I've got you."

I'M NOT sure when I fell asleep—whether it was soon after we left Gobaith or well into our journey. I only know I came in and out of consciousness throughout the night. Eoghan pressed on without ceasing, not even stopping to rest or take a drink from the canteen strapped to his glider.

How long had he been fighting off sleep? How many days has he gone without it? He'd come back from battle to find me and had not rested until we'd reached Bastain, but even then, we only enjoyed one or two undisturbed hours before we were summoned by General Kael once again.

When we finally come to a stop, Eoghan rubs my arm lightly to wake me, and I groan and stretch against him. Eogh unclips from the glider and stretches before helping me off. Then, he sets the glider aside under the shade of the towering walls of a lone structure. Though it resembles Tinemallacht architecture up close, from a distance, it doesn't resemble a building at all. If it's a military base, it's the most magnificent example of camouflage I have ever seen.

"I had thought…"

"It's designed to blend into the dunes," Eoghan explains. "It's the only way to keep it off the radar of the royal military when they fly over in their airships—or at least, when they used to fly over in their airships."

"But why is it hidden?" He takes my hand in his, and I feel the warmth of the sun on his skin from hours surfing along the sand. Strange how I can tell the difference now when he's so warm all the time.

"Because it's not the king's men at this base—it's the Leader's."

He knocks on the large, sand-colored doors, and they make an intrusive, unmistakable sound that tells me they are made of solid, and very heavy, metal. There's only the vacant sound of silence as a response, though Eoghan isn't deterred. He waits for a long moment before he knocks again, and this time, we hear the sound of clicking locks and barricades being dragged away.

"Take a step back," Eoghan commands smoothly. I don't hesitate, and for that, I thank the gods, as the next instant the doors swing open, and at least a dozen soldiers stand there, with their long swords raised, one of which just grazes Eoghan's throat. Eoghan doesn't even flinch. "You'll take an eye out with that thing, Cross."

The man in front of us I recognize immediately as Kimbal Cross, one of the escapees from Báscogar. He sighs and lowers his sword. The other men follow.

"Are you aware of the time?" Cross is annoyed rather than angry.

"Did I wake you, Kimbal? I thought your duties started an hour ago."

Cross steps aside, and Eoghan leads me forward into the

base. There are no windows in this place, and the light is so much dimmer than the sunlight, and I'm momentarily blinded.

"A raven would have been nice. I might have even shaved for you."

"Have I ever shown up announced?" Eoghan speaks in such an urbane manner, I nearly salivate. There's no question he outranks Cross at least ten-fold here. "I'm here in search of something that might be of value. Have the Leader's quarters remained intact?"

Cross leads us down the darkened corridor into the depths of the base. Though it's still an unreasonable hour, there are soldiers everywhere. I try to count each as I pass, but I lose track and give up rather quickly as I struggle to distinguish between faces in the dark. There have to be hundreds of men here. *What were you building, Cai? Someone had to know.*

"We haven't moved most of it since the coup. We were waiting for your orders, actually."

We walk on through the dark halls, men passing with their breakfasts or rushing by with orders in their hands. What could they possibly have to do here now that their leader is gone? Did any of them know?

We reach a door at the far end of a busy hall, and the two men pause in front of it.

"The only thing that's been taken are the Leader's letters. Gálgalesh had them transported to Gobaith, as you know." Eoghan nods, and Cross hands him a key. I almost laugh at the sight of it. What good is a key—or a lock at all—when there's magic to open them? "If you need anything, I'm on duty all morning."

Eoghan thanks Cross and waits for him to leave before unlocking the door with the metal key in his hand. When I sigh dramatically, his lips turn up deviously at the corners.

"Maevie, how much were you taught about magic in that Steel Citadel of yours?"

"Enough to know a key does nothing if someone can wield."

"Oh really?" He continues to fiddle with the lock that proves to be a complicated process of turns in various directions as though in a sequence. "Then why have locks at all?"

"I do not know, Eoghan Kael," I muse.

He simply laughs. "I'll let Gálgalesh fill you in on the futility of human magic later."

The lock gives way, and the door swings open to an office as dark as the Romiodóg winter sky. Eoghan mutters something under his breath, and the room fills with a light brighter than that of the hallway, yet still dim enough to not jar our vision.

The space is large and enjoys similar comforts to that of the warden's quarters at Báscogar. In the room sits a desk in dark wood with several drawers on each side. There are cabinets and large wooden trunks scattered all over the space, and books in the forbidden language are piled high on the desk and along the cushions of the sofa in the corner. The place is a cluttered mess, to say the least.

"Your brother, gods be damned, was not always the most organized."

Eoghan crosses to the desk. I notice three identical frames nearly hidden beneath the chaos there. I follow him and take the photos in. One is of Áine, Cai, and baby Theo, though he is perhaps only a few days old in the photo. Cai presses his lips to Áine's cheek while he cradles the tiny child in his arms, and though the image is only a second in time, his happiness overflows. Another is of Cai and Eoghan, both shirtless and sweaty, laughing together in what I recognize as the Gobaith outpost square. They hold daggers loosely at their sides—no doubt sparring with one another for fun. The third photo, however, takes me by surprise as I see my own face staring back at me, a smile across my lips.

It might be the only photograph of me in existence, and I remember the day—the first time Cai had returned home after he had earned his title of hero and legend in the Third War. I must have been only fourteen or fifteen then, and I had clung to him every moment from the time he arrived. I look so young in the photograph, I scarcely recognize myself at all. My cheeks are round and pink, and my hair falls carelessly around my face in a color that seems so distant, it might as well belong to someone else. She was me, but also only a memory of a ghost now, as much as Cai is.

"He hid that photo after he showed me. I think he was scared I might fall in love with you if I looked at it too long." Eoghan fiddles with a drawer. "The bastard was always right."

I can't say I knew my brother well. In fact, I know him less and less every day. But what has become abundantly clear is that the man they call the Leader loved me more than I had ever been able to comprehend. I'm beginning to think his love was the defining trait that set him apart from everyone else and made others love him too.

"Eogh?" I say as I finally tear my eyes away from the photographs. "Why are we here?"

"We are here..." Eoghan huffs as a long, thin drawer finally gives way to reveal about fifty identical keys. "To find out what was so important about this journal that Cai thought to hide it before he left for your wedding. The date on the first page is less than a year before that day, and I can't read any of what it says, but maybe something in this office might help make sense of it. Give me a hand with these, will you?"

I examine the contents of the drawer. "You aren't serious!

There are hundreds of different possibilities in this room. These keys might go to any one of the cabinets or trunks."

"Well, we better get started then." He scoops up about a dozen keys and lays them into my hands.

———

"Eogh, we are never going to figure this out."

It has been hours since we arrived at Kildar and we have only managed to open one cabinet…which held an assortment of dull daggers that no longer had the power to penetrate fabric, much less flesh. I'm not sure what we expected. With no direction and no understanding of what we're looking for, there's little chance we might find answers here.

"I know." He falls to a seat on the floor, his eyelids heavy with fatigue and his shoulders sagging. "I thought if anything might lead us to answers, it would be here. As always, though, Cai's ways continue to just leave more questions." He rubs the back of his neck with his hand. "Are you ready to head back to Gobaith?"

He hands me the journal and makes to stand. I place my own on his chest softly and push him back to a seat.

"No. You're exhausted. You'll never make it back at this rate."

Eoghan shrugs in a valiant way that tells me I am right, even if he won't admit it.

"How about you rest a bit before we leave?" I crawl toward the sofa and begin to drag the dusty piles of books to the floor. "When you're ready, we can go."

"And what will you do as I rest?"

"I'll make some friends and find us something to eat." I will him up onto the cushions. "I'm at least capable of that."

He takes a dagger from his thigh and passes it to me. I reject it with a silent shake of my head. "I lived at the most dangerous prison known to man for six months, next to the most dangerous prisoner in all of Báscogar."

"Artur Lobo wasn't all that bad." He laughs tiredly. So very like him to make jokes.

"Very funny. I'll be fine without you for a few hours, Eoghan Kael. Rest."

He doesn't like it. He would probably do anything to object, but he's weak with exhaustion, and his body betrays him as he settles down against the soft surface.

"Don't make me have to come save you again," he says as his eyes fall shut, and I barely loose a sarcastic laugh before he's asleep.

I push up from the floor and quietly leave the room. I head up the corridor, unsure where I am going at all, only that I haven't used the lavatory since I had consumed a few too many—very large—glasses of ale. I'll start there, and then maybe I can concentrate on something like a half-decent meal. I wander down the winding labyrinth of passages leading much further than I even imagined the structure would have extended. I imagine that's part of its design, to conceal the truth of this place from any visitor or foe.

Still, I would love to find at least one toilet in this place, and so far, I've come up short. A group of soldiers approach in the opposite direction; I count five in total chatting to one another, and I step in their path as they reach me. At a distance, I had suspected them to be men, from their cropped haircuts to their slim frames. I couldn't have been more wrong. I sigh with relief as five women halt in front of me.

"Excuse me," I begin, the urgency evident in my voice. "Do you know where the nearest lavatory is?"

The women look to one another as though silently deciding who would put me out of my misery while giving me zero acknowledgement at all. It's the smallest in the back of the pack that finally speaks first.

"Down this way and at the next hall. You can't miss it."

Want to bet? I thank her and step aside, rushing down the corridor at a desperate pace. I enter the washroom lined with stone basin sinks and stalls of toilets and thank the gods for small mercies—even when it feels like we haven't been able to find one bit of consolation in months. I rush to a toilet and relieve myself quickly, finish up, and place my hands under the cool tap, thankful once again for the tiny pleasures of clean water after rummaging for hours in Cai's dusty quarters. I dry my hands and then step back out in the corridor… right into the five women.

"Oh!" I say in surprise. I take a step back as the women fill the hall between each wall.

"Do we know you?" one of the women, with blonde hair cut close to her skull and a tattoo running down her neck, asks.

I hesitate. I haven't hidden my identity since I arrived in Tinemallacht, but I'm not about to get killed for it here by a group of women who saw fit to corner me outside the toilets. Regardless of how Eoghan trusted Cai and this place, I'm not sure *who* I can trust anymore, apart from him and Gálgalesh.

I shake my head. "I don't think so."

I give them an apologetic smile as I start to push past them. One of the other women, a brunette with hair to her chin and a sword strapped to her back, places her hand in front of me. *Shit.*

"You look so familiar. Are you a new recruit?"

"I guess you can say that…" I debate trying to move her arm out of the way. I examine the muscles on her and decide against it. Instead, I call on the faerie magic as I face them.

"A soldier or a wife?" one of the women asks.

"Pardon?" *Concentrate on the end of the hall, Maeve.*

"Well, we have soldiers here, and we have wives and

husbands. Sometimes, the women are both or just one, but none of us can figure out which you are."

"I'm…I'm…"

They stand, surrounding me, and nearly all tower over me as they eye me curiously. My heart pounds in my chest as the blonde woman—she must be the leader of the pack—stares me down with an intensity I can't read. *Fuck this*. Every time I'm alone, I find myself in need of saving. Not this time. I refuse to get into more trouble. I lock my eyes on the end of the hall and wield.

Like my center is being pulled by an invisible hook, I disappear from between the circle of women and feel myself travel through space at full tilt then land just a heartbeat later. *Too far!* my brain screams as I slam into the wall at the far end of the intersection of passageways. My boots slide beneath me as I try to keep upright. The group of women wheel around in confusion at the sound and shout as they realize what has happened. I curse and slide as I push myself off the wall, hurling myself down the passageway. A flurry of boot steps echo through the halls as the women race to catch me.

Shit! Shit! Shit! I run harder, my legs exhausted and sore, my mind still unsure where I'm going in the first place.

"Stop!" the women shout in unison as they chase after me.

"Leave me alone!" I shout back. I don't care how far I have to run now. I'm not stopping until I get back to Eoghan or lose these women somehow.

I turn down another hall, and all the women scream for me to stop again, this time more urgently. I throw my middle finger up into the air toward them and make a left at the next, very dark, corridor. Their screams become almost frantic this time—so frantic, it makes me slow down just a tiny bit, just enough for the blonde woman to barrel into me, knocking me over. She tumbles toward the floor along with me.

I tuck my body and roll as I fall while I reach for a dagger at my side. I land on my back as she falls forward toward my face, and I throw my magic out to catch her, just inches from the tip of my blade. She gasps, and the other women halt.

"Leave me alone!" I shout.

"I wasn't trying to hurt you," she pants. "There's a dragon's den at the end of these halls."

I lift my head from the floor and look. Not another one hundred yards down the corridor, the floor gives way to a colossal trench diving down into the blackness of the Earth. From it, the low rumble of a dragon's purr can be heard. Why is there a dragon in the middle of this base?

Like an invisible hand, I call on my magic to push her to her feet and sheath my dagger. Then, slowly, I rise to face her and the others.

"Why did you run?" she asks. I don't answer. She takes a step forward—I take one back. She raises her hands in submission in front of her. "We aren't going to hurt you. Are you…are you Princess Maeve?"

"Of course not." I snap.

"She's a terrible liar," another woman laughs. "But she can't hide those big brown eyes."

I'm not fooling anyone here. "It's just Maeve."

"We knew it!" the brunette with the sword says. "We knew it when we saw you in the corridor, but we thought it stupid to assume. We couldn't figure out why you would be—"

I hold up my hand between us. "I don't mean to be rude, but I am just looking for the dining hall and a bite to eat. Then I'll be gone."

The brunette tries to speak again, but this time, the blonde woman cuts in. "Of course. We can take you there."

———

THE DINING HALL is filled with men and women in matching Tinemallacht Tans, all eating, chatting, and working at long wooden tables situated around the room. It is amazing to me how much Báscogar resembles military life. The women lead me to the food station, and my plate is filled with desert delicacies I've found to be staples no matter if I am at the outpost or at Kael Manor—always piquant and never gray mush.

The others fill their own plates, and we sit at a table near the far end of the room. The blonde woman with the tattoo raises her fork as she nods as if in a toast. I lift my own in acknowledgement before I bring it to my lips.

"I'm Alia," she says. "This is Zara." She points to the brunette with the sword. "Hana, Sofia, and Farah." The other women silently gesture in turn. "Apologies for scaring you, by the way."

They would have scared me by simply breathing after the past few months I've endured.

"It's fine. Sorry I ran away." I dig my fork into my plate. "Do you all live here at the base?"

Alia, who seems to be the leader of this group, pauses as she finishes a mouthful of her own meal. I watch her eyes as she looks around the room, as though she's deciding if it's a suitable place to call home at all. I think back to the previous months in the mountains of Romiodóg. A pang of longing rushes through me, and I can't help but think any place could be home if something makes it feel like you're meant to be there.

"We do. Most of us here do now. Some only come for a few days at a time if they are lucky enough to be from within the borders. We're from the Borderlands, so travel is nearly impossible now."

The Borderlands? After all our weeks of fighting, I hadn't

given a thought as to what might have become of the Borderlands since the Dohertys had taken the throne.

"And what do you do here?" What could be so important that hundreds of fighters stay here with no direction and no reason?

The women's lips curl into a smile. "We are building the start of a new Draíocoinnigh, of course."

"On whose orders?"

"The Leader's, naturally. Do you not know where you are? This was where he was forging a new government. A better Draío for the people—where we would live as equals, regardless of whether we are aristocrats or common folk. It all starts right here, in these walls. We," she motions to herself and the other women, "are charged with making sure there's a place for our kind here. Women have always had an integral role in the Leader's plans."

Excuse me? My fork slips from my hand. Eoghan had sworn to me Cai had not sought to usurp our father, but this is what it might look like if he had. Bringing followers together, promises of a new and better world, the secrets… Even in the letter he had written to Gálgalesh, he had stated his fears of attending my wedding. Had he really not been a part of what happened at all? Could I believe he hadn't had a hand in it, only for it to have gone astray?

"You seem surprised, but you were his sister, were you not?"

"Yes…"

"And are you not here to help in his cause?"

I'm not sure why I'm here anymore. "I'm here for answers I suppose…"

"What answers do you seek, Maeve Moran?"

Where do I begin? I, once again, know nothing at all—less than nothing, except for an enormous hole in my gut that tells me no one is as they seem—and no one is as good as they're made out to be. I reach into my pocket and pull out the leather-bound journal. I place it onto the table between us. Alia's eyebrows rise—not in question, but in interest.

"Have you seen this before?" I ask.

"I have."

"Can you tell me why the Leader gave Ellis Lago this journal?"

She shakes her head. "No, but I can tell you where the others are."

"Others?" I lean forward, abandoning my plate of food. "There are others like this?"

"Hundreds." From her pocket, she pulls a timepiece I recognize as the one so often carried by my brother. It is silver and almost unremarkable beside the engraving of his initials on the case, and it hangs at the end of a long, simple chain. She turns it over in her hand and digs her short nail into an indentation in the back. With a small *pop*, the casing dislodges, and a key falls into her awaiting palm. "Shall we?"

———

"Eoghan, wake up!" I shove his shoulder much too hard, and he groans in protest. "Eoghan!" I shove him again, and this time, his eyes fly open.

"What's the matter?" He jumps up to a seat, his eyes darting wildly around the room, momentarily confused by his surroundings. "Are you all right?"

"I'm fine," I laugh. "Eoghan, this is—"

"Commandant Darwish." Eoghan's tone is reserved as his eyes find Alia by the door. His shoulders square as she crosses the threshold.

"General Kael." Alia steps toward us.

General Kael? *General?* Eoghan is only ranked as a captain in the royal military. Why would she call him 'General'?

Eoghan rises to his feet and tugs at the hem of his tan shirt to straighten the wrinkles that had formed as he slept.

"What is it, Maeve?" I notice his eyes do not leave Alia, even when he addresses me.

"Well, I went to find something to eat while you slept, and I ran into Alia on the way…"

"Nearly ran her dagger through my eye more like it." Eoghan lets out a huff of a laugh.

"Yes, sorry about that," I mutter. "We were speaking and…" My mind is racing, my heart beating out of my chest.

"And…?" Eoghan finally turns his gaze to me, and the intensity of the green and gold takes me by surprise. He isn't Eoghan Kael, my gentle, passionate lover right now. He is Eoghan Kael, the legendary warrior of Tinemallacht.

"I think I might have what you need." Alia holds the key out for Eoghan to see. "This way."

She exits the room. Eoghan places his hand on the small of my back and urges me forward while he keeps pace behind me. Alia winds through the halls, her shoulders back and her gait easy. We walk past classrooms filled with small desks, dormitory halls lined with doors on either side, an armory, a training gymnasium filled with men and women taking their turns sparring. She leads us on until the corridors become darker and quiet, and a muggy warmth settles in the air. Then, she stops.

"Just ahead and down into the pit. There's a single door this key fits." She places the key into my hand.

"Are you not coming with us?" I ask. She folds her arms against her chest and leans against the wall.

"I can't enter the pit. I'm from the Borderlands. Only the Fire Cursed are allowed near the dragon, and she will incinerate everything in that room if anyone except the Leader— or his blood—opens that door. It has to be you."

Lovely. The low purr of the dragon's rumbling snores

filter from the pit beyond. Eoghan's heat rises in anger. He takes a step toward Alia, who only shrugs absently as he approaches.

"Who gave you this key?" he demands. She takes the timepiece from her pocket and dangles it inches from his nose.

"Who do you think, General? You aren't the only person he trusted. Clearly."

There's a long moment of silence—I watch as Eoghan's hand slides across his daggers at his sides.

"All right, I'll go," I cut in before he can gut her. "Unless we want to wait for Theo to do it." Alia smirks, and Eoghan throws her a nasty look. He doesn't like her and she knows it. It doesn't seem to bother her one bit.

"No, Maeve. I'll go," Eoghan says and takes one small but threatening final step toward Alia before turning away. "You aren't one of the Fire Cursed. It's not safe."

"You heard what she said. Only Cai or someone of his bloodline can open that door, or else the dragon will incinerate what's inside…and we need what's inside."

"Fine. I'll kill the dragon first then." He's unsheathing his daggers as he speaks. There is no sarcasm in his voice, but I almost laugh out loud.

"You are *not* killing the dragon. I'm going. You wait here."

I shove the journal into his hands and turn away to face the dark end of the passageway and pit beyond.

"There's a ladder on the righthand side. Try not to step between her claws, or she might kill you for it anyway," Alia encourages.

Well, here goes nothing, I think to myself and disappear down the corridor into the dark.

CHAPTER TWENTY-SEVEN

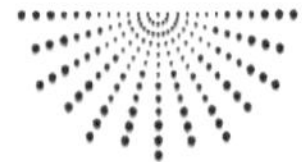

I stand at the edge of the pit and look down into the depths of the darkness. I see no dragon. I see nothing at all besides a small iron ladder leading into the black abyss. Even if I do make it to the door down there, I won't be able to see the lock to insert the key. This has got to be the dumbest place to hide anything. *Or the most brilliant*, I reason. No one would attempt to retrieve anything from here—except me, and I've been known to do the most dangerous and idiotic things known to man.

"Maeve," I hear Eoghan call from behind me. "That dagger I gave you at Báscogar…"

"What about it?" I reach for my thigh and feel for the hilt.

"Hold the blade up over the pit."

If that is not the most ridiculous advice I have ever heard in my life, it might at least be in the top three. I scoff and unsheathe the dagger in the darkness, holding the blade over the pit just as the resting dragon exhales a puff of hot steam that nearly chokes me. As precipitation pearls up against my fist, the blade in my hand begins to glow with a bright purple light, illuminating the end of the passageway and the pit below.

I look down and gasp as a thirty-foot long dragon comes into view, curled up into a nest on the pit floor. She's a burnt red color, with sharp talons and a strip of shimmering scales down her back. Her head rests on her front legs, and her tail wraps around to her front as she sleeps, pointed into an arrowhead at the end.

"The blade is inlaid with dragon's blood and glows when it's in contact with dragon fire or heat from it. Use it to see when you're down in the pit, but don't raise it when you're in her presence; she'll feel threatened and attack you if you do."

"Great," I say sarcastically. "Anything else?"

"I love you, so try not to die. I'd hate for my leave to be cut short and our wedding to be cancelled on account of your death. I was looking forward to a few weeks of rest."

He's decided to be funny now. I loose a dramatic laugh and take one more deep breath as the light of the blade fades and then reignites at the next bit of heat rising up from below. I wipe the sweat from my face. Even in the light fabric of my short-sleeved shirt, I feel as though I'm baking. I cross to the small ladder, place the hilt of the blade between my teeth, and begin the slow descent to the bottom.

Every step I take into the den, the dragon lets out another exhale of breath…and each time, the heat rises up my back and drenches my skin. I thought the dryness of the desert heat was bad, that the unrelenting sun might be the end of me, but this is worse. My palms grow damp and slippery on the iron ladder, and I struggle to grip the rungs as my boots slide along the moisture built up under my feet. I'll be lucky if I don't fall and break my neck—I'm not sure my magic can heal that one.

I continue the climb, nearly wrapping my arms clear around the ladder to secure myself before I can make it to the bottom. Each movement, I find it harder and harder to breathe. If Cai weren't already dead, I might have killed him for such a stupid hiding spot. Red rust covers my arms as it peels away from the metal in disgusting, chalky clumps. I reach the last three rungs, and as I step, the iron gives way under my boot. I stumble and catch myself to keep from falling, but I look down. Of course, the last three rungs have rotted and crumbled into nothing resembling a ladder at all.

"Maeve! Are you all right?" Eoghan shouts as my sweaty hands slide with a loud squeak against the iron.

"I'm fine!" I call back, the dagger still in my mouth. I wrap my hands and feet around the outer edges of the ladder and slide down to the bottom of the pit.

The smell is what reaches me first. Dragon piss. I nearly gag as it fills my nostrils in a nauseating cloud. There must be some sort of spell to keep the smell at bay from the corridor above, because I smelled nothing of it before I reached the floor. I take the dagger from between my teeth, the light of it dimming, all but fading away as the dragon's snores have gone quiet.

Just find the door and get what's inside, I tell myself.

I turn in the darkness to the center of the pit, and something moves in the black that envelops me, like a shadow that makes the hairs on the back of my neck stand. Then, with another hot, wet gust of dragon's breath, my blade ignites and brings me face to face with an angry—and very awake—dragon.

"Eogh!" A dangerous purr rumbles through the dragon's chest as it holds me in its gaze, its enormous teeth bared. "I think it's angry!"

"Fuck!" I hear him say loudly. "Hold on! I'm coming down!"

"No! Just tell me what to do!"

He hesitates. The iron creaks as he leans against the

ladder to peer into the pit below. The dragon's lips quiver, and my muscles tense. It drags its front foot forward, and I step backward into the wall, its snout so close to me, my hands tremble.

"Eoghan!" I shout.

"Bow your head to her. Let her see you yield to her power."

Bowing means I place my delicate head only about an inch from those horrible teeth…and I happen to need my head to stay firmly upon my shoulders. The dragon's breath makes sweat roll down my face, and large droplets to fall into the sand. I'm not sure I can will myself to move, let alone bow to the beast in front of me. The dragon lets out a louder, much more dangerous purr.

"I don't think I can!" I concede.

"Do it, Maeve, or she will eat you." His voice is the angry command of the Leader's General, and my head snaps forward in an instant as I bring my gaze to the floor. I can almost feel the dragon's teeth against my hair. "Good. Now, hold still."

I couldn't move if I wanted to—I'm so paralyzed by fear. I listen to the silence as the dragon's hot breath burns my scalp. My hair, my skin, my clothes are soaked in sweat. Finally, I feel a bit of minor relief as the dragon takes one step backward and places the tiniest bit of space between us. I straighten to see the dragon still glaring at me, its teeth slightly less bared now.

"Now, she will need to smell you. You need to relax and take the dagger to your hand. Make a small cut into your palm and offer it up to her."

"Are you insane?" I am *not* going to offer my blood up to a man-eating dragon!

"Just trust me! You need to relax!"

Easy for him to say! He doesn't have a dragon waiting to eat him!

I take another deep breath and lift the blade to my palm. I press it down against my skin, but with a snarl, the dragon whips its head around and knocks me to the ground. It moves like a streak of deadly red fire and stands over me, its face directly above mine, its claws on either side of my body, its teeth snapping just inches from my face.

"Your blade scared her!" There's panic in Alia's voice as she shouts down at me. "General!" she begins.

"Do it now, Maeve!" Eoghan commands, and I press the blade to my palm and drag it across the surface. Pain sears as blood bursts along my skin. A tribute to the beast. The wound heals with the work of my magic almost immediately, leaving just a dripping streak of red where the blade penetrated.

I drop the blade to my side and shove my hand up between myself and the dragon's gnashing jaws. It freezes as I pant for air. She sniffs my hand in short, testing inhales, and droplets of my blood roll down my wrist onto my face. She pauses, her eyes staring unflinchingly into mine. I stare back. *I have not come this far to be killed by a dragon. I will NOT be killed by a dragon.* Then, she leans forward and presses her snout down against my chest.

The heat is nearly unbearable as the weight of her colossal head presses into my chest, pushing the breath from my lungs. I cough and wheeze as I try to breathe under the weight of her. She's crushing me. I feel myself sink into the sand as she pins me there. If I fight, I'm dead, but if I stay here...well, my fate might be the same either way. I feel the sand begin to cover me as I sink lower. I take shallow breaths, trying to will the air into my lungs. She lifts her head from me momentarily, and I gasp loudly, dragging in an influx of much-needed air. As I do, she presses her head down against me once more with renewed force. I feel the ground beneath me give way as I fall through the sand and disappear under the surface.

I fall slowly, as though I'm a feather gliding softly to the Earth, through an empty chamber until my body tilts of its own accord and my feet land flat on a stone floor. I look up and see a ceiling of sand suspended above me, as if held by some enchantment. The room is circular and large and completely bare, but a small orb of light glows ceaselessly to illuminate the space. On the wall to my right, a single door, metal and etched with an engraving of a dragon, catches my eye.

"Maeve!" Eoghan shouts from above.

"I'm fine! Stay where you are!" I yell back.

I step forward, and the sound thunders through the empty space. I cross the room to the door and grab the knob. It grows hot in my hand, and I jump back in surprise. Across the door, words in red, smoldering embers appear.

> *In the quiet whisper of the dragon's relent to she,*
> *Take in hand the guardian of all mystery.*
> *Thrice to the east, where dawn's light grows,*
> *Turn the key as the soft wind blows.*
> *Once to the west, under fading sky's crest,*
> *Twist it back where the stars suggest.*
> *As secrets stir and whispers flee,*
> *The room shall open, revealed to thee.*

The guardian of all mystery… I feel the key turn warm in my pocket, and I dig it out delicately. This must be the instructions on how to open the door. I place the key into the lock and read through the words across the surface. *Thrice to the east.* I barely know which way is up in this base, let alone east from west.

"When facing the passageway, which direction is east?" I shout. There's a long pause as I wait for Eoghan to answer. "Eoghan, it's a combination lock! Which direction is east!"

"Uh…left!" he shouts back at me.

Left. I spin the key in three, full counter-clockwise turns. *Once to the west, under fading sky's crest, twist it back where the stars suggest.* One full turn to the right then. I turn the key, and the lock clicks with a metallic thunk. The key turns cool, and I let it go as I take a step back. It begins to spin like a top in the lock at increasing speed. I watch it twirl and whirl as the words on the door disappear. Then, the key slows to a stop. I wait for something more to happen, but to my disappointment, nothing does. The door has become lifeless once again. I step forward, and as I do, the door engulfs itself in purple flames that burn fast and bright. I watch as the metal melts away into nothing, and its secrets are revealed.

I blink once, then twice. In front of me, a treasure trove of journals line the shelves of a large vault, leather-bound books in various sizes by the hundreds, stacked high to the ceiling, each just like the one Seren had given me at the pub.

"You're not going to believe this, Eogh!" I shout as I take a step inside and count the books.

I give up quickly. There are just too many. I step deeper into the vault and notice a thin outline of light along the wall. I approach it to find a small, unassuming door. I reach for the handle in the dark and turn it, stumbling as I fall into a dim passageway. I look around, only to see Eoghan's back to me as he gazes into the black pit below.

"Ah-hem," I clear my throat loudly, and he and Alia wheel around on their heels, their eyes wide. I shrug my shoulders casually as I hold the door open to them in offering. "Would you like to see what that dragon's been hiding all this time?"

CHAPTER TWENTY-EIGHT

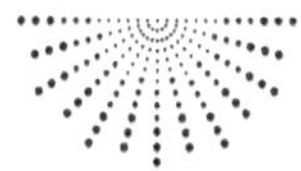

I am seven years old, and the White Night has kept me awake into the wee hours of the morning. Nanny Gwen sits in her chair beside the fire as she signs to the maid, her hands hidden in her lap so I can't see.

"A stupid child. She is slow to learn and easy to fool—just as her father hoped she would be."

I peer on as they speak to one another, mistaking the pile of blankets and pillows for my tiny figure as I crouch beside the sofa. If they catch me out of bed eavesdropping, I suspect I'll feel the sting of Nanny Gwen's hand on my backside for a week.

"The boy has a mouth on him," the maid—who is no more than three years my brother's senior—signs back. "He might be a formidable king one day."

"If King Cashel doesn't decide to do him in first for his insolence. The boy is stupid in his own right. He has no idea he is being raised for slaughter."

"Do you think the king would send his only suitable heir to die in battle?"

"Who says he would ever make it to battle to begin with?"

The maid shifts her weight on the cushions and throws her feet up onto the sofa. It is forbidden to sit on the royal family's furniture in Caisleán Rialú, but none of the servants take the rules very seriously when they aren't in the presence of my father or mother. I slide against the side of the sofa to hide myself further in the darkness.

"Why does he write as though he cannot spell? Does he not have tutors?" the maid asks. Nanny Gwen's eyes are falling tired now, and she lets out an exasperated huff.

"He writes in code. It's to hide from his father, and I imagine us as well. He keeps a sheet of parchment with his codebreaking key in his desk. He has changed it a few times over the years. He's clever for that at least. I don't care what the little prince writes about his wretched father, so I don't bother to read it." The two women laugh quietly to one another before Nanny Gwen rises. "I'm off to bed."

They each throw one more glance toward my bed as I slide silently under the low table at the back of the sofa. I wait for them to leave before standing and tiptoeing to the door, where I peek my head out into the hall and watch the women disappear into the darkness. Then, I sneak from my room in the other direction, toward Cai's.

The room is twice as big as my own, which means it is gigantic, and an even bigger mess. Cai has never been known to be tidy. The door creaks ever so slightly as I turn the knob and push it away, and I pause as I wait for a response. When I am greeted by none, I continue into the room, illuminated faintly by the light of our endless summer night. I creep over to the desk at the far end of the room; It's stacked high with books and parchment and pens empty of ink. Cai's leather-bound journal sits in the center, the pages open to dry the nonsensical paragraphs he's written before bed. A single drawer runs end-to-end underneath the desk, and I grip it in my tiny hands and pull it toward me. I rummage through the contents, nearly too much for it to comfortably conceal, and find the lone piece of parchment at the bottom. I drag it up and begin to unfold it.

"That's not for you, Evie."

He's caught me. I wheel around, and a fifteen year old Cai stands before me in silk pajamas, his hand outstretched. I sigh and hand the parchment over to him, and he guides me back to my room.

———

EOGHAN NEARLY PUSHES Alia aside as he races to meet me. He laces his arms around me and presses his lips to my sweaty hair. Alia saunters over behind him, unsurprised by my emergence into the hall. He rounds on her as she approaches, throwing up his hand to block her advance.

"You knew there was an entrance in this hall, and you sent her down into that pit anyway?" His voice is forceful, strident, full of disdain.

"She *had* to enter through the pit; but now that she has, we can enter this way."

Alia takes a step forward, and Eoghan draws his blade, the tip pressing between her near non-existent breasts. She has no fear of him and leans forward into it, though I don't doubt Eoghan's intentions for a second. He'll kill her and not bat an eyelash. I place my hand on his shoulder, willing him off her. He ignores my touch.

"Easy, General. We're on the same side here."

"Are we?" Eoghan's words are laced with venom. "Last time I checked, no one was sure what side you were on."

"Except the Leader." Alia smiles in a way that unsettles me a bit. "Why else would he have shown me this room?"

"You could have stolen the key." His hand does not yield one inch, and his eyes dance with dragon fire.

"Tsk, tsk, General. A bold accusation from the man who spent four years away and returns once the Leader is dead— and with the Leader's sister on his arm."

This time my blood boils as well. Eoghan steps away from me and into the gap between himself and Alia, still only one move away from a dagger to the heart. I'm not sure what these two have against one another, but I know it helps nothing at all and brings us no closer to answers. I step between the two quarreling soldiers and place my hand on Eoghan's, pressing with my fingertips.

"Enough." That primal, angry growl escapes him as he lowers his arm and sheathes his blade. His eyes hold their glare as Alia smiles up at him, much too sweetly. I take Eoghan's arm and drag him toward the dark chamber filled with leather-bound journals. He only follows as I place his hand against me to coax him to me. I'm sweaty and disgusting…and he does not care one bit. He wraps his arms around me as I lead him into the room. "I think we've found what we were looking for."

Eoghan exhales a soft whistle as he takes in the plunder of secrets hidden in the vault.

"What were you up to, Cai?" he whispers to himself. "We need to get these back to Gálgalesh immediately." This time, he doesn't even bother to release me or look at Alia as he speaks, his voice a firm command. "Commandant Darwish, find Colonel Kimbal Cross and tell him to bring his men here to prepare a large transport to Gobaith."

"Yes, General Kael."

Alia turns back down the hall and disappears at a determined pace, leaving me and Eoghan alone in the dark vault. He releases my shoulders and pulls one of the journals from the shelf to flip through it. I don't bother. Where would I even start?

"Eoghan?" I say, and he nuzzles his cheek against mine in response. "Why was Cai building a new Draíocoinnigh? You promised me he wasn't planning to usurp the throne, but why else would he do it?"

"Maeve, your brother was absolutely *not* trying to usurp your father. Why would he want to? He didn't want anything to do with the throne."

"But Alia said—"

"Alia Darwish," Eoghan groans, "and her husband, Nuri, are hot-headed vigilantes from the Borderlands who would love nothing more than for Draíocoinnigh to fall into absolute chaos so they could enact their own sort of law enforcement. I've never been sure why Cai trusted them at all."

"Nuri?" I turn to face him, and his eyebrow quirks at one side. "I met a Nuri in the Borderlands the night I met Gálgalesh. Tiernan had taken contraband weapons to exchange with him for some gold."

Eoghan scoffs. "Sounds right. Damaris would trust Darwish. Listen to me, Maeve: Cai would not have tried to usurp your father, and as I've already told you, he would never have been involved with what happened to you."

"But—" I begin, and he presses his hand to my lips.

"He wouldn't have done that. I would never have followed him if I thought he were remotely capable of something so terrible. Could you trust me on that?"

I nod, though I'm not sure I truly agree with his assumption of my brother, whom I'm starting to believe fooled everyone in equal measure. I trust Eoghan, though. I trust he would have never followed anything he believed to be wrong —even if Cai had asked him.

"Good. Now, let's get home and figure out what the hell all this means."

———

"I cannot believe you are getting married." Dedra sits on the sofa with her sewing busying away in front of her as she holds a large cup of tea in her hands. "It's so horribly unfair!

Tiernan might never pluck up the courage, and you've been engaged *twice*."

I roll my eyes. The subject of marriage is all she has been able to talk about since I arrived at Áine's this morning. That is, after she gave me a tongue-lashing about wandering off by myself and nearly being killed—again. The last thing I'd like to think about is the impending marriage and entwining ceremony that almost certainly won't be happening in the next month. Eoghan and I haven't even had a moment to speak about it since we arrived in Gobaith last night, but I can't imagine it at all, at least not with everything we still have to figure out and the royal forces getting closer and closer to breaking through the border each day.

"Would you like me to speak to him for you?" I tease as I bounce Theo on my knee. He blows bubbles loudly from his lips and babbles one or two words before giggling to himself. "We're in the middle of a war. It all seems so ridiculous anyway."

"Of course it's not ridiculous. You love him, don't you?" I nod, knowing it's the only thing I am certain of, really. "And you trust him with your life." It's not a question, and we both know it. "Then why would it be ridiculous to trust him with your heart? Timing means nothing in matters of the heart. Besides, I've never seen anyone look at another person the way Eoghan looks at you—like he might die if you were ever to be gone. For his sake, put the man out of his misery and let him share his life with you."

She's right; she always is. I change the subject as my cheeks flush. "Where's Tiernan?"

"Oh, he's at the armory, helping make some weapons to be sent to the border. He thinks he's going to get sent along as well to help fight. I told him he should go. We have no use for him sitting around this house all day, and he's far less charming to me if he's not serving." Dedra laughs.

Theo giggles as he dives for my face, hands outstretched. I tickle his sides and blow raspberries against his cheeks. His tiny hands close around tresses of my hair, and I feel a tinge of desire in my chest for something so small and lovely, with green-gold eyes and a pure, Tinemallacht heart. A tiny Eoghan Kael to love and watch grow.

I rise from the sofa as Lowri enters the room. Dedra straightens and smiles, and Lowri mimics her greeting with a small wink before addressing me with indifference.

"Do you mind?" I hold Theo out to Lowri, and her arms widen as a broad, goofy smile paints her face. Theo squeals in delight as she tucks him close to her chest and smothers him with small, smacking kisses. "I'll see you later. I'm going to go find Eoghan."

Dedra waves goodbye, and Lowri only nods as she takes my seat. I watch Dedra as she moves closer to her on the sofa. Apparently, Lowri is a friend to seamstresses *and* babies…pretty much everyone *except* me.

I exit the sitting room into the kitchen of the over-crowded house. Poor Áine must be going mad with so many people seeking refuge in her tiny bungalow made for no more than three. The kitchen is empty but smells of fresh-baked sweets. I will never get over just how domestic Cai's life must have been here—I never expected it of him, to want something so quiet and lovely for himself, even if the sun and the sand are an absolute pain in the ass.

I head toward the front door and pass by the bedroom near the front of the house. As I do, I hear quiet, almost imperceptible sobs coming from the other side of the door. I pause and listen for just a moment before placing my hand against the wood and pushing it a few inches. Sitting at the end of the bed, Áine freezes, a handkerchief in her hand—her eyes red and puffy with tears.

"Oh," she says quietly. "Are you leaving already?" She makes to stand as I take a step toward her.

"Yes, I think I'm going to go find Eoghan and..." She nods and sniffles as she dabs at her cheeks. "Are you all right?"

There are no words that describe grief more clearly than painful tears flowing ceaseless in dark rooms and quiet halls. I know grief when I see it, having lived it every day for nearly a year now. This—this is something different entirely. Áine's tears flow as though a bit of her very soul has been torn from her chest.

"I'm fine," she lies weakly.

"Is it him?" I guess, and her lip trembles even without the mention of his name.

"Sometimes, I wonder if I'll go on, or if I might just give up. I can't, of course, but I don't understand the point of living anymore. My senses are dull, my heart aches endlessly, my child…reminds me every waking moment of him. Of his goodness, of his love." She runs her hand through her hair in a nervous, sort of desperate way. "His love is still here." She points to her chest. "But it feels as though it's eating me alive, because his heart isn't near."

She begins to cry in earnest again. *This poor woman.* If this is the result of the entwining ceremony, I'm not sure why anyone would want it. What good is being tied to someone if the pain of losing them is unbearable? What if I lost Eoghan? Would *I* feel as though I'm being eaten alive by my sorrow? And what of him? Would he feel the same if he lost me?

"I'm sorry," Áine apologizes and wipes at her face. "I'm terrible company to keep today."

I can take a hint. I nod to her and back out of the room. I wrap my fingers quietly around the door handle and pull it back toward me until it clicks shut softly, and Áine disappears into the solitude of her darkened room once more. Then, I cross the kitchen and exit onto the street.

Eoghan had been called early this morning to the northern barracks to meet with the soldiers and pass out station orders, leaving him with little sleep once again. When I had finally awoken, I found a note on my bedside table explaining his absence with a promise to spend the afternoon naked in bed when he finally made it home. At nearly three o'clock, I am still fully clothed and without Eoghan Kael. I head down the dusty, wood-planked street toward the center of the outpost, hoping I might steal him away from matters of combat to deal with the more pressing matters of the heart. The image of a small child with green and gold eyes and tiny Eoghan Kael features makes my abdomen warm at the impossible thought, and I resolve that the dream of such impossibilities might be better than the reality, though I still can't shake the desire.

I wind my way down into the square, and when the road opens before me, I find him locked in a faux squabble with Finn, the two wrestling each other down into the dirt. Whether due to the harsh heat of the sun or something else completely, my temperature rises as I approach the two sweaty, half-naked men.

"Who's winning?" I ask and come to a stop before them.

"Can't you tell?" Eoghan laughs. Finn's fist collides with his jaw as he speaks and knocks the wry look from his face.

"So Finn, then?" Finn lets out a laugh this time, and Eoghan throws his elbow out, pinning him to the dirt. "Such a temper," I tease.

"Would you like to join us down here?" Eoghan purrs as he turns coolly to look up at me, and my cheeks grow hot and pink. Eoghan takes the opportunity to swipe at the back of my calves, making me lose my footing and fall next to him in the soft sand. "Are you blushing, Mayhem?" he asks as he releases his companion and leans in close.

"Don't tease; it's not polite. I should let Finn finish you off for that."

"As if he could." Eoghan throws his daggers down next to him and runs his fingers into my hair. "He has to leave for the border anyway. He's already late."

Taking his cue to leave, Finn rises and crosses to his canteen and discarded clothes. Eoghan presses his lips softly to mine in that delicate but possessive way that tells me he's thought of nothing else since he last saw me. I melt into him, my hands finding his bare chest and running along it before we finally pull away for air.

"You left me with Dedra all morning," I complain.

"I thought you liked Dedra." He brings his lips to my neck as he speaks.

"I do, just not when she is pestering me about Tinemallacht wedding dresses and entwining ceremonies."

"Ah." His lips curl up deviously against my skin. "Well, it's too bad we Tinemallachts prefer to get married in nothing at all. Tell her to speak to me about the dress if you don't care to discuss it. I could use some new ceremonial pieces while she's at it anyway. Unless you'd like to tell her you don't want to marry me instead?"

I have never been so thankful not to see his exquisite green eyes. He continues to kiss me, seemingly unbothered by the abrupt silence. *You're an idiot,* my mind rightly admonishes. *Who might you be holding out for? Rian Doherty?* I shake off the thought and change the subject.

"Have the journals arrived from Kildar?" My hand finds his jaw, and I run my fingers along its scruffy surface lightly.

"About an hour ago. Gálgalesh is pouring over them now to see what he can make of them. Bryn's helping him sort through them and said they'll come find us if they discover anything." He pulls away, and I whimper unhappily until he presses his lips to mine once more in a short, final kiss. "I don't understand. Why would Cai keep so many of his writings if we have no idea what they mean? What was the point of it?"

I shrug. "I know less about him than any of you. He's always been a secret, though. Ever since I can remember, he always hid from my father and mother and the castle staff. He'd dig holes in the garden and hide things he never wanted them to find or write in words only he could read. I don't think he trusted anyone much, not even me."

"There had to be someone he trusted. If not, why go through all the trouble?" Neither of us have the answer. Eoghan pulls me to himself and presses his lips to my forehead. Then, he replaces his daggers in their holsters and makes to stand before offering me his hand. "Let's go see what Gálgalesh has found."

He intertwines his fingers with mine and leaves his things in the square as we take the short walk to the library. We push the door open, and the dark, cool room comes into view, piles of journals laid out in every corner and Gálgalesh at his usual desk, his head buried in one.

"Close that door, woman. It is much too hot," he says with his back to us, and I push the door closed at his command. "I have no answers for you. It seems the Leader has once again given us a riddle he expects us to solve without a single clue as to what it means."

We approach him, winding our way through the stacks. The library is quiet, and I notice Gálgalesh is alone.

"Where's Bryn?" I ask as I reach Gálgalesh's side.

"I sent him away. I grew tired of his endless optimism and desire to be useful. I ordered him back to the house until I had something worthwhile for him to do."

"You never cease to amaze me with your perfect manners, Gálgalesh," Eoghan goads, and Gálgalesh waves his hand absently. We peer over his shoulders to look at the object of his attention. "Cai really had a knack for nonsense, didn't he?"

I look closer at the page, the familiar handwriting messy, as though in a rush.

"The only thing I have been able to surmise is that the journals are numbered and dated. Beyond this, they are useless."

"They are coded," I say as I work through the letters on the page. "Cai used to code all his writings. I recognize this pattern. It's the one he used when he lived at the castle."

"Can you read it?" Eoghan asks.

I shake my head. "No, but I know where to find the key."

———

"WE'RE GOING to Caisleán Rialú to retrieve Cai's key and decode his journals." Eoghan and I stand in the sitting room of Eoghan's home, facing Tiernan and Lowri on the sofa. Gálgalesh stands by the fire as we speak.

"Are you fucking out of your mind?" Lowri snaps. "There is no way you are getting into Gairdín, let alone the Steel Citadel. Cai had to have kept another key somewhere else. We'll find that one and use it. You are not walking yourself right into the hands of the king who wants you dead."

"Okay, you can go look for the key in Kildar then. The war will be over, and we will all be dead by the time you finally figure out where the hell it is. We are going. Damaris, Maeve, and I will go. Officer Rhodes will get us there, just outside of the Capital, and Tiernan can lead us through the tunnels to the castle walls. There are entrances into the lower levels, and we can be in and out before anyone knows."

"Not to mention, there's been word the king and his son are in Tonnfórsca for the upcoming Parade of Spirits. They might not even be there when we arrive," Tiernan says, and Lowri rounds on him.

"You're willing to bet your life because this one," she points an angry finger toward me, "saw a piece of parchment *once*? You don't even know if it's still there!"

"It's there," I cut in. "I saw it the week before the wedding."

"How do you know any of it is still there? The Dohertys could have used everything you owned for kindling!" Lowri's now nearly crouching on her toes on the sofa cushions.

"The rooms in the Steel Citadel are intact. I overheard a guard telling his partner the Dohertys were instructed by Sir Oli Raven to keep them so. The king is superstitious, and Sir Oli Raven warned him he might anger the gods. They reside on the other side of the castle. I believe Sir Oli Raven had his own motives for keeping the items accessible."

Gálgalesh's words seem to leave Lowri speechless for a long moment, but she recovers as she always does.

"I don't like it. At least give me time to make sure it's safe—!"

Eoghan just shakes his head defiantly. "We leave now. It has to be now, Lo."

"You're going to get yourself killed! You have no plan, no thought as to how screwed you will be if you get caught! Don't say I didn't warn you, Eogh, when this all goes to shit!"

"Noted." There's no give in Eoghan's expression, and Lowri turns scarlet with rage.

She jumps to her feet and stomps out of the room. We listen as she curses and crosses to the door. The house trembles with the slamming of the wood against the frame as she exits. Eoghan shakes his head and sighs.

"We will have time to discuss anything we need to before we enter the tunnels. Maeve knows the layout of the castle better than any of us, and Damaris, you've been there before as well. We'll be fine. Grab what you need from Áine's and meet us at the gates in ten minutes."

Tiernan nods and rises from the sofa. He exits the house, leaving me, Eoghan, Gálgalesh in the sitting room.

"Be safe," Gálgalesh warns. "This might be our only opportunity to figure out just what the Leader knew."

If we get the key, we'll finally find out why Cai needed to build up a secret army for years and what had made him so fearful to begin with.

Eoghan places his hand on my back and urges me out of the room. He grabs his dragon leather jacket from the bench near the door, as well as a second, slightly smaller one he hands to me.

"Dragon leather protects against poisons and acids and nearly anything that can penetrate the skin. Wear it, just in case."

I take the jacket, and he crosses to the door, holding it open for me. We exit the house together, taking long strides that propel us swiftly down the road, making it halfway to where it yields to the outpost square before we hear the door open and then slam shut behind us. Our names echo against the houses.

"Maeve, Eogh!" Bryn comes running to us, his feet pushed into his untied boots and his own jacket slung over his arm. "Let me come with you!"

"Go home, Bryn," Eoghan says, and Bryn's face falls in disappointment.

My heart sinks into my stomach. Though Bryn hadn't been raised in the castle as I had, his family had never allowed him to explore or prove himself. He has been as much a prisoner to this place as I was in Caisleán Rialú. I can't allow it. I can't allow him to be treated as if he's nothing —invaluable, a child.

"He's coming with us," I say.

"No. He's not. Bryn, go home, now." Eoghan's tone is a firm command, and his eyes bear down with such intensity, Bryn loses about an inch of height as his shoulders sink.

"Eoghan! That's unfair!" I complain.

"I don't care, Maeve. He is staying here!"

Red flushes his cheeks to match my own anger boiling to the surface. Eoghan Kael always believes he is right. He always makes demands of everyone and tells them what to do. He would be happy to let Bryn rot here in this stupid outpost and never see the world, never prove to anyone how capable he is—but this is not his call. He will not be the one in charge, not this time.

"I'm not going without him, Eoghan. None of us are." Eoghan opens his mouth to argue, and I hold my hand up to silence him. "We don't have time to argue this. He's coming with us." I grab hold of Bryn's shirt and continue down the street.

CHAPTER TWENTY-NINE

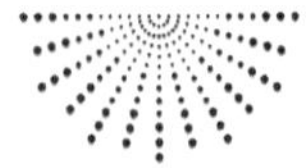

The first days of the White Night have begun to take hold of Golorgleann, and the sky is a tapestry of purples and pinks just outside the city limits. I haven't been back to Gairdín in eight months, haven't set foot in the castle for even longer still. As we wait in a deserted grove of green grass and fruit trees just outside the city walls, a hole deep in the pit of my stomach fills in a way that must only mean I am home. Eoghan leans against the trunk of a tree, and Bryn sits in the grass beside me, running his fingers through it in wonder—the sight and feel of it is just as foreign to him as the sand of Tinemallacht had been to me.

"Damaris should be back soon, so we better discuss our plan one last time before he arrives," Eoghan says. They're some of the first words he's spoken since we left. He's still furious with me, and I am equally angry with him.

When Officer Rhodes dropped us off outside the city limits, Tiernan left us to trade Ama to the people of the tunnels in order to guarantee our safe passage under the city. After he returns, we are to set off under the cobblestone streets of Gairdín to the castle gates. Once there, Tiernan will lead us to the lower entrance of the castle, where Eoghan and Bryn will be charged with eliminating any guards who might get in our way. Then—gods willing—I will lead us through the castle dungeons to the main levels. If we make it that far, the hard part might be over…at least, I hope.

"Bryn, I think you need to go back to Gobaith. I know you want to help, but I think it would be better if you just—"

"Eoghan! Enough! He's here now!" My hands tremble with rage. Eoghan slams his fist against the tree trunk, and the vein in his neck throbs as heat flares around us. I widen my stance in challenge, my arms crossed against my chest. "How many times are we going to go over this? Bryn is *staying*! Ugh! You're such an ass, Eoghan! If you think I'm going to marry you now, you're a fool!"

"Were you ever going to in the first place? Ever since you told everyone we were getting married, you've complained about it as if I'm somehow forcing you to be my wife! I haven't forced you to do *anything*! That was *your* choice, remember?" Eoghan shouts. Bryn's brows crinkle in confusion. "And maybe it's for the best. When have any of your decisions turned out well for anyone?"

Anger tears through both of us like a great chasm. I can't stand him—not when he stares at me with such ridicule, like I'm the dumbest, most ridiculous person he's ever seen. Not when he speaks to me as if he can do no wrong.

"Of course, I'm the wrong one here—never you. Not as you treat Bryn like he means nothing to you and you would rather see him die than—!"

"Gods be damned, fine!" Eoghan's fists dive into his hair. He inhales heavily, his chest rising and falling like the crash of a wave. "Bryn, you stay close. Your job is to help me protect Maeve. I'm counting on you." Bryn nods and goes back to running his fingers through the cool grass. The smuggest of grins coats my features as Eoghan relents. *Good.*

He doesn't get to win, not today. Eoghan places his hand under my elbow and pulls me toward him, just out of earshot. I swipe at him, pushing him away. "Maeve, if you encounter Rian—"

"I won't encounter Rian, Eogh. He isn't here, remember? Besides, even if I did, you wouldn't need to worry. I don't love Rian anymore."

"Yes, but Maeve, if you do. You need to know that his—"

Tiernan breaks through the tree line, and we all turn at the sound of his boots trudging through the grass. His pack is slung over his shoulder, and he looks wary; however, he doesn't beg us to leave, which is a good sign at least.

"The tunnels are secured. I've bought us two hours, though I'd try to keep it to one to be on the safe side."

"Excellent drug peddling, Damaris, really. Let's hope your drugs are better than your weapons." Eoghan's words bite, and I glare at him as he speaks.

"Thank you, Tiernan," I say. I shove Eoghan away as I move toward him. "Let's get on with it before we run out of time."

Tiernan leads the way to the tunnels, following along the city's perimeter walls of large, beige stones. Near the front gates, a circular service hole cover made of steel and embossed with the crest of the new king sits waiting for us. As we approach, I can see one side has already been pried open, and the cover has been left slightly ajar. Tiernan moves the cover out of the way and points into the black descent.

"Ladies first," he says as he nods to Eoghan, who gives a snarky guffaw before beginning to descend the ladder into the darkness. I follow him, and he places his hands on my waist to help me as I approach the bottom. I brush him off, and his hands turn cold for the first time as he drops them to his sides. We wait for Bryn and then Tiernan to join us in the dark chamber. "This way."

We pass through the winding paths of grey stone and vaulted ceilings. The last time I was down here, I should have been dead. My body was so broken and weak, it's a miracle I survived the first night, let alone until this moment. A rush of power surges through me at the thought, and I am reminded that perhaps, I never would have died here at all—perhaps the magic never left me, and instead, I was reborn in these tunnels to become the very thing they hoped would end me.

We walk for what feels like several kilometers in the dark, damp tunnels with bodies of drug-addled men and women strewn throughout. It's worse than any drug den down here. The users could meet their end, and no one would even miss them besides the rats. Bryn pauses as he watches a woman roll around, giggling euphorically as she clutches the front of her cloak, showing it to the invisible spectators. Gods bless him, his heart is still too pure to understand the evils of this place. I place my hand in his and drag him along with me as we continue toward the castle gates.

"Here." Tiernan pauses and indicates to a ladder that leads to the street above. "This will take us out to the military base across the road from the lower entrance of the castle. I'll go first and let you know when the coast is clear."

He ascends to the street, and we wait, listening for his directive. He calls us up one at a time, and Eoghan is the last to breach the surface. I've never seen the castle walls from this side, but I recognize the stones that tower high above the city like a menacing figure of control—to keep something out *and* to keep something in.

Eoghan motions for Bryn to follow him, and they cross the road toward the lower entrance of the castle. They are not gone more than five minutes; when they return, they are placing their knives back at their sides. The toe of Bryn's boot has small droplets of blood across it, and he curses under his breath when he notices.

"I'll clean them for you when we get home," I promise. He gives me a smile so much like Eoghan's, I nearly do a double-take.

We continue across to the hidden castle entrance Cai so often frequented after nights out in the Capital or visits to the military base. This door, too, is slightly open, and a boot peeks out from just beyond the threshold. Eoghan kicks it aside as we enter the lower levels of Caisleán Rialú. The pathways are so familiar, grey stone, a damp mist in the air. The smell of mildew wafts from the dungeons where prisoners were so often kept in the years of my youth. I never went to see them, but my brother had more than once, and the stories of cruelty make my skin crawl even now.

I lead the others past the armory and the old throne room holding the Foundation Stones. I pause as we reach Sir Oli Raven's chamber, the door thrown open wide for all to see. It looks exactly as it had the last time I saw it, vacant only of the red vials of my blood that used to fill the cabinet against the wall. Eoghan places his hands on my shoulder, his lips against my hair.

"Let's leave it, shall we?" He pulls the door closed. "He doesn't exist anymore."

I nod as words fail me and continue through the passageway to the spiraling stone staircase ascending to the main floors. As we reach the bottom step, Tiernan stops dead.

"We need to destroy the acid rain supply," he says.

"I thought it couldn't be destroyed?" Eoghan turns to him as he speaks.

"I didn't say that. It's held just across the road. I know how to get there, and I brought a few items I think could be useful." Tiernan opens his pack, and we all look inside.

Hundreds of tiny bombs sit at the bottom of his rucksack in orb-shaped vials.

"Heat-sensitive bombs?" Eoghan looks almost sick.

"No," Tiernan replies. "Time-sensitive bombs. We set the charge and get out of the base before they blow. It'll be drowned in acid before the night is up."

"But won't it flow out into the streets? We can't hurt the citizens of Gairdín just to prove a point."

Eoghan contemplates Tiernan's suggestion. "No, the city is safe. The base has enchantments in case of such a scenario."

"And accidents happen all the time..." Tiernan adds.

"But we can't leave Maeve by herself." Eoghan shakes his head. "It's not worth it."

"I'll stay with her." Bryn steps forward. "She knows the castle, and I know how to fight. We will be in and out, and if you finish at the base and we aren't at the tunnel entrance, come find us. Tiernan knows how to navigate the Steel Citadel."

Tiernan nods in acknowledgement. It makes perfect sense. The four of us do not need to wander through the castle looking for Cai's key. Eoghan and Tiernan can take care of the other threat and buy our soldiers at the border some time.

"No, I'll stay with her." Eoghan says. "You go with Damaris, Bryn."

"Eoghan..." Tiernan says. "I don't think Bryn will be able to sneak onto the base. He's not officially part of the royal forces, apart from the Tinemallacht ranks your father has given him. If someone sees..."

"No." My voice is firm. "Eoghan, Tiernan needs you. I need Bryn. You go and come back to me as quickly as possible." I close my fist around the front of his jacket and pull him in. "Come back to me soon."

Eoghan squeezes my shoulders, and with a groan that tells me he is absolutely not okay with our plan at all, he turns to Tiernan.

"Let's go."

We part ways, Bryn and I taking the stairs while Eoghan and Tiernan disappear down the lower passageways the way we had come. The pit of my stomach churns as I watch them go. I take the stairs two at a time to reach the main entryway. It's quiet, so much quieter than I've ever heard it. There are no maids or guards rushing through the halls and up the marble stairs. The sounds of my boots against the ornate floors of white and grey ring, as though announcing my arrival, but the floors aren't shiny anymore... I slide the toe of my boot across them, and a gravelly crunch greets me in response. Sand. The King of the Merchants has tracked sand through the once-gleaming halls of Caisleán Rialú. Annoyance fills me. These men killed my family and tried to kill me, and they can't even wipe their boots before they defile our house. Typical.

Bryn turns in circles in awe of the place, and in perfect honesty, I understand his amazement. This castle is so much grander than even the palaces of Bastain. There is nothing that compares to its immense size and splendor, from the priceless art to the gold furniture. Even after spending my every waking moment here for twenty years, it still takes my breath away—yet it's different now. The midnight blue curtains and accents are replaced with ones of tacky sea foam green and the portraits of my father and grandfathers that lined the entryway walls are now completely missing, leaving bare spaces of discolored paint.

"Come on," I whisper to Bryn, taking his arm. We slide and skid against the sandy floors as I rush him toward the staircase. Cai's room is on the next floor in the West Wing of the castle. I look around once more, making sure no one has spotted us, though I would have heard their feet as well if they had approached, and we ascend to the next floor.

When we reach the next landing, we cross the skyway to the bedroom passageway and pause at the threshold. The once-plush blue and gold carpet is caked with a thick layer of grey dust. The portraits on the walls, though as familiar as the back of my hand, are now dull and coated with cobwebs. Nothing has been touched, not a single item removed from this place. I thank the gods Rian and his father had feared them in a way my father never had. He would have turned every bit of it to ash and not batted an eyelash.

"Is this it?" Bryn asks on my left side, scanning the halls for signs of life.

"This is it." I take a step, and a small cloud of dust puffs around my boot. "This way." I point to the left and take careful steps toward Cai's room.

We reach his door, and I place my hand on the golden handle. No one has stayed in this room for years. Cai had last set foot in it when he was twenty-six years old—nearly three years ago now. *I* had last set foot in the room one week before the coup, when Cai's letter arrived notifying me he would be attending my wedding. I had been so excited, I rushed into his room to find his dress uniform and scoured the overly-full desk drawer for his signet ring. I hadn't found it, but I had seen the old piece of parchment he kept there.

I turn the door handle, and it gives way to the room beyond. Suspended in time, it feels as though not a minute has passed, not a moment of grief or pain or anger or fear—except for the shadows of spiders' homes hanging from the chandelier. It smells musty and closed up, though that does nothing to the memories. I can imagine the feel of the soft blankets as I look to the large bed at the far end of the room, the scratchiness of the sofa next to the fireplace. *Home.*

"Bryn, check some of those books while I get the key," I

say as I cross to the old desk. I pull at the drawer, and it sticks as something wedges itself in the way. I yank harder, and it bounces back toward the desk. "Ugh."

I groan and pull once more, and the drawer relents against the force, revealing its contents. I dive my hands into the trove of Cai's treasures and dig around for the parchment, throwing items onto the floor as I go. I find nothing. Maybe we were wrong. Maybe it is gone after all. I push my hands to the very back and bottom of the drawer in desperation, and then I feel the unmistakable: slightly textured parchment under my fingertips. Something similar sits right next to it. I grab both items and draw them from the depths of the drawer, sending items crashing to the floor around my feet. There, in my right hand, is the key, and in my left…an envelope.

For Evie, just in case.

I flip it over in my hands. It's sealed with wax, the Tinemallacht crest embossed at the center. Cai had left this for me before the coup. He must have done so once he'd arrived for the wedding, but when and why? Why would he leave it here, of all places, instead of giving it to me directly?

I pocket both the key and the envelope and turn back to Bryn, who is still dutifully sifting through the piles of books lying out around Cai's room. Had he wanted to hide something in plain sight, this might be the best place. No one would find it among the utter chaos.

"Find anything interesting?" I ask.

"They are all books from Romiodóg, about the history of the villagers there," he replies, not looking from the tome in his hand.

"Well, take a few more minutes and see if there's anything useful we might take. I'll be right back."

Bryn's head snaps to attention, and his eyes meet mine. "I'm supposed to stay with you," he says.

"I'm just going to my room a couple of doors down. You'll be able to hear me shout if there's trouble. Keep your ears open. I'll be back before you get through that stack in front of you."

He doesn't like it. There's an uneasy expression on his face that might be mistaken for fear if I did not know Bryn well. Instead, I know it is disappointment that I haven't asked him to come along with me, but I need a minute alone before we leave this place, maybe for good, and he doesn't push.

I make my way swiftly to the door and stick my head out into the corridor. Empty, as expected. I rush in the opposite direction toward my old room and push the door away. This place too has been left untouched. I have never been a stickler for cleanliness, though my room could be seen as pristine compared to Cai's. The bed, however, remains unmade, the blankets in the same position as when Rian and I left the morning of the coup, when I still expected to marry him. This bed holds so many secrets of forbidden love and forbidden pain. It makes me sick to look at it. I move to my closet instead.

Greens, blues, pinks, yellows, purples, and whites create a rainbow of color along the walls. Dresses with high necks and sleeves, gauzy straps, and skirts that flow across the floor in every shade and fabric. It's hard to imagine that, just a year ago, I wouldn't have dreamed I might not wear one of these dresses every day. Now, I can't imagine what it would be like to wear soft slippers again. I had been a doll dressed for show, without function. I was never of any worth—not even to be shown to the world. I was dressed up and paraded for the portraits and the carpets, to stare at my reflection in the marble floors. At least now, in my endlessly monotonous Tans, I am free to be me, to exist beyond these walls. Still, the colors make me long for a time when I might have both.

I run my hand along the skirts and the toes of the various silk slippers in small square cupboards on the wall. *Nothing had been packed.* My mind rouses the thought that knots my stomach. *They had told you your things would be packed and waiting for you to leave for Tonnfórsca, but nothing had been moved. They never planned on you leaving at all.*

I look down at the empty trunks gathering dust at my feet. They hadn't been moved even an inch since Rian brought them for me three months before the wedding. The hinges had not opened once. I was never going to Tonn-fórsca, whether we were married or not. They always intended on me staying here. That's why my father finally allowed Rian to marry me. He had no need to trade his prized cow because Rian didn't want it from the start.

A loud thud of something heavy falling against rugs and wood shakes me back to the present. *Bryn!* I race from the closet, and as I do, I hear the horrible sound of Rian's voice from the hall beyond.

"It's time to come out now, Maeve."

CHAPTER THIRTY

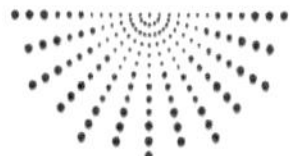

I exit into the hall. Rian and a highdruí in brown robes and bare feet stand just beyond Cai's bedroom. Rian's pale grey tunic is intricately made of expensive fabrics, and his usual gold bangles fill his arm as he holds Bryn around the throat, tucking him close, as though shielding his body with Bryn's. There's a dagger poised in Rian's free hand, pointed toward Bryn's chest.

"LET HIM GO!" I take a step toward them, and Rian's grip tightens around Bryn's neck. Rian and the highdruí take a step backward, dragging Bryn along with them.

"Now, now, Maeve. You aren't coming near us until you drop your knives onto the carpet," Rian says smoothly, and my head spins at the sound of his voice. Something inside tells me I want to please him. I want him to beckon me to him. I want it more than anything. Why would I not drop my knives for him? I feel I might do anything for him if he asked. I unhook the daggers from their holsters and drop them to the floor. Even when my brain asks me why I would disarm myself, my only answer is because I want him to keep looking at me the way he is now. I want him to keep loving me.

"You've always been so good at listening. I bet that's why this Fire Cursed filth here loves you. Though I'll admit, he seems a bit young up close. It's not what I expected from you at all."

"Maeve?" Bryn's tone is fearful now, as I've never heard it. Rian thinks Bryn is Eoghan.

"That's not..." Will he try to kill Bryn if he knows who he is? Is he scared of him now? Is that why his blade only hovers over Bryn's chest? I look at Bryn's wrists and see they are bound with Faebond, making it impossible for him to wield. I am sure Rian can still undoubtedly feel the heat, though. "Yes, he does love me," I resolve to say.

"Yes, you can be easy to love at times," Rian coos, and if he were not holding Bryn to him, I'd demand he take me in his arms. "Tha grá di, Maeve."

Something deep inside me battles against the rush of warmth that greets me as he proclaims his love. I don't understand it. For months, I have felt nothing except hate for this man, but as he speaks, all the love I had once felt for him rushes back. I want him so badly, I might die to be near him. *Bryn will die too then. And what of Eoghan?*

Bryn tries to shake Rian off, the effects of the Faebond weakening him so badly, he can only muster what looks like a lazy shimmy of his shoulders. Rian looks at him and smiles, as if smugly satisfied with causing harm. I have to get Bryn to safety. Everything else in me can wait.

"Have you come to your senses, Maeve? You've given me so much trouble lately. You even killed Sir Oli Raven. Now, that wasn't very nice."

"You tried to kill me first," I say, shaking my head in an attempt at some sort of clarity. "More than once."

"I did. But you deserved it, didn't you?"

Yes. Shame and guilt washes over me. I deserved to die. I don't even know why I deserved to die, yet the knowledge I am still alive makes me feel as though I have disappointed the whole world. I feel like I disappointed him—and I never want to disappoint him. I never want him not to love me. I feel the dampness of tears as they roll down my cheeks.

"Maeve!"

All our heads turn to find Eoghan and Tiernan racing across the skyway into the hall. *Eoghan.* Something inside my chest begins to fight against the guilt and sadness rooted there, something stronger than the cloudiness in my mind. He stops at my side and grips my arms, then turns on Rian. A snarl of anger rips from his throat.

"Release my brother—now!"

"Ah, so this was the brother," Rian muses. "I recognize him now. This one is so like him but so young. You would never, Maeve. You always liked your men older."

Eoghan raises his hands to wield, and I place mine on his as I watch Bryn almost buckle, his body succumbing to the bonds.

"You'll hit, Bryn," I say, and Eoghan's hands drop ever so slightly as he weighs the impossible decision of whether to risk his brother's life in an attempt to save it.

"You can be oh so very wise, Maeve," Rian says, and my head spins again. This time, the feeling of shame is replaced with happiness. "Come now. I'll let this one go if you will just come with me."

I don't even feel my feet move, but Eoghan places his hand on my chest, holding me back as I attempt to close the space between me and Rian. Why would he stop me? I turn to him with both suspicion and annoyance marring my expression.

"Before we made it into the city, I was trying to tell you," Eoghan begins. "I figured out Rian's magic. When we were out hunting, you said you felt like you couldn't place him, like you didn't miss him as much as you should. Then, when he came to the prison, you nearly jumped into the courtyard at the sound of his voice, even knowing he tried to kill you." Eoghan takes my face into his hands and compels my gaze. That strong sense inside me fights again as I meet his green-gold eyes. "He controls emotions, Maeve. What you're feeling isn't real. He's manipulating you." I try to whip my head back toward Rian, but Eoghan keeps me firm in his grip. "Look at me. What you feel with me...*that* is real. *I love you.* He doesn't give a fuck about you. He used you to get to the throne."

Eoghan runs his thumb against my lip, his soft, patient caress bursting something in me. Like a crashing wave, my head clears, and the love I felt for Rian just a moment before turns to pure, raging hate.

"It's no fun once she knows," Rian says, his voice different as it reaches my ears now—menacing and wicked. I realize it always sounded this way, from the moment I met him. How had I never heard it before?

I nod to Eoghan with my understanding, and he nods back, releasing me from his grip. I turn to face Rian again, Bryn slack in his arms now, the blade still against his chest. I am going to tear Rian apart, limb-from-limb, until nothing remains.

"You used me. For years, you made me feel as though I loved you, just so you could murder us and take the throne. I was fifteen, and you used me!"

"That day when I met you in the garden, I had been waiting to catch a glimpse of you. I had overheard some of the rumors that you were vapid and lonely, desperate for love your father would not give you and your mother did not have for you. And then, as we took a break from our negotiations with the king, I noticed you from the windows, playing in the garden with that tiny child like some ridiculous little idiot. I knew then all I had to do was approach you, and you wouldn't say no to me." His wretched smile broadens, making his terrible features even worse. "You were so naïve about everything but so willing to please—even when your father beat you at the mention of my name. There was nothing you wouldn't give to me, and I took it all so greedily."

Disgust and shame wash over me, and this time, I know it's real. It drives me to nearly lunge for him. If not for Bryn, nothing would stop me. Instead, I ask the question ringing through my mind.

"Why? I know your family was on the throne and King Fergal killed them all. It was horrible and cruel, but it has been generations—centuries, even. Why was it fair to make us pay for the crimes of a madman? Wouldn't the trade routes and the wealth be enough? Your father had made himself a king in his own right."

Rian flinches, and I watch as his hand tightens angrily around the hilt of the blade. It presses more firmly against Bryn's chest. Eoghan's muscles tense, and the heat rises between us. It looks like Rian debates killing Bryn for a moment in his rage, but he stops short and lets loose a maniacal laugh.

"Do you really think what we did was about some ancestor who wronged us nearly two hundred years ago? That would be idiotic, even in the name of revenge and honor, Maeve! We have a booming slave trade and more money than the gods have ever afforded even the king. We didn't need to settle old debts long since buried."

"Then why?" I ask. "What was the point of it all?"

"You really are the dumbest person I have ever met. Did you never wonder why all the kings, with their caramel-brown hair and chocolate eyes, looked exactly the same as you passed by their portraits in the halls? Did you never think it odd the kings only last thirty years on the throne? Did you never question why that must be? Of course not— you were too content filling your mind with sunshine and flowers in the castle gardens to realize anything at all." Rian taps his blade against Bryn, who groans as small droplets of blood stain red on his Tans. Eoghan's hand jerks forward, but I hold him back. "We did *not* kill your family because King Fergal killed ours and took the throne. We killed your family because King Fergal was *still* on the throne, and it was time for him to pay for all he had done to us and this kingdom for nearly two hundred years. We will not stop until we kill every last abomination from his line: including you."

I am unaware of the moment my knees buckle, but Tiernan is there to catch me as Eoghan takes his shot and wields against Rian. He throws a dangerous blow Rian's way, his golden cuffs glowing along his wrists. In the same instant, a black veil shoots up between us and absorbs Eoghan's spell. Black magic. The highdruí had been standing so quietly in the shadows, I hadn't noticed him raise his hands to shield them.

"I did you a favor, Maeve. That man cared nothing about you. I'll do this one a favor and give him the hero's death he so desires. He can die knowing at least he tried to save you from what will come."

Eoghan wields again, and again, his spell is absorbed into the black veil.

"Rian, please…" I beg.

"You know what's really pathetic, Maeve? I see it in your eyes—a part of you actually thinks I still love you. You think that maybe, I'll listen to reason, but the truth is, the only thought of you that brings me any joy is that of your head beneath my boot. The Fire Cursed can have the rest of you."

Rian pulls his arm high above him and then plunges the blade into Bryn's chest, directly into his heart. He turns it with a wet, sickening squelch as Eoghan lunges, and Rian discards Bryn unceremoniously onto the dust-filled carpet in front of him. The veil falls away as Eoghan runs directly into it at full speed, and when it does, Rian and the highdruí disappear from the corridor. Eoghan slides to his knees and pulls Bryn to himself, blood running from his chest, puddling in Eoghan's lap.

Eoghan screams, pure rage as the walls shake. He tears the Faebond from Bryn's wrists and throws it onto the carpet, but we know not even that will help him regain his strength now. Pale white as the Romiodóg snow, Bryn lays in Eoghan's arms. Eoghan is pure, hot dragon fire, tears falling as he sobs over Bryn's lifeless body.

The room is silent and deafeningly loud at the same time as my heart pounds in my ears. Time has stopped, just as the world has ceased to spin, and my brain registers only the red pooling thickly under Bryn's tan shirt. I want to open a vein, I want to watch as the color rushes back to his cheeks, but the healing does not yield to others as it had before…and even if it did, it would be much too late now.

"We have to go." Tiernan's voice is soft and full of remorse. I barely hear him next to me over Eoghan's sobs. He makes his way to Eoghan, dropping down next to him on the carpet. "Bring him. They know we're here, and the charges are already set at the base. We need to get out of here before it's too late."

Eoghan turns slowly, his face soaked with tears, and sets his face on Tiernan's shoulder. Tiernan pats his back firmly yet kindly and then helps him rise from the floor. Eoghan scoops Bryn up, his Tans soaked through with blood, and then, without a single word, he leads the way back out of the castle, exactly the same the way we had come.

We make it to the road outside the castle walls and ease Bryn down with us to the tunnels below. Eoghan is boiling, and I fear he might combust from the heat raging through him as he barrels down the tunnel. But there's movement in the darkness ahead, and too soon do we realize we've made a mistake.

"Shit." Tiernan looks at his watch. "We've taken too long. The people of the tunnel are starting to come down from their highs. We aren't going to make it through. They're going to mow through us looking for more Ama."

"Give them more then!" Eoghan demands in a cold voice filled with rage.

"I gave them all I had." Tiernan holds out his hands, and Eoghan growls in frustration.

"We'll go back up to the street and make it through the city on the surface," I suggest.

"No, the gates are locked each night. We won't make it through."

Eoghan's expression is wild, and he grabs Tiernan's jacket with his empty fingertips. "Detonate one of those bombs you have."

"Are you crazy? That'll kill them!" I can't read Eoghan's face in the darkness, but I have a feeling he doesn't care.

"Down that tunnel," he lifts his chin to a dark passageway on our right, "and distract them."

Tiernan shakes his head. "It'll bring the tunnel reinforcers down. We can't."

"And if I wield right now, I'll bring the whole fucking city down around us. Do it." Eoghan does not blink—does not give. "We detonate it and wait in there," he points to the opposite side of the tunnels, "until they come to see what it was. Then, we sneak past them. If we come across any stragglers, we'll kill them if we must. Do you understand?"

We both nod, certain we don't want to know what Eoghan might do if we don't relent. Eoghan and I make it to the far side of the tunnel and crouch in the darkness as

Tiernan sets his charge. Then, he races back to where we sit, waiting. He takes a deep breath and counts off the charge. Five…four…three…

Boom! I cover my ears as an explosion rocks the tunnel, the ground shaking. There is no flash of fire or light. There is no visible explosion to be seen. It's not the one we were expecting—it had come from somewhere above us. *Boom! Boom! Boom!* Two more explosions from above and the one in the tunnel explode at the same time, ringing filling our ears. We watch as the large metal tunnel reinforcers fall to the stone floor with six clamorous bangs…and then, realization hits us as droplets of water begin to fall, sizzling as they hit the stone floor. We have just blown up the tunnel directly below the weapons storage at the military base, as well as thousands of orbs full of acid rain at the same time.

"RUN!" Eoghan shouts as he pushes us from our hiding spot, Bryn still in his arms.

We dash through the tunnels as fast as we can, Tiernan in the lead and Eoghan at the back. We make it down the next tunnel before we hear the crash of the ceiling giving way and the rush of a river of acid running fast and lethal behind us. Then, we hear the unmistakable sound of pounding feet as a mob of tunnel people come running our way.

"MOVE!" Eoghan shouts, and we let him race ahead of us, the sound of the incoming deluge growing louder. He wields at the oncoming stampede, and like a violent missile being released through the center of the tunnel, their bodies fly into the walls, leaving just enough space for us to move. Again, he wields, and more bodies fly as we pass. "KEEP MOVING!"

We run, and as more crazed, glassy-eyed tunnel people rush toward us, Eoghan wields again. Then, like a horrible nightmare, so much like the attack on Bellrúg that it makes my stomach queasy, screaming begins from behind as the deadly torrent finally claims its first victims. The screams are close—much, much too close. We don't stop, and neither does the flood. We see the tunnel exit just ahead, and Eoghan throws Bryn's lifeless body over his shoulder as he ascends to the surface. A woman screams somewhere near my boot as Tiernan shouts for me to climb, and faster than a blink, I call forth the faerie magic and wield.

A bright blue wall fills the tunnel as the acid rain crashes into it, blocking its advance.

"Maeve, come on!" Tiernan pleads.

"I have to hold it off! You go!" I concentrate as the potion rises, screaming drowned out by the flood.

"Come on!" I shake my head, and Tiernan grabs me by the waist and throws me over his shoulder. "Hold that shield," he commands as we move together to the surface.

CHAPTER THIRTY-ONE

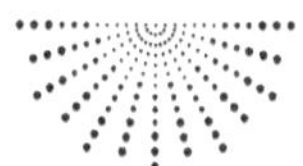

We burst through the service hole onto the grass just outside the city gates, and as we do, I drop the shield, and the flood washes over the last bit of the tunnel. I wield and lift the metal cover, setting it down in its place as acid splashes at our feet.

"Maeve, tell Officer Rhodes to come get us." Eoghan pants as he cradles Bryn in his arms. He is covered in blood from his shoulder to his boots, and Bryn…his eyes are lifeless and cold.

I tug on that ever-present hum of magic and call on Officer Rhodes. I don't know if he hears me through the ceaseless screams in my mind, and I feel nothing but the tinge of grief, waiting for me to let it free. I call out for him anyway, not bothering to calm the rush of my thoughts before I do. In no more than two minutes, Officer Rhodes stands in front of us, Gobaith just beyond him. His jaw falls slack in shock as he takes us in. Ever quietly, he moves aside with a dutiful shift of his body as Eoghan steps forward without a single word. We pass through the portal and into the hot desert sun. Eoghan doesn't stop walking when we reach the gate, or the medic's outpost, or the square. He doesn't stop as he continues up the red sandy road to the house he shares with Bryn; he doesn't even stop to turn the door handle. He kicks the door clear off its hinges and enters into the sitting room, where he lays Bryn's body onto the sofa.

"Get my father and mother," he says to Officer Rhodes, who says nothing before he disappears to Bastain. "Damaris, find Lo and Sawney."

Tiernan watches him for just a moment and then turns and leaves through the demolished front door. I take a step toward him, but he lifts his hand to halt me in my tracks.

"Not right now, Maevie." His voice is hollow; still, he calls me by the gentlest name he has for me, to show he's not angry with me or seeking to be rid of me. He runs his bloody hands through his hair, and the sun-bleached highlights turn red. He doesn't seem to care. His fingers tremble so violently without ceasing, he looks as though he's shivering against the cold that does not exist here.

I step back toward the corner of the room as Gálgalesh, Dedra, and Áine rush through the door. Horror strikes them as they look down at Bryn lying lifeless against the cushions. Dedra and Áine begin to sob, muffling their tears in their hands. Gálgalesh's expression falls, and his lips turn down at the corners as he shakes his head.

Another moment later, the sound of an opening portal lets us know General Kael and Mari have arrived. They step into the room and take Eoghan in, his eyes downcast, his hair and clothes covered in Bryn's blood, his face soaked with tears. Then, they find Bryn on the sofa, and Mari shrieks as she falls to her knees beside him. General Kael takes a step toward him, and his eyes become clouded as he places his hand on Mari's shoulder. He does not make a single sound, but his grief fills the entire room.

The seconds feel like hours as the wails of Mari Kael drown out all other sound. She clutches at Bryn, as if she can pull him close enough to her that she might breathe her life into him—but there is no remedy for death, and we all know that terrible reality too well. I'm not sure there will ever be enough emotion in the world to sufficiently feel all the grief Bryn's loss has brought.

The heavy sound of footsteps on tile rouse us as Lowri bounds into the room, Sawney and Tiernan behind her. She freezes in the doorway. Her hands quake as violently as Eoghan's, her eyes overflowing with tears, as rage distorts her features. She looks around the room to Eoghan—then to me.

Faster than I can react, she closes the space between us and presses me into the corner of the room as her fist collides with my face once, then twice. The whole room takes a loud, collective inhale, and Sawney shouts for Lowri to stop.

"I'll fucking kill you!" she screams as she takes hold of my shirt and slams me into the wall. "YOU KILLED HIM!"

She draws a dagger from her side and holds it to my neck. Eoghan quickly catches her arm before she can run it through me. She snarls like a wild animal, our noses nearly touching. She resists Eoghan's grip, but he has her, and Tiernan grabs her other arm, trying to will her off me.

"You do not belong here, *princess*! You belong in a grave! Not him! NOT HIM!"

"I-I—" I begin, tears streaming down my jaw.

"OF COURSE! IT'S ALWAYS ABOUT YOU! YOU ARE A SELFISH, STUPID, DANGEROUS WASTE OF SPACE, AND I AM GOING TO DRIVE THIS DAGGER THROUGH YOUR HEART JUST LIKE THEY DID TO BRYN!"

Lowri heaves every bit of effort against the two men's grips, and the dagger comes down toward me. The men pull her back again, and this time, it's an effort to move her away from me even the slightest bit. She's going to kill me. She's not going to stop until she does.

"Enough." General Kael's voice is stern and even. Lowri's sobs take over, and she drops the blade to the floor, releasing my shirt. Eoghan and Tiernan will her away from me. "That is enough, all of you. Close his eyes, Mari. Let him rest. We will prepare for his burning passage. Leave him here and go home. I want no more violence, for Bryn." He pats Mari's shoulder and coaxes her to stand. "Did you get what you were looking for?" I nod, even though I feel like it means nothing anymore. "Well done."

He turns to Officer Rhodes, who acknowledges him and prepares to send them back home. Mari stands on wobbling knees, her sobs still filling the space, and he guides her through the portal as they disappear. Lowri shakes Eoghan and Tiernan off as she stares daggers into me and then turns and finds Bryn. She throws herself down beside him and leans over, sobbing quietly against his cheek. She kisses him over and over again, her hand running through his brown hair. She takes him in, unable to let him go, and finally, when her tears have nearly soaked his lifeless body, she stands. She wipes her face on the back of her hand and clears her throat. Sawney meets her and takes her arm to lead her away. The others file out behind them.

"The key?" Gálgalesh asks. I reach into my pocket and draw it out, keeping the envelope hidden. I hand it to him. "Thank you." He runs his hand gingerly up my arm before disappearing from the room—Eoghan and I are the only ones who remain.

"Eogh—" I begin, but he passes through the sitting room without looking at me.

"I'm not good company at the moment, Maevie. I'm going to shower and head to bed."

Then, he leaves me alone with Bryn in the sitting room.

———

I WAKE with the depression of the mattress next to me. It's still much too early. The outpost outside is quiet, and the low rumble of the nighttime dance of the dragons still vibrates through the floors. As I lift my head and rub my eyes, I watch Eoghan leave the room with a stack of clothes in his hands, one for me near my feet.

I didn't speak to him for the rest of the evening. It seemed everywhere I was, he was not. He fled from the shower as I went to join him and from the room when I climbed into bed. I was asleep before he made it back later in the night. Now, it seems he is avoiding me again.

I notice a small note on top of the pile of clothes, and I reach for it. There is only a short scribble of words across it.

When you wake and get dressed in these. We have Bryn's burning passage at dawn. - Eogh

I sit up and stretch, brushing my hair from my face. The clothes laid out for me are the brightest white and as I unfold them, I notice there is a skirt of light linen and a matching top, cropped short just under the breasts and exposing the arms. A pair of brown sandals sit on the floor next to the bed. I plant my feet on the floor and stand to get dressed as I listen to Eoghan brush his teeth in the bathroom. When I finish, I head to join him, but he pushes past me and heads down the stairs. I brush my teeth in silence, alone. I leave the bathroom and cross the landing, careful to avoid looking expectantly toward Bryn's room where he would so often spend his days, and then I descend to the ground floor.

Tiernan, Gálgalesh, Dedra, Áine, and baby Theo wait quietly in the kitchen. Bryn's body has already been removed from the sitting room sometime during the night. They're all dressed as I am, in white linens, and Dedra and Áine's skirt and top match my own. Eoghan comes around the corner, pulling his boots onto his feet.

"Ready?" he asks, and when we all agree, he is the first to reach the door and exit onto the street.

I try to catch up to him as he leads us through the outpost and out toward the gates. His stride is too long, though, and I can't will him to look at me—let alone slow down. We continue as though we are the saddest parade the world has ever seen, exiting the outpost into the open desert barrens. Ahead, I can see a small platform at least to my chest, Bryn's body dressed in white upon it. The blood is now gone, his body cleaned. He looks as though he might just be sleeping. Beside the platform at attention stand General Kael, Mari, Lowri, Sawney, Colonel Hayes, Officer Rhodes, and Finn, all dressed in their mourning clothes. Eoghan stops near the platform, and we follow suit. I find a spot beside him and intertwine my fingers with his. He doesn't pull away; instead, his fingers squeeze my hand in a tight and loving embrace. When we all fall silent and still, General Kael steps forward.

"To the gods, a tribute. A life lost is a treasure gained. A heart returned is a soul remained. Dualdanas, Urrir, Ghlóiriant."

"Dualdanas, Urrir, Ghlóiriant," the Fire Cursed repeat.

Then, from under the sand, one small dragon rises at Bryn's feet. He lifts his head, his dragon's snout in line with Bryn on the platform, and lets out a morose cry—the melody of the Tinemallacht battle song. The sound of it is so beautiful, I have to force myself not to burst into tears all over again.

"Bryn wasn't meant to fight." Eoghan's voice is low, just

between us, as the dragon's cry continues. "He was good, though he would never tell you so. So good, in fact, that he was accepted to the military academy at seventeen, just like me. But my father worried about him after nearly losing Lo in the Battle of Buaeth. He asked her to walk the path of Bryn's future. She had never walked one before without a destination in time, so she guided herself to his death. She saw him die, with a dagger to the heart in Golorgleann—his requested home base after the academy." The dragon sings on as Eoghan clears his throat.

"My father and mother became fearful, unwilling to lose him in any sort of fight, so they didn't tell him of his acceptance to the academy and had him enlist unofficially in my father's Tinemallacht squadron instead, where he could stay under the command of my father within the borders of the territory. Rather than send him to battle or promote him through the ranks, they stationed him at Gobaith under our care and sent him on orders to a one-man post on the Iranndair border, one next to a small village that runs no risk of trouble. He always hated it, but at least he was safe."

Lowri had seen how Bryn would die, and the family tried everything they could to keep him safe, even to his disdain, even when they knew he resented them for it. Eoghan had begged me to stop when I demanded Bryn come with us, but instead of trusting them all, I had forced Eoghan's hand. I hadn't known, and it had been the thing that killed him.

The dragon falls silent and then purrs once before opening his mouth to let its fire engulf Bryn's body. It remains cool against our skin as we watch, burning only the intended.

"I'm sorry, Eoghan. I didn't know."

"I know, Maevie," he assures me. "Another secret I didn't tell. It's my fault, not yours. I should have told you. Lo should have come after me, not you."

I watch the fire rage in silence, and then I remember Bryn had been due at the station near the border tomorrow, that someone would be waiting for him there—expecting him.

"Eogh?" I say under my breath.

"Hmm?"

"Can we go to his station near Iranndair? Tomorrow?" Eoghan's eyebrows quirk even as his gaze remains on the fire.

"Why do you want to go there?" he asks.

"There might be someone I need to see."

The flames die down around the platform. Bryn's body is gone. In the center, however, sits a large gemstone as big as a human heart, purple and pink and gold. We step forward in unison as the dragon descends back under the sand. *A life lost is a treasure gained. A heart returned is a soul remained.* Bryn's heart, as beautiful as he ever was, marred only by a single mark from the blade wound, sits in front of us as our last reminder of the son, brother, and friend who lost his life because of me.

"Tomorrow, we'll go," Eoghan agrees as he runs his thumb over the backside of my hand.

———

WE RIDE on Eoghan's glider to the border station. It takes us all day, and by evening, we arrive exhausted, our skin darkened by the sun. The small border station is little more than a single room and a bath. It is definitely smaller in every way than the one-bedroom cottage in Fáintìrean, but as we take it in, we find Bryn made it his own. It's filled with Tinemallacht-crested packs, blankets, and blades of all lengths and sizes, photos of Eoghan and Lowri and some of Bryn, a beautiful dark haired woman on his arm...against his lips...his hands entwined in her hair. Ovidia.

Eoghan looks at the photos curiously as understanding washes over him. He traces their faces in the photographs with his fingers.

"She's Iranndairian," he whispers.

"Yes," I say.

"Did he love her?" he asks me, and I hear the unmistakable remorse in his voice. I only nod.

Eoghan leaves the station house and stands in the sunlight of the endless day. His brother had been stolen from him too soon, but more than that, he is learning how it feels to discover secrets once it's too late. He crouches into the sand and runs his hand across the surface.

"Bryn?" I hadn't noticed her make her way from behind us, but as we turn, the young woman from the photographs looks on at Eoghan, a basket of baked goods in her arms. She falls back a step. "Oh," she says as she registers his features.

"Ovidia?" I ask quietly, and she nods in confirmation. "I'm Maeve Moran, and this is Eoghan Kael, Bryn's brother."

"Where's Bryn?" She takes a cautious step toward the border. "Bryn?" Her voice is louder now as she calls for him, and when he does not answer, she turns to run.

"Stop!" Eoghan jumps to his feet. She freezes. "Stop. We aren't going to hurt you." His eyes are wet with tears. He reaches into his rucksack and pulls out the gemstone that is all that is left of Bryn, and her eyes survey it, knowing on her face.

———

Eoghan spends hours sitting in the red sand, speaking to Ovidia, sharing stories of Bryn. I busy myself in the small border station and wait as he laughs with her, cries with her, places his hand on her back to comfort her as he shares Bryn's last moments. She loved Bryn, had met him more than a year ago and spent every moment not with him pining over when they might be together again. And he had loved her. He had promised himself to her in stolen kisses and warm embraces, saving their final union for when he could promise her an entwining ceremony and one of her own people. He had been good to her, a love that had been forbidden yet lasting, one she might not ever lose, even without the formality of entwined hearts.

It's morning by the time we head back to Gobaith, and Eoghan helps hook me into his board before he hops on behind me. I lean back against his chest in a lazy, tired cuddle, and he plants a kiss against my hair.

"Thank you," he whispers. "For everything."

"Eoghan?" I say as we head north through the barrens.

"Yes, Mayhem?" I can hear his smile in his voice, subtle as it may be.

"I want to marry you," I say, and I feel his body shift against mine in an almost startled way.

"Are you sure?" he asks.

"No," I laugh and place my hands against his. "But I know for certain there will never be a heart I want more than yours, never another person I want to give mine to. I want to be your wife, and I want you forever, Eoghan Kael."

"You have me," he promises as the wind crosses our sail and pulls us over the sand dunes. "I'll marry you, Maeve, and tie my heart to yours. I will love you until the sun gives out in this desert. But first, let's figure out what the hell Cai wants us to do next."

CHAPTER THIRTY-TWO

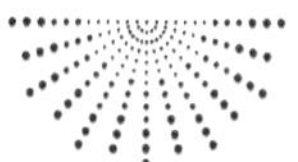

Dedra and Sawney sit with their legs entwined on the sofa in Áine's sitting room. Lowri left two days ago, when Eoghan and I had finally announced the date of our wedding and entwining ceremony, and hasn't been seen since. Sawney assures us she just needs time to clear her head—I'm not so sure there will ever be enough time to ease her hatred of me.

"Spin around a bit," Dedra commands as Sawney runs her hands through Dedra's straw-colored hair. "I want to see how the skirts move."

Dedra has spent the past two days sewing an impressive mock-up of a dress for me. She used old, light curtains and scratchy scraps of fabrics she found around the outpost, though Eoghan has promised her the most expensive fabrics and sewing accessories money can buy when she is finally ready to make the real thing. I spin slowly, and she twirls her finger in midair, urging me to go faster. The skirts spin out like blossoming flower petals as I move.

"Perfect. You can take the girl from the flower fields, but you can never take the flower fields from the girl." She leans back against the cushions and exhales deeply. "It's very romantic, Maeve."

"Is it?" I ask as I examine the dress critically and wonder if perhaps the skirts should be longer.

"Of course it is," Sawney agrees. "He's marrying you on his birthday. A day that is his, he's making yours as well. You'll share everything then: a day, a life, a heart…"

"He already shares that day with Lowri, remember?" I pick at the fabric, and Dedra snaps her fingers at me to stop. "She's going to hate that I took that from her too."

"She'll come around," Sawney assures me as Tiernan joins us, leaning over the sofa to give Dedra a quick kiss on her lips. "Me too!" Sawney coos and grabs his arm playfully. He plants a small peck on her forehead.

"Not you." Tiernan points his finger toward me, and I feign disappointment. "I've met your husband. I want none of that sort of trouble."

"I'm not her husband yet—though you're a wise man, Damaris." Eoghan crosses the threshold with a freshly baked cookie in his hand. He seems different now, his mood lighter since our trip to meet Ovidia, though the grief is still evident. We all shout at him to leave, and Dedra throws a pillow his way, urging him out the door of our makeshift atelier. He holds up his palms in surrender and turns, exiting the room as he laughs.

I pull at the straps of the dress and drop it to the floor, leaving me in my underwear. Tiernan swears in surprise as he diverts his eyes to his feet. I grab my discarded Tans from the small chair in the corner and exit to find Eoghan leaning against the wall outside. He raises an eyebrow as I walk through the door into Áine's kitchen.

"I thought Tiernan was just saying he'd like to keep his life… Funny way of doing so." He takes my clothes from my arms, holding each piece out to me in offering as I pull them on. "You could get married in Tans, you know. You don't have to go through the trouble."

"Eoghan Kael, I have very few pleasures in life. Let me have one dress." I drag my hair from under my shirt collar.

"I'd give you a new one every day if I thought it might make you happy." He rights himself and takes me in from my head to my toes. "I have a feeling you're much too sensible for that now, though." His eyes narrow, and I wonder if he knows the longing I felt in those scarce moments alone in my old room back at Caisleán Rialú. "I think, perhaps, there might be something else that makes you much happier than dresses..."

I watch as Tiernan, who had been listening from the sitting room, crosses back into the kitchen with us. He leans on the doorframe and folds his arms over his chest.

"Gálgalesh has begun to decipher Cai's journals, and he would like you to come see what he's found."

I freeze. For days, Gálgalesh has been hidden away in the outpost library, pouring over Cai's journals, hoping to use the key to crack the coded writings Cai left behind. It's proven slow and infuriating work, though now, it seems we might be finally getting somewhere. I push past Eoghan and find my boots by the door. I shove my feet into them and fiddle with the laces, but then Eoghan drops to his knee, pushing away my hands to take over. When he's finished, he rises back to his feet, a towering figure who makes me weak at the knees.

"Shall we?" I reach into my pocket and find the envelope I have kept with me since we returned from Gairdín.

"Let's go."

———

"Your brother was clever," Gálgalesh begins. "Much more clever than we ever gave him credit for. Woman, when was the first time you remember the Leader keeping a journal for himself?"

I wrack my brain for my earliest memory. I can't seem to remember any time when he had not poured over his daily writing. "For as long as I can remember," I admit finally.

"Curious—it seems as though our dearest one had suspected something amiss as early as the age of twelve. Though I have yet to decipher much of what has been written, I have found his journals span almost sixteen years of his life and not just tales of his own journeys and the ponderings of a young, growing heir. No, there are full histories of Draíocoinnigh rewritten in these tomes, and theories and legends and accounts from countless individuals Prince Cai sought to find. It appears the Leader has left us more than two hundred years of mysteries solved, and if we are lucky enough to seek the answers, we might find the truth hidden in these pages as to why we are all standing here today."

Cai had spent nearly the whole of his life searching for answers to questions I do not even have the sense yet to ask. Why had he done it? What might it lead us to find? My hand dives into my pocket, and I pull forth the envelope addressed to me. The others examine it curiously as I turn it over in my hands.

"When we were at the castle in search of the key, I found this in Cai's desk drawer. It had not been there in the days before Cai arrived for my wedding. He must have left it there for me just prior to the coup."

"What does it say, Maevie?" Eoghan asks.

"I don't know. I haven't opened it. After all that happened..." I stop short, and I know I don't need to speak the words. Tiernan, Eoghan, and Gálgalesh know exactly why I had not touched it until now. "I suppose it's as good of a time as any."

I push my nail under the envelope flap and will it to open. It gives way as I loosen the wax seal with the Tinemallacht crest embossed at the center. I pull the single piece of folded parchment from its resting place and begin to read.

Dearest Evie,

If you are reading this, that means Father has already killed me and has—by some great fortune—spared your life...for now. I'd say we would be lucky to hope for days or weeks before he decides to take your life as well. Caisleán Rialú is no longer safe, Evie. I'm so sorry I couldn't get you to safety sooner, but now, I beg you to heed my warnings.

Head to the military base in the city center and find Captain Tiernan Damaris. You will recognize him as a trusted friend from the small flame insignia on the underside of his uniform collar. He is the ONLY person in Gairdín you can trust.

I have instructed Tiernan, on my death, to seek you out and take you to a faerie named Gálgalesh Devenallt, the Warden of Báscogar Prison. You must agree to follow him, whatever the cost. Evie, you must take the key to my journals with you. When you reach the prison, stay with Gálgalesh, and he will lead you to Eoghan

Kael. Together, you must unlock the secret that might save Draíocoinnigh before it's too late.

When you find him, look to my journals, and please start from the beginning. I have a story you'll both want to hear.

My love endlessly,
Cai, Leader of the Resistance

I drop the letter on the table. "Tiernan, you—" My mouth goes dry, and my eyes fill with tears as he raises the side of his jacket collar to reveal a small flame embroidered just out of sight.

"I told you I had promised to take care of you long ago," Tiernan says. "I had no idea why or what might happen, but I never would have let him down when it came to you."

I dip my head and turn to Gálgalesh.

"At the praying tree, when I agreed to help him, he had told me one day, the Princess of Draíocoinnigh might seek my protection. When she did, he asked me to help her *and* to help her to find the Tinemallacht Warrior by the name of Eoghan Kael. When he showed up at my gates a few months later, I only knew I must keep a room next to 264 free at all times and instructed the guards it might only be filled if a woman were to be taken prisoner. I never thought you might be the most incessant, insolent...and important woman I would ever have the good fortune to meet."

"You told me to stay away from him..." I breathe.

"I knew you would never listen to a single word I had to say, especially not about Kael. I just had to wait for him to give up on killing you long enough to place you together."

"And you?" I turn to Eoghan, whose eyes have not left the parchment.

"I was told to not give up, at any cost. I still find that to be one of the most difficult promises I've ever had to keep; still, it led me to you."

I cry in earnest now. Of all the secrets kept from me, the secret to keeping me alive and safe was the greatest of them all—and Cai had done it. By sheer accident, it had all fallen into place, just as he had hoped. I wipe my eyes on the back of my arm.

"So, we begin at the start...and where might that be?" I look at the hundreds of journals scattered around the dark space. Gálgalesh pulls one from his pocket instead.

"Here." He lays it on the table and turns to the first page. Then, he hands me the deciphering key, and we begin to decode the first entry.

Across the ravine, the wisest are seen, selling souls to the faeries of old. They beg for their lives, not gold be the price; they are given for the power they hold.

The tale of madness and power begins in a small village in the Romiodóg mountains known as Fáintìrean. Seek out the faerie leaders of Dún to uncover the truth.

Our mouths fall open as we look at one another in silence. Eoghan is the first to speak as he clears his throat and straightens, his eyes on Gálgalesh.

"Are you ready to take a short trip back to your homeland, Gálgalesh?" he muses, and a wicked sort of smile plays on his lips. Gálgalesh's expression fills with trepidation as he contemplates the kingdom he left behind more than three hundred years ago.

"I do miss the snow," he finally concedes. "Woman, I'll need to teach you a few more spells before we go."

ACKNOWLEDGMENTS

To my family: Jess (dad), Dawn (mom), Jess, Kellen, and Wyatt. Thank you for always supporting me through this process, for loving me despite the long hours I spent cooped up, missing time with you so that I could write.

To Megan Brebner, my best friend and biggest fan. Without you, this story would never have come to be. Thank you for never leaving my side through the ups and downs of publishing. I wouldn't be me without you and these books are yours as much as they are mine.

To Tyler Brebner, Kevin Easley, and Freddy Lopez. Thank you for listening when I have something to say. Thank you for seeing me when I feel unseen.

To my PA team: Summer, Danielle, Hannah, Angy, Brie, Daph, Sarah, and Kirsty. I could have never gotten through this launch without you. You have held my sanity in your capable hands and without you, the Steel Citadel Series would not have found its readers.

To Sophia DeSensi for your continued support and encouragement of my writing and your unwavering friendship. I would not have made it through this gruelling year without you.

And last but not least, I want to thank my Creator for blessing me with the words to write this novel and the courage to bring it to the world. I am forever grateful to You for all You have done in my life.

ABOUT THE AUTHOR

Whitney Welsh Gibbs is a storyteller at heart, with a love for history and a curiosity for discovering new worlds—both real and imagined. She grew up on California's Central Coast, where the fog-draped mornings and salty sea air helped spark the imagination that fuels her writing today.

She holds a Master's in Intelligence and Security Studies from the University of Leicester and honed her craft through a blend of academic work and years of creative writing. Whitney has self-published three novels—Lucas Taite and the Mysterious Armor of God, Broken Anchors, and Lucas Taite and the Mountain of Örlög—each one earning praise and a growing base of loyal readers.

Her latest series, The Steel Citadel, brings together her love of layered plots, complex characters, and rich, magical worlds.

When she's not writing, Whitney can usually be found reading, exploring new places, or catching up with friends— often gathering sparks of inspiration along the way. She currently lives in Burbank, California.

ALSO BY WHITNEY WELSH GIBBS

THE STEEL CITADEL SERIES

The Land of Frost

YOUNG ADULT FANTASY

Lucas Taite and the Mysterious Armor of God
Lucas Taite and the Mountain of Örlög

STANDALONE ROMANCE

Broken Anchors